EMPIRE'S PASSING

IMPERIUM SUCCESSION SAGA #1

JW MORRIS

ACKNOWLEDGEMENTS

To the two women in my life who married me and then put up with my writing crap. Fran, I'm sorry you didn't live to see this and to see our grandson. Janeen, besides being my wife, you're my live-in editor and my best friend. Thank you for helping me through a very difficult time and making this possible.

I'd also like to acknowledge Streetlight Graphics for their wonderful cover and their help and support in publishing this work.

PART I

DUKE

"A leader is a dealer in hope."
Napoleon Bonaparte

PROLOGUE

———◆———

EARTH IS GOING TO DIE.

The phrase hung fluttering in his mind, a banner to the Imperium's malaise. Duke Alexander Landsman of the planet New Meyer scanned the opened tactical data windows projected through his optic nerves by his neural implant. All of Sol System lay before him. The Goths had breached the thin defenses at the two jump points a month ago and were advancing on Earth like a tsunami approaching a seaside village. Behind the advancing fleet he made out huge Goth tugs towing hundred-meter-diameter asteroids. *At least two hundred of them. I watched them gather the asteroids as they closed on Earth. It was like watching the assembly of a firing squad.* Five hundred Goth cruisers led the armada, each armed with deadly rail guns and their smaller ship-killing kinetic projectiles.

He gauged their closing velocity and did the numbers in his head. *Contact in three minutes.* The Home Fleet Tactical

Officer's voice confirmed his time estimate. "Contact in three minutes, four seconds."

Not bad for an old fart. His attention kept wandering to the open e-window image. The image of the mottled blue-green sphere hanging against the dark, heartless black of the universe drew him back with an almost primeval force. This was the ancestral home of his race and the capital of the Imperium. He had never seen Earth until he arrived a year ago to help plan her defense. Now she was going to be bombed back into the Stone Age.

He forced himself to the matter at hand. Tactical calculations and streams of data cascaded through his implant from the battleship's operations center. The fleet was as ready as he could make it. His entire flag conn crew lay encased in their General Quarters nanodiamond spidersilk protective cocoons. All communications occurred through implants. He took comfort in hearing the soft murmurs of his staff as they conversed through TacNet, or the fleet tactical network. He sighed with gratification as he listened to the exchanges among his staff. *They're working together as a team, just the way I trained them.*

He gave the order to ready an implant recording for transfer to the message drone he had left in deep stealth at the jump point. He owed his children that much. *I need to say goodbye and let them know what happened here.*

Goth cruisers moved in and launched their waves of kinetic projectiles. He didn't react as tendrils of alien thought slithered into his mind.

Goth Cruiser Kelth, Sol Star System
20 January 684 IP (13 April 221 New Barwick Standard Calendar)

The capital of the Imperium is dying.

A virtual image of the now gray-black Earth hung in the center of the compartment. Dust from the impact of the asteroids raining down on its surface darkened its atmosphere. The High Priestess of the Goddess Nearyahn stood rigidly straight, as if in the throes of a standing orgasm. Her eyes closed as she savored the taste of the passing of a world and its people. She shivered as she feasted on the terrified despair arising from Earth as the asteroids landed. The emotional tidal wave of billions of beings dying washed over her. Ten billion minds all cried out in pain and horror. She inhaled the death of Earth and fed on the dying souls until satiated.

Her eyes opened and reflected back at her in the mirror across the cabin. Large violet pools of nebula-like luminescence glowed with the demons inhabiting her Granacian humanoid body. She wore only a filmy robe hiding nothing and emphasizing all of the lush amber-skinned Granacian body she inhabited. Her eyes, still alive with invitation, had calmed to a more indigo now. Her large rose-pink lips were moist and tempting.

She had flooded the compartment with pheromones to aid in her control over visiting humanoids. Sex served her as a major weapon of hers, though the designation "she" only applied to the humanoid body she currently occupied. She had completely subjugated and integrated the host Granac mind to hers. *We're fully Merged. Neary and Granac.* That a Neary's intelligence and power only came when Merged with a humanoid didn't disturb her. *So be it. Besides, these sexual feelings that come with the Merge are, well, refreshing and serve other purposes. They lead to and enhance feeding. They help me control humanoids.*

There was a knock on the door and in walked Al'Rik O'Rathll, her husband and High Adept in the Nearyahn religion. He served also as King Al'Rik of the Goth Alliance and High Admiral of the Fleets. She acknowledged him and smiled. *Other Granacs consider him rather good-looking.* She used his firm, hard body to seduce and dominate females for her own purposes. His hooded scarlet eyes now burned deep with a star-hot desire. She tasted his excitement about Earth's destruction along with his raging lust for her. Raw energy emanated from him, almost tempting her to nibble despite her current satiation. She clamped down on her desire to feed. *I need this one.*

She reached out and connected with the piece of his mind inhabited by her implanted splinter. Unlike her own host, whom she totally dominated, only a small fragment of her mind inhabited his through the splinter. She used it to control him without his knowledge and without exercising complete control. The splinter enabled her to influence his actions while keeping his basic personality intact. Besides fueling his hatred of the Imperium, she had implanted a fanatic desire for workouts and body building. His looks, when combined with his political power, enabled him to bed many female Granacs, allowing her to feed on his conquests.

The pheromones were probably overkill for her husband. She controlled him far more deeply than by mere sexual arousal and mind control. He was totally unaware of the alien presence in his mind and responded to her thoughts as if they were his own. He grasped at some level his addiction to her body as a servant to his Goddess but found it natural, the result of her conditioning his mind. She smiled to herself, almost giggling. *After all, as a Goddess, aren't I entitled to be worshipped?* Her smile grew to a Granacian equivalent of a wicked human grin.

Al'Rik as grand leader of the Goth Alliance had continued his grandfather's efforts to bring enough disorder to destroy the Imperium. An image of another blackened husk, the former Imperium capital Meyer, joined in her mind with the one of Earth floating overhead now. *That was seventy five-years ago. I didn't think the Imperium could survive Meyer's destruction but Humans are stubborn and resourceful, making them such good feeds. Al'Rik has continued what started with his grandfather. I'm in a better position to help him than I was with his grandfather when*

10

everything was so new to me. First Meyer and now Earth. Soon, New Meyer, too, will go the way of its namesake.

Al'Rik wore just a pair of briefs, and, upon approaching her, fell immediately to his knees, his head bowed, staring at the floor. She felt the stream of emotions and raw sexual heat from his mind flow into her as the influence of the pheromones took full effect. Still, he managed to control himself somewhat. *He's a strong one which is why I need him.* She motioned him up.

"Mistress, it is done. We have destroyed Earth," he said in his deep resonant voice. "The Imperium has been weakening and splitting into factions. The fall of Earth will divide them further. I'm sure you're aware of all this."

"Yes, well done, husband. Still, we must bring some of the more independent-minded Goth chiefs back in line." *Yes, from your point of view it's going well and yet I'm still concerned. Despite our recent success the Goth Alliance is also fracturing.*

He nodded. "Yes, Mistress, I'm aware of the situation. The ones who have shown independence do not have Nearyahn priestesses or Adepts as wives. I am addressing that."

And you think you thought of that on your own? She nodded her approval. "We have influence with many of the other Imperium leaders. Now we need to deal with New Meyer. The planet may seem to be just a Tier Three world but its Duke almost thwarted our attack on Earth." *And New Meyer keeps reappearing in my visions of the various timelines.*

"Yes, Mistress, you're right," he admitted. "But he is dead."

"His son and nephew represent even more potent threats. New Meyer must be destroyed, too."

"New Meyer's destruction is in the plan, Mistress. We initiated an attack with what forces we could spare on New Brazil, the other rich world in their chute. When we destroy New Brazil no one will be available to aid New

Meyer. We won't need to use the overwhelming numbers of ships required here. That will allow us to attack other worlds and hasten the destruction of the Imperium."

This time she smiled tenderly at him and absorbed the cascading emotions from his reaction. *I need him.* "Yes, the plan goes well. I think you've earned your reward." This time she spoke as his Goddess. She stepped into his powerful embrace. As she lost herself in his almost fanatical lust she again had to tamp down her desire to feed. She wouldn't miss the energy.

Part of her mind luxuriated in the sensual intimacy with her husband. She tasted his strength and let it flow through her without consuming it. The Neary part of her considered other things. *Right now I need the Granacs as the core of the Alliance.* Her plans for the dissolution of the Imperium were proceeding just as she had expected. The Goth Alliance would continue to disrupt the Imperium

Humans provided a far richer source of life force than any of the other races in this section of the galaxy, including the Granacs. *Eventually I will personally inhabit a Human. Once the turmoil in the Imperium is complete and its structure destroyed, chaos will reign. In the ensuing anarchy the Church of Goddess Nearyahn will rise and take control of thousands of the humanoid worlds.* Then she would have a new supply of energy rich Human cattle for her race and no concerns about interference. *Be patient. All in good time.*

CHAPTER 1

Landsman Manor, New Meyer
1 February 684 IP

EARTH IS DESTROYED. THE IMPERIUM is dying.
The acting Duke of New Meyer, Baron of Courtney Michael Landsman, woke up with a start, a nightmare about his father fading back into his subconscious. The chime from his neural implant tinkled again. Years of military training and conditioning kicked in as he shrugged off sleep.

"Yes, Wallace, what is it?" he grumbled subvocally into the implant.

The implant-created avatar of Ian Wallace, Landsman Manor Chamberlain and Majordomo, floated in front of his eyes. "My Lord, I'm sorry to bother you. A message drone has arrived with word from your father. The message was downloaded automatically to an implant chip for your Eyes-only."

Michael sat up immediately and ran his fingers through his hair as if he were trying to rake the sleep from his body. "Okay, meet me in the sitting room." *Eyes-only chip. It can't be good news.*

Michael stood up and slid into a robe conveniently hanging on the bedpost. He strode through the darkened room, using his implant's low-light augmentation to amplify the dim ambient light that leaked in through the door's sill and the closed window. Outside a blizzard raged. He glanced over his shoulder at Donna. She lay in her usual position on these cold nights when she wasn't cuddling with him. She slept on her stomach, with just the top of her lustrous auburn hair and one shapely leg poking out from beneath the covers. *Why did someone who was so obviously snuggled up against the room's coolness have to keep one leg out in the open?* A brief smile. *Maybe she's using it to breathe.* He sighed and stepped through the door into the sitting room.

A short, squat man with a large handlebar mustache waited for him. Worry and concern replaced Wallace's normally cheerful expression. In the thirty-two-years Michael had known him Wallace had never looked so grave. His blue eyes, normally vibrant and pulsing with life, were dark and troubled, and his face showed none of the usual dry sense of humor that Michael so appreciated.

Wallace handed the chip to Michael, bowing. "I'll be in my quarters if you need me, My Lord."

Michael just nodded absently. He completely focused on the small oblong object in his palm. It glowed in response to his DNA and the wireless data transmission began. Tendrils from the ever-present social networks tried to worm their way into the transmission but were easily blocked by the Manor's security software and his implant's filters.

Suddenly he found himself staring into his father's hard, steel gray eyes. It was like looking in a mirror with an older version of the same square chin and slightly oversized nose. Duke Alexander's features were the grimmest Michael had ever seen.

"Son, by the time you receive this I'll be dead. Our worst fears will have come to pass, only decades earlier than expected. Earth will have been sacked and the Imperium will be on the verge of collapse. I'm linking now. See for yourself."

The image switched and Michael was looking out of his father's eyes at the busy flag conn of battleship *Duke of New Meyer*. There were a couple of open e-windows connecting to the TacNet floating in front of him. One immediately caught his attention. It contained no data, only the image of a blue and brown sphere shining against the black canvas of the universe. *Earth.* Something about those colors merged deep down inside him creating an emotional tie that was almost irresistible.

"Catches you, doesn't it?" his father asked softly.

Michael had to stop himself from answering out loud, remembering it was only a recording. *Yes, it's true. A beautiful world.* Something kept drawing his gaze back. He let the sounds of the battleship's flag conn flow around him. The implant could not and did not catch his father's thoughts, only the sensory inputs streaming in through sight, sound, and smell. Still, Michael couldn't shake the feeling of actually being on the battleship and inside his father's mind.

"Our idiot Emperor has really done it this time." His father continued with the clipped speech of subvocal communication. "Do you believe his stupidity? He sent Admiral Kamarov off with half the fleet on some show the flag tour. You can see the tactical realities as well as I can. We're outnumbered three to one. The longer range of our blast cannon to their kinetic projectiles won't make that up."

Michael tensed as the two fleets sped toward each other. *Why hasn't the Home Fleet opened fire yet to take advantage of their blast cannon's longer range?*

He almost had to smile as his father's recording seemingly answered his question. "Our glorious Emperor has ordered holding fire until we can be sure of a higher chance of hits. Geez, son, maybe the Imperium deserves to die," Alexander muttered subvocally, his voice only slightly muffled and distorted. "Duty, Honor, Imperium. Maybe we should add stupidity to that."

Goth cruisers on the open sensor windows moved in and launched their kinetic projectiles. At a predetermined distance from the Imperium fleet the projectiles exploded and released hundreds of baseball-sized submunitions in rapidly expanding waves. They covered an area that would prevent the target ships from dodging them. The Imperium fleet's point defense rapid discharge lasers opened fire. Hull mounted countermeasure tubes launched a dust cloud of nanocrystalline materials designed to damage or destroy the incoming submunitions.

Despite the stout defense, submunitions crashed into Imperium hulls. Incandescent energy flared as the dense nanocrystalline spheres impacted the electromagnetically reinforced hulls. Ships began to die. The Imperium battlewagons opened fire with their heavy blast rifles, sending sun-hot bolts of plasma into the lightly armored Goth cruisers. Bodies, shards of armor, and equipment floated from smashed hulls on both sides of the battle.

The fleet's return fire grew ragged, even from undamaged ships. His father appeared dazed. Why isn't he reacting? Michael's teeth clenched as twenty submunitions headed directly for his father's ship. No point defense fire countered their approach. His father still didn't respond.

Michael barely had time to react as the whole world exploded and the image went black. Involuntarily, he screamed.

"Hon! Hon! Are you all right?" It was his wife's voice.

Stunned, Michael looked over at Donna who had entered the sitting room. "He's dead. My father's dead. The Emperor is dead! The Imperium is dying!" His vision blurred as he reached for her and let himself find the warmth of her bosom. As she held him tight, he tried to let the tears come. Only they wouldn't. Outside, the raging storm battered the Manor's stone walls.

CHAPTER 2

THE LATE WINTER BLIZZARD WITH its howling, gale-force winds continued to wail outside of Government House. Michael shivered slightly from an imagined cold draft even though the Government House Artificial Intelligence (GHAI), or Guy as they affectionately called it, maintained the room at a comfortable twenty-four degrees Celsius. The Privy Council chamber always seemed slightly cold to him. *Is it because I hate politics so much?* Or is it just a hangover from the memorial service?

A single phrase, as old as civilization and carried deep in racial memories, kept popping into his head. *Barbarians at the gates.* With it came a deep chill. Earth was gone, the second Imperium capital sacked in seventy-five-years. *Now what stands in the way of the marauding Goths and their hatred of the Imperium? When will the Goths come through New Meyer's jump point and do the same to us?*

He took one last glance through his implant at the projected e-window floating in front of him. Nothing had changed in the daily Intelligence report. New Meyer was still a Class Three world with a population of three hundred million. The destruction of the New Meyer ships in the defense of Earth left New Meyer with an almost non-existent defense force. *Just a couple of old cruisers and destroyers along with a couple dozen corvettes.* Few outside this Council knew how many ships his father had taken with him.

Now we have to rebuild. If we can buy enough time then maybe we can survive the collapse of the Imperium. He smiled bitterly. *Yeah, and entropy can be reversed.* With Earth gone, and the Emperor dead, the remnants of the Imperium were almost as much a threat as the Goths. The words from Intelligence in the report jumped out at him. "At least four Dukes are claiming the throne. None of them are of Landsman descent." *Yes, it's starting already.* The intelligence report continued. "New Meyer's reputation for technical prowess and advancements makes us a valuable prize." *So much for lying low.*

With a final soft internal sigh he closed the implant window and turned to the conference table where the members of his Privy Council gathered. They had just finished viewing the message on his father's chip. Many of these men and women had been his father's advisors and close friends. *They must become mine now.* He glimpsed the pain in their eyes, but was pleased to see no apparent panic. *Grief, yes. Maybe even a touch of despair.* Yet, one by one, they drew themselves up and turned to him with expectant looks. *Geesh, do they expect me to have the answers?* He sighed silently. *Yes, you idiot. You're the Duke now. What do you expect?*

A slightly nutty and spicy aroma from Wallace's wonderful coffee wafted across the room from the large pot on the rear credenza. He mechanically lifted his mug and sipped. The coffee's bitter taste surprised him. *This isn't up to Wallace's normal standards.* Another sip. *No, it's not the coffee, it's me.*

He clearly wasn't alone in these thoughts. Mugs of steaming coffee on the conference table went untouched. Sweet-smelling pastries piled high on plates in the center of the table sat uneaten. By this point in the meeting they would normally have been well on the way to being devoured.

He glanced around the table again. Because of the foul weather a couple of the Counselors attended the meeting remotely from their homes by connecting through their P-Net Avatar. These artificial constructs used the interconnectivity of their personal neural implants and the worldwide Planetary Net or P-Net to attend the meeting without being physically present. The conference room's AI created a lifelike image with a holograph projector of the absent person in his seat. Two others were off-world and therefore unable to attend. His cousin Mitch was on a mission to New Brazil and his sister Carol was visiting one of the Lagrange Point production habitats.

"This was not unexpected," Bryan Landsman, Earl of Newberry and Michael's uncle, said as the replay of the flash message ended. He spoke as if he said something profound. "My brother was always impulsive and I think sometimes he lacks good sense, particularly in matters of honor." He gave what Michael could only describe as a theatrical sigh. "What did he expect to happen?"

Michael stifled a grim smile. He found this behavior typical of his uncle's penchant for stating the obvious and acting as if he were revealing some great truth. *He's not smart enough to realize the effect is just the opposite of what he intends.*

"Yes, My Lord Earl, the Imperium is faltering, but way sooner than expected," replied Admiral Shirohito Murray, commander of New Meyer's Imperium Navy contingent, to the Earl's comment. Shiro was a longtime friend and ally of Duke Alexander. "Way too soon," Shiro repeated, running his hand through his thinning red hair. He sat ramrod straight, his wiry, square shoulders braced as if standing for inspection. Though not a big man, the intensity in his dark eyes added to his stature.

"My Lord, you need to take charge," Emil Aurelis said to Michael while trying to tame the shock of graying hair he always seemed to be fighting to keep in place. "You must follow your father's instructions and become Duke," Emil insisted, following the script he had laid out with Michael before the meeting. "This is not a matter of choice or preference. We're facing the survival of this planet. We simply don't know how much time we have. We don't know when the Goths will arrive here."

Emil served as his father's principal advisor and Michael's former tutor. *That wild gray hair gives him a somewhat professorial look. He's a man with an immense intellect tempered by a compassionate streak. I trust him implicitly. He will become my rock now.*

"I think you're being premature," the Earl interjected. "We don't even have official confirmation that the Duke is dead."

Michael glanced back at his uncle, keeping the disdain off his face. The Earl was a tall, thin, elegant man, with salt-and-pepper sideburns and a bushy mustache that added an air of dignity and maturity to his cultured image. Like many of the Landsman clan he had steel gray eyes, but to Michael they seemed to lack depth and conviction. Michael remembered a conversation with his father, "Watch out for my brother, son. He has never gotten over being born second." The Earl seemed too soft and self-absorbed to Michael. He valued his creature comforts too much to be a good Duke. The Earl's current twenty-six-year-old, blonde bombshell, trophy girlfriend was a symptom of what was wrong with his uncle. *It's a mid-life crisis on steroids. I can't afford to indulge him now. I can't shut him out either. He is still the Earl of Newberry.*

Emil struggled to hide his distaste for the Earl as he responded. "My Lord, with all due respect, I don't believe this is the time for hesitation or any sign of indecision. I think the general message plus the Duke's private message to the Baron, made it clear he didn't expect to survive." He turned back to Michael and used the ducal form of address for emphasis. "Your Grace, you're popular with the media and the general populace. We're about to enter a time of huge uncertainty. They need to know their leader is in place."

Michael turned to the congressional leaders present. "Can I count on Congressional support?"

Petir Sanches, Speaker of the House of Representatives, nodded. "Of course, Your Grace. The House will back you," he said simply. He then turned and raised an eyebrow at his Senate counterpart.

"Of course, the Senate will too, Your Grace." replied Senate Majority Leader Agnes Chen in response. "This is no time for politics. Petir and I will introduce a joint motion this afternoon endorsing you as Duke."

Michael stifled a momentary grin at the interaction between the two political rivals. Sanches and Chen represented opposing political parties, their antics often raising Michael's frustration with politics and Congress. The New Meyer legislature consisted of a House of Representatives and a Senate. House members were elected for fixed terms from districts much like the old U.S. House of Representatives on Earth. Term limits restricted them to five two-year terms, and no one from the Peerage could be a member. The Senate consisted of a mixture of twenty Peerage and twenty elected non-peerage members from twenty large Senatorial districts. The non-Peerage members were limited to two five-year terms, while the Peerage members had no term limits and were appointed by the Duke.

"Any word on the frontier?" Chen asked.

Michael considered. The Goths were not the only Imperium enemies who would benefit from Earth's destruction and rising chaos as the struggle for the Imperium throne became more violent. The Shaallit, a race related to the Goth Alliance Granacs, had been humanity's foe for more than six hundred years since the inception of the Imperium. All of the Council expected the Shaallit to take advantage of the Imperium's weakness. *The bigger question is can the ISDF survive the collapse of the Imperium and keep the Shaallit contained?* The ISDF was the Imperium Salient Defense Force charged with maintaining the blockade that kept the Shaallit confined in their salient of eight hundred worlds. The Shaallit's original unprovoked attack more than six centuries earlier had led to the creation of the Imperium and the crowning of Emperor Michael Landsman I, Michael's direct ancestor and namesake. Michael I had rallied the crumbling Coalition and pushed the Shaallit out of Imperium space. After assuming the throne, he formed the ISDF to keep the Shaallit confined in their finger-shaped space sector.

"I'm sure nothing has changed," Emil interjected. "The ISDF is largely independent and will be able to hold out on its own for a while."

"I agree, Your Grace," Shiro interjected. "The important thing now is a unified front by Your Grace's government. What's left of our Navy will fall in behind you. Uncertainty is our worst enemy."

"Your Grace," Charles Atwood, the Minister of Defense, said with his usual sharp twang, "I believe we need to accelerate frigate construction and move them to high priority. Means we need to increase the defense budget..." he trailed off looking expectantly at the two congressional leaders.

Michael grinned to himself and fought an urge to wink at Emil and Shiro. Atwood was right on cue, playing his role perfectly. A short barrel-chested man with wild unruly hair who didn't look the part of Minister of Defense. *Those who didn't know him would never suspect that he was a retired*

Marine Colonel with the Medal of Honor. He spoke with his usual slow drawl that Michael had come to appreciate as a way of disarming his opponents.

"I agree, Charles," Michael said, looking at the two congressional leaders. "I know Congress is going to scream about the expenditures, but so be it."

Sanches returned Atwood's stare placidly. "Mr. Defense Minister, you would use this to push your shipbuilding program." He smiled wanly. "Unfortunately, you're right. Shoring up the Navy will help reassure the public. However, you won't have carte blanche." He turned to Michael. "Your Grace, I can pledge our support."

Michael studied Sanches. His stocky build gave the impression he had once been in shape despite a fairly well-developed paunch. His eyes were a commonplace brown but seemed to be alive with a sparkle that reflected his humor. Many of his political opponents didn't realize the glint hid the intensity of his beliefs. He had a deep-seated intelligence and political savvy not matched by many on New Meyer. As Speaker of the House his duties were reminiscent of those of a Prime Minister in parliamentary systems.

"Thank you, Petir," Michael said. He looked at the Senate Majority Leader. "And you, Agnes?" he asked, meeting her eyes.

A small, compact woman, Agnes Chen worked hard at appearing tough and hard. She wore severely cut and tailored clothes to make her look more businesslike and to disguise her good looks. This only served to add a sense of sourness to her public image. She couldn't hide her large dark eyes that many found her most attractive feature. She wore her hair short but still long enough to frame her face with its small nose and thin-lipped mouth. She used just enough makeup to hide some of the lines on her face. *A no-nonsense hard-headed career politician.* Not one of

Michael's favorite people, but one to whom he'd entrust the planet despite their differences.

"I agree with Petir. Now's not the time for political divisions. We'll vote to confirm your ascendancy as Duke and we'll support the increases to the military budget." She paused, smiling in a way that Michael interpreted as something like a feral cat showing her teeth. "Not a blank check mind you, but we'll increase emergency funding for the Navy."

Had to add that didn't you? "Thank you, Agnes."

I'm no longer looking at the Council through the prism of sitting in Father's chair on a temporary basis. This is now my chair and my chair alone. His ascension to Duke forced him to look at all of the Privy Councilors through the eyes of a Duke, as the leader of this planet, as the person responsible for defending this world and keeping its people safe.

He gazed around the table again. *They must become my people now, not my father's. So this is what it's like to be Duke.* His father had pounded into his head that leading meant taking responsibility for a decision. *Now I'm beginning to understand better what that really meant.*

The Earl responded to the glance by bowing his head. "I stand behind you, Your Grace. If it's your decision to declare your father dead and assume the Dukedom, then so be it."

Michael sighed to himself, relieved there would be no confrontation. His Uncle's acceptance of the inevitable avoided that for now. *Or was it something else?* He didn't have time to worry about it.

"Your Grace, we need a statement from you for the public. Time is running short," Shareen Chavez, Director of Communications, pointed out.

Michael looked around the table at his advisors. "I'm not my father in making speeches and public speaking. No need to tell you all I'm grateful for your support and that we face many grave challenges. If we work together I think we can make it through this. New Meyer can become the center of learning and civilization envisioned by my father and grandfather. But only if we hold together." He stopped, embarrassed. "I'm sorry, I didn't mean to preach."

Shareen grinned, "Your Grace, I think you've just made your statement."

"Now if I can only remember what I just said," Michael said, with a smile. Suddenly the coffee smelled better, almost back to its usual piquancy but still better.

"Don't worry, Your Grace, we have it recorded," assured Colonel David Ben-Levi, the Duke's head of security, and commander of the Duke's Guard Battalion, a unit of elite Marines assigned to protect the lives of the Duke and his family.

"Download to my implant," Michael ordered with a sigh. He would use the implant as a teleprompter during the speech. He sighed again, envying his cousin Mitch on his soft cushy diplomatic run to New Brazil in command of a warship.

He sipped his coffee, noting that even though it had grown cold the bitterness bothering him earlier seemed to have lessened. Outside, the wind and snow still battered the Government House's stout walls.

CHAPTER 3

New Meyer Corvette *Harrier*, **Deep Space, New Brazil Star System**
8 March 684 IP

"UH-OH, THIS ISN'T GOOD," MUTTERED Commander Mitchell Landsman, the newly appointed Baron of Courtney of New Meyer. He shifted his hundred kilo frame in the tight confines of the corvette's small command chair while studying open tactical e-windows. *We arrived two minutes ago out of the jump point and no challenge. Way too long.* He queried an open e-window to show data from the ship's hull-mounted passive sensor arrays. The data came back negative, detecting no New Brazilian ships nearby. *Not a good sign. Earl of New Brazil takes his jump point security and customs inspections seriously. We should've been challenged. Something is wrong.*

He considered his options. A radar search when entering a friendly star system was considered bad form. *Sitting here blind is a worse option. To hell with politeness.*

"Radar! Sweep of the surrounding area. Full ping!" he ordered.

Radar data replaced the passive sensor data in his

implant's open e-window. Still no sign of any of the customs corvettes or the supporting cruiser and battleship force normally guarding the jump point. He gritted his teeth as imaginary images of raiding Goth cruisers pushed their way into his thoughts. *Don't jump to conclusions. Wait for the reports. There must be another explanation. Maybe they're stealthed for some reason.*

He was on a diplomatic mission, carrying personal messages to the Earl for his cousin Michael, the new Duke of New Meyer. The mission afforded an opportunity for some deep space training for his crew. He checked his implant for any sign of radio contact. *Still nothing.*

His radar tech sat up suddenly and his implant images changed. "Skipper, debris fields. Lots of them. At least two dozen ships," the radar tech, Master Chief Petty Officer Andrea Josilene Grove y Alves, reported. Mitch sensed a slight rise in the tone of her normally unflappable voice. She bit her lower lip in concentration as she dove deeper into the radar return data.

Imagination-generated images of the Goths rampaging through the New Brazil system returned. He pushed them away again and returned to the electronic-generated radar scans. *No sign of any intact ships, no less a Goth force. Should I go to General Quarters?* He needed more data.

"Deploy the Twenty-Two," he ordered, working to keep his voice calm.

A hatch on the ship's hull swung open. A tractor rocket fired, extending a thin super strong cable of spun nanotubes and man-made spider silk attached to a small winch. When the cable reached maximum extension an impulse cartridge fired, triggering a line cutter that guillotined the cable attached to the rocket. The nanos imbedded in the expended rocket case dissolved the molecular bands holding the rocket together. At the same time, a gas generator inflated the TSA-22A Towed Sensor Array into an almost invisible sphere comprised of billions of sensitive nanosensors. The array became a sixty-meter-diameter telescope capable of "seeing" in every frequency of the electromagnetic spectrum including X-ray and gamma rays. Developed by New Meyer's Institute of Technology (NMIT), the Twenty-Two, as it was nicknamed, marked a significant improvement in array technology over the standard Imperium TSA-17A's. The array began to passively probe the star system, vacuuming up all stray bits of man-made emissions and feeding the data into a specialized artificial intelligence with almost magical algorithms to glean data from the merest shreds.

I can't risk the ship. "Battle stations. Sound General Quarters," he said. His own calmness almost startled him as he shifted into a command mode, a response dictated by his training as a naval officer. He relegated the earlier churning fear to some distant part of his mind.

The biting, irritating sound of a klaxon reverberated through the small ship. He winced. *The klaxon isn't really necessary. Everyone else is already at their jump stations.* He shrugged. The ship's AI was just following regulations.

He donned his emergency softskin pressure suit, feeling it mold to his body's contours. His command chair reclined and encased him in a spidersilk and nanodiamond composite fiber cocoon for added protection during combat. He now viewed the world outside the cocoon through his implant.

"Captain, I'm getting first sweeps of the system from the Twenty-Two. The star system is pretty dark. No emissions from the asteroid manufacturing centers and the planet itself," reported Lieutenant Joshua Ben-Levi, *Harrier's* executive and tactical operations officer.

"Any signs of Goths?" Mitch asked. *A star system like New Brazil this dark?* He tried not to think about the implications to New Meyer. This star system was too important to his homeworld. *The whole crew must now suspect the Goths are in this system*

"No, sir, not yet." Josh replied, his voice in a clipped monotone showing no emotion.

Goths. The word brought a sense of dread that wrapped around Mitch's mind like the hood used at executions. He queried his implant and another e-window opened, this one containing a three-dimensional star map. The purple of Imperium space spread out a thousand light years from Earth, interrupted by the angry red blotches of Goth controlled worlds and the yellow smears denoting "out-of-contact" worlds. The name Neo-Goths had been coined by some Emperor centuries before who had been enthralled by the history of the Roman Empire. Now they were just called Goths. The current map didn't show any reds near the New Meyer/New Brazil jump chute. Mitch smiled wryly to himself. *I guess the map is out of date. Stop jumping to conclusions!*

So what is the situation? New Brazil was a Class Two world with a rich technological society and a population in the billions. Class Twos sported a large and sophisticated enough economy to retain the technology infrastructure required to support jump drive technology. To be almost electromagnetically dark meant one of two things. Either New Brazil had already been bombed and sacked by the Goths or it was under attack and had instituted an emergency EM blackout. The Earl of New Brazil retained a strong Navy presence. *I believe the Earl's forces should be strong enough to resist most incursions. With two jump points he keeps his main forces near the homeworld, allowing him to respond to threats from either jump point. So the battles may be occurring closer in.*

Mitch turned to his options. *Harrier* was a diminutive, poorly armed warship massing only a bit more than a thousand tons. *Information is the weapon here. The Duke needs to know what's going on.*

"Institute Manta," he ordered. *I shouldn't have waited this long.*

With that command he imagined the corvette fading to a virtual ghost blanketed by her new Manta stealth system. *If this works as designed, it'll be a major advantage. Harrier* became many times more difficult to detect than any other Imperium stealth protected ship.

"Manta nominal," the ship's AI reported in his clipped professional persona.

"Standard Manta procedure," Mitch ordered.

Standard Manta limited his drive options. *Harrier* had two primary propulsive systems. She carried a high powered fusion drive, nicknamed the torch, capable of sprints up to ten gravities for short periods. She also had a virtually undetectable gravitic drive capable of up to one g for long periods. There was a secondary gravitic drive for use in orbit that was of no consequence here. *Can't use the fusion drive.* A fusion drive's flare would show outside the stealth field and would therefore stand out like a signpost that could not be masked. *Speed vs. stealth.*

"Contact!" Josh said. "*Kuhl*-class patrol ship. Heading inward at three gravities. I have her torch flare. She's at least five hundred thousand klicks ahead of us," Josh reported.

Kuhl-class! Goth. "Too small to stop even us," he said to the crew over *Harrier's* ShipNet or S-Net. "Must've been posted to intercept message torps. Let her go." He switched to a private command channel and pulsed his tactical officer privately. "Your thoughts?" he asked Josh.

Josh answered without hesitation. "Captain, we need to find out the depth of this incursion and the status of the New Brazilian forces." He paused. "We can't tell New Brazil's condition from out here."

Mitch studied his exec. *Damn! How can he stay so calm?* Then he sighed. *What else would I expect with his background?* "Yeah, I agree," Mitch replied. "My thoughts too. The Goths in-system won't realize we're here for more than an hour thanks to the lightspeed limit of any message sent by the *Kuhl*. Of course, that's assuming the Goths are concentrated around New Brazil. If they have a presence in the asteroid belt then they will know a lot sooner. Do we trust Manta to keep us hidden and head on in to find out?"

Josh's ShipNet avatar shrugged. "I understand Manta's a new technology, Skipper. I took part in the final testing. It works. Manta and the Twenty-Two will give us a decided advantage over any Imps or Goths we encounter. The Twenty-Two can penetrate Imperium stealth at a half-million kilometers and Goth stealth at twice that. In the tests we ran, the Imp's seventeens couldn't detect a Manta protected ship beyond ten thousand klicks."

For centuries Imperium stealth technology had been limited by a ban imposed by Emperor Claudio II who had been terrified that a potential assassin could sneak up on his flagship undetected. Even after his death the ban had never been lifted and Imperium stealth technology stagnated. NMIT researchers had rediscovered a forbidden technology hidden away in a two-century-old database that was supposed to have been destroyed. Twenty-five-years of research and development went into bringing the technology to reality. Now New Meyer probably had the best stealth system in Imperium space.

Mitch studied his exec's avatar again for a moment. Josh carried himself more like a military officer than an academic, despite being only a reserve officer and a member of the NMIT faculty. He came from a family with a rich and storied military history. His brother, David, commanded the Duke's Guard Battalion protecting the Duke. His father had been a legendary special operations officer. Ben-Levi children were cultivated for a military career starting at a young age. Josh didn't look anything like a typical academic. He more closely resembled the Special Ops operators his family had long produced. Slender in build, but also rock hard, he worked out rigorously to keep his body in something approaching the fighting trim of a SpecOps operator. The intensity in his blue eyes along with his close-cropped blonde hair only added to Mitch's impression of Josh's military demeanor. Mitch chuckled to himself. *As big as I am I still wouldn't want to meet him in a dark alley somewhere.* And yet, Josh had graduated NMIT near the top of his class in astrophysics. *I wonder if the iron discipline that must have been imbued in him by his father might have contributed to his academic success. I bet it certainly contributed to his demeanor now.*

"Ok, Josh. I agree. We go in. There's no other choice. The Duke needs to understand the size and threat of the incursion. Most of all he needs to know New Brazil's condition. I'm not sure there's much the New Meyerian Navy can do about it but at least they can prepare themselves. Maybe they can add more externally mounted missile tubes to all the ships, and accelerate *Courtney's* launching. All of that will probably take too long if the Goths are successful here." *If the Goths are successful here we're fucked, truly fucked.*

In addition to the new stealth and upgraded array technology *Harrier* carried another NMIT innovation. She carried externally-mounted missile launch tubes containing new Venom anti-ship missiles armed with nuclear shaped charge warheads. Historically, nuclear armed missiles had proven ineffectual against major warships. Nuclear explosions in space, unless a direct impact, only provided a strong Electromagnetic Pulse or EMP. While EMP was capable of frying some electronics, most warships were shielded against such threats. These new shaped charge warheads were supposed to be different. *If they work as planned they'll revolutionize the current hidebound Imperium naval theory of big ships pounding each other at close range.* The four tubes *Harrier* carried gave the corvette enough punch to possibly disengage and escape from an encounter with a larger hostile ship. New

Meyer was hurriedly adding these strap-on launchers to every warship they had.

New Meyer's hope for survival depended on their new class of ships. *Courtney*, designated a frigate, was the first ship designed to fully take advantage of these new NMIT-developed systems. *We're hanging our survival on unproven technologies. They all worked during testing. Real battle is always a different thing. And Courtney's still weeks, if not months, away from launch.*

Mitch sighed and opened communication to his sixteen-person crew. "Ok, we're going in to find out what's going on. Duke Michael needs to know how bad this incursion is. It must be serious if the Earl wasn't able to get a message out to warn us. With luck, it's just a raid and the local New Brazilian Navy contingent is handling it. If we're facing a full-scale incursion then New Meyer is in deep shit. No need for me to tell you to be on your toes so we can get the hell out of here and get the news back home."

He looked over at the astrogator. "We'll go in at one point five gravities for a couple of days and then reduce to gravitics only and go into Manta then. To hell with fuel consumption and stealth. Plot us a course that brings us within three million klicks of New Brazil. We'll stay in Manta. Secure from General Quarters. No need at this point to keep you all cooped up. We'll go to DefPost Two." Defensive Posture Two put half the crew on station for four hours and half off for four hours. Normal ship operation used DefPost Three with the crew divided into three watches of six hours on station and twelve hours off.

As the conn settled down into routine, Mitch considered the implications for New Meyer of a New Brazil incursion. New Brazil anchored the other end of the New Brazil-New Meyer chutes. Transportation between star systems was accomplished through jump points. Jump chutes represented the locus of all the worlds that could be reached by the linked jump points between New Meyer and New Brazil.

Of the seventy-three star systems accessible through the NMNB chute, the New Brazil star system was by far the richest. Its second jump point on the other side of the star system led toward the Imperium Heart Worlds through a connection to the New Brisbane/New Phoenix chute. That jump point represented New Meyer's most direct access to the Imperium Heart Worlds. Without the New Brazil connection, trips to the Heart Worlds would require two or three extra jumps, adding two months or more to the trip. Trade would become more difficult and more expensive.

Who would have thought that Earth, capital of the Imperium, would have been overrun by the Goths? So my uncle had to go off and try to rescue the Emperor while leaving New Meyer undefended. Shit. And now this.

As the ship's acceleration increased, the internal gravitic field struggled to keep up. Mitch was back trying to find a comfortable position in the captain's chair, now even more uncomfortable under the increased gravity. He had always worked out with Marines when possible but there were no Marines aboard *Harrier*. He and Josh had worked out together to keep each other in shape, but their schedules did not always coincide. His workouts in *Harrier's* confined space left him feeling deprived and unfulfilled. *It's not going to get any better on this trip.*

He sighed. "Ready a message drone with an upload of the log and launch it back to New Meyer. Ready two more and launch them in loiter mode ready to jump at a moment's notice. We'll maintain a tight laser contact with them while constantly updating the log recording. Program them to jump if we break contact for more than an hour."

He settled into his chair and thought about getting a mug of his special rich blend of New Meyerian coffee. While the coffee might not cure his discomfort it would certainly make it seem better.

CHAPTER 4

Somewhere in the Universe
Somewhere in Time

THE COUNCIL MET, A MEETING different than one defined in human terms. None of the beings were physically present since they were spread out across the brane in space and along the timeline. Nor did they use the full capacity of their prodigious minds. Not quite at a nuisance level, the meeting functioned as a distraction.

"One, what is so important to call this Council?" Seven, the seventh being to arrive at the meeting, asked, though the act of asking involved nothing even closely related to speech. Conversation between billion-year-old beings occurred in a manner beyond the understanding of human physics and knowledge. "The next Brane Touch is still far in the future in this universe's timeline. So what can be so important?"

"A Chosen Race Faces a major crisis," One replied. "The Humans are in distinct peril."

One, the first to arrive at the meeting, wasn't concerned about the touching of the two membranes that would end all life in this membrane and start over with a new

Big Bang. That was still trillions of years in the future, using the human race's limited sense of time. By then, Humans would either have ascended to join his race in the totality of the brane or would have perished. *That's why the Humans are one of the Chosen races. They have the potential to join us.*

What did we call ourselves long ago? Ah, yes, Passimians. One's race now existed outside of time, travelling freely up and down the timeline to the past and up into an infinite number of potential futures. On his last trip up the Humans' timeline he found the change.

"These young races always face a crisis," chided Twelve, the twelfth entity to arrive at the meeting node. "You love to dabble with these lesser races, so why can't you fix it?"

If a billion-year-old entity with no physical form could be said to sigh, then One did. "This is a true crisis. It involves the Neary." He paused as he sensed a sudden interest from the now hundred or so gathered entities. "We knew at some point we'd have to deal with them. They're a freak mutation we shouldn't have allowed to continue. They exist because of us and now we must remedy it. They've discovered one of the Chosen Races and are moving to subjugate and feed."

"This cannot be allowed."

"Preposterous."

"We cannot allow this."

"Unacceptable. They're parasites. They are an infection and must be eradicated."

The responses continued. It wasn't easy to catch the interest of a race that had been around for a billion years with little or no physical connection since the Discorporation to the real universe. One, as one of the youngest, had maintained the most contact with the Chosen Races, those selected for their potential to grow toward their own Discorporation at some far point up the timeline.

One didn't feel satisfaction about making a satisfactory

argument. The term "his" was only a momentary referral since in Discorporation they had no sexual identity or all sexual identities. "We must act now," he said

He received their agreement with a series of "take care of it," and then the meeting dissolved.

One contemplated their abrupt departure for microseconds and then immersed himself in a study of the timelines. Passimians could travel in the past but they couldn't change it. That would violate chrono entropy. Direct action against the Neary wasn't allowed by their terms of Discorporation because that would make him a God, and that was forbidden. Somewhere he'd discover a timeline providing a solution within his limited means. Then he would take action to make the probability of its positive outcome approach one hundred percent. *At last, a challenge.*

CHAPTER 5

Landsman Manor, New Meyer System
8 March 684 IP

"Y OUR GRACE?" A SOFT FEMALE voice floated from the study's doorway.

Michael turned to face his wife, the Duchess Donna Ariel Ben-Levi Landsman. He sat in his favorite high-backed pseudo-leather chair with his legs crossed at the ankles and stretched out on a matching hassock. The chair's nanos massaged his back, deftly working to relieve the tenseness and exhaustion accumulated through another long day of political wrangling, public appearances, and two brief media interviews. Soft pop music from some singer he didn't even know played in the background adding to the relaxed atmosphere. A bottle of lager beer dangled in his right hand, his arm supported by the plush leather of the chair's armrest. He faced a hand-carved, natural stone hearth with a roaring fire crackling in the firebox. Well-appreciated warmth radiated into the softly lit room. A flickering display of wraithlike shadows danced across the den's hardwood paneling and scores of old-style books packed into ceiling-high shelves. The faint aroma of fruitwoods added to the rustic illusion. *Wallace takes the building of a fire to an art like everything else he does.*

Michael's eyes widened at the image Donna presented standing in the entrance from the hallway. She stood with one hand on a hip and the other bent, leaning against the doorway. Light from the corridor backlighted her robe, emphasizing every marvelous curve of her body. She wore a filmy, not quite transparent, floor-length dressing gown belted around her waist. *Am I imagining I can see the beginnings of pregnancy? She's only in the second month. No matter, she's even more beautiful.*

Her lustrous auburn hair fell to her shoulders and framed her oval patrician face. Her large green eyes had attracted and entranced him the first time they had met. They still did so. He disagreed vehemently with those in the media who deemed her "attractive not beautiful." They judged her eyes and nose as being a bit too large for her face. He couldn't disagree more. *Everything about her is perfect, especially those marvelous eyes.* Arranged marriage or not, he had fallen in love at first sight.

"M'lady?" he asked while trying to appear nonchalant.

"Am I disturbing you, Your Grace?" she replied in a soft, inviting voice.

He struggled to sit-up. All of the emotions of the past couple of days were welling up in a tidal surge demanding some sort of relief. His quiet moments in front of the fire had helped. The burden he was carrying demanded something more. He wore only casual shorts and a tee shirt which did little to hide his arousal. "Disturbing me? No, of course not, my love. I'm just sitting here thinking about the hearth. Did you know the stone was hand-cut when the Manor was built? I doubt if you could find a stonecutter on New Meyer, certainly not one who cuts stones like these by hand now." *I'm babbling.*

"Hmm, Your Grace, I think you need some distraction,"

she said with a faint smile, her eyebrows lifted in what Michael took as exaggerated consternation. She glided in and poured herself spring water from a crystal pitcher into a goblet bearing the New Meyer Ducal Crest. She sat down in the sister leather chair facing the fire, tucked her long legs under her, and gazed at her husband.

"So, love of my life, what can I do for you? something you wanted to speak with me about?" Michael asked, trying not to show his true thoughts.

"You seemed quiet and contemplative at dinner. I thought you might need a soft shoulder," she said with the trace of a smile telling him he wasn't hiding anything from her.

"If your shoulder comes with the other soft parts of you, how can I resist?" he asked with a fake leer. The sensuous fragrance of his favorite perfume wafted across the small distance separating them. Her nearness stimulated him even more. Part of him just wanted to bury his head in those soft breasts and let the world pass him by.

"Are you OK?" she asked, her voice almost a whisper.

Her green eyes locked with his, and her emotional warmth flowed to his need. He sighed before responding. "Am I Ok? I guess physically I'm fine, except maybe a bit tired. This is my first free moment in the past week."

"I'm more concerned about your emotional health," she replied.

"So many emotions whirling through my head I not sure which ones to grab. Do you realize I don't really mourn my father? I'm pissed at him for taking those ships on that ridiculous crusade of his." The anger, fear, and frustration of the past weeks began to pour out of him. "Why did he have to be so fuckin' stupid and noble? God, honey, he was a guy who I thought was a great leader, the rock holding this place together. Instead, he goes off on a wild fool's chase and leaves us here with the Goths just a couple of fuckin' jumps away!"

She reached over and placed her hand on his. "Your Grace, you would've done the same thing had the responsibility been yours. He was a Duke, a member of the Peerage, sworn to protect the Imperium and his Emperor. Your Landsman clan takes your oath and honor seriously. How many times have I heard you use the phrase 'Duty, Honor, Imperium?' Why do you think the people on this world trust you and your family so implicitly?"

"But he left us defenseless."

"Us defenseless? Or is it that he left you?"

He turned from the fire and looked into her eyes. "You think his leaving me is what's bothering me?"

She smiled again. "Hey, I'm no psychologist, just a poor medical doctor who hasn't practiced since I was betrothed to a dashing young Baron."

He almost giggled, but it came out as a deep-throated chuckle. "The media had a ball with us, didn't they, when my father announced the betrothal?"

They both smiled at the word betrothal, a not-so-private joke between them. "This is the 30th Century Earth time you know," she grumbled. "There are no arranged marriages."

He chuckled again. "Well, it wasn't arranged in the medieval sense. We were pushed together and subtly encouraged."

"Subtly?" she asked, her eyes twinkling. "Your father didn't understand subtle. His idea of subtlety was a two by four."

This time his grin reflected the warmth in his eyes as they brightened with images of his father's actions leading up to their announced betrothal. "Well, I guess featuring us at the Planetary Ball before we were even barely introduced might be one person's idea of subtle, but not mine."

"Yes," she replied with a smile. "It did cause a stir in the media. They had us married before the Ball was even over."

"So did I," he said, taking her hand in his. *I knew from the first time I met her I was going to marry her. She completes me in ways I couldn't imagine.*

"Have you picked out a gown for the ball this year, my love?" he asked, dreading the long-scheduled Planetary Founding Day Ball in three days. *Of course she has, you idiot.* The Council had decided to hold the affair to reassure the populace and maintain a semblance of normalcy. Even the congressional leaders had agreed. *I'm not sure I agree.* A sense of normalcy was good to help prevent panic. On the other hand, he wanted to foster a feeling of urgency and sacrifice he believed the planet needed to survive. He mentally shrugged. *Maybe the ball will be cancelled because of the weather. Nah! No such luck.*

"Of course, I picked out a gown," she replied.

"Nice and modest, and matronly, now that you're in a family way?" he teased.

She stretched out her long legs, her robe parting to reveal creamy white thighs with the slightest hint of auburn curls at their juncture. She thrust out her chest to expose more of her ample bosom. "Are you sure, My Lord, you want matronly?" she asked, her eyes the deepest green he had ever seen.

He put down his glass, stood, and took the two steps to her chair. He leaned down, and grumbled, "Maybe in a hundred years," as their lips met and her arms went around his neck. Her hair smelled of vanilla, his favorite scent. Her skin warmed to his touch as he stroked the back of her neck. Their lips welded as the kiss grew more passionate. The world with all its problems faded as he focused on his physical senses and the moment. She seemed to sense his need and responded in kind, her hand caressing the tender spot on his earlobe she knew drove him crazy. This only added to the passion and heat in the kiss as they slowly slid to the floor and onto the thick rug.

Later that night Michael awoke with a bit of a start.

He'd been dreaming though he couldn't remember what the dream was about. Despite the presence of Donna's warm body, the room was cold and dark. He staggered to his feet and padded nude over to the hearth. He stoked the fire with an ornate cast-iron poker. Bright red sparks flared and a couple of tiny flames rose as if in a last gasp of life. The bed of coals still glowed. He placed some smaller kindling and three pine logs on glowing embers, waiting until they caught before adding two larger oaks. When he turned back to Donna she was propped up on an elbow watching him.

"Cute butt," she said. "And an even better view from the front."

Michael felt his face reddening. He chuckled to himself. *I've always been a bit of a prude. Probably got it from my father.* He slid down beside her on the soft rug and sighed with contentment he couldn't have imagined a couple of hours earlier. He reached out and caressed her shoulder, relishing the softness of her skin and the warmth radiating from within.

"You're crude," he whispered while nibbling lightly on her neck. Her sweet fragrance mingled with a trace of saltiness from the sweat of their lovemaking.

"Mmm," she replied. "Keep doing that and you'll see how crude I can be."

"Is that a threat or a promise?"

"Both," she said, rolling over on top of him.

Later he muttered, "You're going to kill me, girl," as they lay side by side out of breath.

"Hell of a way to die, isn't it?" she said back to him.

He reached up and handed her water from an end table. He grabbed his beer and took a swig. "Thirsty work," he said.

"Work? Is that what you call it?" she pouted.

"Work is force times distance, an expenditure of energy. And I did expend lots of energy. Therefore, work."

She rolled her eyes. "God, you military men are so romantic."

Michael grinned. "Er, I think this was a bit beyond romance. You know, like hot, passionate sex?"

She batted him with a pillow they had pulled off a nearby couch. Then her expression changed. "Feel any better?" she asked.

"Yeah, I should think so, but now I'm physically a wreck."

"A big strong hunk like you?" she pouted again.

"What's the old saying about a tiger by the tail, whatever a tiger is?"

"A large carnivorous cat on Earth," she replied, stretching languorously.

"Oh, yes. I remember now. I wonder if any survived the kinetic bombardment?" he mused.

"I think they were already extinct. How bad was the bombing?" The humor had left her eyes.

"Reports are still sketchy. At first they only bombed all of the power plants, spaceports, and parts of the major cities. They also took out seats of government and military bases. Ten billion people without power or access to help. In other words the Goths wanted the anarchy that followed. Then they came through and looted the cities. Right now any survivors are experiencing subzero temperatures due to the all the debris thrown into the atmosphere. There's no government, and no electrical power. I don't think a hundred million people are left alive on the planet out of ten billion. Probably a lot less. We're still short on details."

"My God! That's barbaric!"

"Why do you think we call them Goths? Their goal is to destroy the Imperium to make up for their perception of six centuries of persecution."

"Michael, what about the Shaallit?"

"What about them?"

"Wouldn't they take advantage of the situation? I know I would."

Michael shrugged. "From what we can tell the Imp forces on the Shaallit border are still intact. Naval Intelligence reports Goth incursions have not reached the Salient forces yet. Different reports indicate the Shaallit are facing problems of their own with the Goths. How can the Goths be in the Salient but not yet reaching the ISDF? So the reports conflict." He grinned. "What else do you expect from the Office of Naval Intelligence? We'll have to wait and see how things turn out."

"Hmmm, sounds like you have a lot on your plate, m'lord," she said. "Still, I think there's something else bothering you."

"The Plan. My grandfather believed the sacking of Meyer and the ever-present Goths foretold the fall of the Imperium. He and my father set out to make New Meyer self-sufficient so we'd be in a better position to make it through the chaos. They searched out technology to give us enough of an edge to survive. They also worked to hide New Meyer's capabilities in Imperium databases. All of this to buy us time to grow."

"And? I sense a 'but' coming," she asked, resting her head on his shoulder, her hand gently stroking his chest.

"Hon, we're a planet of a little over three hundred million people. We're at the bottom edge of the size experts say is required to sustain a high-tech civilization in the long run, even with the extensive use of automation. How can New Meyer hope to withstand an onslaught that Meyer and Earth couldn't? They had the resources of ten thousand worlds to draw from. How can we as one planet ever hope to survive?"

"By playing small and hiding? Not drawing attention to ourselves," she replied. "I know the Plan."

"I don't think the Plan's going to work. We didn't expect the collapse to come so soon. But I'm afraid along the way we've burned too many bridges here in the chute. The Earl of New Brazil is barely talking to us."

"Michael, who was that ancient German general you keep quoting?"

"Uh, you mean Clausewitz?"

"Yes, Clausewitz. Didn't he write about no plan ever surviving the first minute of battle or some such stuff?"

"Well, yes, but..."

"Go with it. You're the Duke now. Make the Plan yours."

Michael nodded. "Yeah, but I need to deal with the Earl of New Brazil. We've shirked our responsibility to the chute. My father let him keep his power because it suited our purpose and the Plan. My grandfather and father focused on New Meyer's development and basically ignored the chute, leaving that to the Earl of New Brazil."

"And you believe that was a mistake?" Donna asked.

Michael responded, "I do now. We can't survive without New Brazil's help. They're a Class Two World with far more resources than New Meyer."

"The Plan calls for us to lay low and let the Earl of New Brazil worry about chute defense," she replied.

"And the Plan expected the Imperium to be around longer than it obviously will be," Michael retorted, and then bit his lip. *She's just playing devil's advocate.* "How do we get Earl Sakomoto as Earl of New Brazil to yield his position in the chute to me? After all, he's indicated he resents us and our position."

"I may have an idea," Donna said. "You designated Mitch as the Baron of Courtney. Declare him as your regent if something happens to us and as your heir if our child or children don't survive. You need to name your successor. Carol has stated so many times she'll refuse the appointment. She's your sister. You must honor her wishes," Donna replied. "Besides, she's doing a fine job running TSP. We need her there. So all of this fits."

"Mitch will make a fine regent should something

happen to us. He'd take good care of Alex." *We've named him already and he's still only two months in the womb.* Then a bit of a wistful smile. "Mitch needs to settle down a bit."

"I believe we can we can kill two birds with one stone," she said with a smile.

Michael stared at her. *You can't be suggesting what I think you are.* "You're joking, right? Mitch will murder us."

Her smile grew broader. "I hear Earl Sakomoto's daughter, Claudia, is beautiful and intelligent. They'd make a good couple."

Michael shook his head. "This is the 30th Century. We don't do marriages of state."

"Of course we do. It's done all the time throughout the Imperium. How about us? We just follow the legal fiction that we don't."

"And you think Sakomoto will agree to a marriage?"

"To have his grandson become a Landsman? Does he know you're twelfth in line for the throne?"

I don't know. In this day and age being a Landsman might not be such a good thing," Michael replied. "The Sakomoto lineage is a good gene line and goes back to the founding of the Imperium. A good match." Donna had been lying in the crook of his arm. He pushed her away a bit and stared at her hard before asking, "Why aren't you on my Privy Council?"

She giggled, her hand stroking his cheek. "I am, only on a more private privy council."

He laughed. "Mmm, I do love you," he grumbled, hugging her tightly. "But be aware, I'm adding you to the official Council. No arguments..."

His words wee smothered by a mouthful of kiss.

"Of course, dear, if that's what you want," she grumbled as they came up for air.

The next kiss was interrupted by the urgent chiming of his implant. Three chimes in quick succession, the code for an emergency. He reluctantly opened a communication window. Shiro appeared, his face gaunt and alarmed.

"Message from Mitch. Possible incursion in the New Brazil system."

Fuck!

CHAPTER 6

—◆—

"JANAÍNA LUNAR SYSTEM IS DARK, Skipper, but the Lansan colony is untouched," Josh reported.

Mitch nodded. *Harrier* was deep in-system and immersed in Manta. *Everything depends on Manta's effectiveness.* He activated his implant and entered ShipNet, floating across the simulated conn netspace to observe over the tactical officer's shoulder. Josh was immersed in his open sensor windows. An image of a gray, red banded Jovian-class planet, Janaína, filled one of the windows. *Harrier's* array also served as an excellent optical telescope and the image of the huge planet was clear and well-defined at thirty million klicks.

A moon transited across the planet's face, allowing the array to reproduce an excellent image of the reddish white disc. Another open e-window contained the brownish-red image of the moon, Lansan, the system's largest satellite. The grayish white of the surface-girding ice crust was clearly visible, with cracks crisscrossing the entire surface. *The sea below the ice is important. Lansan is covered with an ocean that is filled with minerals and edible life harvested for export to the asteroid belt mining colonies.* A colony of three million mined the ocean. The moon's cold and thin atmosphere provided insufficient warmth to keep the ocean liquid by itself. Lansan didn't get enough radiation from the New Brazil system's sun. Janaína provided the gravitational heating to keep the ocean liquid. Mitch checked the ShipNet database. Terraforming equipment now augmented Lansan's thin oxygen atmosphere with artificially released carbon dioxide to help institute a greenhouse effect. Humans might be able to survive unprotected on the surface in a couple of centuries. The Earl thought in long term.

An image of the colony from the ship's database showed a series of moderate-sized domes covering entrances through the ice to large underwater habitats. Water temperatures were above freezing while the surface conditions were at minus two hundred degrees Celsius.

A colony of three million. A domed colony is especially vulnerable to attack, even with most of the population under the ice. He shuddered. Another e-window showed a closer image of the moon's surface. The domes appeared intact. *What must it be like hunkering down in Lansan waiting for the world to end? Of course, it probably isn't much better on New Brazil itself.*

"So the colony is untouched? Good news, Josh," Mitch said. "The incursion is confined to the inner system?"

"Appears that way," Josh replied, pointing to a smaller, less-clear image of New Brazil still two hundred million miles away. "New Brazil is still dark, so whatever is going on isn't over yet. No telltale signs of bombardment. The atmosphere is still clear."

How in the hell can he see all that from here? He grinned to himself. *Of course!* As a trained astrophysicist he reads things from the arrays a normal tech couldn't. Mitch sank back against the backrest of the Captain's chair, nursing his coffee mug. He let the coffee's aroma fill him. *So no signs of kinetic bombardment on New Brazil itself.* "So the battle isn't lost yet with new Brazil still intact," he mused out loud. "The incursion obviously started at Jump Point One, and progressed inward. Why did the Goths skip Lansan?"

"Intercepted by New Brazil units?" Ben-Levi suggested.

"One possible answer. Or maybe they aimed for New Brazil first and figured to take the colony later," Mitch suggested.

He was bringing his mug of coffee to his lips when his thoughts were interrupted by Josh. "Captain, nine contacts moving in our general direction. Range is about two million klicks." He pointed to another open e-window showing a track of nine dots moving through space. "They're heavily stealthed. I can tell they aren't Imperium ships, which is why we were able to pick them up at this range. We've identified them as *Veign*-class cruisers and designated them as contacts Golf One through Nine. I'm bringing up library images now."

The image of a smallish rectangular ship with a railgun running lengthwise along the ship's hull appeared. *A Veign-class cruiser, the primary ship used by the Goths.*

Mitch's eyes darted reflexively to another e-window showing system status. *Manta's still engaged and functioning.* He sighed and smiled to himself. *Of course, it is or I would've been told.* "Are they on an intercept course?"

Josh's blue eyes crinkled for a moment in Mitch's implant avatar image. "No, sir. Their apparent target is somewhere in the near asteroid belt. Their course doesn't lead anywhere close to the belt's industrial centers."

"So they're not hunting us?"

Josh ran some quick simulations before replying. "No. I don't think so, Skipper," Josh replied when he was done. "Their radar is not active and their course is not nearly reciprocal to ours. I don't think they've spotted us. They're trailing arrays, so they're searching for something. Possibly us, but I don't even think anyone knows we're here."

"What if the *Kuhl* scout reported us?" Mitch asked.

"Even if it had reported us we're on a new random vector. I don't believe they could have tracked us since we shut down the torch and switched to gravitics only. Not with Manta operating and protecting the ship from detection. The course change could not have been detected. No, I think they're looking for something else."

"How can you be so sure?" Mitch asked and then winced. *Stupid question. I know the answer to that one.*

Josh glanced over his shoulder at his Captain to make live eye-to-eye contact. "Skipper, Imperium databases are pretty firm on Goth tech levels and their array effectiveness. Their arrays are less capable than the Imperium's Seventeen by a pretty good margin. The Imps couldn't have tracked us either. No way Goths could've picked us up, even if they were pulsing us actively with their radar." He grinned. "I guarantee it."

"I guess we'll find out firsthand how accurate our intelligence is and how much your guarantee is worth, Mr. Ben-Levi," Mitch replied, returning the grin. *No matter how well Harrier's stealth functions, there is always a risk of being detected.* "Just remember about assume."

Josh's grin didn't waiver. "Yes, Skipper. I had the same lesson in tactics. Assume makes an ass of you and me. Skipper, even if they had Imperium level tech we'd still be virtually undetectable."

"You're assuming again, Josh."

"About Imp detection tech and Manta? No, I'm not," Josh replied in a firm tone. "You forget I served on the Manta's development team. We tested the hell out of the arrays. No, sir, I feel comfortable with my guarantee, at least at this range."

Mitch nodded with a wry smile. "Ok, I'll go with your

guarantee. Of course, if you're wrong and they detect us, I probably won't be able to collect that guarantee from you."

"They won't detect us," Josh reiterated.

Mitch smiled to himself. He agreed with his tactical officer. He had seen the Manta test reports, since he was slated to get the first new frigate. At this range, with Manta engaged, the odds of winning the New Meyerian planetary lottery were better than being detected.

Switching gears, he turned to his conn crew. They all seemed focused on their tasks with no outward signs of fear or nervousness. *None of them has seen combat. Then again, neither have I.* They all looked young. *What do I mean looked so young? They are young. The old Duke took all of the experienced hands with him.*

"Ok, everyone else, this'll be just as we drilled," he said to the entire crew. "Your training taught you what to expect. Stay on your toes. We're staying to find out what's going on. Let's determine where those Goths are headed."

No one showed any outward reaction nor had he expected any. *They all had known they were going to stay. They expect nothing less from me.*

CHAPTER 7

Argula City, New Barwick, Okra Star System
16 March 684 IP

THE HIGH PRIESTESS LEANED FORWARD in her comfortably padded chair and tasted the building passion of the blonde Human girl desperately thrusting against a Human male Adept named Gregory. *The time is almost right.* She smiled, sipping the emotions flowing from them. Gregory had been her first Human convert and had proven to be a good one. He was being allowed to participate in the transfer as a reward. He would get to enjoy the body of this conditioned Human female while fulfilling the sexual function his High Priestess required.

She stood and walked over, dropping her gown. She leaned in and kissed the girl with as much passion as her Granac host could muster. The girl recoiled from the alien kiss. The Priestess smiled an almost gentle smile before using her prodigious mind to press her image as a highly desirable Human into the girl's malleable mind. The Human female let out a sigh and responded to her bisexual conditioning. Gregory had been conditioned to love the touch of Granac females as well as Humans and didn't recoil. He responded by leaning over and kissing the Priestess' soft amber inner thighs. A torrent of lust erupted in all three of them. She sensed the girl beginning to orgasm and she clamped down with her mental prowess to prevent the pending climax. She required more energy from the girl to make the transfer. Her hands roamed the girl's soft creamy skin as she drove the girl even wilder. Her own body began its rise to climax, adding to the emotional feedback loop she had formed with the girl and Gregory. Everything Gregory and she felt was doubled and returned to the girl as her own feelings. The girl writhed in approaching orgasm but was never permitted to reach climax until the right moment. The Priestess viewed the girl's life energy as a pulsing, golden luminescent ball. *The time is about right.* As the girl began to explode in pleasure she made the insertion. The buddling flowed from her mind into the lust-filled open mind of the girl and met no resistance. The transfer was successful as the girl screamed in pleasure. Torrid emotions further intensified the spiraling feedback loop. The Priestess' Granacian body writhed in a burst of orgasm. Even through the mix of energy and passion flowing through her she managed to sense the buddling and the girl's mind Merge as they should.

The High Priestess lay in a heap with the other two, exhausted but not yet satiated. She wanted to feed more. Later, she and Gregory would couple, and she would nibble enough. Gregory would sleep it off the next day. She had to be careful. She needed both of them.

Yes, this girl is perfect to bring down the Earl of New Meyer. Acolyte Jessica. I can use her name now. She's more now than just a girl. The High Priestess preferred to send an Adept or Priestess to New Meyer. None were available who matched the body and personality type that would appeal to the Earl. Jessica fitted almost perfectly. Blonde, with an athlete's lithe body and piercing blue-green eyes. Just what the Earl favored, if the Alliance Intelligence profile was accurate. Jessica was educated enough to hold her own in company as the Earl's trophy wife.

When her buddling matured enough Jessica would inject a splinter and gain complete domination of the Earl. Prior to the insertion Jessica had to rely on the same mental and sexual control techniques used during her own conditioning process. Without the splinter, the Earl, in some circumstances, could still break free. Jessica's use was initially limited to mischief-making and building up her Nearyahn religious cell. Once the splinter was inserted his resistance was no longer possible. *I can use Jessica to control the Earl to disrupt the planet's government and maybe even foment a revolution, or at least a civil war, making New Meyer vulnerable to attack.* Then New Meyer will no longer be the threat to the timeline. The visions were just probable timelines of the future. *There's still time. I can and will prevail. I will have all Humans as feedstock.*

CHAPTER 8

---◆---

"**M**AINTAIN COURSE," MITCH ORDERED, KNOWING his curiosity got the better of him. He had elected to decelerate and match trajectories with the Goths. *They're after something and I must know what. Why are they going to this portion of the asteroid belt, well away from its manufacturing center?* A simple raiding mission would put them on a different course, heading for the rich mining and processing facilities vulnerable to a quick grab and run.

The nine Goth ships flew in a loose formation, and had not activated their radar. This helped *Harrier* avoid detection as the distance closed. *At what range will the new Manta stealth lose effectiveness? Josh indicated less than the effective missile range of 50,000 kilometers.* He had heard numbers as low as 10,000 kilometers. *I hope we don't find out.*

Harrier approached now less than two hundred thousand klicks from the Goth ships, closing at a relative velocity of slightly less than a hundred klicks per second.

If everything stays the same we'll be in missile range in about twenty-five minutes. I'll break away before then. My mission is not to engage the Goth ships, and besides, with only four missiles I can't engage all nine. Still, he was tempted to test the missiles and Manta to see how well both worked in real life. The data would prove invaluable to NMIT and to the Duke. *Trouble is we might not survive the encounter to report our findings, particularly if Manta or the warheads don't work as advertised.* He sighed. *I'm still tempted.*

Mitch checked the tactical summary. No sign the Goths had activated their radar. Manta looked good and was operating in expected parameters. *What in the devil are those ships out here for? There's nothing out here!* Not that he was complaining because they weren't using their radar and were relying only on their passive array sensors. The Goths' arrays were known to be less sensitive than *Harrier's*. This gave the corvette a potential detection advantage. He was also confident the Manta and the Electronic Counterwarfare system, or ECW, could handle Goth radar at this range. *I guess this new tech will get a good test today.*

Now the *Harrier* and her crew faced the dreaded waiting game that was the hallmark of war down through the centuries. Shiro Murray's comment in tactics class came to mind. "The lot of a soldier at war involves long periods of boredom broken by shorter periods of sheer terror before dying."

He went back to the command briefings he received when he took command of the newly refitted corvette. With her new Manta stealth activated, *Harrier* literally became a hole in space. Her stealth field bent light and other electromagnetic waves such as infrared and even x-rays around the ship. This made the stars behind the corvette appear visible with minimal distortion to an observer. No occultation or blocking of stars by the corvette meant no visual giveaways a photo-sensitive array could detect. Even the cosmic background microwave radiation left over from the Big Bang was bent around the hidden scout. There was no interruption in its uniformity.

This part of the hunt was a thousand years old, going back to the submarine warfare of the 20th and 21st centuries. He had studied accounts from submarine captains and submarine hunters of that era to get a feel for this sort of situation. The new stealth capabilities would lead to change in the standard tactics taught at the New Meyerian Military Academy. Imperium's stealth didn't support this kind of prowling, at least not at the close-in ranges he was anticipating. *Harrier* now operated under a whole different set of paradigms than the Imperium's doctrine of toe-to-toe shoot-outs. This was more akin to the proverbial cat and mouse game. *Except in this case the mouse had claws and the hunter could change to the hunted rather quickly.*

"Captain, I have a good estimate on their detection technology," Josh reported. "It's roughly comparable to standard Imperial, but not up to ours. The Goths made some improvements."

How the devil did he do that? Estimate the sensitivity of an array at this distance? "Good work, Josh. Care to explain how you arrived at your deduction?"

"Reflectivity of the array gives me a decent idea of its composition," Josh explained as if he were answering a student in class. "They don't have the transparency capabilities ours do. Good ol' albedo. You know the reflectivity of a surface. Goths' arrays are not nearly as stealthy as ours. We were able to filter enough to give me an idea of what the albedo is."

Mitch chuckled to himself. *Albedo. Thank the gods of space for an officer who was also an astrophysicist. Let's hope that none of the Goths were as good as Josh.* He sincerely doubted it. In fact, he doubted that any other detection tech or officer in the Imperium could have done what Josh had just done. *Unbelievable. Detecting a towed array.* "Very good, Mr. Ben-Levi," he said formally with a grin. "Carry on."

For the next hour Mitch restlessly watched the scenario unfold. He let his curiosity get the better of him and ordered a course change to parallel the Goths'. *What is so damned important out here in the middle of nowhere? What the hell is going on?*

Josh interrupted his thoughts. "Captain, you're not going to believe this, but we're picking up a large space battle ten million klicks from New Brazil."

Mitch sat up in his command seat. "Battle? How can you see it from this far out? It must be like picking out gnats in a rash of fly shit."

"Uh, Skipper, I think you mixed metaphors, but anyway, we can pick it up because the planet is so quiet. No EM emissions to mask the battle."

"Can you make out any details?" Mitch asked.

"I think the Imps are winning," Josh replied. "I make out about two dozen raiders racing for the transfer point with Imp ships in pursuit. Even at this range I can sense the difference in their drive flares. No stealth by the Goths. They're hell bent in retreat."

"So what the hell is going on out here?" Mitch asked.

Josh hesitated before replying. Then he nodded. "Skipper, I think I know the answer. Four new contacts designated India One, Two, Three, and Four. They're stealthed Imperial ships, about one hundred thousand klicks from here. I also detected a stealthed asteroid. The ships seem to be guarding it."

"Stealthed Imperials? Stealthed asteroid? Out here? Of all the freakin' luck," Mitch muttered, leaning forward and rubbing his large hands together. "Do you think the Goths spotted them?" he asked.

"I'm not sure," Josh replied. "They shouldn't have but

they're on a course heading for approximately where the Imps are. We only picked the Imps up by luck, and our arrays are better than anything the Imps or Goths have."

Luck? No, Josh, not by luck but by the fruits of your magnificent abilities. "I highly doubt luck was involved, Mr. Ben-Levi. But what the hell is going on?"

"I believe the Goths are searching for that asteroid. I don't know if they realize it's guarded. The Imps' stealth is working well even by Imp standards."

"Can you make out what the Imps are?"

"Not sure, but my guess is a battleship and three destroyer escorts," Josh replied. "They're leaking a little trace EM our arrays can pick up. I don't think the Goths can."

"A battleship and three destroyers against nine raiders? Not fair odds at all," Mitch mused out loud. He then came to a decision. "Maintain max stealth and ready ECM."

"Max stealth. Aye, Captain," Josh repeated. Then he added, "It'll make targeting more difficult if we need to fight."

"It's a risk I'll take. We're about to get involved in this. We're still an Imperium Navy corvette and have a responsibility to protect those ships. Also activate our Imp transponder. Put it on passive to respond only if the Imps query us."

"Battle stations?" Josh asked.

Mitch nodded his agreement. The crew was currently at their stations but not buttoned up in their cocoons.

"Battle stations," Josh commanded and the klaxon sounded.

It took less than three minutes for the readiness boards to turn green. *Well done.* "Let's see how close we can creep in before we launch," Mitch ordered. *What is so important about that asteroid?*

Then he remembered a top secret report. The whole situation coalesced for him. *New Brazil's Earl and/*

or his family must be on the asteroid. This is their hidey hole. If that's the case, it leaves me little choice. As an Imperium naval officer I must engage to protect a Peer or a Peer's family.

"We must intervene," Mitch said to his entire crew. "We're still in the Imperium Navy until told differently. Those Goth ships are looking for something instead of running to the jump point with their brethren. It must be something damned important. I think there's a member of the Peerage, or at least his family, hiding on a stealthed asteroid. The damn Imps don't realize they've been detected, or, if they do, they're sitting tight hoping they can avoid contact."

Mitch bit his lip. *I face two options here, neither optimum. I can remain hidden, and not get involved, which would allow me to slip away and report to Michael. Or I can stay and come to the aid of the Imp ships as is my duty as an Imperium officer.* The first option violated his oath as an Imperium officer. The second risked the mission. *There isn't a real choice here. With the life of an Imperium Peer or his family at stake I know what my duty is. I'll rely on the message drone to get the info back to New Meyer.*

Now that the decision was made he began work on a plan. In a straight up battle, *Harrier* stood no chance against a Goth raider. The corvette's diminutive 90mm popgun wouldn't be of much use, and she had little armor to withstand the cruiser's kinetic weapons. *On the other hand, this isn't a straight-up knuckle to knuckle bar fight. My strongest asset is surprise, provided Manta keeps working. And provided the new missiles work.*

However, once he fired the four tubes strapped to the outer hull he was basically unprotected until he could reload. That required extravehicular activity taking a couple of hours. So, at best, he could take out four of the Goth cruisers. That would certainly help even the odds for the Imps. His attack would add another element. Complete surprise and the resulting terror of being attacked suddenly by an undetectable enemy. *That, of course, assumes the Manta works.*

"Mr. Ben-Levi, prepare to engage the enemy."

I'm going to be optimistic and assume I can assign one Venom per target. We'll take out the middle three Goth cruisers and one of the last three. That allows the Imps to finish off the first three and then deal with the last two, if they hang around after seeing their four sisters magically destroyed. *Assuming the technology works.* "Mr. Ben-Levi, do you have firing solutions for Golf Four, Five, Six, and Seven?" he asked formally despite knowing the answer from reading the ShipNet data flowing past him.

"Yes, sir, we do," Josh replied just as formally.

"Time to launch?"

"Nine minutes."

"We'll launch from stealth. Launch a radar buoy in six minutes."

"Aye-aye, sir."

The minutes passed slowly. Through his connection in ShipNet he sensed Josh taking data and busily updating his firing solution. *I envy Josh. At least he's doing something. As captain, I can only watch and wait.*

The Goths came on without showing any change. *They don't know we're here and were hoping the Imps would reveal themselves.* About five minutes into the wait, the Goths switched on their active radar.

"Between Manta and ECM we're handling their radar," Josh reported. "I don't think they've detected us, but they may have a return on one of the Imp ships."

Mitch nodded grimly. "Launch radar buoy," Mitch ordered. "Reel in the array."

A small package floated free of the corvette. The buoy's gravitic drive pulsed, accelerated at fifteen gravities before burning out as it diverted away from the parent ship. Three minutes later the buoy activated its powerful phased radar and began tracking the four targets. A tight beam laser sent tracking data back to the corvette. The laser locked onto a tiny nanosensor antenna extending out beyond the ship's stealth field. The buoy also provided updates to the *Harrier's* missiles as they flew toward their target when launched.

One of Mitch's e-windows traced the Goth's own radar pulses back to their ships. *They're not using buoys.* The Gothic radar emissions helped Josh firm up the attack solution for the missile launch, as they searched wildly for the source of the buoy's radar.

"Launch!" he ordered.

The corvette bucked as the four missiles were hurled electromagnetically from their tubes. Aided by the launchers' magnetic compensators, the ship's gravitic generator strained to cancel the effects of four successive launches.

The Venoms flew deep in stealth on gravitic drive. At a thousand klicks from their target, the missiles' fusion drives flared on and the missiles sped forward at five hundred gravities acceleration. Mitch idly wondered what the thoughts of the crews onboard the Goth ships must be. *Four fusion drives and an attack radar pulse must've materialized out of nowhere.*

The four missiles accelerated toward their targets at almost five kilometers per second squared. Every second they added another five kilometers per second to their closing velocities that had started at about a hundred kilometers per second. He did the math in his head. *About twenty seconds.*

He watched the Goth ships jink to avoid the incoming missiles. *Not enough!* The Goths appeared not to have much in point defenses either. "We got them!" Mitch grumbled to himself. *That's if the warheads work as planned.* "Helm! Prepare for evasive action if required."

Harrier was creeping away at almost one gravity on its gravitic drive while immersed in deep stealth. The radar buoy, now almost five thousand klicks from the corvette pinged the enemy in an effort to draw attention away. *Harrier's* ECM system was in constant action now as all nine raiders frantically searched with their radars for the attacker. Meanwhile, the four Imperium warships dropped their stealth and pounced on the first three raiders.

Mitch's tactical summary monitored the four Venoms flying unerringly toward their targets. They were undeterred by the Goth's relatively primitive countermeasures and light point defense fire designed to take out smaller kinetic projectiles of other Goth ships. Imperium warships rarely used missiles against other warships because of the ineffectiveness of a nuclear explosion in space. *The Venoms are designed to change this paradigm.*

When the range closed to warhead effective kill radius, a small nuclear charge in each warhead surrounded by densely packed helium exploded. A five hundred kilogram nano-insulated molybdenum conical shaped liner was driven forward. The insulators ablated, protecting the liner for microseconds from the full heat of the explosion but not from the compressive force. The liner collapsed under a torrent of radiation and the pressure wave from the helium. A singularity generator produced a momentary pulse of high gravity reinforcing the liner collapse and jet formation before it died. The liner stretched into a plasma-like jet and impacted the cruiser's armor at close to five thousand kilometers per second. Unlike shaped charge warheads used against tanks, the jet didn't impact perpendicularly, but swept across the target in a slash, much as a sword slashes an opponent. The Goth armor failed catastrophically, sending huge chunks of spalled or shattered hull throughout the ship across a sixty-meter long gash in the hull.

Josh let out an exultant shout, "Got 'em! Skipper! Four hits. Golf Four and Six are broken in half. I mean it. Two radar returns for each. Golf Five and Seven are powerless and are spitting air. Four kills."

A minute later Josh reported, "Skipper, Golf Eight and Nine have fired forward fusion drives and are breaking off. Golf One, Two and Three are being handled easily by the Imps."

Mitch forced himself to relax. *Everything worked. All of it.*

Fifteen minutes later Mitch stretched in his connchair, fighting a mixture of nervousness, excitement, and impatience. He had splurged after the battle and brought out some of his private stock of coffee to celebrate with the crew. The crew relaxed at their stations with large steaming mugs and sweet pastries he had also released from his private stash. Despite his wealth and Peerage, he ate the same fare his crew did. However, as Captain, he needed little goodies like this for the sake of crew morale.

The Imperium ships had held their own against the three Goth ships they had engaged. The data *Harrier* had gathered about the battle was priceless. For the first time, New Meyer had its own direct data of the Goth weapon systems in action. He now had a better understanding of the Goths kinetic railgun capabilities. This data would be invaluable in helping the design of the point defenses for the new frigates.

"Captain, the Imp battleship is hailing us. She's the *Don Pedro*."

The *Don Pedro* was an old battleship design launched almost two centuries ago. "Put the com through."

The virtual image of Earl of New Brazil's visage materialized. His oval space-black eyes blazed with emotion. *Anger or left over emotion from the battle?*

"My Lord?" Mitch queried.

"What ship are you and what the devil did you do to those poor Goths?" the Duke replied. He spoke in slightly accented English.

"Corvette *Harrier*, Your Grace, out of New Meyer." *Can't you read our transponder?* "Baron of Courtney, Mitchell Landsman in command."

"Hmmmmph. Now, Baron, explain to me what you did to those Goth cruisers."

"Your Grace, all I can tell you is that we used missiles. The details have been classified Top Secret by the Duke of New Meyer. I'm sure we'll be able to share them with you but through formal channels. I bring communications from the Duke for you."

"Fools," he muttered, "keeping technology like this from us." Then the Earl nodded and regained his poise. "Very well. Send the messages over. I'll give you a response to take back. We're heading back in system but I'll delay until I give you a reply. I need to discuss some issues with your Duke. The raiders jumped in from our joint chute, meaning they had penetrated the chute through one of the unguarded jump points. They could still be in the chute somewhere."

He's your Duke too. Have things in the chute gone that bad? "Thank you, Your Grace. I think Duke Michael will need to know that," Mitch replied, now wondering if New Meyer was under attack.

CHAPTER 9

Main Gate, TSP Plant #1, New Meyer
19 March 684 IP

THE CLOVERLEAF SPIRALED OFF THE elevated highway, giving Michael a clear view of the sprawling twenty-thousand-acre plant. He pulled over to the side, his fusion powered electric car kicking up pebbles and small stones on the soft shoulder. New Meyer's wartime economy precluded using gravitics for personal transportation. Michael, as Duke, owned a gravitic sled, but kept it for official occasions only.

He glanced over his shoulder and grinned. No one was following him yet. His gaze turned to the giant facility at the foot of the exit ramp. TSP Industrial Facility's #1 gate sat at the foot of Gavin Bay. Piers dotted the headland's northern shore, a continuation of the natural horseshoe-shaped harbor serving the city. Five large chemical cracking towers covered the southern shoreline, rising above the shorter manufacturing shops. A massive steel and metalworking mill filled the southeast quadrant.

He scanned the plant and quickly found his favorite structures. Four squat concrete buildings, each covering almost two thousand square meters, housed the cradles in which star drives for jump-capable ships were born. These set New Meyer apart from most Class Three worlds. Not many Class Threes can manufacture their own star drives. We need more than four of those star drive assembly plants if we're going to build the ships we require to survive the oncoming chaos. Problem is they're so fuckin' expensive. He shook his head and sighed. All in good time, my boy. I just hope we have the time. He exhaled again and took a deep breath before sliding back into the car.

The guard at the main gate stepped out from his glass enclosed booth to check identification. "May I help you, sir?" he asked. The bored look turned to one of surprise. "Your Grace! I apologize, I didn't recognize you. Where's your escort?"

Michael waved his hand as if to brush off the answer as the guard electronically opened the gate. He ignored the question. "Have a nice day, Bill," he said as he drove through. A robotic security point would violate my ducal full employment policy. What else would Bill be doing if not working as a guard here? He's an ex-Marine retired on partial disability. His physical impairment restricts what jobs he can fill. I think I'm doing the right thing in mandating full civilian employment at the expense of the robotics industry. The military is using plenty of robots, enough to keep the industry growing.

A well-landscaped road led to the twenty-six story glass and plastisteel tower housing the corporate operational and administrative hub of TSP in this star system. He pulled into the Duke's permanently reserved parking spot. An armored utility vehicle arrived with a screech of tires and his security detail piled out. Michael sighed and turned to meet them.

Marine Master Gunnery Sergeant Ralph Goodson snapped to attention in front of him. Michael interpreted his expression as the reproachful father catching his son in the middle of some prank. "Your Grace with all due respect..." Goodson began.

"Can it, Master Guns. I don't want to hear it. You can wait out here." Michael retorted.

"Yes, Your Grace," the non-com replied with a hurt look on his face.

Michael couldn't help but laugh. "Always the actor, Guns," he said. "It's not going to work. I'll go see my sister at my secure company headquarters without you trailing behind me." He put an extra emphasis on the word secure.

Goodson bowed his head. "As you wish, Your Grace. With all due respect, I'm not sure how the Duchess will react to your taking off on your own again."

"Now, Guns, that's not fair and you know it." He sighed. "Ok. You win. Come in."

The five Marines formed their usual box around him with Goodson at the point. He sighed again and decided there could be worse things. *My lot in life as Duke.* The guard at the front desk buzzed them in without the slightest hint of surprise at his unannounced visit. *Bill let him know I was here.*

The elevator door slid open to reveal the Lady Carol's personal assistant waiting. Michael grinned. *The staff here is efficient as always.* Word had spread quickly. The Duke had arrived unannounced. *Carol prefers live assistants to robotic ones.*

"Right this way, Your Grace," she said with a bow, leading him to a large double wooden door to Carol Landsman's spacious office. It smelled of something flowery and feminine but resembled any other CEO's lair with its proliferation of communication electronics, mahogany desk, and nanoleather covered furniture.

The Lady Carol Landsman rose and bowed. "Welcome, Your Grace."

"Sis, what's with the Your Grace bee ess? If I hear one

more Your Grace I'm going to take you over my knee the way I used to when we were kids."

Carol giggled. "I don't remember it like that, brother."

"Well, Father, said he'd kill me if I ever did that to you again," he complained with a grin while flopping down on a dark leather couch. Two large picture windows overlooked the bay. A ship with red metal containers piled on its deck made its way through the bay's protected waters toward the ocean beyond. "Please cut the 'Your Grace.'"

Carol grew serious. "Get used to it, Michael. You're the Duke now. There must be formality even from relatives."

He grinned at her. "Well, as Duke I proclaim you call me Michael in private."

"Yes, Your Grace," she replied automatically and then chuckled. "I mean Michael."

She poured him rich, aromatic coffee from a large but simple ceramic pot with the TSP logo on its side. He took it without comment. She sat facing him with a cup of tea in her hands. "Ok, Michael, why are you here unannounced?"

He studied his sister before replying. She followed the standard Landsman mold, tall but slightly stocky with deep-set gray eyes and black hair framing her face. The dark hair only served to emphasize the burning intensity in her eyes. She wore a fashionable, conservatively styled charcoal business suit that didn't hide the curves and fine tone of her body. He remembered she worked out regularly with her Marine bodyguards. Though she had no steady man in her life she was far from celibate. *Ask her and she'd tell you she hadn't met the right one yet. Still, they call you the Dragon Lady of New Meyer for a reason.*

"To bring you some news you aren't going to like," he said to her. "I wanted to give it to you in person."

Her eyes widened and she shot up to her feet. "You wouldn't!"

"Yes."

"You wouldn't! You can't! I won't accept it!" She placed the mug down to avoid dropping it.

Michael rose and took her hands. "Sis, I'm afraid neither you nor I have any choice in these matters. I didn't want to become Duke either. So, it'll be official for you tomorrow. I require your support on the Council. As the new Baroness of Freehold you'll furnish the clout I need. I require sound advice I can trust."

"Please! No!" she pleaded. "I don't want titles. I'm happy here."

Michael shook his head with a sad smile. "With Dad gone it's just you, Mitch, and me. I need you. You can still stay here and run TSP."

For years she had resisted her rightful position in the Peerage hierarchy on New Meyer, content to run the TSP operation and stay away from politics. She had replaced her uncle three years before, and under her tutelage the company had grown significantly. Her no nonsense business demeanor had earned her the nickname "Dragon Lady," a mantle she wore with honor. But "Dragon Lady" and politics did not mix. "Sis, the public needs to see us together as a family. So does the damned media. I would much rather be off commanding *Courtney* when she's launched, but Mitch will have that privilege. These are things we must do as members of the Landsman family.

"I'm submitting your appointment to the Senate for approval. You know the consent will be automatic. You're now the Baroness of Freehold, in line behind Mitch until my son is of age. This is a ducal order. By rights you should be Baroness Courtney behind me. Be thankful I'm putting Mitch ahead of you."

She sighed, lowering her head. "Yes, Your Grace."

"You will assume your rightful place on my Privy Council as the Baroness Freehold, not just my economic advisor."

"Yes, Your Grace."

"You'll be a Senator as the Baroness of Freehold."

"Oh, God! Do you hate me so?"

Michael laughed. "No, Sis, I want you on the government team precisely because I love and respect you so much."

She just nodded and sighed again.

"This wasn't an easy decision for me. Sis, your work here at TSP is even more important now. I'm placing a large burden on you. You can use an avatar or second for routine Senate sessions. TSP controls more than fifty per cent of military manufacturing on this planet and all of the military ship production. I need you involved in the difficult industrial decisions the Council will be forced to make. You'll be in a position to help raise production at other facilities besides TSP's. I want you to kick ass and take names. I also need help with Congress. This New Brazil incursion shook many of them up. I need your straight head to guide them."

One more sigh and then she straightened her shoulders, "As you command, Your Grace. I'll be honored to accept."

He grinned. "Good. Now, how's *Courtney* doing?"

She smiled. "That I can handle. *Courtney* is really moving along. She'll be ready for Mitch when he returns."

"And the spacedock?"

"Three berths are dedicated to launching the new frigates at one a month. Build time for the next group of frigates is three months. By then an additional two more berths should be on line. You can run the numbers. This spacedock will max out at six docks for frigates. The other limitation we face is star drive cradles. We have eight cradles available. Assembly cycle is two months per drive, so we can barely maintain the buildup."

"And the new cradles?"

"At least four or five months away," she replied with a sigh. "Too many supplier limitations. Even with nanos you can't build one of these cradles in a day. Crystal maturation takes three weeks alone. They can't grow any faster and maintain the purity."

"The new spacedock?"

"Construction will begin as soon as we finish the current one. I just don't have enough spacers to build both at the same time."

Michael nodded. "Sis, you've worked wonders here. I'm sorry I'm making you do what you hate so much." He sighed. "Duty calls all of us."

Carol shrugged. "I understand. It's the lot of the Landsman clan not to shirk responsibility. I won't let you down, brother."

"I know you won't," he replied with a warm smile. "If there's a certainty in the universe that's one of them."

CHAPTER 10

---◆---

Low New Meyer Orbit, Frigate Courtney
15 April 684 IP

THE ACRID ODOR OF WELDING and soldering filled the ship's conn as five civilian workers worked diligently on the compartment's control stations. Star-like sparks from cutting torches cast garish shadows, providing glimpses of the exposed wiring on the still incomplete installations. Two men stepped through the open hatch and stopped to survey the compartment. The workers briefly glanced up and nodded to the first visitor, the Spacedock Superintendent. They turned back to their work, paying little attention to the Navy officer with him. Many of those came through almost every day for tours or to check on progress. The second visitor, a Commander, paused. Since he wore the standard jet-black Naval uniform with no peerage badges or decorations, the workers didn't recognize him as Baron of Courtney Commander Mitchell Landsman.

Mitch surveyed the conn, the combination bridge and combat information center serving as the heart of the ship. In deep space there was no need for a separate bridge like a ship at sea. He sighed to himself in anticipation of taking command. Despite the apparent incomplete construction and disarray, *Courtney* was now only a week or so from completion as the result of three weeks of overtime work. *As Prospective Commanding Officer, or PCO, I appreciate the effort. A Priority One can do amazing things.*

"Welcome to your domain, Commander," Spacedock Superintendent Carlos Sanchez said, bowing and sweeping his hand across the scene.

Mitch smiled at Sanchez' gesture. He walked over to the high-backed chair near the center of the compartment and absently rubbed the pseudo-leather nanocomposite, feeling its unworn smoothness. As the commander of the first ship in a new ship class, he inherited the responsibility to prove out the whole frigate concept. He grinned appreciatively. *At least this command chair will be big enough and more comfortable than Harrier's.*

"It's okay, Commander. You can sit in it," Sanchez said with a gentle smile. Then he grew serious. "With Earth destroyed and the Imperium in turmoil, *Courtney* is going to be needed more than ever. That's why she's been moved up on the priority list."

This was nothing new to Mitch. He looked over to Sanchez, nodding sagely as if accepting this tidbit of information. "I understand, Superintendent. *Courtney* represents a whole mind change on how space battles will be fought. I appreciate Spacedock's efforts in expediting her completion."

Courtney had originally been Michael's ship, but now as Duke he would command task forces and fleets, not mere frigates. *I can't help wondering if I've been given Courtney because of my rank as Baron of Courtney.*

Sanchez studied Mitch for a second. "Commander, many new PCOs face a moment of doubt. She's yours. Don't think for a minute that you don't belong here."

Admiral Murray had assured him he was not a political

choice. He had supposedly been slated after Michael to get the next *Courtney*-class frigate available. Still his rank and relationship to his cousin certainly played a role in putting him in that position. He thought of at least three or four officers who were senior to him and more qualified to command *Courtney*. *But they're not first cousin to the Duke. Whatever the reason, Courtney is my responsibility now.*

He turned his attention to the compartment, focusing on the quartermaster's station. Two panel covers, exposing unfinished electronics in the console, lay on the floor around the already installed seat. Communications fared no better, but Detection, Engineering, and Guns were in final assembly. *Reminds me of a trauma center with major stomach surgeries going on.* This was a normal state of affairs for a ship at this point in its construction. *Could she possibly be ready for her commissioning next week?*

Again Sanchez must've sensed his concerns. "She'll be ready, Commander, come hell or flare," he said softly. "That I promise."

Mitch merely nodded and continued studying the compartment. *The conn is the heart of the ship, its brains. Here he had complete domain as captain. He was master in this small world of technology and flesh and blood. His words were law and his crew lived or died by those words. In space, while aboard this ship, I command by naval rank, not peerage.*

The Captain's chair was a lure he couldn't resist. The chair's nanocomposites were not yet activated so it didn't conform to his body. To his surprise, even without the nanos, the chair fit. Somehow everything seemed right. He had commanded other ships but never from their birth. Serving as a ship's founder was a rare opportunity. *Courtney* would always be special to him, like someone's first love.

One of the workmen glanced up, noticing the officer sitting in the command chair. No visitor in uniform would dare sit in the Captain's chair unless he belonged there, particularly in the presence of the Superintendent. Then he must have recognized Mitch because he stiffened slightly. He flipped back his welder's mask and bowed his head in acknowledgment. "Yours, My Lord?" he asked. The worker was silver haired with a weathered face Mitch thought of as almost grandfatherly.

Mitch nodded, trying to maintain some sort of outward calm and dignity. "Yes, I'm the PCO," he replied.

The workman beamed a broad smile. "She's going to be a good one, My Lord."

Mitch grimaced, and then forced a smile. "Take good care of her," he whispered.

The workman grinned. "We will, My Lord. Very good care."

Mitch stood and pirouetted, taking one last look before walking toward the hatch back to the small two-man shuttle. He stopped as his eyes focused on another hatchway whose hatch wasn't installed yet. Five long strides took him to the entrance. He poked his head into the unlit compartment. Enough light filtered in from the conn to allow him to make out the contents. Its five stations, housing four USV controllers and the ship's assistant tactical officer, were almost complete. *A controller for each of the Raptors.*

He looked back over his shoulder to the opposite side of the bridge to an identical opened hatch. The compartment's five stations were barely visible in the dim light. It would be unmanned during most missions but would serve as a flag conn for when the Duke or Admiral Murray were aboard. As the most modern ship in New Meyer's tiny fleet, *Courtney* had been designated as a flagship. *Having a frigate as a flagship says something about the state of New Meyer's Navy.* On subsequent *Courtney*-class ships the compartment would be used for other things, designed to be configured to the mission. It could also serve as a backup Raptor command center. *The wonders of transmutable electronics.*

He turned to the Superintendent and shook his hand. "Superintendent, thank you for the quick tour. I'm going to set up my office. I'll come back to tour Weps and Engineering after I settle in and spend a little more time with her plans and specs. I don't want to take too much of your time."

Sanchez nodded. "My pleasure, Commander. And don't worry about the time. I gave you my best Yeoman. She knows her way around and will help you with what you need."

Mitch nodded, took one last long look, and exited through the hatch into the ship's corridor on the way to the spacedock portal.

CHAPTER 11

———✦———

Corvette Aguia, Deep Space, New Meyer System
24 April 684 IP

A GUIA, A *HAWK*-CLASS CORVETTE ASSIGNED to customs duty, hid in deep stealth in an orbit fifteen thousand kilometers from New Meyer's jump point. Captain Richard Bassett, Lord Baron of New Leicester, formerly of the planet New Britain, occupied the command chair at the center of *Aguia's* cramped conn. The corvette's "Twenty-Two" trailed behind, searching for the telltale glimmer or spike of energy that would reveal the arrival of a ship through the jump point.

Rich squirmed in the tight Captain's chair that squeezed his broad hips. *You'd think with so many corvette captains complaining about the conn chair width the Navy might actually do something about it. Nah!* He was a product of New Britain's higher gravity which led to his stocky stature and wide hips. No ships were due for a while and he settled back to relax for a moment. Images of New Britain from eighteen years earlier surfaced as a near-lifeless planet, bombed and pillaged by the Goths. They were memories he'd been fighting over those years and he never knew when they'd resurface. *I should've done more.* He sighed. *No, I've got to stop these bouts of blaming myself. I did what I could. The Goths paid heavily but not enough.* Visions of the hundreds of Goth cruisers swarming through the jump point and overwhelming the New British Navy forces interfered with his view of the open ShipNet e-windows. The images were still raw and real after all these years.

He closed his eyes and let them come. They came anyway, no matter how hard he fought to suppress them. New Britain defense forces harassed the onrushing Goths for the weeks they drove implacably into the system. *Too many of them and they just kept coming.* The Goths intended to destroy New Britain based on its membership in the original Coalition that had destroyed the Granac's and Braum's homeworld centuries before. They did not intend to occupy the planet. Revenge was on their minds, not conquest.

He was back on the bridge of the *Sheffield*. The cruiser led a convoy of merchantmen loaded with refugees in a desperate flight to safety as the Goth-launched asteroids began falling on New Britain. The Goths ignored his band of ships, apparently content to allow their ships left at the jump point to intercept them. Rich elected to take a long circuitous route toward the system's one jump point, powering everything down to avoid detection. *Maybe they'll forget about us.*

As they approached the jump point he separated his force. *Achilles* and three destroyers led six empty decoy freighters to distract the Goth ships, coming from a different direction than *Sheffield* and her charges. All ten ships died in the attack but the diversion worked. The convoy made it through the jump point. The Goths pursued them after a day or two delay in getting started. The chase sped through three star systems. Unfortunately, those systems' forces were only able to slow the pursuing Goth ships. That bought them time to prevent the Goth warships from catching the slower merchantmen. *Thank God the merchantmen were military attack transports with military gravitic drives with higher acceleration capabilities than standard commercial ships. Still, it was close.*

Closing his eyes didn't erase the image of the cruiser *Norfolk* exploding under a hail of Goth kinetic projectiles. She died to let them jump into one of the uninhabited star systems in the New Brazil-New Meyer chute, or the NBNM chute as it was commonly referred to. A week later they jumped into New Meyer system, a cul-de-sac system with no other way out. Duke Alexander had a long-standing offer of asylum that he had hoped the Duke would still honor.. The Duke did. Six New Meyer battleships at the jump point made short work of the ten remaining Goth cruisers. *Those six battleships are now shattered wrecks floating somewhere in Sol System.*

Forty merchantmen had left New Britain. Thirty-four made it to New Meyer. *I know I should be okay with what I accomplished. It still doesn't overshadow the death of my homeworld.* Eleven thousand New Britain refugees were granted asylum by Duke Alexander. *New Britain will live in us.*

All eleven thousand had insisted on staying with him. Together they formed the basis for the fast growing New Leicester Township. He now owned a substantial plot of land outside the town proper and was a member of the Senate. He rarely went to Senate sessions, content in sending his son, Jeremy, as his Second or substitute. *Geez, I feel like a damned feudal lord.*

Two-years ago the old Duke persuaded him to come back into service. He had grown tired of moping around his estates and was bored to death with the Senate. *So here I am, commanding a flotilla of corvettes on customs duty.* He grinned to himself. *Not a capital ship but I'm out in space and in command again.*

Finally the memories faded and he returned to the

insistent whisperings through his implant of the ship's sensor suite processing incoming data. He looked forward to the scheduled arrival of TSP's thirty-thousand-ton freighter *Space Flower,* due within the next hour. The brief appearance of his old friend, Jonathan Craig, her Captain, served to break the monotony of dealing with the hundred or so other arrivals every day.

Almost on cue the ship's AI dinged in his ear, its voice programmed with a distinctly British accent. "Captain, breakout is imminent."

"Very well. Alert the other ships to go to max stealth." *No need to submit the crew to the rigors of GQ every time a ship emerges from jump. Not with a hundred a day. We'd be living in our cocoons.*

He used ShipNet to peer over the detection tech avatar's shoulder. The energy readings at the jump point rose asymptotically toward infinity and dissipated rapidly as the ship emerged. He read the transponder code. *Space Flower.*

"Drop stealth," he ordered.

Moments later, the com beeped. "Captain of *Space Flower,* sir," *Aguia's* com tech, Chief Petty Officer Aliane Valques y Stafford informed him.

A wizened old face, burned by many years of exposure to the radiation of space, materialized in front of him. "Jonathan," Rich said with a warm smile.

"Ahh, Richard, it's you," replied Ship Master Jonathan Craig with a broad smile. His accent identified him to Rich as a fellow New Britainer. Jonathan's blue eyes were bright with an intelligence one didn't always expect to find in the captain of a tramp freighter.

"Looks like you made it back in one piece," Rich said.

Craig grimaced. "Yes, but a close thing. Imperium space is in chaos with five Pretenders to the throne and Goths running wild." Craig also held a commission as a Commander in the New Meyer Naval Intelligence

Service. His ship not only pursued trade and profits but also intelligence. A tramp freighter could go places a warship couldn't.

"As long as they stay away from New Meyer," Rich grumbled. "Go ahead. You're clear. I'll let orbital customs back home do the formal search and check." The tramps were as cramped and crowded as the corvettes. Rich allowed himself a brief smile. Jonathan wanted a shower and hot fresh food more than anything but he still had five weeks travel in-system at the quarter g acceleration of a merchant ship.

"Thanks, Richard. When will you be home? Thalia and I would love to have you and Edith over for dinner."

"Not for another couple of months. Thanks, Jonathan, the offer is appreciated."

"Damn, I'll be gone then. Next time. Catch you on the way back out." He blinked off.

Rich sank back in his seat and watched the freighter ponderously accelerate away at a quarter g. Two minutes later the alarm bells interrupted his thoughts. His detection tech barked, "Breakout imminent and it's something huge!"

"Sun of a bitch! What the bloody fuck is that?" Bassett grumbled as the energy signature surged.

CHAPTER 12

———◆———

Argula City, New Barwick, Okra Star System
24 Aprivil 684 IP

J'AN D'TOR SHIVERED IN HIS old tattered down coat as the icy wind knifed in between Argula City's tall skyscrapers. He grinned. The coat was old but relatively warm. Some rich person had thrown it out two weeks ago and he had been in the right place at the right time. He pulled his woolen cap down over his ears and pushed forward as another gust stirred scattered papers and trash across the cracked concrete sidewalk. He had earned a few dollars last night sweeping the floor of a dilapidated bar that catered to military and the working class. This, after scrounging a few dollars from patrons by keeping an eye on their vehicles parked out front, meant that he had a few hireks in his personal credit account. *Not a bad night. At least I'll eat tomorrow. It'll be hot and it won't be that tasteless slop served by the Goddess' mission.*

He was a street waif, orphaned by the war with the Imperium. He lived by scavenging and hustling on the streets of Argula City, Capital of the Goth Kingdom of Orath. New Barwick's society did not spend on safety nets though the Goddess of Neary's Missions did form a little bit of a lifeline. He turned the corner to the alley where the cardboard hovel he called home was located. *Maybe I'll even have enough left over to add a bit to the cache. I don't have enough yet to get a permanent place but every little bit helps.*

A screech of tires behind him. He turned and eyed the van sliding to a stop at the curb. Two males jumped out and approached him. Before he had a chance to react they swept him up and manhandled him into the open car door. *Slavers. Or maybe even one of the Alliance Navy's press gangs. Shit!*

A rough hand ripped off the cap and slipped a hood over his head covering his eyes. One of the goons pushed him back into the seat. "Move and you're dead," a deep Granacian voice growled at him. *Certainly not military. Not even slavers. Too much effort for one victim. Slavers would just stun me with a blocker and throw me on the floor in the back of a truck.*

He didn't move. The ride didn't seem to take all that long. They dragged him from the vehicle and marched him into a building. He heard the automatic doors whirr and close. The hood was swept off. Before he could react to the bright light, a stream of hot water pushed him up against the wall.

"Take off those clothes," came the same guttural voice again. A bar of soap was flipped to him. "Clean yourself real good. The Goddess doesn't take to dirty boys."

The Goddess? All of the street stories ran through him like the coming attractions of some vid. She was the most beautiful woman in the world. She was a monster. People called before her became unbelievably rich and powerful. Or they disappeared. So many different versions. He didn't know how to feel so he faced it with a mixture of terror and anticipation. He washed and scrubbed, and scrubbed some more. *Maybe this is a break.*

The taller of the two thugs handed him a simple one piece tunic to wear and nothing else. "Follow me," he commanded.

Another relatively short walk and he was ushered into a large chamber. Sweet fragrances assaulted his senses and seemed to make their way immediately down into his groin. He stopped and gawked. He had never seen a female so beautiful in real life. Tall and big-busted, she oozed sexuality, all aimed at him. At seventeen, he had never been with a woman. She wore a robe parted in the front, providing tantalizing hints of what lay beneath. Sexual desire overcame fear. He was already erect and hard.

"Undress, little one," she said, her voice melodious and driving deep into his soul.

Without hesitation he pulled off the one-piece, knee-length tunic. His hands worked as if they were not his. Not that he wanted to resist.

"Don't be afraid, little one," she purred. Her voice filled his mind with images of raw hot sex that had been the subject of his teenage fantasies.

He was raging hard now, entirely focused on the woman before him. He somehow grew harder with anticipation as she reached up to drop her robe. She was everything he expected. Lust pulsed through him like the blaring of a marching band. She stepped back onto the bed behind her and motioned him over. Thoughts of refusing never even entered his mind. She represented the fantasy of every humanoid sex-starved teenage male in the galaxy.

J'an's legs started towards her without any thought on his part. She reached out and pulled him to her. Her mouth pressed on his and he found a warm breast in his hand. He would have exploded and climaxed right then and there but something clamped down on his mind preventing him. *Not yet* came the command. He didn't know if the thought was hers or his. He wasn't even sure if she had spoken.

She pushed him flat on his back and hovered over him.

The dark tawny triangle between her legs contrasted with the velvety amber of her thighs. He gulped as all of his fantasies seemed to be coming true. Her eyes glowed violet, locking his gaze. He couldn't look away no matter how hard he tried. Soon he didn't want to look away. He just wanted to fall into those shining pools and let his mind dissolve. He no longer thought about anything, his mind lost in waves of lust and shrouded in a haze of nothingness.

She lowered herself onto him, sending a bolt of exquisite pleasure up through his entire body. Her movements were calculated to drive him to climax but the mental clamp in his brain prevented him ever reaching it. When he reached the point she wanted the block evaporated and he began to explosively release. She responded in an outburst of soft moans. The eruption of his white-hot raw sexual energy spread through him like waves of fire filling his entire being with exquisite pleasure and sensuality. He convulsed from head to toe in paroxysm after paroxysm of release. Something else appeared in his mind but before he could react he felt nothing at all. Nothing ever again.

The High Priestess disengaged herself. The young male's life force had filled her Neary with the energy needed to bud and create additional buddlings for insertion into new Acolytes. She watched impassively as two mind-wiped male servants lifted the body between them and left the room heading for the incinerator in the temple's basement. The Granacian side of her brain was satisfied and content.

CHAPTER 13

Corvette Aguia, Deep Space, New Meyer System
24 April 684 IP

"SHUT THAT BLEEDIN' ALARM OFF," Rich ordered. "Now easy, Ms. Hu, take a deep breath and report." *GQ? No, I'll wait a second.*

Warrant Officer Beverly Wu took a deep breath as ordered and studied the readouts on the panel in front of her. "Captain, large unidentified ship escorted by two Imp destroyers and a cruiser. The contacts are designated as Bogies One, Two, Three, and Four. Bogie One must mass a million-tons if not more."

"Imp destroyers and a cruiser," Rich mused out loud, "escorting a million-ton spacecraft. No Imp battleship is anywhere close in size by almost two orders of magnitude. I don't think the Shaallit and the Goths have anything that size."

Wu's voice sounded surprised. "Captain, they're squawking Imp IFF. An old code." IFF Identification Friend or Foe.

"Can you identify it?"

"Trying, sir," she replied. Her eyes furrowed as she scanned the ShipNet database. "Got it! ISDF!"

Rich pondered her identification. ISDF, Imperium Salient Defense Force, the legendary forces who held the Shaallit at bay for six hundred years. They were almost a separate service now from the mainstream Navy. *Holy crap! If that's what I bloody think it is...*

Hu continued. "I've ascertained the vessel as a *Langley*-class tender. Identified as *Yakumo*."

Rich pulled up an image of a *Langley* from the database. A huge cylinder with three rows of hollow spokes around its circumference. Each protruding spar was the equivalent of a spacedock. *There are good and bad implications here.* The *Yakumo* would be a great asset to the New Meyerian Navy. *Almost like adding a number of spacedocks. Langleys* serviced the ships patrolling the border between the Imperium and the Shaallit Salient. *On the bad side, what in the hell was it doing here? Is the Salient open?*

"Captain!" Hu sounded embarrassed. "I can't believe I missed this. The big ship is unpowered and is being towed by four tugs. I guess the breakout scrambled our sensors more than I thought."

"You're doing fine, Beverly," Rich said, using her given name to reassure her. *They're all so damn young.*

The information jived with what he knew about *Langleys. No main propulsion of their own and towed by tugs.* The database article indicated the few times a *Langley* had to make a jump they were towed to the jump point. The tugs were stored on board the tender, and the jump was accomplished by a strap-on singularity generator. *Probably why Beverly didn't detect the tugs.*

"The tugs were stored on the *Yakumo* for the jump," he told her. "That's why you couldn't detect them."

The ISDF had been formed to contain the Shaallit within the Salient, the eight chute finger extending into Imperium space. *Eight chutes might not sound like much when* compared to the Imperium's hundred and sixty. Each of the Shaallit chutes contained an amazing three to four hundred mostly Level One and Two terraformed worlds. Shaall is a rigid, genetically modified caste society, a dictatorship the likes of which had never been seen on Earth. Their entire racial energy is directed toward the goal to become strong enough to destroy the Imperium.

The ISDF's mission involved fortifying jump points in over a thousand systems, many of them without inhabitable planets. This meant small fortified asteroids were moved into position and reinforced by fleets of ships. The ISDF had been successful for hundreds of years in containing the Shaallit and defending the Imperium against incursion after incursion. Occasionally they would need to be supported by regular Imperium Navy when the Shaallit incursion grew too large. Maybe twice in the last two centuries. The last option is no longer available with the Imperium in shambles. They're on their own now.

Geez. There's another possibility here. A scary one at that. A Duke Viceroy ruled the ISDF. Outside of the Landsman royal family he was the highest ranking Duke. If the current ISDF Duke ever decides to claim the throne, there would be few who could resist.

The ISDF had created the Sentai Haramaki, or Protector Fleet, crewed by descendants of refugees from the Southwest Asian War of 2039. China, India, parts of Russia and all of Southeast Asia had been decimated by the war. They had adapted to the isolation of the Salient with almost a religious fervor, evolving a code reminiscent of the code of Bushido. Ships like Yakumo became home to thousands of workers and families for generations. Who knows what the ambitions of the current Duke Viceroy were concerning the throne? Someone in his position might consider himself a savior of the Imperium.

"Message from Yakumo, sir."

Another space radiation-wizened face materialized in

the same spot where Jonathan Craig's had been a few minutes before. The almond shape of his eyes and high cheekbones left little doubt of his Asian descent. The darker color of his skin hinted at some Indian or other southwest Asian blood.

"I am Lord Bassett, Baron of New Leicester, and Captain of the corvette *Aguia,*" Rich said. "You've entered New Meyerian space. Please identify yourself."

"My Lord, I am Captain Badri Takahashi, Captain of the tender *Yakumo,*" he said with a trace of a smile. "Please inform your Duke that Taki is here to see him."

"You're acquainted with the Duke of New Meyer?" Bassett asked, keeping his surprise from his voice.

"Alexander, er, I mean the Duke and I served together on the *Renown* for three years. We've kept in touch since."

Ahh! I thought he looked too old to know Duke Michael. "Captain Takahashi, Duke Alexander is dead. He died defending the Emperor at Earth a while ago. His son Michael is now the Duke."

"Alex is dead?" Takahashi grumbled. "The universe is a duller place without him. And Mikey is Duke now?"

Alex? Mikey? Is this Captain Takahashi daft or did he know the Duke that well? "Captain Takahashi, if you've been in contact with Duke Alexander why aren't you aware of recent events?"

"I am proud to say the former Duke and I are lifelong friends. We corresponded three or four times a year and managed to see each other every couple of years. I haven't heard from him for more than a year. I've been concerned. I've been out of contact during the journey here. We took a path here favoring uninhabited systems. The trip took months longer than a more direct route but there was less risk. I heard about the fall of Earth but had no details."

That explains his lack of knowledge. "So, Captain, what are you doing here with *Yakumo*?"

"Seeking asylum," he replied.

Rich's stomach roiled at the thought of Taki abandoning his post. After a moment's thought he calmed. *There's something more to this.* Beneath the man's informality he sensed a toughness one would expect from someone brought up in the Samurai tradition of the Sentai Haramaki. He pulled up Takahashi's record from the *Aguia's* database. *We received an Imperium update three years so the data isn't too aged.* He studied the record. *Takahashi must've spent more than half his career away from ISDF as a liaison to the Imperium Navy. Two citations for extreme valor, including the Emperor's Medal of Honor.*

"Asylum from what? And why aren't you at your post with *Yakumo*?"

Takahashi's eyes narrowed. "Asylum from the chaos out in the Imperium. The Duke promised my family and me asylum when things started to go to hell, which they have. As for bringing *Yakumo*, I was ordered to bring her here by the late Emperor."

Rich raised his eyes at the mention of the Emperor, but he decided to refrain from a comment. *I'll leave it to the higher ups to sort this out.* "Taki, I will inform the Duke of your arrival."

CHAPTER 14

―――◆◆――――

New Meyer Cruiser Francisco Cibola, Deep Space, Star System New Brazil
30 May 684 IP

"UNIDENTIFIED SHIPS, STATE YOUR IDENTITY and business," came the immediate challenge from a New Brazilian warship as *Cibola* emerged from the New Brazil jump point. The face materializing in front of Michael had a grim look, and one of little patience.

Michael grinned at the *Cibola's* Captain, Eric Burton. "Unfriendly cusses, aren't they?" *What's this all about? They're aware of our pending arrival. A message to us? Can the Earl be so pissed at us?*

Burton grinned back, his smile illuminating an Imperium standard bronze complexion derived from North American stock. His dark brown eyes twinkled as he smiled at his one-time Naval subordinate, now turned Duke. "You would be too, Your Grace, after what Baron Mitchell found. I suspect they're ignoring our transponder out of heightened security."

No, this is a message to me. They're pissed. Michael recognized the officer as Captain Luis Fernando de Silva y Correa, a first cousin to the Earl and Heir Regent to the throne until the Earl's children reached thirty. *At least they've shown the proper respect with a high ranking official greeting me.*

"I am Duke of New Meyer on a state visit to the Earl." Michael said.

The face relaxed. "We've been expecting you, Your Grace. Please forgive my harshness, but in these times of chaos..."

Michael waved his hand. "You're doing your job, Captain....?" *The message is received.*

"Captain Luis Fernando de Silva y Correa, Your Grace," Silva stated formally, bowing his head. "I was sent here by Earl Sakamoto to receive you."

Michael suppressed a grin. He half expected to see Silva cracking his heels together and snapping to attention. "Captain Silva. No offense taken."

"Your Grace, I am to escort you to the meeting. My astrogator will forward destination and trajectory information."

"Thank you, Captain."

Silva's ship, *Cristobol Ruiz*, matched *Cibola's* course. She was an *Esteves*-class cruiser, pretty much a sister to *Cibola* before her upgrades. *Hard to believe Cibola was retrofitted so quickly.* Taki had jumped right in, putting his crews on a twenty-six-seven schedule. Using a mixture of robotics and highly trained, dedicated technicians, *Langley* completed *Cibola's* conversion in less than two weeks. *Amazing.*

"Your Grace, Captain Silva accepted our invitation to dine with us," Burton said, this time through the privacy of implant communication. "He and his exec will be here for dinner at 1800. We're heading to an asteroid about forty kilometers in diameter and only noted on the charts as a number. Right now it's not showing up on our sensors, which means stealth. ETA is four days."

Michael nodded. "Same one Mitch reported, I presume."

"Yes, Your Grace," Burton confirmed.

"Very well. I'll let Wallace know about dinner," he replied, activating his implant and sending a brief message to Wallace.

He sighed and returned to his thoughts. Little was required of him at this point. *As Duke I'm just extra baggage.*

Two hours later he arrived at the receiving area in front of *Cibola's* main airlock for the piping of a distinguished visitor aboard. Four Marines clad in dress black uniforms, accompanied by four crew members in dress whites stood at attention. The Bosun of the Deck was positioned on one side, his personal old-fashioned metal bosun call in hand. Michael smiled. Master Chief Withers was a traditional sailor. He loved naval traditions and took them seriously. No recording or an electronic call for him, not when he had his own metal one. *I once asked him how old the pipe, no, call is the more formal term, was.* He claimed it had been handed down in his family since the days of Horatio Nelson.

A ship-to-ship transfer while accelerating at one-g was tricky but they accomplished it perfectly. A slight jar and a dull clang announced the shuttle docking. Two minutes later the airlock swung open, "Whoooee!" Withers' call rang out, initiating the fifteen hundred year old "tending the deck" tradition tracing its roots back to the sailing ships of the British Royal Navy. Captain Silva stepped through, followed by his executive officer, Commander Gabriella Larissa de Oliviera y de Santana.

Michael grinned. *The New Brazilians do like their long names.* Silva stiffened ramrod straight and snapped a tight salute towards the *Cibola's* stern. He faced the Officer of the Deck, Lieutenant Juan Chavez, and saluted again. "I request permission to come aboard, sir. I have an appointment with the Duke."

Chavez responded, "Granted, sir."

Commander Santana repeated the process.

Michael studied the two officers. Silva looked the part

of the dashing officer described in the intelligence briefing though he was no longer a young man. He sported a large black bushy mustache that matched his dark eyes and longer than regulation hair. He wore the standard black Imperium Navy dress uniform of a tunic and trousers with embroidered gold stripes down the pant legs. A blue and white ribbon with the five pointed bronze star of the Medal of Honor adorned his neck. A silver star hung from his left breast *Medal of Honor and Silver Star. I knew that from my intelligence briefing but still impressive. Assuming, of course, those were truly earned and not awarded by the Earl as payment to a relative.*

He turned to Santana. She wore her raven-colored hair long and down for this occasion, highlighting her large dark eyes and framing her aristocratic cheek bones. *By any standard she is drop dead gorgeous.* She was tall and long limbed. Her black dress uniform hid little of her formidable feminine curves. *Her bearing is regal but professional. I wonder if she considers her looks a help or hindrance in her career.*

He returned the New Brazilians' salutes and welcomed them aboard. "May I present my wife, the Duchess of New Meyer?"

Silva clicked his heels and bowed. "Your Grace." He spoke in a deep tenor with the barest trace of a Portuguese accent.

While English served as the lingua franca of the Imperium, many worlds retained their ancestral language. On New Brazil, Brazilian derived Portuguese was spoken as much as English.

Santana bowed and said in a slightly accented soprano voice, "Your Grace."

Michael introduced Emil as an advisor. "Shall we proceed?" he asked.

"At your service, Your Grace," Silva replied.

Cibola's flag accommodations included a private dining

room for use by the resident flag officer or dignitary. Michael grinned as he entered the small compartment, nodding to his Chamberlain who stood guard. Wallace had insisted on coming along on the trip to New Brazil. "I'm not about to let some uncouth simpleton Navy orderly take care of my Duke," he had said in a tone that brooked no argument.

Michael scanned the room. The table setting for six was as immaculate and perfect as shipboard conditions allowed. The china and silverware were at least five hundred years old, handed down through generations of Landsman-commanded ships. Wallace had complained about the settings, being unsuitable for someone of the Duke's standing and peerage. Michael had smiled and shooed him away with the order to "buck up and make do." As they seated themselves, a peppery fragrance drifted up from the sashimi appetizer of a delicate white fish from New Meyer's Tibbett Sea over a bed of lettuce covered with a lightly spiced sauce. He inhaled and settled in with anticipation. *Wallace at his best. Simple but complex.*

They started the meal off with a toast. While many North American Navy customs dominated the Imperium's Navy, having "dry" ships was not one of them. He raised his glass filled with champagne from New Meyer's Calistoga region. "To the Imperium!"

"To the Imperium!" came the customary reply from everyone else at the table.

With no Emperor, Michael skipped the traditional toast to His Imperial Majesty. "Captain Silva, I wish to welcome you aboard *Cibola*," he said. Then he smiled. "Now that we're alone we can drop a lot of these blasted Navy traditions and have a good discussion. I assume you expected this to be a working meal?"

Silva and Santana looked at each other and then broke into smiles. "Yes, Your Grace. Truthfully we didn't know what to expect," Santana said.

"Ah, so you expected some sycophant?"

"Er, no, Your Grace," Silva replied. "The brief time we had with Captain Ryan left the impression you're certainly not one of those. If I may be frank?" He waited for Michael's nod. "We didn't know what to expect because so many of today's peerage are products of a culture not lending itself to the true military conditions and realities we're facing."

"You mean we're soft and pampered, don't you?" He held up his hand as the two officers began to protest. "I agree with your assessment. However, if you knew my father and my grandfather, you'd know there was no chance in hell they'd ever pamper anyone."

"Your Grace, his Lordship the Earl said the same thing. Did you know he was under Duke Alex's command at Barq Seven?"

Michael nodded. "My father spoke highly of the Earl." Michael didn't mention his father's comments concerned the Earl's administrative and logistic capabilities, not his fleet tactics. "To get to the point, I guess you're wondering why I'm here?"

"Yes, Your Grace," they both answered.

"There is a deep tie between New Meyer and New Brazil we've allowed to fray in the past few years. Novo Éden was originally a New Brazilian colony before being purchased by Emperor Harold III and renamed New Meyer. We have a substantial Brazilian/Portuguese derived population and it's reflected in our culture. Note the name of this ship. I know some on New Brazil still resent Emperor Harold's actions. I think it's time to change things up a bit.

"The Imperium is in chaos. We've come to a realization. We simply can't go it alone. Our original plan of lying low and hoping we could stay below the radar long enough to make it too costly for anyone to attack us is not going to work. We've concluded things have changed. We need allies and I must reassert my authority as Duke of this chute."

Wallace pulsed him through his implant to ask if he

could bring in the next course. Michael assented and paused while Wallace removed the sushi plates and placed a bowl of cold broth in front of him. Michael tasted it, and inhaled deeply. Sweet and spicy at the same time.

Silva looked at Wallace. "My compliments to the chef. Both of these first two courses were exquisite."

Wallace bowed and withdrew.

Silva smiled. "I gather Wallace is your personal Chamberlain?" Michael nodded. "Then, Your Grace, please share the secret of how you can eat magnificent food such as this and keep yourself in such fine shape?"

Michael's reply was a broad grin. "You haven't met Master Gunnery Sergeant Ralph Goodson of my personal guard yet, have you? Then you'd understand."

Silva returned the grin. "Ahh! I do, Your Grace. I have Master Chief Petty Officer José de Guaraná." His grin grew broader into a wide smile. "We both understand, I see, who really runs the Navy."

Michael smiled back and nodded. Then he grew serious. "To answer your question, Captain," he continued, while still savoring the shrimp bisque. "Yes, our jump chute extends two hundred and fifty light years and terminates at New Brazil. In between are seventy-three other entry and exit points to star systems. Sixteen are uninhabited cul-de-sac systems with no exits from the chute so they can remain unguarded. This leaves us fifty-seven with potential entry from other chutes. Twenty-four of those are inhabited in some form while the remaining thirty-three are uninhabited. We need early warning sentinels with sufficient forces in each of those non-cul-de-sac systems to at least buy time for a quick reaction force to arrive. Another incursion by the Goths is not an if, it's a when. I don't need to tell you this. You just suffered through a raid."

Santana started to say something, but bit it off. Michael noticed it and responded, "You can speak frankly,

Commander. I suspect you're going to say the attack on New Brazil occurred because my father neglected his duty to protect the chute."

Santana nodded.

"I agree, Captain. While my father had many strong points he also had flaws and blind spots. He focused on the technology at the expense of the welfare of the other worlds in the chute. I intend to remedy that. As I said we need to place sentinels in all dual jump point systems and organize a chutewide rapid response force."

"An ambitious project, Your Grace. The Earl had been advocating this with Duke Alex for years."

Michael nodded. "Yes. There's another reason why we need your help. We can't accomplish this alone."

Santana tilting her head slightly, as if studying Michael. "New Brazil will have to bear the brunt of this expansion in chute forces, won't we? With all due respect, Your Grace, New Brazil's industrial capacity dwarfs New Meyer's, doesn't it?"

"Yes true, up to a point. However, there's an element balancing the burden a bit. You both witnessed *Harrier's* actions."

"Yes, Your Grace." They both responded.

Michael pointed to the Medal of Honor. "You won it there?"

Silva blushed. "Yes, Your Grace. The Earl authorized it in the absence of the Emperor."

"Very well. You'll have to tell me the story some time. As for authorizing it without the Emperor's approval, I'm afraid that's going to be standard procedure for a while. There's no Emperor right now and in my opinion a high probability there won't be a new one. We expect the Imperium will fracture into small kingdoms or political entities.

"If I can make sure this chute survives technically and we hold on to spaceflight then I'm doing the Imperium a great service. Too many worlds are going to lose their tech bases. I also suspect the Heart Worlds will eventually fall by attrition to Goth incursions. In a century or less, spaceflight may become more of a rarity. We're facing a dark age paralleling the collapse of the Western Roman Empire on Earth. We can mitigate the depth of the fall by surviving with a tech base. Maybe we can become the source of a Second Imperium."

"So that's your family's plan?" Silva asked.

"Our plan," Michael replied, "was to hunker down and hoard technology, keep a low profile, and let events pass us by." Michael smiled wanly. "How ironic my grandfather and father, two extremely aggressive Dukes, would select such a passive survival path. I decided we can't go down that route. We need to strengthen the chute and then work outward. The problem is, of course, as we become stronger we become a bigger target." He shrugged. "I don't see how we can avoid it."

He paused as the compartment door opened and Wallace entered with the next course. He sipped the wine to calm his emotions, allowing the piquant, slightly fruity essence to roll on his palate. After Wallace left he took a bite into an explosion of flavors. He closed his eyes and savored the mix of spices. Michael couldn't identify the light sauce over the dish of finely sliced beef and wild rice. He tasted a citrus base enlivened with chilies of some sort with the slightest hint of cilantro, Michael's favorite herb. *Master Guns, you're going to have to work me real hard after Wallace is done with me.*

They all ate in silence for a few minutes before Michael continued. "The technology New Meyer has may at least balance out the resource inequity between our two worlds. It's what we have to offer. Securing the chute will be a huge drain on both our worlds. As part of the alliance, I have a deal for the Earl..."

The talks went on well into the night.

CHAPTER 15

Newberry Manor, New Landsman City, New Meyer
8 June 684 IP

ARL BRYAN LANDSMAN SAT IN the private office of his penthouse apartment contemplating the unfairness of it all. Art he had acquired over the years decorated the walls and bookcases. He didn't apologize for the extravagance, and offered no justification to his sanctimonious son and nephew. The two of them pretended to be too good for the Peerage. *Bah! What's the value of wealth and being an Earl if you can't flaunt it?*

On the other hand what good is wealth and the Peerage if they don't bring you power? Duke Alexander had made the succession clear. Michael became Duke upon Alexander's death, not he, the Duke's much more mature and experienced brother. Michael designated Mitch as his successor should something happen to him or his future son. So here he was, in late middle age, with no place to go, just because of the accident of birth as the second son. *Imagine, I might have to bow to my own son.*

Of course, he didn't have a bad life. As nominal head of the New Meyer TSP division he had a planetary business to worry about even with Michael's sister becoming Chief Operating Officer, relegating him to Chairman of the Board and Chief Executive Officer. *As much as I hate to admit it, Carol is doing a better job than I did. On the other hand, I now have time to enjoy my bennies.* He smiled at the images of his previous evening with a buxom twenty-six-year-old he had met at some party. *Yes, wealth attracts women.*

So now Michael was off to New Brazil and Mitch was off on *Courtney's* workup. *With Carol deep into TSP, that leaves me tacitly in charge. Murray is still here to keep an eye on me and Carol could always step in if necessary. Still, plenty of opportunities will present themselves for me to take advantage, and perhaps gain control. But to what end?* He sighed. *Yeah, what do I really want?*

He absently sipped the brandy Ogden had left on his desk. Its fragrant musk, combined with the heat as it went down, drove some unusual clarity into his mind. Did he really want to be Duke with the planet so much at risk? *Can I expect the populace to accept me the way they follow Michael, or even Mitch?* He shook his head. *Now I know why.* No matter how he turned the facts and tried to put them in a better light, he still didn't like the answer. The public, so often easily misled, somehow grasped the truth about him. *I understand why Grace left me. It wasn't just the other women. I'm a coward and she saw it.*

He stared this self-knowledge in the face and it stared right back at him. *I'm a coward. I let Carol take active control of the company because I was scared. That explains why I'm not taking advantage now while Michael is away.* He caught an imaginary whiff of Jessica's perfume, the blonde he met last night. *She's still in my bed.*

He stood. "AI. Cancel all my appointments this morning." He strode out of the office toward the safety of his bedroom and the willing arms of Jessica.

Newberry Manor, New Landsman City, New Meyer
8 June 684 IP

Jessica Lowery luxuriated under the soft covers in the king-size bed, her mind deep in the memories of passionate sex. She sighed with pleasure. The Priestess of the Goddess Nearyahn dominated her thoughts. It wasn't that she hadn't enjoyed her time in bed with Bryan. He was an accomplished lover and she was conditioned as an Acolyte to relish sex with whomever she was with. It was just that nothing could compare to that evening a year ago when she met an exotic, alluring Granacian female in a tavern on Belliard III who seduced her and led her through a night of erotic adventures beyond anything she had ever imagined.

I never thought of having sex with a Granacian. Until that night I barely thought about them at all and certainly not in a sexual way. The next morning she had resigned her post on a tramp freighter. She received a buddling from the High Priestess herself after undergoing nine months of sexual and mental conditioning. She emerged as an Acolyte skilled in the use of sex, mind control, hypnosis, and other nefarious methods of manipulating people. She was now dedicated to the Goddess of Nearyahn and to expanding that religion across the galaxy. Along the way she also picked up and transmitted information useful to the High Priestess and her High Adept O'Rathll. She had been dispatched to New Meyer with a target in mind.

Now she was weaving her magic on the Earl. He had been her target. She found him to be a weak-willed man with delusions of becoming the reigning Duke. She might still make that happen, but for right now she was content using him as a conduit for information while she conditioned him to be her servant. It had been easy to make her way into his bed. *He's placed to get me into positions of power on this world. Then soon this world will know the bliss of the Goddess.*

She almost sneered as she heard the door open. *Right on schedule.* She kicked off the covers to expose her body to him. His reaction told her that he was well down the road to the submission she sought. She activated her new genetically enhanced glands. Pheromones filled the room, amplifying his desire. She smiled and held out her arms, tasting his lust and luxuriating in it before feeding it back to him as his own cravings.

He quickly shed his clothes, his slight pot belly his only unattractive feature. He kept himself in relatively good shape. *I'll make it better. If he's to entice women for me then he'll need to be even more attractive.* He slid into the bed next to her and into her waiting arms. They kissed ardently. She fed his rising passion directly back to him in a loop that drove his lust to an even higher level. His emotions drove her own and she orgasmed, driving him to an explosion. His life force flowed into her. She reduced the feedback loop. She had fed enough and didn't want to kill him. *I need him.*

She watched as he fell into a deep sleep. *He'll wake up ravenously hungry and not know why.* She exhaled in frustration. She wasn't ready to implant a splinter into him. Her own buddling was too immature. The piece of the Goddess inhabiting her mind needed time to grow. *Not for another year or two.* She'd have to rely on other means of control. She sighed and grinned to herself. *Well, at least it'll be pleasurable.*

CHAPTER 16

"To a LONG-LASTING FRIENDSHIP!" TOASTED Alfonso Joaquim de Vargas Sakomoto, the Earl of New Brazil.

"Here! Here!" came the unified reply.

Michael downed his glass of champagne and sat back in his high backed, dark hardwood chair. Oriental dragons and Japanese mythical figures decorated the furnishings in the compartment. The furniture and table settings were much too ornate for his taste and he found the chairs uncomfortable. *They must reflect both of the Earl's ancestral Brazilian and Japanese backgrounds.*

He looked around at the six people seated at the table. The Earl and his wife Countess Stefania sat at the head and foot of the table respectively with Michael and Donna, Emil, and Admiral Luis Victor de Rodriques Kevorkov, the New Brazilian equivalent of Admiral Murray seated between them. Like his dinner with Silva, this was meant to be a working session, with the meal providing some of the informality. Placing Donna and Stefania next to each other allowed them to converse if they became bored. Michael grinned to himself. *They don't know the Duchess. I suspect the Countess is the same.*

Michael studied his host and considered his resemblance to Silva. The Earl and Silva shared jet-black hair and deep-set dark eyes with a slightly oversized nose and mouth. They both wore a mustache and were the same height and build, though the Earl sported the beginnings of a middle-aged paunch. Michael wondered if the two men had a relationship similar to his with Mitch. *No wonder he trusts Silva so much.*

They completed the meal quickly with a minimum of ritual and only small talk. While the food was excellent, it wasn't nearly as memorable as Wallace's preparations. He did enjoy the Cachaça, the traditional Brazilian drink that resembled rum in many ways. The New Meyer version was not nearly as smooth as the one served at the dinner. *A good import/export item. I'm surprised it wasn't already.*

Michael followed the Earl's lead and kept to pleasantries and general discussions of their respective worlds. Over coffee the discussion began in earnest.

"Your Grace, this so-called deal of yours intrigues me," Earl Sakomoto said. "But I must say, trading a cruiser for a frigate is hardly a fair trade."

Michael shook his head. "My Lord, you misunderstood. The deal includes more than trading a cruiser for a frigate. We'll also refit one of your existing cruisers with our new systems and also supply you with two corvette upgrade kits. This means we're increasing your missile-capable ships four to one."

"I understand that, Your Grace. Do you really believe your weapon systems are so superior that I really want to convert my cruisers?"

"You viewed them in action," Michael countered with a grin. He turned to Admiral Kevorkov. "What do you think, Admiral?"

Kevorkov was a short squat bear of a man, with hooded eyes making them difficult to read. "Your Grace, I wasn't there. I was busy fending off the raiders attacking New Brazil. I studied the sensor files and discussed the engagement in detail with Captain Silva. Still, the particulars aren't that clear yet."

"Earl, if I may use your AI?"

"Of course, Your Grace."

Michael keyed his implant to the AI. "Upload File Duke 4."

"As you wish, Your Grace," the AI replied.

"This," Michael said, "is the *Courtney*-class frigate." He waited as a three-dimensional image of a rectangular solid spaceship materialized above the dining room table. "She masses 3900 tons and is capable of the usual ten g emergency acceleration. Her primary guns are 125mm laser rifles, four of them."

"She's undergunned," remarked Kevorkov.

Michael grinned. "True, but only important if the guns were her primary weapons."

He pointed to two large round hatches on each side of the hull. The hatches opened, exposing the roundish flat disks of the USVs mounted vertically, looking somewhat like two New Meyerian black-wing bats clinging to the side of a cave. He panned to the side directly opposite on the frigate showing two more USVs perched the same way. He waved his hand and the four disks detached. The view moved to a close-up of the Raptors.

"This is the Raptor, an unmanned space vehicle controlled by a high order AI and by tight beamed laser commands from the command ship. The Raptors are capable of a three hundred gravity sprint acceleration for one minute, have the same stealth capabilities as the frigate, and are armed with four Venom anti-ship missiles. You saw the Venom's effectiveness against the Goths. I guarantee you they're as effective against Imp ships,"

Michael rotated the image to show four stubby cylindrical missiles tucked neatly into indentations on the bottom of the USV's hull. "We're developing a Raptor II to carry six Venoms. We've developed an alternate to the Venom that is slightly smaller and easier to make. The Stinger is slightly less effective than the Venom, but we can make them in much greater quantities. The Raptors will be able to carry eight of them, making up for some of the performance loss due to a less effective warhead."

The Raptors spread out from the frigate. "Engage stealth," he ordered verbally. The four USVs disappeared. "This is not an exaggeration. The Manta makes the Raptors extremely difficult to detect."

A Goth task force materialized some distance away and the Raptors altered course, visible by a red line track produced by the simulation.

"They can be directed by human controllers aboard the frigate or independently by the onboard AIs. The AIs were difficult to develop because their design operates at substantial distances from the *Courtney* and they need to function independently due to speed of light considerations. For example, when they're ranging a million kilometers ahead of the frigate there's a seven-second communications delay between USV and frigate, three plus seconds each way. Add in human delay and you just can't provide tight human control. Our technologists developed a unique set of learning algorithms that enabled these AIs to mimic their controller's responses. Not really human reactions, mind you, but trained responses developed through relentless simulations and live fire exercises.

"We all know that Artificial Intelligences or AIs have been under development for a thousand years. We've heard the debates as to whether they are really intelligent or just sophisticated calculators." He paused and grinned. "Hell, our scientists can't decide on a definition of intelligence and sentience. AIs make trillions of calculations per second and therefore make complex decisions. On the other hand, we humans don't do that, at least on the surface. However, we're able to make decisions based on some other process. The big difference between the artificial minds and us seems to be in pattern recognition. AIs accomplish this by comparing known patterns and running through a database library. If none match they start using probabilities. They run their calculations at a terahertz rate and, therefore, are accomplished quickly. They can also extrapolate if there's a defined relationship they can track. We Humans, on the other hand, accomplish all of this almost instinctively without the terabit comparisons. You all know there are many theories explaining humans' abilities to accomplish this pattern recognition that run the gamut including a religious explanation called the soul.

"We train our AIs with pattern recognition and responses based on what their controller and their senior officers will do in a given situation. It's analogous to how we train our crews. The new AI algorithms enable this." He paused and waited. When no questions came he proceeded on. "The other key to the Raptor is the new stealth."

Beams of yellow light swept out from the Goth task force, simulating search radar. The Raptors simply flew through them. No resulting glimmer or re-materialization indicated detection.

"So where did this new stealth come from? What was the breakthrough, Your Grace?" asked Kevorkov.

An impish smile appeared on Michael's face, his dark eyes twinkling. "Who said it was new?" he asked.

The New Brazilians looked puzzled. "From what I observed your stealth is certainly better than anything the Imps and we have, Your Grace," Kevorkov replied.

"You just got the tense wrong. We uncovered the principles in a 4th Century Imperium Period data file that had been buried. Apparently, Emperor Claudio II was, shall we say, a bit paranoid. He wanted to make sure that no ship could sneak up on him. He constantly worried about assassinations and coups. He eventually outlawed the newest stealth technology. He required all ships to have it removed in favor of a less powerful version. Then he purged Imperium databases of all references to the new stealth. He made it a death sentence to pursue, develop, or possess any stealth technology that rendered a ship undetectable closer than fifty thousand kilometers by his flagship's sensors. For some reason that particular edict has never been repealed."

"Why, that's insane!" muttered Kevorkov. Then aghast at what he said, he mumbled, "Excuse me, Your Grace but..."

Michael waved his hand quickly and replied, laughing, "That was my reaction, too. I have a few Landsman ancestors of whom I'm not proud. I guess it's inevitable in the Imperium structure.

"Anyway, he and his minions missed this little file. My grandfather had teams out scouring every database they could uncover for the lost, undiscovered, or ignored gem. This and the Venom are only part of what we discovered buried in an old monastery on a little known Class Three world. How it got there we have no clue."

"Interesting," Sakomoto mused. "I wonder what's buried in our own archives."

"You should assign a couple of hotshot grad students to it. You'd be amazed what might turn up. We were." He grinned. "Besides, we all know that grad students are cheap. It's a low-cost, high potential payoff investment."

"Your Grace, you mentioned something about refitting cruisers?" Kevorkov asked.

"Yes, Admiral." He explained the modifications. "So, in short, two cruisers jump into New Meyer and you receive a refitted one back and a brand new *Courtney*-class frigate, as well as upgrade kits for two of your corvettes. You also receive enough missiles to arm your new ships."

"And why won't you just give me the plans?" the Earl asked.

"Because I need to control the technology. Can't risk it falling into a Pretender's hands. No offense, but right now the consensus among my people is that we have to limit access. I don't agree, and I expect to lift that sometime in the near future. I had to fight hard enough for these concessions." He smiled a bit wanly at the Earl. "My Lord, you know as well as I do that you and I are far from absolute rulers. Politics... We'll give you some spare modules so if something fries you can replace it. I can't stop you from trying to take them apart or x-raying them, but they'll be protected against tampering."

"Your Grace, I'm still a bit puzzled," Kevorkov said. "You need our cruisers because you're a year or two away from building a cruiser-sized spacedock. Then how and where can you turn around the cruiser refits so quickly?"

"Ahh! Admiral, sometimes Murphy takes a day off and something good happens. A new addition to our vast fleet arrived recently, the *Yakumo*."

Kevorkov's eyes widened at the name. He clearly recognized it. The Earl looked puzzled. "The *Yakumo*?" Sakomoto asked.

Kevorkov answered the question, "My Lord, she's a *Langley*-class tender used by the ISDF."

Sakomoto nodded as if understanding the answer. Then his eyes opened wide, too. "A *Langley*-class tender, Your Grace? Is the frontier open?"

"No, it's not. Our late Emperor ordered the *Langley* in payment for my father's service in defending Earth."

"Four corvette mods," Sakomoto said suddenly.

"Three," Michael replied.

"Deal."

CHAPTER 17

"THE DUCHESS OF NEW MEYER," announced the Countess's lady, a short blonde-haired woman of about thirty.

The Countess Stefania Joana Mendes Sakomoto rose and bowed. "Your Grace," she grumbled, "thank you for consenting to share lunch with me today."

"Countess," Donna smiled in reply, seating herself, "I hate these titles. Will it offend you if we drop them in privacy here?"

Stefania seemed momentarily surprised at the informality. After a brief moment she returned the smile. "As you wish, Your Grace. My friends call me Steffi." She almost giggled at the name, her gray-green eyes twinkling with almost childish delight. "I know Steffi sounds a bit childish, but it helps me survive the aristocratic pretense."

"Call me Donna. And this will be our secret, Steffi. I suspect we're going to have a long relationship and the survival of our worlds may not depend on us getting along, but it will certainly help."

They settled down at a small circular table. One of the Countess' handmaidens came in and poured them both tea in fine china cups decorated with the Earl's crest. Stefania held the cup up. "This is a tea transplanted to our own New Santa Catarina do Sul province. It took to the New Brazilian soil but developed a distinctive flavor over the next five hundred years. This particular vintage comes from the Earl's private reserve."

Donna sniffed its bouquet politely and then sipped the tea. She nodded appreciatively. "I see why the Earl keeps it for himself."

"Rank hath its privileges," Stefania quoted, shrugging her slim shoulders. "It may look to you like we take advantage of our position and wealth. Part of it has to do with the expectations of our people. They take pride in their Earl and insist that we look like planetary rulers. In these difficult times I guess they want it even more. It gives them a sense of security." Her long patrician fingers almost completely wrapped around the cup.

Donna nodded in agreement. "The Duke also hates all of these protocols and ceremonies. He's okay with naval ones, but the Peerage formalities drive him crazy..." she trailed off, taking a sip of her tea and allowing its delicate jasmine flavor to focus her thoughts.

"So when are you due?" Stefania asked.

"In about six weeks," Donna answered with a wry grin. "We can't stay here too much longer. I don't want to break my water on the way home."

"I'm surprised you even came, my dear."

"I think meeting here at Refugio is working better than travelling all the way to New Brazil. It will let me get back home earlier to have the baby. If we had to meet formally on New Brazil we would have delayed the meeting to after the birth. Even so we're cutting it close. We brought along my obstetrician just in case. *Cibola's* sick bay is well equipped."

"A wise precaution." Stefania paused for a moment before reverting to a more formal air, "Your Grace, I asked you here to discuss a sensitive matter."

"Yes?" Donna drank the tea to hide her excitement.

"I truly believe this alliance is critical to the survival of our worlds. I think we need to formalize it."

"Formalize it? I thought the treaty would do that," Donna replied, allowing puzzlement to slip into her voice. *This may be easier than I expected. GMTA? Great minds thinking alike?*

Stefania hesitated. "I think we need an extra strong bond between our two worlds." She brushed a strand of auburn hair back from her eyes.

Clearly she's nervous. Donna kept the confusion on her face. "Are you speaking of a marriage? Who? Certainly not my son. He isn't even born yet!"

"Of course, not your son. However, I understand Michael has a cousin of marriageable age."

"Mitch?" Donna looked truly surprised. *Could they have been reading our minds? Or had they bugged our quarters?*

"We have a daughter slightly younger than he, and I can honestly say she's special. She's beautiful and smart. In fact, we're planning to send her to New Meyer as a Special Minister on a good will visit. It would be an opportune time for them to meet."

Donna laughed. Stefania looked surprised. Donna explained, "Steffi, that's how Michael and I ended up together. It was a marriage of convenience. They couldn't and wouldn't force us to marry, but they pushed us together enough to make it happen."

"So you'll arrange this?" Stefania asked eagerly.

"I'll try. This won't be the first time he's been matched. He's never shown all that much interest."

"He is interested in women?" she asked cautiously.

Donna laughed again. "Oh yes, interested, but just not in settling down. We do need to work on him. He's in line for the Duchy should something happen to Michael and me."

"So, Your Grace," she asked formally. "Do we have a deal?"

Donna giggled, "Mitch is going to kill me." *Of course she doesn't know that Michael and I already discussed this possibility.* "Yes, Countess, we have a deal." She raised her tea and they touched cups conspiratorially. *I love it when a plan comes together.*

Earl's office, Asteroid Refugio, Star System New Brazil
9 June 684 IP

"So, what do you think, Your Grace, do we have the framework for an alliance and an agreement?" asked the Earl of New Brazil, his eyes showing traces of tiredness.

In contrast, the whole process of negotiating the new treaty exhilarated Michael. He wasn't tired at all. For the first time in months he viewed the future with a sense there might be a chance for New Meyer to survive the oncoming holocaust. He took a deep breath to calm himself down. Now that the broad outline of the deal was worked out, their respective negotiating teams could hammer out the details. *Of course, the devil is in the details. Still, both worlds will benefit from this agreement.* We've been nominal allies and this would tighten it up even more. Better yet, Donna had pulsed him on her implant with the welcome news of the marriage deal. *I'm sorry, Mitch.*

Michael glanced at Sakamoto. "What do you think? Shall we call it a day and leave it to our teams?"

The Earl grinned in relief and sighed. "Yes, I think so, Your Grace."

"Well, I have one more requirement," Michael said.

"What now?" Sakomoto said, sounding irritated. He then smiled ruefully. "Forgive me, Your Grace, I am tired."

"My requirement is you call me Michael in the privacy

of these get togethers. This 'Your Grace, My Lord' stuff just grows old. We've both heard that our bonds are going to grow even tighter as our families unite. This 'Your Grace and My Lord' stuff is a royal pain in the ass."

The expression of shocked surprise on the Earl's face melted into a wide grin. "As you wish, Your, er, I mean, Michael. Please call me Jack."

"Jack?"

"Better than Alfie," Jack replied with a big smile.

Both men laughed.

Michael realized he liked the Earl. Despite a trace of stuffiness bred in by the New Brazilian approach to the Peerage, the Earl seemed likeable. In fact, Michael sensed a bit of a kindred soul. *There's an age difference, to be sure, but, in these days of one hundred twenty year life spans, ten or fifteen years isn't much.*

"Ok, Jack. We have a deal. Please don't call me Mike. I hate that."

"As you wish, Michael," Jack replied, and then burst out laughing.

Michael sighed as the earlier exhilaration began to morph into exhaustion. He managed to return the laugh and said, "This is rapidly deteriorating. I think we've had enough for one day. Besides, what do we have staffs for?"

"True, Michael. Let them sweat the hard details."

CHAPTER 18

———◆———

"GET OUT OF MY SIGHT!" the High Priestess screamed. O'Rathll cringed. She took a little solace in Al'Rik O'Rathll, great Goth War Leader and High Admiral of the Fleet, quailing like some errant school child in front of an angry headmistress. She tasted his fear and was tempted to feed. *It's not his fault. You still need him.* She calmed herself.

"I'm sorry, Al'Rik," she said in her most silky voice. "It's not you I'm mad at. Let me have some time alone."

As the door slid shut behind him the anger returned. *Almost three months. Four good feeds and no buddling.* Again she fought to control herself. This was not so unusual. It had happened before. Something in the Merge between Humans and Neary limited the number of offspring she could bud. *But it's becoming more difficult to bud. Is it time to transfer to a new body?* She fought down the other thought but it kept coming back. *Or is the Neary part of me finally reaching its limitation?*

It had happened once before. She had to bud and then

transfer her mind to that buddling after it grew to sufficient maturity. *But that'll take years and I don't have years now. The Humans are ripe. I need more Human Adepts and Acolytes.* Unfortunately, a number of her buddlings were infertile. They were capable of making splinters but not the more complex buddlings.

She sighed and gave an order. The door slid open and a slim human female of about eighteen clad in only a nightgown entered. At the sight of the Granac she cowered. The Priestess took a deep breath and calmed herself. She reached out and tasted the Human. This one had not been prepared and conditioned. Slowly she explored the girl's mind. When she finished mapping she knew where to push. Still, she had to go gradually. Push too hard and the mind might fold. She needed maximum emotional commitment from her so she'd have a good feed.

She found the first pressure point. Gently she pressed, feeling the resistance, careful not to raise any alarm in the girl's mind. Suddenly the resistance at that point was gone. The girl now saw the Priestess as a beautiful human female of her own age and forgot the Granacian form.

One push and suddenly they had been lifelong friends since infancy.

Another gentle push in the right region and suddenly the girl was attracted to women. The priestess stood and dropped her gown. The girl's eyes opened wide.

The Priestess smiled, "Yes, it's OK. I know you've wanted this for a long time."

"Yes," the girl breathed.

"You've wanted this for a long time, haven't you?"

"Yes, I've wanted it for a long time," the girl agreed, her hips squirming slightly.

"You want this more than anything, don't you?"

"Yes, I want this more than anything," came the whispered answer.

"Then come here. And you don't need that nightgown, do you?"

"No."

They embraced. She began to feed. A couple of minutes later she watched as her mind wiped slaves carried out the husk.

Maybe this is the one.

CHAPTER 19

Frigate Courtney, Star System New Faroe
15 July 684 IP

COURTNEY MATERIALIZED IN THE NEW Faroe star system in a burst of blue Cherenkov-like radiation that disappeared as quickly as it appeared. A thousand kilometers away, her single escort from New Brazil, the *Falcão-Peregrino*, or the *Peregrine Falcon*, also popped into real space. Both crews took a few moments to recover from the jump while the AIs maintained control on a previously selected heading. At the same time they deployed their TA-22A Towed Arrays. Though New Faroe was part of the New Meyer-New Brazil chute, contact with the planet had been sparse recently. Since the Goths had penetrated the chute during the New Brazil incursion, Mitch wasn't taking any chances. *Courtney* was too valuable to risk. *We're not sure where else the Goths went other than New Brazil.* Almost immediately after deployment *Courtney's* array registered contacts, while at the same time the ship's ECW or Electronic Counter Warfare system bleated a warning. "Attention! High intensity radar painting this ship!"

The announcement jerked *Courtney's* bridge crew into

action, helping them shake off the aftereffects of the jump. "Contact, Captain," Joshua Ben-Levi reported. He shut off the alarm. "Two contacts! Distance fifteen thousand kilometers. They're painting us with ZN-167A radar!" Josh also served as the frigate's executive officer.

ZN-167A is an older generation Imp radar. Mitch nodded in response. *Not unexpected from a system at this level.* "Let's contact them before they get itchy trigger fingers," he ordered.

"I have them identified," Josh reported. He reclined in his acceleration couch, his azure blue eyes seemingly focused on nothing as he studied the data flowing through his implant. "Two old *Feline*-class corvettes," he added after a moment. "But something is different."

"*Feline*-class corvettes. They're still around?" Mitch muttered.

"Message coming in on Imp standard frequency," reported the com technician, Chief Petty Officer Elijah Patterson.

"Unidentified ship, identify yourself," a disembodied voice demanded.

"Any visual?" Mitch asked.

Elijah shook his head. "No, m'lord."

"Elijah, how many times do I have to remind you, aboard ship I'm Captain or sir, not My Lord or m'lord?" Mitch said. "Remember that, Mr. Patterson."

"Yes, sir," Elijah responded.

"Open our reply," Mitch ordered. "This is the New Meyerian Frigate *Courtney* representing Duke Michael."

"Frigate? What the devil is a frigate?" the gruff voiced asked.

"A big enough warship to kick your butt, Mister," Mitch replied. "I am the Baron Courtney."

"Forgive me, m'lord," the voice replied hastily. "I'm Lieutenant Commander Lars Hansen of the New Faroe Planetary Guard Corvette *Black Lynx*. The other ship is the *Red Lynx*. My Lord, may I ask your business here?"

"I'm here to speak with your planetary leader, Baron Harold Nielsen."

"M'lord, the Baron Harold died two months ago. His son Niles is now the Baron of New Faroe."

"Captain," a voice whispered in his ear, "*Abby* and *Betty* are ready for launch."

"Very well. Launch in max stealth," he ordered through his implant.

Mitch watched through opened e-windows as the two Raptors silently detached from the *Courtney* and glided away on their grav drives, swathed deep in stealth.

"What did you just do?" Hansen asked, forgetting the appropriate way of addressing a Peer.

"Do?" Mitch asked, trying to portray an injured innocent party.

"Excuse me, My Lord, but we thought you launched something. I guess we're mistaken."

"Captain," Josh whispered through his implant, "these corvettes aren't right."

"What do you mean aren't right?" Mitch replied subvocally.

Josh hesitated before answering. "They've been seriously modified. I'm having trouble getting a good radar lock on them. I can detect that they're there, but the image is about ten percent of what I expect and it's fuzzy. Difficult to make out details."

"Do they have their stealth field on at low power?" Mitch asked.

"No, sir. *Felines* don't have sophisticated stealth systems. They're meant more for patrol and customs duty. They don't have the power for a real stealth field. No, this is something else."

"Can you get the Raptors close enough for visual?"

"Will do," he replied. "*Abby and Betty* are closing."

Meantime, Mitch kept busy exchanging information with Hansen. *They don't trust who I am. Can't really blame him. We appear out of nowhere, a previously unknown ship design claiming to come from the Duke that has ignored this system for years. Now he's suddenly sending his second highest ranking peer to restore relations. I wouldn't be surprised if they gave us the finger.*

Finally Hansen appeared satisfied with Mitch's identity and whom he represented. Still without a visual, "M'lord, I'm forwarding your info to Planetary Control. Our policy is to have ships wait here for clearance from Control."

Mitch reviewed the star system parameters, pulling up data to refresh his memory. The primary for the New Faroe system was a K1 V star, smaller and cooler than Sol or New Meyer's. Because the system was smaller with a less massive star, the jump point was located an average of only about one billion klicks from New Faroe. Radio or laser transit time was a little under a standard hour each way. At least two hours round trip, not to mention all the bureaucracy the message has to go through to get to the Baron. *I'll bet it takes at least eight hours.*

"Very well, please send a personal message to your new Baron. Duke of New Meyer conveys his warmest greetings. He introduces his envoy, the Baron Courtney, and requests top level discussions."

"As you wish, My Lord."

Mitch checked the progress of the Raptors as they crept toward the two corvettes.

"*Abby* is being pulsed by radar," reported Technician Mate Jacquie Chou, Raptor Able controller. "No return. Stealth functioning nominal."

"*Betty* is being pulsed," reported Technician Mate Angela Jimenez, Raptor Beta controller. "Stealth functioning nominal. Manta and ECW are handling it. No return."

"Captain, there's something wrong with these corvettes," Josh repeated. "The returns are all wrong."

"Wrong?" Mitch asked, finally paying attention to what Josh had been saying.

"Like I said before, their radar signatures are smaller

than they should be and they're distorted. Using the arrays I can detect no evidence of a stealth field. It has to be something physical."

"You mean like the Goths use?"

Josh pursed his lips. "Hmm, that might be it."

"So they've resurrected some of the original stealth stuff with RAM and geometric shapes?"

Radar Absorbent Materials (RAM) were first developed in the late 20th century. They were composite materials that changed the reflection of radar. Early stealth technology also used angular shapes to deflect and distort radar returns. Most of this technology went out of fashion with the development of the stealth field. But the Goths, coming from a technology-poor region had resurrected it. *And now I find it here at New Faroe. So are they trading with the Goths or did they just follow the same path the Goths did? Of course, we also resurrected the materials for the frigates to enhance Manta. Am I being overly sensitive?*

The first visual images of the two corvettes arrived. Instead of the squarish structure with stubby protrusions that were standard Imp design, he could see the modified profile that intended to alter the reflection of radar waves. But two other items were surprising.

He heard the surprise from his weapons officer. "Captain, they're refitted with 150mm rifles! Is that a railgun along the keel?"

Those rifles are way too big for a corvette. They lack the power to cycle them at any reasonable rate of fire. "Yes, I think it's a rail gun, Mr. Santiago." *Another Goth weapon.*

"Captain, a 150mm on a ship that size has been tried before. Their fusion generators just can't recycle fast enough, particularly if they don't have anti-matter injection."

"Mr. Santiago, if you're desperate enough you'll try anything."

Stealth technology and railguns. What am I getting into? Could this world be in contact with the Goths, maybe helping the New Brazil incursion force? He shook his head to himself. *No, the merchant skippers who visited here reported nothing unusual. Still, I'll have to proceed with caution.*

"Josh, anything else around? Sweep for stealthed ships."

"I have, Captain," Josh replied. "The only thing I found is this area over here." He sent him an image. "Could be a stealth field or just a local disruption in the magnetic fields. The discrepancy is within instrument error. Best I can do without the high power radar. Passive only told me what wasn't there, not what was there."

Now that he had made contact with the customs ship, protocol required him not to use Courtney's high powered battle radar and to retract his 22A. While *Courtney* wasn't blind she was hampered. The USVs became her eyes. He studied the e-window with Josh's data. "Damn, it does look like a stealth signature, but of what? It's too small to be a task force." He chuckled at a thought. "We certainly can't ask them."

"Captain, I have a far out idea."

"Let's hear it."

"Captain, the *Feline*-class corvettes are too old and small to carry sophisticated stealth systems, particularly the way they've been modified. That's why the larger *Hawk*-class was developed."

Mitch nodded. "Go ahead. I know that."

"What about a stealth buoy? A small powered structure that provides a localized stealth field that a couple of ships can hide in. It has its own self-contained power supply and a stealth field generator that can cover a couple of small ships."

"Where'd you come up with that one?"

He smiled. "I learned about it during my stint at NMIT while working on the Twenty-Two. Of course, our new corvettes are well stealthed, but the older ones aren't."

Interesting. Advanced technology mixed with more

primitive technology. Maybe they're just a planet trying to survive using the resources they have on hand.

"Sounds reasonable, Josh. We'll go with it until we know otherwise. Well done. So we can expect a couple of more corvettes hiding at the buoy?"

"My guess, Captain. Though they could be hiding a destroyer or cruiser, but then with ships that size why use a stealth buoy?"

So what do I do? If I send Abby in-system and Nielsen denies my request she'll be stranded here. My mission is to find out what I can about this system. We've lost too much contact with them over the years. And Nielsen wouldn't dare refuse a Duke's request. Not now.

He came to a decision. "Ok, here's the plan," he said, using his implant to ensure the entire bridge crew including the Raptor controllers heard. "Launch *Cassie* and have her keep an eye and a lock on the buoy. Have *Abby* make a high speed run in system and check things out, while *Betty* keeps an eye on these two corvettes. I won't leave *Abby* here. I'm betting we'll get the okay to pay the planet a visit. I don't think they want to piss off the Chute Duke even based on past lack of interest by that same Duke."

Then he settled back to wait for the Baron's reply.

CHAPTER 20

E IGHTEEN HOURS LATER MITCH RECEIVED permission to proceed to the planet. The response took a bit longer than expected even with the most inefficient bureaucracy at work. Still, he was used to dealing with planetary bureaucracies. He never knew one that could move beyond a snail's pace. Some good things came out of the delay. *Abby* penetrated deep into the small star system and found nothing out of the ordinary. No Goth ships discovered waiting to ambush the unsuspecting frigate. *Abby's* Twenty-Two acquired a good read on the planet's EM emissions. The data gathered by Abby showed an industrialized society with signs of higher than expected CO_2 levels and low neutrino emissions. *Smog. They're reverting to fossil fuels and related technologies to provide industrial capacity. Typical of colonies of this type. And now with the Imperium collapsing and interstellar trade more restricted, it's going to be difficult for them to maintain an industrial civilization. We can offer them the aid to keep their technology, besides offering protection down the road.*

"Captain, incoming com."

Mitch took a sip of his special blend of coffee. *I'm not going to show them I'm impatient. They can wait.* "Put it through," he ordered. "Let's have them wait a bit. Take your time." *I don't like playing these games but eighteen hours is way too long a delay.*

An avatar of a ruddy faced man appeared on the front of the bridge. His skin color, combined with the fact that he had almost no hair, reflected long exposures to the radiation of space. *I bet he was an asteroid miner. This system has a pretty decent asteroid belt.* "Yes, Lieutenant?" he asked, allowing the merest trace of annoyance to sift through his otherwise professional demeanor.

Hansen bowed his head in acknowledgment. "My Lord, I have the response," he replied.

"Go ahead."

"His Lordship, Niles Johannes Alvaldur Nielsen, the Baron of New Faroe, welcomes you to New Faroe. You're invited to visit with him to discuss matters of importance. He adds that he is looking forward to this meeting."

"What the devil took so long?" Mitch asked, letting his impatience and displeasure show.

Hansen looked uncomfortable in his reply. "The Baron was out of touch, sir."

"Out of touch? In this day and age?"

Nielsen's discomfort grew. "He was incapacitated."

"Incapacitated. Is he ill?"

"No, m'lord. Not exactly."

Mitch sat patiently not saying a thing but letting his rising impatience show.

Finally Hansen pursed his lips. "He was out hunting and was incommunicado. He had only one companion with him and both had their implant communicators shut off."

"You said he was incapacitated but then you said he was incommunicado hunting. Which was it?"

Hansen looked even more uncomfortable. "M'lord, it

was both. He was out hunting with a female companion. They both, er, had too much to drink."

Mitch laughed lightly as if getting the inside joke. Meanwhile he was working to hide his irritation. "There, was that so hard? The Baron has the right to some rest and relaxation," he said with a real effort now to show patience.

Hansen didn't say anything though Mitch swore he heard him mutter something about "that's all he does."

So he's one of those, a spoiled Peerage brat. "We're free to depart in-system?"

"Yes, My Lord. When should I tell him you will arrive?"

Mitch weighed his answer. It was typical to ask for a flight plan, in case of an emergency and contact was lost. He could significantly reduce time by using the fusion drive but there was no guarantee he'd be able to replenish his propellant supply.

"I'll forward the flight plan. Probably five days."

"Very good, My Lord. Have a safe flight inward. New Faroe Customs out."

"Prepare for departure in system," Mitch ordered. "Bring in Betty. We'll pick Abby up on the way in. Have *Peregrine* stay here on watch."

The trip in system was proving uneventful. Mitch studied the data that *Abby* transmitted back and found few surprises except possibly how far New Faroe had regressed in some ways and yet still managed to maintain spaceflight. Both the Jovian and asteroid belt had signs of habitation – of the type used by Earth in the late 21st Century, early 22nd Century. Abby detected j-divers scooping hydrogen from the Jovian planet. The Raptor also detected a fairly sophisticated mining complex in the belt, one that appeared to be active and inhabited. The propulsion systems used to transport the materials in-system indicated their level of development as mid-21st century. Solar sails. However, all the warships detected were both gravitic and fusion powered, though all were old and obsolete, and had obviously been built elsewhere. Worse, none were bigger than a corvette. Modern fusion plants required gravitic technology to allow for anti-matter injection. That in turn required sophisticated electronics and nanotechnologies that were difficult to maintain with any world below a Class Three. The economies of scale weren't there nor was there sufficient infrastructure to maintain the technologies. A Class Four world like New Faroe might purchase an automated nanotechnology or electronics plant but where were the trained personnel and support structure when that automation needed repair or replacement? New Meyer was a Class Three world and had created and maintained the infrastructure to allow it to maintain an intrinsic gravitics capability thanks to the strength of NMIT and a concentrated effort by the succession of Dukes. Clearly, New Faroe as a Class Four had not. That it maintained space travel with such a small population base indicated the strength and vitality of its people.

New Faroe had done a respectable job of maintaining at least some spacefaring capability. They obviously had sufficient technology to modify those corvettes. He didn't necessarily approve of the changes, but then, he didn't come from a planet struggling to stay in space. It also meant that they should be interested in what he had to offer. The question was what did New Faroe have to offer in return? Trade would be better than outright aid.

My uncle failed this chute. We let it down following a misguided plan. New Faroe showed itself as an innovative world responding to the crisis and chaos as best as it could. *How many other worlds are like that?* Of course, that's assuming these ship mods were homegrown and not the result of Gothic influence. He found that unlikely considering the actions of Hansen, who was acting just as a suspicious customs agent. Letting Cou*rtney pr*oceed unescorted probably indicated that his own fears of Goth influence were unfounded or at least overblown.

He sighed. Duke Alexander had worried that defending worlds like New Faroe would be a drain on New Meyer's resources. *Maybe so, but the planet represents a source of trade, a new market to be opened that could help New Meyer's economy grow.* So which approach was correct? Pull in a hidey hole and concentrate on defending the one system or expand efforts to defend the Chute and grow its economy? The more he thought about it the more he thought that the Plan, with its isolationist driving force, was wrong. *No, the ultimate result would be stagnation, first economic and then eventually technical.* New Meyer cannot grow fast enough, even with the government encouraging large families.

He studied images of New Faroe gathered by Abby. New Faroe was a cold planet with no large continents, only three large islands, with the remainder of the landmass in the form of archipelagos. The climate in the equatorial zone was only a bit warmer than Northern Europe on Earth. Native life on the planet had never risen to a robust level. Land-based life was primitive with a slow metabolism. The colony founder had managed to pay for seeding the seas with Earth sea life, which took very well, exploding in population quickly. He had also paid for some limited land seeding, a mixture of domesticated livestock and wild animals, including predators. The Earth-derived species had a much higher metabolism rate and no natural enemies. Large bison herds, hunted by wolves, ran free on the largely unpopulated high plateau on the smallest of the three large islands named Nye Eysturoy. Most of the planet's population of thirty million were scattered over the other two islands.

The largest of the three islands, Nye Steymoy, straddled the equator and was about the size of Australia on Earth. Its climate was reasonably temperate with mild summers and relatively mild winters, at least when compared to the rest of the land masses. The planet's capital, Faroe City, was located on its east coast and sported a large horseshoe-shaped bay that Mitch could see was filled with shipping of all types. The other two major islands, slightly smaller, also contained numerous bays where cities had sprung up. *There's a lively sea trade going on down there. This looks like a vibrant colony.*

"Captain, I have tapped into the planet's Net," Josh reported. "It's not all that sophisticated and the AI had no problems penetrating its security protocols."

Mitch queried his implant and accessed a torrent of data as it fed into the ship's computers. Current planetary population was about forty million, higher than he had expected.

Mitch sank back in his captain's chair as a plan formed. He asked the AI to run some simulations for him and then continued studying the planet while ground control organized its customs inspection. By some quirk, New Meyer's asteroid belts were not nearly as metal rich as this system's. Because this star system was much smaller than New Meyer, the jump points lay just outside the asteroid belt. He ran the calculation. A three day journey for a merchant ship at a quarter gee from jump point to the belt's largest manufacturing center. Their belt mining operation could supply *Yakumo* with much needed raw materials. *It's a basis for trade. We can add fish exports, too.*

"Captain, we have permission to land a shuttle as soon as customs inspection is done with us," the com tech reported.

"Very well. Inform the Marines."

CHAPTER 21

---◆---

C OURTNEY'S SHUTTLE SETTLED DOWN ON the worn, cracked nanocrete spaceport pad, rocking momentarily on its landing gear. An official-looking squarish vehicle powered by a hybrid internal combustion engine pulled up and two uniformed men clambered out. The shuttle lowered its stairs and the entry hatch slid open. Master Gunnery Sergeant Roger Brassard, clad in his standard soft combat armor, stepped out, but with rank and insignia showing and his suit's chameleon field shut down.

One of the officials at the foot of the stairs remarked sarcastically in accented English, "Is this an invasion, Master Guns?"

Brassard tilted his head and stared down. "Not bloody likely. There's nothing on this godforsaken world anyone would want."

The speaker guffawed and raised his hand in a mock salute. "Sergeant Major Nick Tobias, Imperium Marines, retired, now in New Faroe Planetary Customs."

"Mastery Gunnery Sergeant Roger Brassard of

the New Meyerian Imperial Marines, still in service," Brassard replied.

"So, Master Guns, what brings you to this godforsaken world of ours as you called it?"

Brassard shook his head. "You know damn well why we're here, Sergeant Major," he snarled, showing his impatience.

Mitch stepped out. "A problem, Guns?" he asked.

Brassard eyed the other sergeant with mock distaste. "Nothing I can't handle, My Lord."

"My Lord?" Tobias picked up the reference. He bowed his head, "M'lord, welcome to New Faroe. I hate to trouble you with minor details, but we do have Customs to pass through. I'm here to usher you through quickly."

Mitch put on his best imperious nod. "Get on with it."

Tobias whipped out a small ancient handheld computer and began asking questions. "Please identify yourself."

"Baron of Freeport from New Meyer," Mitch said, handing him an Imp ID chip.

"Sorry, m'lord, but we don't have the technology to scan these anymore. The last scanner we had failed about a year ago."

"Then I guess you'll have to take my word for it, Sergeant Major," Mitch replied, using Tobias' former title as a sign of respect.

Tobias nodded his head. "Of course, m'lord. May I ask the purpose of your visit?"

"Above your classification level, Sergeant." Mitch replied, this time a bit brusquely.

This is just a stalling tactic. "Sergeant, where is your Baron's representative? I'm not accustomed to waiting like this. As an official envoy of this chute's Duke I expected to be received as such. No disrespect intended, Sergeant Major. You're not of the level one expects to greet a visiting dignitary from the leader of the chute." *I don't need a brass band. However, I do expect some show of respect.*

"I assure you this is just routine, My Lord," Tobias replied calmly. "We're a small world and your visit was not planned or expected."

"Bullshit, Sergeant Major. You had five days' notice of my arrival. Where is the Baron? What the devil is going on here?" he demanded, using his best command voice.

"My Lord," Tobias replied slowly. "I'm sorry about this, but I assure this is merely routine."

"Like hell it is," Mitch snapped. "Is this how you deal with the official representative of a Duke?" He nodded to Brassard and started walking back up the stairs. "Master Guns, let's go. This is a waste of time. They obviously don't think we're important enough."

Tobias sighed, his voice firm. "Please, My Lord. The vehicle sent for you by our Baron has broken down and I was sent to stall."

Mitch stopped and peered down at the former Imp sergeant. "You're still lying or covering something up. Oh, hell! Did your Baron just forget?"

"No My Lord, I assure you he didn't forget."

My God! The Baron must be too drunk. Do we really want to deal with him? Or am I jumping to conclusions? He turned to walk up the stairs when two vehicles raced from behind the small terminal building, red lights on their roofs flashing. One was a limousine of some sort, the other a black van. They screeched to a halt in front of the shuttle. To Mitch's experienced eye they were clearly internal combustion powered, and both looked old from the outside, though well taken care of. *Obviously imported.* The rear door of the limo vehicle swung open and a tall, lean, distinguished-looking middle-aged man dressed in a simple military uniform stepped out. He strode over and stopped in front of Mitch, bowing. "My Lord, please forgive the delay. I am Colonel Hans Spehlman of the Baron's Guard. Welcome to New Faroe." He turned and pointed to the two vehicles. "Our rides await us. The second car is for your bodyguard."

Mitch caught Brassard's look of displeasure and raised a hand to forestall the non-com from replying. "Very well, Colonel, let's proceed," he said coldly, letting his displeasure show. He didn't want an incident to derail the meetings before they began. *Besides, they have a right to resent us. We've ignored them for so long. Maybe this is a ploy to let us know of their displeasure, an official snub.*

Mitch sighed, still wanting to avoid a major incident. The rear door of the first vehicle was held open by a uniformed non-com who snapped to attention when Mitch stepped past him. The interior of the limo smelled new though the electronics were clearly old and obsolete, maybe by hundreds of years. The seats were leather and well appointed. *They've refitted the interior seats and furnishings but not the electronics. How far have they regressed?*

"So, My Lord, what brings you to our end of the universe?" Spehlman asked conversationally as the car accelerated smoothly onto a main road.

"Sightseeing," he replied with a trace of a smile.

Spehlman chuckled. "I didn't realize New Meyer was so wealthy it could let you go off on a holiday jaunt with one of its new frigates."

The reference to the frigate caught Mitch's attention. He struggled not to betray any surprise. "*Courtney*'s on workup, so a diplomatic-trade mission to reopen contacts with you provided a good use of the time. We trained and drilled the crew over the trip. My visit here will hopefully re-establish an obviously broken relationship. Our new Duke is reasserting his authority over the chute."

Spehlman nodded. "Yes, My Lord, we've begun to get a sense of that. I guess with the situation the Imperium is in, you want to secure all external paths into the local chute?"

Who is this guy and where does he get his info from?

"True, Colonel. We're entering into a long term alliance with New Brazil to share resources and protect the chute. As I said, this is all part of Duke Michael's efforts to better organize chute security. To cut to the chase, I think we can make it worth your while to participate in this joint defense with an increase in trade between our worlds. We've neglected the chute for too long."

Spehlman raised an eyebrow. "As you probably observed on your way in we have a few obsolete corvettes and armed merchantmen. Enough to prick a serious incursion for about ten seconds."

It was Mitch's turn to nod. "Even with your stealth buoys you're still at a real disadvantage. Your corvettes are just too small and too weak to challenge anything, even with their 150's. The rail guns are also of limited effectiveness."

Spehlman's eyes widened slightly. "Pretty sophisticated stuff you have to detect all of that. I didn't think the Imps could."

"As I said, I believe we can help with your security," Mitch replied smoothly. "It's to our advantage to make you secure. It's not altruism. It's self-preservation."

"My problem," Spehlman said, eyes focused on Mitch's, "is that we have nothing to offer for your technology."

Mitch paused for a moment, evaluating the conversation. *He certainly gets to the point quickly. What do I know about this guy? We gleaned all of our information about him off their P-Net.* Colonel Spehlman commanded the Baron's Guards and most likely acted as his security advisor. So is this an advance talk to set the stage with New Faroe's leader? Or is Spehlman overstepping his authority? Or maybe Spehlman was the de facto leader of the planet, based on the innuendo Mitch had picked up from Hansen and Tobias that the Baron was nothing more than a figurehead. Interceptions from the P-Net indicated the current Baron left much to be desired. The chatter seemed to encompass more than the usual displeasure with the ruling class of a planet found on P-Nets.

Mitch replied carefully. "I believe your system possesses things of interest to New Meyer. During my journey in-system I made a quick calculation. The New Faroe system is much smaller than New Meyer. Your jump point is much closer to your asteroid belt. We have a," Mitch hesitated, not wanting to reveal *Yakumo's* existence, "habitat where we can repair ships on station near our jump point. This allows us to keep more ships on alert. It also serves as a base for a quick reaction force for our allies. Anyway, we need raw materials that your belt can supply."

Spehlman nodded. "Might work. Though I don't know if enough income will be generated to really grow us back to the Imperium norm."

"We can provide your corvettes and armed merchantmen with upgrades in weaponry, stealth, and detection that should increase their survivability."

"My Lord, there's more to this than just mutual security, isn't there?" Spehlman suddenly asked coldly.

Michael nodded. "Yes, as part of the alliance, your Baron would need to reaffirm his allegiance to my Duke."

"So, there it is. The crux of the matter. My Lord, if I may be forward and blunt. This is just a power grab in the Imp vacuum isn't it? After all your Duke is a Landsman."

Mitch shook his head. "No, Colonel, it isn't. The Duke of New Meyer is responsible for the local chute. When the Imperium was stable the previous Dukes saw no reason to worry about this." *That's a lie, but we'll stick to the polite truth. My uncle was blinded by his belief in the Plan.* "Now, since the fall of Earth, we have to deal with Goth incursions, rogue Imp units, potential Shaallit incursions, and, of course, the so-called Pretenders. Duke Michael is trying to stabilize this chute. The terms for fealty are not all that stringent. We'll use the standard Imperium oath. However, if we are to commit our forces to your defense, then the Duke needs some assurances you'll use those forces to defend the chute." *I won't add that these assurances include a no resale clause. They will not be allowed to sell this technology.*

"You really plan to do that? I mean you'll commit forces to protect our security?" Spehlman sounded surprised.

"Yes, Colonel, we will. We've got to bolt the back doors so to speak. We learned lessons from the New Brazil incursion. As a result, we plan to have a rapid reaction force available, one that can respond to an incursion in any of our dual jump point systems. We're already dispatching ships as pickets to uninhabited systems with outside connecting jump points. This should be accomplished well before the end of the year. Sometime in the near future we will have sufficient forces to station a couple of frigates here for increased security."

Spehlman looked a bit disappointed. "Frigates. No offense, My Lord, but they look like hopped-up corvettes to me."

"No, Colonel, I assure you they're a lot more than a hopped-up corvette. Things often aren't what they seem."

Just then the car arrived at a large estate gate opening automatically to let the vehicles in.

"Care to join me for lunch where we can continue this discussion?"

"Ok with me. Will the Baron be joining us?"

"I'm afraid not, m'lord. Affairs of state require his presence elsewhere," Spehlman said with an unconscious emphasis on the word affairs. "He sends his regrets. A local emergency requires his attention. He should be available in an hour or so."

Mitch wasn't surprised in the least.

CHAPTER 22

Faroe's Haven, New Steymoy, Star System New Faroe
23 July 684 IP

BRASSARD HAD BEEN TO HUNDREDS of bars like this across the Imperium before settling down on New Meyer. They all had the same sweet smell of dope, the same bored naked girl dancing on the stage, and the same patrons lost in their own memories. He ignored the furtive glances cast his way when he entered, sensing only minor hostility. His black Marine fatigues had few distinctive badges to identify his unit. *These are all ex-military. They know what I am.* Most turned away as he walked past. *Interesting. I'm sure they know I'm an active duty Marine and yet there are no Imperium Marine units here and probably never were.* He grinned to himself. *In places like this it's best to mind your own business.*

Tobias was casually dressed in jeans and a sweatshirt but he carried himself in a similar manner to Brassard. The only difference was that the bar patrons knew him and were comfortable with him as one of their own. Tobias motioned Brassard to a secluded booth near the back. As he slid onto the cracked pseudoleather seat, Tobias pushed over a bottle of beer and a small bowl of hard bread with a dish of dip.

Brassard eyed the beer for a moment and then took a swig. *This stuff is good, better than most similar bars on New Meyer. Gotta let the Baron know.* Maybe their beer can be an export. And this herring dip, too. Good luxury exports. He studied Tobias. *He's easy to spot as an ex-Marine.* Close-cropped hair, sharp creases in his clothes, braced shoulders.

"So, Sergeant Major, how did you end up on a dump of a world like this?"

Tobias grinned. "How do you always end up at a place like this? A woman."

Brassard rolled his eyes. "Should've known. How did you meet her? I mean this place doesn't exactly export much. I'd bet you never visited here while in the Marines."

"Easy. I finally got fed up with the Imps and the prissy fops who became officers. You wouldn't believe what the Corps has come to."

Brassard nodded. "Yeah, tell me about it. Exactly why I like New Meyer. They're serious about their Marines and about their military."

Tobias continued, "So anyway, I quit and needed some work. Found a job on a tramp as head of security. Thought it would give me an opportunity to find somewhere a Marine is appreciated. The freighter visited here and I met this barmaid. Prettiest little woman you'd ever want to meet. Had one of those benders and the damn freighter left without me. You know, I'm not really in the customs service here."

"No, duh. Baron's Guard?"

"Yeah, I work directly for the Colonel. He's trying to hold this place together despite our Baron. The old Baron was okay but the son is a spoiled brat. He needs a couple of months at boot camp to straighten him out." He took a swig of beer. "And you?"

"The Baron Courtney's uncle, the late Duke, came on a recruiting tour ten years back while I was recovering from wounds taken at New Bresford Heights." Brassard grinned at Tobias' raised eyebrows. "Yeah, I was there. What a cluster fuck that was. Anyway, this Duke comes marching into the ward and right up to my bed. He says, 'Son, how would you like to be a real Marine again?'"

"No shit?"

"No shit. He was the real thing. Tell ya, I wouldn't want to have met him in a dark alley. He was a Duke but he could've been one of us just as easy."

"Working for a livin'?"

Brassard laughed. "I might not go that far, though I guess I could see him as a Sergeant Major. Close enough to an officer for government work."

"Fuck you, Guns," Tobias grunted but with a smile and raised his beer in salute.

A waitress glided over. "Another round, boys?"

Brassard looked into her dull eyes. She might have been pretty once but the years had taken their toll. Still, he caught an inkling of animation in them. *She's learned how to divorce her work from the rest of her life. It helps her stay human.*

"'I think we can have one more," he said gently.

He watched her walk away. She had one hell of a body. *Down boy, you're a married man.* "So, am I to believe that your Baron leaves something to be desired?"

Tobias hesitated and looked around. The bar wasn't busy and the few patrons at nearby tables had their attention on the stage or their beers. "He's typical of many of the Imperium's peerage these days. A freakin' fop who spends his time with booze, drugs, and women. The only reason this place is held together is because of Colonel Spehlman."

"Why don't you replace him? There's no Emperor left to interfere and up till now the Duke didn't care."

"Why do you think? Spehlman likes it this way. He's behind the scenes and the media leaves him alone. He gets less attention than if he kicked that idiot out and declared himself Baron. Between you and me, I don't completely trust Spehlman. I think he likes power and manipulating people. In my opinion he doesn't like responsibility, which is why he stays in the background." Tobias hesitated and looked around again before continuing, "To be honest, I think he's a bit of a coward. I managed to hack into his personnel dossier once. He's a staff puke. Never had a combat command in his life."

Brassard sank back in the booth and sipped his beer. *How lucky is New Meyer to have men like Duke Michael and Baron Mitchell.* "So why do you stay?"

Tobias shrugged. "Where else would I go? This is an out of the way world and not likely to be a target for a while. Besides, I married that barmaid from way back and have family and roots here now."

"You mean there's a rash of little Tobiases running around? Future Sergeant Majors? Thank God I'm heading back to New Meyer," he said with a grin.

"Fuck you, Master Guns," Tobias said and took a swig of beer to hide his smile.

Hotel Denmark, New Steymoy, Star System New Faroe
23 July 684 IP

Mitch sat in a high backed chair in his suite's sitting room with Brassard seated next to him in a similar chair. A small table with two bottles of the local beer on it separated them. Occasionally, they each reached over and took a drink. Mitch held up the bottle. "I think you're right, Guns. This stuff is good enough to export along with the herring dip. Adding some high-end luxury items to supplement their supplying Yakumo with material from their asteroid belt will further aid their cash flow."

"So we're going to help them, m'lord?" Brassard asked, slightly slurring his words from the effect of multiple bottles of the beer.

Mitch nodded. "I don't any other choice. With two jump points, this system is a back door into the chute. We must monitor and defend it. We're not in the conquest business so we're left with two options. We can hold our nose while supporting the current Baron to plug the gap, or we can leave a back door open. The choice is obvious."

Mitch took a swig and continued, "I met with their Baron. I guess he had a relatively sober moment. Actually, he's not a bad sort, just spoiled and afraid of responsibility. Though, if what you say is true, then Spehlman has manipulated him. The Colonel's in charge and the Baron doesn't realize it. Or maybe he does and likes it that way. On a good note, the Baron agreed to study whether to re-swear fealty to the Duke. I guess he thinks it would mean one less responsibility for him. Let Duke Michael make the important decisions. He'll learn quickly that won't happen." He took a big gulp of beer and then put it down. "Damn, this stuff is good. Well, one hole plugged for the moment. All in a day's work. I'm turning in." He sighed. "Have a good night, Master Guns. Well done. Good info."

"Thank you, My Lord. See you in the morning."

Mitch nodded and watched the non-com depart. *Good man. We're lucky to have him.* Mitch sighed and walked into the bathroom to get ready for bed. He had not brought along an orderly. *I'm an adult and can take care of myself.* Five minutes later he was in bed and asleep.

The sound of Josh's voice in his implant startled him awake in what seemed like no time though the opened timer e-window indicated he had slept three hours.

"Captain, we have an incursion at Jump Point Two," he said.

Mitch sat up, any thoughts of sleep gone. "Any identification?"

"We intercepted a message. They're Imp forces. Rogues, I suspect. They're demanding supplies and tribute. Past-due taxes to the Imperium they call it."

"Crap. okay, bring in all of the Raptors and get them refueled and armed. I'll be up as soon as I can. Get the ship ready for immediate departure."

"Aye-aye, sir," Josh responded.

Mitch spoke into his implant again, "Master Guns."

"Here, m'lord," came the instant response.

"Don't you ever sleep?"

Brassard chuckled. "Hell, m'lord, I'm a Marine. I don't need no stinkin' sleep."

Despite the gravity of the situation, Mitch couldn't resist a tight smile "You heard about the incursion?" he asked. *Josh would've informed him.*

"Yes, m'lord. The boys and me are ready to move out."

"Figured that. Meet you downstairs. Hopefully Spehlman and the Baron are awake, and we'll work this out."

As Mitch expected, downstairs was in turmoil. People were running in all different directions. Baron Nielsen stood in the middle of the lobby with Spehlman standing by his side.

Nielsen spied Mitch coming down the stairs, "Ah, Lord Courtney. You've heard, I see. Can we count on your support?"

Mitch saw the fear in the man's eyes, yet outwardly he seemed calm. "Lord Nielsen, my responsibility is to my ship and to report back to the Duke. I have orders not to risk the ship unnecessarily."

"Lord Courtney, you can't be serious," Spehlman interjected. The panic in his eyes reflected pure terror. "It's your duty as an Imperium officer to help defend this world." His voice broke.

"From other Imps?" Mitch asked with a raised eyebrow. "Besides, at this time, we don't even know if there is an Imperium. I'm returning to my ship and we'll depart this system."

"Lord Courtney," Nielsen said, "I offer my immediate fealty to the Duke of New Meyer in return for your support."

The fear in his eyes had receded, replaced by a coldness of purpose. *So now we see he does have some mettle, unlike Spehlman there.* Mitch nodded. "On your honor as a Peer and a Gentleman?" he asked.

"Yes, Baron, on my honor," Nielsen replied, not even looking at Spehlman. His voice was perfectly calm and his eyes clear.

Yes, he does have a spine. "Very well, I need transportation to my shuttle."

"A Guard jumpjet is on the way,"' Nielsen replied. He stuck out his hand. "My Lord, good luck and Godspeed."

Mitch took his hand. "Luck will have nothing to do with it."

CHAPTER 23

Frigate Courtney, Star System New Faroe
26 July 684 IP

MITCH SLID INTO THE CONN'S command chair moments after the shuttle docked. "Com, see if you can contact that Imp Task Force. Use the Duke's authorization code."

Due to light speed limitations and the distances involved no response was expected for more than an hour. Tactical data from Josh flowed into his implant. One open e-window showed a three-g departure trajectory. He weighed the energy consumption and decided it was worth the expenditure to make contact away from New Faroe. A quick subvocal command and the high-g klaxon blared. His chair automatically reclined, and its high-g contours enfolded his lower body, acting much like an old-fashioned g-suit. Moments later he was slammed back into the chair's deep padding as the fusion drive kicked in and the frigate accelerated from orbit.

The trip out took three and a half days. Three hours at three gravities followed by an hour at one g made the trip barely tolerable. His enhanced nanoskeleton and cardiovascular systems were standard issue to all Navy crew members to help them survive long periods at high acceleration. Enhancements or not, three gravities still felt like three people sitting on his chest for hours at a time.

As he closed on the Imps they still refused any contact with *Courtney* and simply repeated their demands to Nielsen.

"Captain, Baron Nielsen rejected the Imps' requests again," Elijah Patterson, the com tech reported.

Forty minutes later a brief message arrived from Lieutenant Commander Ricardo Costa of the *Falcão-Peregrino*, the New Brazilian corvette at the jump point. Costa's dark eyes were hard, and his normally calm features showed anger, his mouth a grim line, as he reported, "Imps have opened fire, My Lord. They disabled the customs corvettes and started moving in system. The New Faroe stealthed corvettes then attacked and scored some hits. Minor damage." His face grew even grimmer. "The battleships opened fire and destroyed the corvettes. No survivors. I'm trailing the Imps in and will send course and position updates. Manta is holding. We haven't been detected. Costa out."

"Good job, Commander. We're proceeding to intercept," he replied into a recorded message to be sent. "Here's our projected course."

Mitch studied the opened tactical e-window containing *Falcão's data*. One massive *Ivanov*-class battleship, three smaller *Moscow-class* battleships, three cruisers of unknown class, and four standard *Crecy*-class fleet destroyers. Against his one frigate. Mitch grinned wolfishly. *Maybe I'll hold back one of the Raptors to even the odds. Nah.* He admonished himself for his cavalier attitude. *Hopefully action can still be avoided.* "Launch Raptors." The frigate shuddered slightly as the hanger hatches opened, and the Raptors drifted free.

He settled in for another bout of three-g acceleration.

Frigate Courtney, Star System New Faroe
28 July 684 IP

"Captain, they're finally acknowledging us," reported Patterson when the frigate and task force were only separated by a couple of light-seconds.

The avatar of a balding older man materialized. His eyes were a sparkling blue but icy cold and almost devoid of emotion. The large mustache he sported did nothing to soften his features. "I am Lord Admiral Jacques Leblanc of the Imperium battleship *Peter the Great* and the personal representative of His Imperial Majesty Wolvein."

Mitch used his implant to pulse the ship's database of Imperium Peerages. *Wolvein? His Duchy is over 800 light years away. Another fuckin' Pretender.* "When was Duke Wolvein crowned as Emperor? We heard nothing of it here," Mitch replied.

After a maddening seven-second delay, Leblanc shrugged. "We installed Emperor Wolvein three months ago. He swore to bring stability back to the Imperium."

"I assume he was approved by the Senate over all of the Landsman heirs?" Mitch asked, matching LeBlanc's icy stare. The seven-second delay was beginning to diminish as the gap between the ships closed.

"There are no Landsman heirs. They're all dead," LeBlanc said almost nonchalantly. "As is the Senate. Once order is restored Emperor Wolvein will reinstate the Senate and restore the government. And I ask again, who are you?"

No Landsman heirs? Have you been hunting them? "I am Baron Courtney of New Meyer, the personal representative of His Grace, the Duke of New Meyer."

Leblanc frowned. "Duke of New Meyer? Never heard of him."

"His Duchy encompasses the entire New Meyer-New

Brazil chute. This world is part of His Grace's chute," Mitch replied, increasing the hardness in his voice. "We don't recognize Duke Wolvein as Emperor, not without Senate approval."

"There is no Senate, I tell you," Leblanc repeated, irritably. The delay was down to five seconds now.

"If that's the case, then what is to stop anyone from declaring himself Emperor? Until the Senate is reconstituted His Grace does not recognize anyone who merely claims to be Emperor. If your Duke Wolvein thinks he should be crowned Emperor, let him call the Council of Dukes and let them declare him Emperor. My liege will recognize the choice of that council in the absence of a Senate."

"Council of Dukes? Impossible!" LeBlanc snapped.

Mitch shrugged. "Then, as the representative of the Duke of New Meyer, I must ask you to leave this system."

Leblanc stared at Mitch. "You dare demand that we leave your system? I don't think so. No one demands anything of the Emperor's representative."

Mitch sank back in his chair and sighed. *I see which way this is headed.* He closed his eyes and concentrated momentarily on the background chatter through his implant between the controllers and their Raptors' AIs.

"They're pulsing us with radar," reported Abby's AI. "No lock, still undetected. Range to *Peter the Great*, 4800 kilometers."

We've gotten in missile range without being detected. He heard similar by-play from the other controllers and AIs. *The Imps can't penetrate our new stealth!* Abby was less than five thousand klicks from the flagship and still remained undetected. That meant the stealth field was handling the Imps' optical sensors too. *Either they're incompetent or the Manta is working better than expected. Maybe a combination of both.*

He returned his attention to Leblanc who was still

castigating him about Mitch's demand for the task force to depart the system.

"Do you have any more of those popgun corvettes of yours?" Leblanc was saying derisively. "And what kind of toy are you piloting?"

"Heavy probing, Captain." Josh reported. "Full countermeasures operating. I'm letting him think we're a large corvette."

Everything's working as designed. They haven't detected the Raptors and don't know what Courtney is. He weighed his options. At any moment the Imps might break the Raptors' stealth and then things would turn nasty in a hurry. *I'm still trying to avoid a confrontation. These are Imps, not Goth raiders. I'm not comfortable shooting at them.* He felt the taste of bile rise at the thought of civil war and fratricide against fellow Imps. *Was this how Roman legionnaires felt at Pharsalus and Philippi? Or American soldiers at Antietam and Gettysburg? Or Imp crewmen at New Bresford?*

"We have missile locks, Captain," Josh reported. "We can launch any time you're ready."

Those are fellow Imps out there. Do I really want to launch? If I let them go and they report back, no doubt New Meyer will become a place of interest. That's if he really represents Wolvein and isn't some rogue pirate using Wolvein as a cover. After all, Wolvein is four jumps and 800 light years away. How can I check Leblanc's credentials? And how do I make him leave without a battle? Then into his subvocal, "Josh, don't open fire until my command. Then take out their lead destroyer. Be prepared to engage additional targets and to go to deep stealth."

He looked back at the Admiral and sighed. "Admiral Leblanc, I must repeat my demand for you to leave this system at once."

The Admiral's face turned a bright red. "You dare? You

demand?" His eyes bulged as the anger quickly spread across his face.

"I don't. Duke New Meyer does," Mitch said calmly.

"This is outrageous!" Leblanc growled.

"Admiral, I will not say it one more time. You are to leave this system now by order of the legitimate governor of this chute, His Grace, the Duke of New Meyer."

"Or what? You're going to shoot me with your little popguns?" Leblanc laughed.

"Things are not always what they seem," Mitch said calmly, still desperately trying to avoid the upcoming engagement. "Admiral, the Duke of New Meyer is the legitimate Peer responsible for this chute. I am his representative. If Duke Wolvein is crowned as Emperor by the Senate or Council of Dukes my Duke will gladly offer his allegiance and fealty. Right now Duke of New Meyer's responsibility is to defend the worlds of this chute."

"Enough of this! You are impeding the official business of an official representative of the Emperor. I'll show that little toy of yours what it is to defy the Imperium. Mr. Flint," he said to someone off-screen, "prepare to provide a lesson in respect."

Courtney was at what would have been maximum effective blast cannon range for *Peter the Great's* 300mm blast rifles if the frigate had been the corvette LeBlanc thought she was. As a frigate, she had additional armor, almost as much as that of a cruiser. She could take a few hits before suffering critical damage. Mitch was not going to test that out.

"Back five gravities!" he ordered.

It was the ship's AI who instantaneously responded, a full three-quarters of a second faster than the human quartermaster. The frigate's forward fusion drive flared while the aft drive shut down immediately. Mitch felt the punch in the stomach of the sudden acceleration as *Courtney* backed away.

Peter's first salvo of fiery plasma bolts narrowly missed. Mitch sighed as his options to avoid the conflict rapidly dissipated in LeBlanc's fit of rage. *Damn him!*

"Launch!" he ordered.

He heard through his implant the interchange between the controllers and the four USV AIs. *Betty* had a lock and let loose with one of her missiles at short range. The flare of the missile's fusion drive registered momentarily on every ship's infrared sensors. That signal was soon overwhelmed by the pinpoint of bright light followed by a gout of sun-hot flame from the bow of the lead Imp destroyer as the Venom's nuclear shaped charge warhead literally split the ship in half.

Mitch balled his fists in anger. *Damn you. This didn't have to happen. That was an Imp crew I just killed.*

"What the hell just happened?" LeBlanc demanded. Then his face began to twist in anger, his mouth transforming into an uncontrolled snarl. "You dare?" he screamed.

"Take out the second destroyer. Launch!" Mitch ordered, swallowing the rising bile.

Another missile hurtled from *Betty* and flew directly into a second destroyer. The result was even more spectacular as the warship disappeared in an expanding sphere of white-hot gases.

"Depart this system immediately," Mitch ordered, trying to keep his voice firm. "We have no wish to continue this."

He heard LeBlanc scream, "Open fire, you idiots!"

"Stealth! Now! Launch countermeasures," Mitch ordered. "Fire on all targets."

Courtney shut down her fusion drive as she slipped into her shroud of EM invisibility. Following a pre-programmed plan, the frigate's AI initiated the port divert gravitics and the frigate invisibly danced to the right. Mitch watched the ensuing engagement with a mixture of exultation and fury. *This isn't a battle, it's a slaughter.* Leblanc's battleship took a slashing hit and immediately began spewing atmosphere and bodies from a sixty-meter gash in her hull. Moments later a second jet of plasma plunged into the battleship's engine room, penetrating the compartment's main fusion bottle. The aft end of the battleship evaporated in a ball of stellar-hot gas, a small nova momentarily lighting up the star system. The remnants of the battleship began to tumble end over end. There was no one left alive to respond. The other Imp warships fared no better. It was over in two minutes.

Mitch just sat their shaking with a mixture of anger and horror as *Courtney* decreased her acceleration. *Over two thousand Imp crewmen killed! Did I just plunge New Meyer into a civil war?* "Good job, all," he said as calmly as he could.

He stood up and walked into his ready room just off the conn and quickly entered the lavatory where he promptly vomited.

CHAPTER 24

Duke's Office, Government House New Meyer
15 September 684 IP

"BARON COURTNEY IS HERE," WALLACE whispered into Michael's implant.

Michael stood up as his cousin walked in. The two men embraced and sat down, each on one of the facing couches in front of the desk. Wallace placed a tray of coffee on the table between them. The coffee's aroma was bittersweet, a blend Wallace didn't often select. He also left a plate of simple butter cookies, favorites of both men.

"All the new stuff worked," Michael whispered.

Mitch poured himself a mug of coffee and popped a cookie into his mouth, enjoying the intense sweetness that embodied his warm feelings about his return home. He followed with a sip of the coffee which seemed to jerk him back to the matter at hand. He nodded. "Far better than any of us imagined. The Imps were unable to penetrate the stealth at all. The Raptors all functioned as designed, as did the Venoms." He paused and sighed before continuing, his voice almost a whisper. "This wasn't war, cousin. The engagement was slaughter. They had no chance."

Michael leaned over and put a hand on his cousin's

shoulder. "I know, but it's what we need to survive," he said softly. Then a bit firmer, "Besides, they deserved it. They broke their oath to the Imperium."

Mitch nodded, letting the warmth of the mug reassure him as he lifted it with both hands. "They wouldn't have hesitated to do the same to me. I recognize that, but it doesn't change the reality. For all practical purposes, we executed them."

"Your sense of honor, cousin?"

Mitch shrugged. "I guess so."

"Mitch, this separates us from them. We remember who we are, and what we stand for. 'Duty, Honor, and Imperium' means something to us. To them, those are just words. Are we old-fashioned and behind the times? I certainly hope not. If we are, then not only is the Imperium doomed, so is civilization. LeBlanc and his ilk are sharks. Lone predators out for whatever they can get. You and me, cousin, we're wolves. Dangerous predators who are loyal to the pack, to the Imperium, to society as a whole. We believe in a social contract to protect the people of the Imperium." He paused. "Sorry about preaching. Remember they would have done the same to you if they had a chance, and they would have done it without the guilt."

"You sound like a raving liberal, cousin," Mitch replied with a grin.

Michael grinned back. "Call me whatever you want. I just take my role here as Duke seriously. My job is to protect the worlds in this chute from people like LeBlanc. Besides, you're aware how I hate stacked decks that prevent people or planets from reaching their full potential. As I said, LeBlanc was trying to do to you what you ended up doing to him. Only you did it in self-defense. You were defending a planet of forty million people from a shark. Human predators can be far more destructive than their counterparts in the animal kingdom."

Mitch nodded. "It's still not any easier even if you have justification. You're right, though." He sighed and straightened his shoulders. "So you wanted to see me about something else?"

It was Michael's turn to sigh. "We've received word that Lady Claudia will be here 16 December."

Now Mitch looked even more stricken. "You're going to make me go through with this, aren't you?"

"Yes." Michael replied firmly.

"That's all you have to say?"

Michael shrugged. "We're between a rock and a hard place, and we need New Brazil. This is the quickest way to seal our relationship. I'm asking for a sacrifice to help us survive. They sent some additional pictures and info about her. You can download them from the AI. I peeked. You could have done a lot worse." He grinned wolfishly and clapped Mitch on the shoulder. "You're getting a lot of woman there. I think you'll find her an asset." Then the grin grew broader, to a smile. "Maybe even a bit of a challenge."

Mitch exhaled slowly. "I guess it could be worse."

"Yeah, maybe. She might be downright ugly and stupid. She's obviously neither. Let's see what happens. You know, I would or could never force you into a marriage that obviously wouldn't work. I won't do that. All I can ask is for you go in with an open mind."

Mitch nodded. He opened an e-window to peek at the files as they downloaded. He stared at the image of the raven-haired beauty. She seemed to be gazing intensely back at him with large, intelligent eyes. He imagined those eyes would penetrate his soul when they were in person. Michael was right about her being neither ugly nor stupid.

Argula City, New Barwick, Okra Star System
15 September 684

The Shaallit female orgasmed again and again, her breath coming in short raspy gasps. The High Priestess felt her buddling offspring pass into the Shaallit. Intense emotions and life force flowed into her. She struggled not to continue feeding and reluctantly pulled away as the Shaallit passed out in sheer exhaustion. In the coming weeks she would condition this newly enslaved female herself. This one was too important to leave to others. She smiled in anticipation. Sex would play a large role in the conditioning. *I will get to feed a bit and enjoy conditioning her.* During the process only a taste would be allowed. *But what a taste!* After training, the female was to be sent back into the Shaallit's capital to begin the seduction of the Shaallit royal family.

She smiled her equivalent of a human feral smile. The Shaallit were as easy to control as the Granac, since they belonged to the same racial stock. Their homeworld now held a dozen temples to the High Priestess of Nearyahn. This new female Acolyte was not destined for those temples. Instead, she was destined to become a plaything for His Majesty the Emperor-Protector of the Shaallit. She had been selected for her sexuality and her appeal to the monarch's tastes. Big busted and narrow waisted, but short in stature. A bit of a spitfire. Just what the Emperor-Protector likes. The challenge was to keep the new Acolyte's spirit after conditioning. *That I can do. I did it with my husband and I'll do it with her.*

She'll become and remain the Shaallit Emperor-Protector's plaything for only a short time before moving up to Favorite and then Consort. *By the time she becomes Consort her buddling will have finished growing and her ability to control other Shaallit will be well developed.* A satisfied smile. *The Emperor will be easy to control.*

Her smile disappeared. *I should be satisfied with the Granacs and Shaallit. They are adequate as feedstock.* Adequate, but not nearly as tasty as Humans. Her visions showed that if she didn't conquer the Humans they would eventually destroy her. Those visions of Human victories persisted and were becoming more frequent. *And New Meyer is at the center of them.*

The Shaallit were readying an incursion into Imperium space. A large incursion. *Only now with the influence of the new Consort its focus will change.* Her visions only showed probabilities. A definite future was unknowable, just an infinity of probable timelines. *For the Imperium a new Emperor will rise.* In some envisioned timelines she succeeds in killing the new Emperor before he assumes the throne. In others, she kills him later. Unfortunately, in the vast majority, she fails. He reunites and strengthens the Imperium and then destroys the Goth Alliance and the Shaallit. *I never survive those defeats. So I have to change the probabilities. New Meyer appears to be the key. Why that small, unimportant world is so significant is a mystery. I must eliminate New Meyer. I need alternatives to increase the probabilities.*

With her new influence on the Shaallit Emperor-Protector, the planned Shaallit incursion will not be aimed at Longhorn, the new Imperium capital, as it was now. Instead New Meyer will be the target. *I'll have my Goths strike at the same moment.* Other Human entities under her control will join in the assault. *New Meyer will not survive this onslaught and neither will the new Imperium Emperor.* Then the collapse of Human civilization will be ordained and the Nearyahn Religion will rise in Human space. *I will then be free to bud fully and feed.*

CHAPTER 25

M ITCHELL LANDSMAN, BARON OF COURTNEY, stood shivering on the field as he waited for the orbital shuttle and the arrival of the woman he was expected to marry. He arched his back trying to ease the tightness stemming from nightmares in which he was badly burned aboard the doomed Imp ships and trapped in a compartment leaking air. Death by vacuum promised to offer relief from the agony of scorched skin. Only, he seemed to continue breathing as the air leaked out. In another nightmare, Leblanc's faced morphed into Michael's just as he gave the order to fire.

He refused to take any drugs to provide relief from the nightmares or even tell anyone about them. Somehow, the dreams seemed a form of penance for the battle, though his rational mind justified the actions as necessary. He sighed and pushed away the stiffness and the doubts for the moment.

He glanced up at the dull gray sky. He smelled snow coming as the edge of the northern horizon turned an ugly dark purple. He still seethed at his cousin and wife for engineering this whole thing. *We're in the 30th century for God's sake. No one arranged marriages anymore.* He exhaled again. *Actually, not really true. The Peerage did it all the time in the name of planetary or family need.*

The nature of interstellar communications limited his access to more information describing his future bride and her life. The P-Net made info about almost any person on New Meyer abundantly available. However, lightspeed limitations constrained data availability from other worlds. Therefore, data had to be carried via spaceship or com drone from one star system to another. Interstellar communications cost too much in energy and money to waste on frivolous content. Maybe the Heart Worlds could afford com drones on a daily, if not hourly, basis or by use of the regular parade of ships passing through the jump points. While no law required them to do so, most ships at a jump point accepted message packets to be broadcast immediately after the jump in return for a drop in customs fees. Thus, the busier the jump point, the more info crossed from other star systems. However, for the non-Heart Worlds, out-system communication and news were much more limited. Though fairly busy by some standards, much of the media content never seemed to cross the New Brazil-New Meyer jump point. Mitch had been frustrated by a dearth of data about Claudia Maria Mendes Sakomoto on New Meyer's Net. He found a couple of pictures of her, though none as recent as he'd like. She certainly was attractive. *Actually, downright beautiful.* The few articles he read indicated she showed no fear in expressing her opinions. The new files Michael gave him seemed to support that conclusion.

Beautiful and opinionated. Sheesh! What am I getting into? The supplied files were obviously public relations stories released to the media. While they gave a good idea of her physical looks, the insights into her personality seemed nominal at best. *Well, at least she's not some ugly frump.*

So here he waited for a woman he had never met but was expected to marry to cement the alliance between New Meyer and New Brazil. He could have sent his majordomo to meet the Lady Claudia and then make a grand entrance sometime later in the day. *No, not my style.* Claudia was his guest here at the Courtney Manor for their get acquainted meeting and he planned to be the consummate host. *Damn the ridiculous Peerage Protocols!* Like his cousin, he hated them.

The shuttle dropped in and flared up as its jets kicked in and brought it gently to the landing pad, a concrete circle lined with high-temperature nanoceremets and a GPS transponder. The transport rocked briefly and then settled. Mitch fidgeted as he waited for the landing ramp to be extended. A cold icy wind gust roared in, knifing through his old-style western parka. Outside of the spaceport, leaves and other trash churned in spinning eddies. The field itself was constantly policed for debris, so the wind just tugged at clothing and hats.

Two crew members emerged first. Mitch stomped his feet with a mixture of impatience and an attempt to keep warm. For a moment he regretted wearing throwback American West outerwear rather than a more modern nano-controlled parka. A conservatively dressed middle aged woman with a dour face appeared next. *Chaperone. Aunt.* Finally, Claudia appeared, followed by two ladies in waiting.

Mitch took a deep breath. She wore an outfit more suited for the ski slopes of New Meyer's Artesia Resort. Dark sun glasses hid her eyes and her long jet-black hair was covered by a stylish black and white knit beanie. The simple and stylish nano-insulated pullover sweater she wore offered a hint of her lush figure. Her charcoal pants hugged her body, indicating to Mitch the rest of her was nice, also.

Mitch walked over and greeted her, bowing. "My Lady, I am the Baron of Courtney —"

The older woman interrupted him. "Senhor, how dare you? Where is your sense of propriety? And a member of the peerage, too. To address a Lady without proper introduction —"

"Tia!" Claudia snapped. Then in near-perfect English, "Please forgive me, My Lord. My aunt is a bit old-fashioned and overprotective." She returned the bow.

I must've breached some form of etiquette. He bowed in return and then bowed to the older woman. "Ah! You must be the Lady Claudia's Aunt Iris. I was warned of your elegance and beauty."

Iris returned the bow with a nasty smile on her face. "My Lord, I understand that this is a former Norte Americano descended colony and therefore forwardness is accepted as the way."

"Tia! I said enough!" Claudia smiled at Mitch and sighed. "There are elements on New Brazil who are trying to return to old ways as a defense against the uncertainty of our time. The inclusion of my Aunt on this trip is, shall we say, an acknowledgment by my father. And now this marriage thing."

Mitch smiled back at Claudia. "To be honest, m'lady, I am not real happy about this arrangement either."

She giggled. "My Lord, that makes two of us."

"Well, let's get out of the cold." He motioned to three servants to grab the luggage, as a black limousine glided up.

"No, grav sled, My Lord?" she asked.

"No, My Lady, we're on a war footing now and all civilian grav generators are appropriated for military purposes. I refuse to use my rank and privilege to keep one. We've reverted to more ancient forms of transportation including automobiles and helicopters, though they are all powered by microfusion generators and not internal combustion engines."

"How quaint, My Lord" she giggled again. Then more seriously, "We're doing the same, though many of the New Brazilian Peers aren't as conscientious as you are."

"My Lady, this My Lady thing is going to grow old real fast. So will senhorita and senhor. Will I be too forward to suggest using first names?"

Claudia glanced over at her Aunt. "Tia, I'm okay with this. No, Mitchell, of course not."

"Mitch, if you please."

"Mitch it is," she replied.

He opened the door to the limo before the chauffeur walked around, and bowed with a sweeping hand, "Lady Claudia. Lady Iris. Another vehicle will carry your staff."

Claudia gawked at him askance. "I thought you said no 'Lady and My Lord'".

Mitch grinned. "Peerage prerogative to be flexible when it suits me."

She chuckled and rolled her eyes before climbing into the limo. Much to Iris' chagrin, Mitch ushered the older woman to the jump seat facing her charge and then slid in next to Claudia. Mitch fought down a chuckle at the aunt's reaction. He sensed Claudia was reacting the same way he was. The barest trace of a smile appeared momentarily.

The limo departed smoothly. The ride to the Manor took only a couple of minutes through a stark landscape contrasting with the Manor's lush spring and summer green. Empty horse corrals with the horses safely in their barns portrayed preparations for an oncoming snowstorm. The Manor still operated as a working horse farm, a carryover from earlier colonial times when things were less advanced.

The squat stone structure of the Manor seemed constructed more for functionality than elegance or aesthetics. Built-into the side of a small mountain, the natural stone provided excellent insulation in summer and winter. The rock shielded the building from the worst winter blizzards and summer thunderstorms, as well as the occasional tornado. *The Manor isn't quite a cave dwelling but close. Legacy from the early colonial period.* Mitch could easily afford to build a new, more elegant manor. However, he cherished the old house and its history as the second-oldest manor house on the planet, next to the Duke's. His father, on the other hand, despised the place and lived in a penthouse condo in New Landsman City nicknamed Newberry Manor. Mitch didn't miss him and his self-centered actions.

He studied Claudia. With her sunglasses off, her large hazel eyes with the barest trace of the Asian almond shape reflected her mixed Japanese–Brazilian ancestry. Her slightly pointed nose and mouth complemented each other in a way Mitch couldn't describe. *They're just perfect. In fact, she's one of the most beautiful women I've ever met. Careful boy, don't let your lust ruin this.*

"You can't appreciate the beauty of this country at this time of year. It's so dreary and dead-looking, so stark," he was saying.

"I don't agree, Mitch," she replied in an almost melodious mezzo-soprano with a sweetness reaching deep inside of him. "New Brazil is more tropical and I don't experience this kind of weather much except for the occasional skiing holiday. It may be stark, but it reminds me of the cycle of life."

Whoa boy! Don't talk yourself into anything. You don't have to like this woman. You can still tell Michael to stuff it. But he found her attractive and he didn't want to tell Michael to stuff it. *At least not yet.*

They pulled up in front of the manor. A long semicircular driveway allowed vehicles to line up during the occasional social or business function. The manor's majordomo/chamberlain, Eric Caldwell, waited out front.

Eric opened the limo door and bowed. "Welcome to Courtney Manor, My Lady," he said, extending a hand to help Claudia out. "I'm Eric Caldwell, at your service."

He then helped out Iris. "And you must be Lady Iris. We are honored to have you at our Manor, My Lady," he said, bowing his head and kissing the back of her hand.

"Jesus, Eric," Mitch subvocalized into his implant, "you don't have to lay it on that thick."

Caldwell hid his grin but even the subvocalization could not hide the trace of humor. "Trust me, My Lord, I know this type."

Iris blushed and giggled. "At least someone here knows how to treat a lady."

Claudia shot her aunt an angry frown, unaware of the brief conversation between Mitch and his majordomo. She regarded the landscape and the front of the building. "Interesting."

Mitch cleared his throat. "Let me show you in." *Cool. Real cool.*

Eric raced ahead to grab the large right wooden door. He swung it open. Mitch rolled his eyes as he walked past. Eric just grinned. They entered through a foyer opening into a vast great room large enough to hold a cocktail party or even a small ball. The décor was simple and somewhat rustic, with roughhewn stone walls and dark leather-covered hardwood furniture.

"Definitely has a male feel to it," Claudia remarked. "Yet, it's nice."

"Really?" Mitch asked before almost kicking himself for the stupidity of the question, as if she were going to answer it.

"I like the simplicity and lack of pretentiousness. I gather there's much history associated with it?"

"Some," Mitch answered with relief. "Courtney Manor was the second one built on the planet when things were much simpler. I like it for the same reasons you do."

"Interesting," she grumbled. "So where am I staying?"

"My bedroom is on the ground floor in the back. Guest rooms are upstairs. Nice and separate," he said with a grin.

"Well, young man, at least you got that right," Iris snapped. She turned to Eric. "Show us to our rooms."

"Yes, m'lady," Eric dutifully intoned.

Mitch watched Eric struggle up the spiral stairs, lugging two large suitcases. Three other servants trailed behind with more. *Maybe I should get a couple of robotic helpers to ease the burden on poor Eric.* He brushed the thought aside and focused more on Claudia's rounded, shapely rump as she walked up the stairs. He was looking forward to an interesting next couple of days.

CHAPTER 26

Courtney Manor, New Meyer
17 December 684 IP

THE WIND FROM THE DAY before was gone, as if pausing to regain strength. Two saddled horses stood waiting as Mitch and Claudia emerged from the main building. The ranch hand holding the horses' bridles nodded and lowered his head in respect.

"Good morning, Hank," Mitch said, taking both the reins and handing one set to Claudia.

"Good morning, m'lord, m'lady." Hank Álvares replied. "We lucked out last night. Not anywhere as severe as predicted. Looks like a break in the storm for a couple of hours."

Mitch nodded. "Enough for a ride to show the Lady Claudia around the near pastures." *Also gets us away from Iris for a couple of hours.*

He admired how easily Claudia mounted her mare, reaching down to pat the horse's neck as she settled on the western saddle. She smiled back at him as he swung up onto his horse. He marveled how her smile lit up her face.

She quirked an eyebrow at him. "I've been riding almost

as long as I've been walking. We own a ranch too, though not a working ranch like this one. More of a vacation spot for our extended family. I spent my summers there as a youth."

Something more in common. He nodded at Hank and flexed his knees. The large roan started forward, following a path he knew well. Less than a centimeter of snow had fallen the night before despite the forecasts of blizzard conditions. The storm had petered out. *Meteorologists still can't get their predictions right.* They rode through a world of dark and white contrasts. A fine white layer of snow and ice glistening in the early morning sunlight covered the stark branches of winter-stripped trees and the dusky greens of the pines.

Mitch was riding his favorite, a bay roan named Spacewind, a good-sized range horse, strong and smart though maybe not the fastest. As a working horse, Spacewind was comfortable in the snow. Claudia rode next to him on a smaller mare, Starwitch, another working horse also confident in the snow. Claudia seemed at home on horseback. *Thank God, Iris wasn't, so she stayed behind, protesting, but overruled by Claudia, who clearly wanted more time alone with me.*

Courtney Manor stood on an eight-hundred-meter high plateau straddled by a mountain range running the entire north-south length of the New Arthur continent. With a mild climate, much like North America on Earth, the Manor's location in the mountains away from the tempering influence of the ocean, led to harsher winters and more frequent snowstorms. The Manor was a working ranch raising horses and cattle. The ranch owned three thousand acres of plateau meadows located adjacent to another ten thousand acres of state-owned land leased for grazing rights. *Not the largest ranch on New Meyer, but comfortable in size. The cattle provide a modest profit over the expenses of maintaining the Manor House.*

The cold, biting air revived him, cutting through the layers of lower-technology clothes and touching something primal in him. He loved it out here where he could just be, even in the dead of winter. He wore traditional old-style clothes and eschewed the popular nanofiber outerwear with built-in climate control. A lined buckskin-colored suede jacket with a fur collar covered a heavy sweater and jeans. Synthetic bullhide boots, a simple black Stetson with ear coverings extended down, and leather gloves completed the outfit. *I almost never wear the modern stuff. Why wear something like that and bother to go out?*

Being out here with Claudia is special. She had surprised him by wearing similar North American western-style clothes instead of dressing more in the Brazilian gaucho style of her homeworld. They had begun bonding the night before at dinner despite the limiting presence of Iris. The conversation had been light and general. He had sensed the older woman warming a bit to him as she learned more about his life. After the meal, Iris had gone to bed leaving the two of them alone in the study by a roaring fire. *I guess that was a small victory, her leaving us alone.*

"So you grew up on a working ranch?" she had asked.

"Yep, for my early years. Went to public school in Courtney only twenty-five miles away. Cute city. I'll take you after the storm. Not that big, maybe a couple of hundred thousand. I think that's part of a plan by the old timers to keep the city quaint. Economy focuses on tourism and ranching, though the Baron of Courtney Manor and its position in the government brings in quite a few jobs."

"Public school? Not me. Only the best private schools and tutors. I also spent my summers on the ranch, but with tutors, though not all taught academics. By ten I was an expert marksman and could survive reasonably well outdoors by myself. At fourteen I served on a training cruiser as a junior midshipman."

"Sounds just like me," Mitch replied, refilling her wine

glass. "I did the same. I had a tutor, a retired Marine gunnery sergeant named McAdams. His job was to toughen me up. Like you I learned how to shoot and survive. He also taught hand to hand and much more about being a soldier. Best of all Michael was with me. He spent his summers here, too."

"So you're more than just cousins?"

Mitch nodded. "I guess so. We became inseparable though we had a friendly rivalry in everything we did. Neither of us had a brother so I guessed we filled that role for each other."

"Why such small families? I thought to protect the line you'd have large families?"

"My parents led very different lives and grew apart. They were separated for many years before the divorce. Michael lost his mother at an early age and the Duke never remarried." Mitch grinned. "I think he was quite arrogant and couldn't find another woman who would put up with him."

Claudia laughed. "I heard similar things on New Brazil said about him. The word was insufferable. Same about your father, with a few other unflattering descriptions. No offense."

What a beautiful laugh. "You mean like self-centered? Elitist? I'm sure there's more. I always wondered how Duke Alex put up with such a fop of a brother. He may be my father but I have no illusions about him. He's the opposite of his brother."

The conversation had continued on well into the night.

"This is beautiful country, Mitch," she said, interrupting his thoughts. "I can imagine spring here."

"Wildflowers all over," Mitch replied. "Horses and cattle grazing on Earth-green grass. I'm told our skies are the same blue as on Earth though I've never been there." *Guess I won't anytime soon. I don't think Earth's skies are blue anymore.* He pushed the thought from his mind, not wanting to ruin the ride.

New Meyer had been a prize, an earthlike planet requiring little terraforming. A few domesticated food animals had been imported early on to fill some niches. The planet's natural wildlife, though Earth-like, lacked some of the critical nutrition required by humans, so animals were imported from New Brazil, Meyer, and Earth. Bringing in outworld steers, goats, and horses had another advantage. New Meyer's homegrown wolf-like predator, called a caolobo or dog wolf by early settlers, didn't show much interest in Terran animals. *Almost as if it instinctively recognized these animals lacked essentials for survival.* Terran grasses and grains also survived well and fit into their required environmental roles. Ranching and farming, while requiring some importation initially, were now self-sufficient and profitable. Due to natural and directed crossbreeding, few plants or animals were purely native or imported. As a side effect of the hybridizing, the caolobo now showed more interest in cattle and goats. Mitch carried a pulse rifle just in case.

"A true working ranch," she remarked.

"One I don't get the opportunity to work much anymore. I have a crew with a good foreman to handle affairs here."

"Do you live here year round?" she asked.

Mitch shook his head. "Only when I can. This is my official home as Baron Courtney. However, with so many things going on now I'm spending way too much time away, particularly in space."

"You love that, too, don't you? I mean, being in space?"

"Perceptive of you. I don't know. Maybe being in space with a crew of highly trained personnel is not different than being out on the range with a group of wranglers. Less rugged surely, but more isolated and you have to depend on each other for survival. I think it's the comradeship and dependence I like so much. Still, I miss my horses."

He continued on. "A young colony like New Meyer can't afford the use of gravitics for ranching. Ranchers use a mixture of four-wheel-drive electric vehicles and horses for wrangling. No gravitic sleds like on the Heart Worlds. Some of the larger, wealthy ranchers also own a fusion-electric helicopter for ranching use, mainly for mapping and spotting. Horses still provide a good deal of the transportation here on a working ranch. I love it out here on horseback."

They rode silently side by side for a while, Mitch studying her out of the corner of his eye. This was a woman he was expected to marry to cement a relationship between two planets anchoring the local jump chute. He considered. She was drop-dead gorgeous, intelligent, witty, and sharp. *So what more can I ask for? Do I need to love her? This is supposed to be a marriage of convenience. Am I willing to accept that? On the other hand, what are my choices?* He pursed his lips. *Take a step back. If I met her on my own would I be attracted to her? Hell, yes. For a one-night stand? Hell, yes. For a longer relationship?* Then an internal sigh. *Yes. Well, so far.*

He pondered for a while, considering he had met her only twenty hours or so earlier. In his normal life he probably would have tried to bed her at some point. If that turned out well then he'd most likely see her again and life would take its natural course. He didn't bed all the women he dated on the first date or even the second. So much depended on the woman and their mutual intentions. *Where would I have placed Claudia?* The more he thought about it the more he realized he would have pursued her even if he had been rebuffed. *I am attracted to her for so many reasons. So, where does that leave things?*

"So you're trying to figure things out, too?" she asked, disturbing his thoughts.

Damn, does she read minds? "Yeah. And you?"

They were moving at a slow walk. The lack of wind left

a deep stillness undisturbed by the sounds of life. *Most animals are either hibernating or have gone south for the winter.* The silence around them made it easy for them to converse. *It's almost as if the world is pausing to hear this conversation.* He grinned to himself. *And I call my father self-centered?*

"Me, too," she admitted.

"This is damn awkward. They say this isn't an arranged marriage but dammit, what else can you call it? What do you think would happen if we said no?"

She laughed. "I don't think no is an option."

"Dammit," he growled. "This is the 31st century!"

She turned in the saddle and met his eyes. "Mitch, let's get down to the core of this. I've been truly alone with you for a grand total of three hours and one-night, no forty-four minutes. So, at least, I've garnered a first impression of you, and I think you've been pretty straight with me. I like that about you. I've been thinking about whether I would have been attracted to you in another life. The answer is yes. I wondered whether I would have slept with you. Again the answer is probably yes." She paused as she saw his eyes widen. "Does this shock you? I assure you I'm not like what Iris would like me to be." She stopped again as he began laughing. "What is so damn funny?" she demanded.

He managed to catch his breath. "I was thinking exactly the same thing. I mean whether I would've been attracted to you, and whether I would have pursued you. My answer is also yes."

"Does that mean we're compatible?" she asked with a giggle.

"Er, no, not necessarily, but it does mean that we're on the road in that direction."

She looked at him oddly as if coming to a decision. "So back to the core of this. If this were five-years or even two-years ago I would've told my father to stuff this. But, like

176

you, my upbringing stressed a sense of responsibility and duty. I haven't always let these direct my life. On the other hand, we're living in really bad times now. Sometimes you do what you have to do and not always what you want to do."

"And?" he asked with a mixture of hope and suspicion, and maybe a touch of dread.

"I'm moving in with you. I will share your bed starting tonight. And we'll see how it goes."

Mitch nearly fell off his horse. "You don't have to do this, you know," he whispered.

"Yes, I do," she stated in a tone indicating to him she had made up her mind.

"Claudia, despite the tough times and our obligations, do you believe that our marriage is required for this alliance to work?"

"No, I guess not, but it will help greatly. Look, I'm one of the darlings of the New Brazil Media and Net. People follow me everywhere I go and my pictures are broadcast over P-Net. God forbid, I have a slip and the barest hint of a nipple appears while I'm at some function. Don't believe that nothing can move faster than the speed of light in this universe. A picture of that slip will, as will a rumor that I'm involved with some guy. So if we get married, the New Brazilian Media will set up direct communications between our planets. I expect daily, if not hourly, message drone jumps between our systems. This'll help bring our two worlds together."

He considered for a moment. "Do we have to wait for tonight?" he asked with a sly grin.

She looked around and gestured at the snow. "I think it's little cold out here. I don't care how hot our passion might be," she said with a wry chuckle, "but I'm not freezing my buns off. There's a limit to my dedication."

He grinned back, giving her a fake leer. "There's an

emergency cabin a couple of klicks up the road we use when working the range. It's fully stocked."

She studied him with a suspicious air. "And how many women have you brought there?"

"Who me?" he asked innocently.

"Show me this cabin," she demanded.

"What about Tia?"

"She's not as naive as you might think. We've already talked about this."

"God, I should've known." He spurred the horse up the road and said, "Follow me."

CHAPTER 27

THEY LAY ON THE BOTTOM bunk of the wood framed oversized bunk beds in one corner of the cabin. Another set of beds lay a couple of feet away. *Not the most comfortable but this is an emergency cabin.* Her head rested in the crook of his arm, momentarily dozing after a bout of rather athletic lovemaking.

A fire burned noisily in the stone fireplace, filling the room with radiant warmth smelling of burnt New Meyer's versions of oak and pine. *What do I do next? Things are moving faster than I anticipated.* Claudia touched him in ways no other woman ever had. Now he was beginning to feel the loss of control associated with a relationship turning serious. In the past, he would have just run from it. *That's not an option. I need to deal with these feelings.*

The expected snowstorm moved in, though only the lightest of flurries drifted down, excited by a swirling wind. Mitch pulsed P-Net with his implant and received a satellite image of the storm bearing in from the northwest. *If we leave now we can make it back to the Manor. Otherwise, we'll probably have to remain here for three days, judging by the size of the storm.* This was an early season blizzard coming in on the heels of the season's first snowstorm. *It'll be a cold, unpleasant ride back but doable and not all that risky.* With his access to GPS there was little chance of getting lost. This would be one time he wished he had the nano-warmed coats rather than the old-fashioned pseudo buckskin he preferred. *One has to live by one's choices and take the consequences.*

He looked around at the cabin, a one-room affair, about nine meters by six meters, with a couple of thermal pane insulated windows. A small enclosed lavatory with a heated shower took up one corner. The cabin's water came from a deep well that was in no danger of freezing. The nano-enhanced log walls exhibited increased insulation and also resistance to mold and rot. As such, the cabin was not as drafty as the original log cabins on Earth but still maintained some of the same visual rustic appeal. He grinned. *Modern technology at work again.* The cabin's small fusion thermoelectric cell supplied power for years. *okay, so those two break the rustic charm but we do live in an advanced technology world.* A well-stocked pantry contained plain, ready-made food for at least a week. A microwave and a wood stove provided the cooking arrangements. He had also discovered a couple of small packets of spices last night. Most importantly he found plenty of coffee.

The spartan furniture included a small couch and a bare wooden table with a couple of straight-backed chairs. Two old-fashioned stuffed chairs with foot rests sat near the fireplace. *Not luxurious, but enough to be comfortable riding out a storm.*

Their implants provided them with a link to the P-Net and, therefore, he'd never be out of contact. They could also connect and download some entertainment sims if they needed some diversion. They could even explore some of the sims linked together in a virtual world. That would certainly give them some more insight into each other's views. Disposable jump suits stored in a small closet allowed them to change clothes. Not flattering, but okay for their intended use. Intrinsic nanos would size the suits to fit their wearer. *Besides, I wonder how much we'll be wearing clothes.* He still had more than two weeks on his official thirty-day leave from *Courtney*. He chuckled to himself. *I wonder if Michael considers this official duty.*

The horses were protected from the storm in a small heated enclosure near the house with plenty of food and water. *So why return? Because to stay implies some sort of commitment and I'm not sure I'm ready. This is all way too fast.*

He looked over at her only to see her looking back at him with her lovely hazel eyes. He cleared his throat. "I was thinking —"

"Of staying here and riding out the storm?" she interrupted, her voice a soft, husky purr.

Mitch looked at her in surprise. *How does she do that? How does she always know what I'm thinking? Or is it we're just thinking alike.* The lovemaking last night had been more than just pleasant and more than satisfactory. They seemed compatible in their sexual tastes. They had both enjoyed exploring each other's bodies and with that came the thrill of discovery. As the night progressed and they learned each other's tastes, the passion grew. *Or was it just lust? It's still too soon to define what it really is.* Three days alone here would either drive them stir crazy or allow them to get to know each other.

He nodded. "If we stay much longer we're stuck here for three days."

She smiled at him and sighed, batting her eyes coquettishly. "All the lovemaking last night really tired me out. Don't think I can make the ride. I already pulsed Iris and told her that."

"Hey, who's the Baron here?" he asked with mock ferocity. "And who's in charge here?"

She grinned demurely. "We women usually let the men think they're in charge. Even in the 31st century."

He sighed. *Exactly what I'm afraid of.* "We're nice and cozy here," he replied, ignoring her implication. "Horses are protected. Plenty of food, water, and conveniences."

She leaned over and kissed him. "Why go anywhere then? We have everything we need right here," she whispered in his ear, the sweet fragrance of her hair stirring desire.

"Yeah, why don't we stay?" he grumbled, lost even more in her scent and the touch of her skin. "I need to let Eric know," he said trying to resist his rising passion and thinking he still needed to go out and bring in some more wood.

"No need. I already told him," she replied.

Yeah, who is in charge here? "I need to get some wood for the fire," he grumbled.

"I'll keep you warm," she replied. "Besides I feel some hard wood right here." Her hand had slipped down to his groin.

"I'll pay for this later when I have to go out in the storm for that damn wood. What the hell? No big deal." He let himself go and inhaled deeply her musky fragrance He began kissing her body, sliding his lips down off her neck. *"Yeah, what the hell."*

CHAPTER 28

Corvette Raven, Star System Back Door One
22 March 685 IP

T HE STAR SYSTEM DIDN'T EVEN have a formal name, only a New Meyer catalog code and a classified codename, Back Door One. Officially, Imperium databases showed it as NBNM-64 but the New Meyer Navy referred to it as BD-1. The New Meyerian corvette *Ravenhawk* swung on patrol in an almost lazy, slow orbit around the system's star, a million and a half kilometers from Jump Point One, the jump point leading to the NBNM chute. Under the command of Lieutenant Commander Carmen Escobar, the corvette trailed her TA-22A Towed Array to detect in-coming jumps and to identify arriving ships. Three stealthed sensor buoys monitored Jump Point Two while searching for the betraying signs of a ship jumping into this godforsaken system. Due to lightspeed limitation, data from those sensors took more than a light hour to arrive.

The system's primary, an unnamed Class M red dwarf, glowed a dull red against the blackness in an open e-window. Carmen closed the window after a moment's reflection.

Middle of nowhere. Its only two planets, both Jupiter-sized Jovian planets, orbited relatively close in and would have made interesting viewing. Neither of the two Jovians were anything special, just cold, dull red-banded gaseous spheres with a couple of small pockmarked rocky moons. With no inhabitable worlds, the Imperium Survey Service never explored the BD-1 system beyond a cursory probe. Jump point two, however, connected to an external chute, leading to a back door into the New Meyer chute. *Thus its name.* Carmen could think of quicker ways of getting from here to there within the Imperium. Jump point two connected to a backwater chute. On the other hand, two weeks travel by a military ship between jump points barely left time for defensive forces to organize themselves. *Worse yet, jump point one connected directly into the New Meyer or New Brazil star systems.*

The system's two small gas giants also provided means for refueling of the valuable hydrogen and helium 3 needed by an invading task force. Strategically, this system proved a huge risk, and the New Brazil incursion showed it required monitoring. Naval Intelligence considered this system as a probable entry point by the Goth raiders that had attacked New Brazil.

We're assigned here as a sentinel to provide early warning. A tedious, and yet critical role for a corvette. Carmen eyed the flow of sensor data through her implant with a mixture of boredom and a trace of distaste. *In the last month we've had eight tramp freighters pass through and that's it.* She grinned. *Customs checks are the highlight of the cruise. They give us something to do.* She reflexively brushed back a thin wisp of jet-black hair that had worked free of the tight bun keeping her hair out of her eyes while on duty. The long hours of watching an empty star system was not her idea of a fun assignment, but she took the long periods of monotony as a challenge. All through her life tight self-control had been the difference maker. Her iron self-discipline explained why she was a Lieutenant Commander in the New Meyer Navy and not a near-minimum wage service worker like many of her childhood peers.

She had been born in the slums of Brasilia on Earth. Her family had been randomly chosen to migrate to New Meyer in a planetary lottery sponsored by Duke Alexander. New Meyer was always looking for new immigrants to grow its population. The relocation had led to a dramatic change for the Escobar family beyond the implications of the move. Her father had also been selected for retraining as a technician in the colony's New Landsman City TSP plant. Suddenly her peasant family went from abject poverty to lower middle class.

She closed her eyes and remembered the difficult adjustment that had faced her family. Many of her fellow immigrant children had struggled with culture shock. This despite New Meyer's Brazilian sub-culture connection to New Brazil. Her passion for soccer and an iron discipline gave her a way out. She exhibited a talent for the game, enough to help her high school win a couple of provincial and planetary titles.

That trip to the first Junior Planetary Tournament made the difference and changed my life. It gave me focus. She let the images of that day rise and push out the e-windows. Her excitement as she settled into the suborbital shuttle's padded couch seemed as real now as it did then. The one and a half gravity acceleration barely phased her as the shuttle raced upward. She looked out the window and took a breath in awe. New Meyer lay beneath her , a quarter arc of fluffy white clouds under the blue haze of the atmosphere. Behind it the black of space glittered with a glimpse of the non-blinking stars. *That's my world down there. And the stars...* She took another deep breath in a mixture of wonder and excitement.

She hadn't dared to look out at space during her

emigration from Earth. A five-year-old's fear of the eyes of God had deterred her. Besides, they had been transported in what could euphemistically called cattle cars with few viewports. *No chance to look out even if I could have overcome my fear.* Now it was different. *Up here is where I want to be. This is how I'll pay back my world for what it's given me.*

Carmen opened her eyes and the images faded. When the opportunity came in her junior year she applied to the fledgling New Meyer Military Academy. Her high school grades had been decent and her soccer talents helped her get into the Academy. *The Academy had its own challenges.* As a plebe she hade been singled out because of her immigrant status by arrogant New Meyer natives who looked down on an upstart immigrant. She grew angry thinking about those morons, as she called them. *Everyone else on New Meyer is a descendant of an immigrant. We're growing this world, making it vital and varied.*

She used her discipline to resist the intimidation and harassment. Suddenly, after scoring two goals in her first game as a freshman playing on the varsity all the extra harassment disappeared. The victories that followed cemented her status on campus. She was never harassed again. Her academics also excelled. She had graduated number two in the class behind Josh Ben-Levi. She grinned to herself. *Not a bad one to lose out to.*

So here she was, patrolling Back Door One, hoping that all of the intrusion simulations she'd been running were not needed, and yet secretly hoping for something to break the monotony. If an Imp taskforce or Goth raiding party were to come through Jump Point Two, the invaders would have only a few options. They could head directly across the system to Jump Point One and then onward into the NBNM chute or they could head for one of the Jovians for refueling. Both Jovians had hydrogen-rich atmospheres that any Jovian atmosphere J-diver could easily handle.

Most task forces, even the Goths', included a tanker with J-divers.

She ran sim after sim to determine the expected loitering time at the Jovians as the invading force refueled. For these runs, she assumed the tanker class which would then determine the number of J-divers available and how long they'd have to stay in orbit to accomplish the refueling. Still, the scenarios gave her some judgment on how long they'd linger in the system. The simulations gave her crew and her something to do to pass the time.

She absentmindedly scratched the tip of her nose as she narrowed her eyes in thought. She was lost in one of her simulations when the shrill clamor of the alarm disturbed her. *Another false alarm.* When she queried the AI and the sensor readouts materialized, her eyes opened wide and she sat up straight in her command chair. *Holy shit! It's real!*

The actual composition of the intruder took a few minutes to form. *This is an impressive task force.* She read off the list generated from the sensor input. Seven battleships. Three cruisers. Six smaller escorts, probably fleet destroyers. Five support ships, at least one tanker. All standard Imp classes. They squawked the Imperium's Top Level IFF code.

"What the devil?" she asked aloud.

"Ma'am?" one of the bridge crew asked, looking up at her.

"Sorry, Mr. Lehman, just thinking out loud," she replied.

So who in the hell are they and what do they want? Another task force from Duke Wolvein seeking retribution and revenge for the destruction of LeBlanc's task force? Or one of the competing Pretenders? A different rogue? Intelligence had scoured all of the recordings of the New Faroe confrontation. The data definitely showed no surviving Imperium ships. LeBlanc had not even left the customary ship at the jump point to observe and report back to Wolvein if anything went wrong. It may have been arrogance, but most of the experts had concluded that it pointed to him being a rogue. *He had no one he needed to report to.* That, in itself, was disturbing. *Imp regular Navy acting as pirates?* The few survivors recovered in escape pods had been low-level crew members. They believed LeBlanc was on a mission from the newly crowned Emperor Wolvein. None of them ranked high enough to have any firsthand knowledge of what was really going on.

She studied the squawks. *Does one of the Pretenders actually believe he is Emperor of the Imperium? Is that why his ships are flying the Imperium's flag?* She sighed and checked the IFF data. She verified the Imp Top Level Identification. *Strange. Not one normally associated with the Pretenders. The squawk is from a frontline Home Fleet unit. I thought they were all destroyed at Earth.* It became even stranger. *The squawk indicates the flag of Star Admiral Nicolai Kamarov. Kamarov is dead. He died in the effort to relieve Earth, after its fall. This makes no sense.* The data on her screens flashed as the task force began to accelerate on a trajectory toward the nearest Jovian. The Imps made no attempt to hide their transponder squawk, nor did they attempt to engage stealth. *They want to be identified.* She directed *Raven's* AI to load all the pertinent data into a message drone that was launched through the jump point to New Meyer. Without hesitation she ordered the corvette towards the Jovian while remaining in deep Manta. *Careful what you wish for. You may get it.*

CHAPTER 29

Corvette Raven, Star System Back Door One
27 March 685 IP

IN THE SIX DAYS SINCE the emergence of the Imp task force, little had changed. Carmen had received a quick response in the form of a message drone from New Meyer acknowledging the message and ordering her to follow standard procedure. She had continued moving toward the Imps under stealth. Now, six days later, the situation had not changed. The Imp task force was still proceeding at a leisurely pace toward the Jovian. *They'll achieve orbit in a day or so.* They still squawked Imp IFF and had not instituted stealth. *Raven* closed to almost five light minutes away from the Jovian, a bit further than the Imps. The Imp task force had not detected the corvette, or at least gave no indication they had.

She sighed and opened an e-window in her implant to a view of surrounding space. She often used that particular image when she needed to think. The stars stared back at her, cold and heartless. She fought the urge to stick her tongue out at them in defiance, chuckling to herself. Many people thought a view like this to be the face of God.

To her, the view reflected the realities of the universe, a cosmos unconcerned with what she did. *Not a heartless universe, just an indifferent one.* Besides, if God existed, he should be too busy to worry about the likes of her. Not that she wasn't religious. She practiced New Catholicism, the reformed version of the old religion founded by Pope Leo the XVII. Of course, his reforms had split the church as things like that often do. But with Humanity spread out among thousands of star systems there was enough room for every religion. The Imperium frowned on religious wars and clamped down at the first sign. She wondered how many people would turn to religion and God as their salvation in the coming chaos as the Imperium collapsed and space became far more dangerous. Maybe religion would play the same role it did in the Middle Ages by providing a structure and hope for a Messiah to save them all. She shook herself and switched off the view of deep space with one last mental sigh. *This is doing no good.*

She turned and looked around the corvette's crowded conn. To the uninitiated the sight might appear strange. Some crew used their station's physical computer displays to monitor their incoming data, while a couple did it through their net implants and seemed to stare blankly into space. Regulations didn't favor either approach but left it as a matter of personal preference. She encouraged the use of the physical systems to keep the crew better anchored in reality. This approach also led to more personal contact. *To each her own.*

Carmen sighed as she studied the situation for the umpteenth time in the last five days. *Why haven't they tried a system-wide broadcast announcing their arrival and their intentions? They're still squawking Kamarov's IFF pennant code. What the hell gives?*

Carmen sensed a slight stir, and Lehman reported from the detection console, "Captain, breakout from Jump

Point One. It's small. Clearly another message drone. Incoming message."

Raven had deployed sensor buoys to monitor Jump Point One, similar to the buoys at JP2 that had detected the arrival of the Imp task force. Small, only a few meters in diameter and virtually undetectable, they carried the same sort of array used by the corvettes though more compact. The buoys also acted as relays. The incoming drone "knew" the buoys' locations and directed its message to one of them.

In a few moments she keyed the half hour old incoming message into her implant and watched Admiral Murray's image appear in front of her. "Good job so far, Commander. I approve your actions and your plan. However, stay clear and avoid contact until reinforcements arrive. We'll arrive in eleven hours or so. Murray, out." A stream of data followed

Reinforcements? So they intend to intercept them here rather than wait and see their destination. No surprise. She downloaded the plan and studied it. Simple enough. The reinforcing task force was going to arrive at the jump point in eleven hours and accelerate inward using gravitics under stealth protection. *Deep stealth. They won't rendezvous here for seven days.* She was to wait until ordered to take *Raven* in closer, then drop stealth, and make contact. She would act as a go-between while the New Meyerian Task Force closed in.

She settled back in her command chair for more of a long and boring wait. *Another seven days. Raven* was decelerating to match orbits to get within a million klicks of the Imp task force when it achieved orbit. That was a good range with the new stealth to watch without risking detection. *If the Imps make contact at this distance it'll mean a six-second communication delay between us, three seconds each way. Right now we're facing a couple of days at least of hanging about here. The Imps have shown no inclination to make contact. Probably means they don't know we're here and won't, unless they can penetrate Manta. Drone emergence is difficult to detect from this far away. Their emergence signature is designed to be small.*

Most space travel consists of long, boring trips with not much to do. Patrols never seemed to end. Add the waiting for the unexpected and space travel could be downright unpleasant and unhealthy from a stress standpoint. Crews passed time by working out to keep physical tone. One-sixth gee was considered the minimum required to prevent long term muscular degeneration and bone loss. *Raven* kept her internal gravity at a quarter g when not accelerating. At that level, physical workouts were mandatory, even in the confined spaces of a corvette.

Carmen spent an hour or more daily working out to help pass the time and stay in shape. She also studied courses from New Meyer's Naval War College as part of her preparation for promotion to Commander and beyond. Her endless simulations brought their own brand of monotony as she ran them over and over, trying to glean some trace of new insight. She also added crew drills to ready them for the upcoming encounter. Even with all of this activity time passed slowly with a sense of dullness and tedium. The lure of a pending confrontation in a week or so with the Imp force just added a combination of anticipation and tension to the mix. Needless to say, the eleven hours until the arrival of the New Meyerian force seemed to pass at a pace that made Carmen check the flight data to make sure they weren't experiencing some sort of relativistic time dilation.

Finally she heard the report, "Breakout at Jump Point One."

Another twenty-five minutes passed before she received a message. The face of the Duke of New Meyer materialized. His dark gray eyes were hard and focused and his lips compressed in the tight line of seriousness.

"Commander, well done so far. I assume you're still deep in stealth since we can find no sign of you and the buoy indicates it's still in contact with your ship. Admiral Murray and I agree with your assessment. They're not acting in a manner that I would expect of the Pretenders. As you pointed out, their security's almost nonchalant. They seem to want to be detected." He paused. "Wait three days and let us close in a bit to shorten this damn delay. Then let's see what they're all about. *Cibola, Ikaga,* and *Leyte Gulf* will approach using Imp level stealth. If they detect us it'll be nothing unusual. The remainder of the task force, four frigates, will approach under maximum stealth. Of course, they probably have detected our jump in and may elect to try to communicate earlier. Duke of New Meyer out."

Three more days of waiting. Three more days of inching in. She didn't want to get too close and be detected. She didn't want the Imps to gain a hint about their improved stealth capabilities. She inputted her plan. *Raven* was going to close within about a hundred thousand kilometers of the Imp task forces with a resultant vector not directly in line with the Imp position. If they proved hostile she wanted to get the hell away.

She spent most of the next three days on the conn, taking quick naps when she couldn't stay awake any longer. She had run out of simulations to run. You can only run the same one so many times before it became really old. The crew was tiring of the drills for the same reason. Nothing to do but wait. She found herself constantly on the ship's net "looking" over the ECM technician's shoulder. She also found herself holding her breath every time an Imp radar beam came sliding by, but the new stealth system held. *God bless the NMIT.*

CHAPTER 30

THE DUKE LOOKED GRIM. "OKAY, Commander, start easing back your stealth and let them detect you. Maintain tight laser beam contact with us and relay both sides of your conversation with them."

She switched to the open channel to the crew. General Quarters, everyone else.

She waited until the GQ indicator flashed green. "Ok, listen up. We'll begin to ease up on the stealth. Let them detect us so we can challenge them and find out who they are. Stay alert. We may need to get out of here in a hurry. Godspeed. Mr. Lehman, reduce stealth, if you please."

When the stealth reached Imp levels Lehman sang out, "Skipper, picking up a radar pulse. There's a return!"

She heard the ping through her implant, an audio manifestation by the computer of a radar pulse. She had asked her instructors at the Academy where the sound of the ping had originated, and had been told that it had originated with the sonar scans used against submarines in the twentieth and twenty-first centuries. The Navy's respect for traditions didn't change it. More and more pings became audible. *okay, they're locked and are pinging us with their battle radar to warn us to drop stealth or risk being fired upon, though we're out of their range.* One of the Imp destroyers swung out of orbit, its fusion drive flaring a bright long plume, as the warship accelerated toward them at three gravities.

"Drop stealth," she ordered, feeling a mixture of excitement and relief. The long wait had ended.

A few moments later Lehman reported, "Laser com contact. They're challenging us."

Here goes nothing. "Put them on," she commanded.

The image of a stern-faced middle-aged woman of indeterminate ancestry materialized. "Identify yourself," she demanded without preamble, her voice hard and with a slight rasp. Carmen had no doubts this woman expected immediate compliance. She wore the standard uniform of the Imperium Navy. No shoulder patches were visible to allow Carmen to determine her fleet unit. The uniform, however, came straight out of Imperium manuals with none of the modifications often added by Chute Dukes.

Carmen took her time responding, taking care not to let herself appear intimidated. "Imperium Navy, New Meyer Corvette *Ravenhawk*, Ma'am. Lieutenant Commander Carmen Escobar in command," she replied. After a pause she added, "And you?"

The woman did not seem surprised or taken aback by Carmen's demand. "Captain Larissa deJenais, Imperium Navy. New Meyer, eh? You still consider yourself part of the Imperium?"

Carmen replied with a grim smile, "Until told otherwise, yes, though most of us aren't sure there still is an Imperium, Ma'am. Just a group of Pretender wannabes."

deJenais broke into a broad smile that lifted the hooded veil from her face. Her dark brown eyes twinkled. "Well put, Commander. Pretender wannabes, I love it. I'm sure Admiral Kamarov will appreciate that."

"Admiral Kamarov? The Admiral Nikolai Kamarov?" Carmen asked, her composure dropping. *He's supposed to be dead, killed trying to retake Earth! The implications if he's still alive are enormous.*

"The one and only, Commander," she said with the barest trace of a smile. "The rumors of his death have been greatly exaggerated."

Carmen gave a silent whistle. *Maybe she's right and the Imperium isn't dead yet.* "So, Captain, what brings your task force to our tiny part of the galaxy?" she asked. "We're a backwater area with little to offer."

"Au contraire, Ms. Escobar," said another voice, a male one with a distinct accent. "This is the supposedly deceased Admiral Kamarov."

Carmen's avatar stiffened in response to her own actions. "Yes, Admiral, I gather we've been mistaken about your condition. So what can we do for you?"

"I'm here to see your Duke," he said, "I need to speak directly to him and I suspect you're in contact with him even if we can't detect his ship. So, please notify him that I respectfully wish to speak with him on a matter of the utmost importance."

"Very well, Admiral." She spoke into her ship command channel. "Secure from GQ." She sighed. *This is going to be interesting.*

Cruiser Cibola, Star System Back Door One
1 April 685 IP

Michael's communicator chimed. All of the tension of the past days seemed to sit squarely between his shoulders. Even his chair's nanos were fighting a losing battle to relieve the tight muscles in his back. *Why did Kamarov travel all the way here to speak with me?* He found the question troubling. He had an inkling that filled him with dread. If it proved true his life was about to change dramatically. In fact, dramatically was much too mild a term. *No use guessing and getting riled up about something that might not happen. Yeah, and if pigs could fly...* With a determined effort he pushed all of the speculation and the associated tension from his mind to focus on the upcoming meeting.

The contact with Kamarov came in ship-to-ship and, therefore, piped through the two ships' AIs as a security precaution. Unlike implant-to-implant which utilized avatars to mimic the individual's expressions, this method provided face-to-face contact, allowing both participants to better read each other. Of course, the image might still be spoofed and an avatar used. Imperium com protocols supposedly prevented this from happening. Michael shrugged to himself. *I'll take what I can get at the moment. I don't think I can stand another day of speculation while the fleets rendezvoused to wait for a face-to-face.*

A hologram of an older man with long, silver hair down to his neck and a bushy, flowing gray mustache materialized in front of Michael. Large, piercing blue eyes stared back at him. Now he understood why the admiral took on the persona he did. Kamarov's bio pointed to flamboyance but that was a misinterpretation. *How many people underestimated Kamarov because of the façade of shallowness his smokescreen created?* The hair and mustache distracted anyone studying his face from seeing the depth and vibrancy in his eyes. *He does look like the old pictures of a nineteenth-century dashing cavalry officer.*

Kamarov smiled, as if reading Michael's mind. "Yes, Your Grace, I'm me. On my honor, this is me, not an avatar. Contrary to popular myths and reports, I wasn't present at Earth for the final battle. Our glorious Emperor," he couldn't hide the scorn in his voice, "sent me off on a show of force to the Heart Worlds trying to raise additional forces to take back the Kronin Duchy. He believed we needed their resources for our tax base as well as their shipyards. I protested the order as putting Earth at too much risk. He blew me off and reiterated the order. The order came from the Emperor. I was obligated to obey. He deprived Earth of my task force and left your father in charge with inadequate forces. Your father mounted a truly marvelous defense. You should be proud. He almost pulled it off.

"The rumors that I died trying to retake Earth are obviously not true either. The Goths bombed and then sacked Earth. They left long before I returned. We did engage a rearguard task force and both sides lost a significant number of ships. I lost too many ships to continue chasing the retreating Goths, and while my flagship suffered damage I wasn't hurt. I decided until we declared a new Emperor we would keep my survival classified. Why let the Goths know I survived? They must be feeling pretty good right now."

Michael closed his eyes. His implant, sensing his eyes closing, blanked out the image being fed into his optic nerve and for a moment he lost himself in blissful blackness. Even the last image of his father from the message disappeared, not from the implant's actions but from his own force of will. He lost himself in its comforting softness for a couple of seconds. He shook himself and opened his eyes. Both his father's and Kamarov's images reappeared, one from in an implant opened e-window and one from the window of his mind. He pushed his father's image back down. "So, Admiral, why are you here?" he asked. *As if I don't know.*

After the maddening six-second delay, Kamarov replied, his face remaining bland and impassive, "To bring the next Emperor of the Imperium to his throne."

Michael's heart skipped at those words. The dread returned. His worst fears materialized. *Next Emperor of the Imperium? There is no Imperium.* He said the same to Kamarov.

This time Kamarov smiled a grim smile. "Oh, but, Your Grace, the Imperium still exists. Maybe a bit smaller and in grave danger, but it still exists. All the Imperium needs is its Emperor."

Michael sagged back into his seat. "Who," he asked, dreading the answer about to come, "is this new Emperor you seek?"

The six-second delay only allowed Michael to fret about the expected response. The answer seemed obvious, though not one he sought or wanted. He couldn't come up with any other reason as to why Kamarov had traveled all this way.

"I think you already know the answer, Your Majesty. The Imperium needs a new Emperor, a legitimate one. Even if I were to declare myself Emperor as some suggested, I'd just be what you call another Pretender. You're the next in line who has the lineage to make the claim."

"But I'm merely a Duke of a small Duchy well removed from the line of succession," Michael argued, knowing full well that what he was saying was an officially sanctioned lie.

Kamarov's voice came back cold and hard and his response indicated he had little patience for legal fictions. "You're a Landsman, and we both recognize your father was twelfth on the succession list even though the databases don't show it that way. Your grandfather did a good job of hiding that fact, but he couldn't get to all of the protected military databases, even with the Emperor's sanction. We both understand that Spec Ops always has an independent streak. Don't worry. None of the so-called Pretenders can access that particular unaltered database. As far as they're concerned they've killed all the few surviving Landsman heirs. Eight Dukes and their families have been assassinated or died in battle in the past six months."

Michael felt drained and numb. *Kamarov is respected for his reputation as an adept political player as well as his military skills.* He had served as Star Admiral to three

Emperors and had almost singlehandedly held the Imperium together during that time despite the incompetence of his Emperors. Kamarov had the reputation of being fiercely loyal to the Imperium. The throne could have been his if he had wanted it. Kamarov was correct in his assessment of what would happen if he declared. Many would rally to his side because of his long service to three emperors, but legally he would have no more right than any of the other Pretenders.

Kamarov continued, "I am aware, at least in broad terms, of the plans for New Meyer. Your father apprised me of your family's plan. The most recent Emperors had never been briefed. I approve of the basic concept, but, Your Majesty," Kamarov said, using the royal honorific, "I don't believe the Imperium is done yet. I'm not so blind to the Imperium's current state and the potential for a near-term collapse. To believe otherwise would be narrow minded, and, believe me, I don't have those blinders on. I do think with a strong Emperor and a little luck we can stabilize the situation and prevent this sector of the galaxy from falling into complete disorder.

"New Meyer's plan can still serve as a Plan B and a fall back. As Emperor, you can focus attention away from New Meyer while providing it with a few more resources. The Heart Worlds are the prize attracting the Goths, and with a crowned Emperor, the Pretenders will face some hard decisions. They're relying on the support of Imperium naval units, but with a legitimate Emperor many of those will return to the fold. All of this will take the focus away from New Meyer."

Michael shook his head. "Admiral, I'm not sure I agree with everything you said. I think New Meyer will become a target when they find out that after me there is another Landsman adult male and an adult female, not to mention my Uncle."

Kamarov's face softened even more. "Your Grace," he

said, reverting back to the Ducal honorific, "your father and I had long discussions about his family. He was proud of you and your sister. He spoke highly of your cousin, too." He stopped and grinned impishly. "He didn't speak highly of your uncle, his brother." Then the grin disappeared and his face grew serious. "I think New Meyer will still be well served if you accept the throne and make Mitchell Duke. It's your right of heir selection without a son at majority. I will work hard to conceal New Meyer and protect it. I promise you I'll do everything in my power to protect New Meyer."

Michael sat quietly for a moment just letting the impact of this discussion to soak in. *How much can I trust this man? With the Emperor dead, Kamarov holds the reins of power in what's left of the Imperium now. Why is he in such a hurry to give them up?* He could only think of one answer. *Things haven't become so bad in the Imperium that there still aren't men of honor left.*

"Admiral, why come here and wait without contacting us? You've certainly been taking your time refueling."

Kamarov grinned revealing perfectly white teeth. "Your Majesty," again reverting to the Imperial honorific, "I was testing you. If you weren't guarding this system and didn't challenge me here then you aren't the man I want for Emperor. I've had my fill of fools."

"Did I pass?"

"Yes, Your Majesty. So tell me, I recognize the class of cruiser carrying your flag, but she seems to be missing a couple of turrets. And the stealth system of yours..." He trailed off with raised eyebrows.

It was Michael's turn to grin. "I could tell you, Admiral, but then I'd have to kill you."

Kamarov guffawed, a deep bass bellow. "Touché, Your Majesty. I think we're going to get along just fine."

It was Michael's turn to be serious. *I wish he'd stop*

calling me Your Majesty. I haven't accepted yet. But he knows I will. "I need to discuss this with my advisors."

Kamarov nodded. "I should hope so. If you were impetuous enough to accept on the spot then I would know that you were the wrong choice. I'll forward you an update on Imperium status and will await your response. Besides we need to get closer to get rid of this damnable delay. Just one more thing. I can't afford to be away too long so you don't have an unlimited time. I need to get back. Contact me when you're ready to discuss this further."

Who's in charge here? "Very well, Admiral. You have my leave." Michael countered.

Kamarov laughed again. "I know now I'm really going to like you."

CHAPTER 31

MICHAEL, SHIRO, AND EMIL SAT around the small table in *Cibola's* admiral's quarters, each with a mug of steaming coffee in front of him, and each lost in thought. Michael inhaled the aroma coming from the steaming mugs, taking solace in something familiar. He smiled to himself. He felt no guilt in bringing Wallace along. The Chamberlain had started in the Imperium Navy as a ship's cook and had worked his way up to Admiral's orderly before joining the Duke's staff. Wallace was possessive and would never allow someone else to take care of His Duke, even in the face of potential space combat. Michael grinned to himself. *He's so good at setting a mood with his choice of food or beverage, using all the tools at his disposal including smell and sight, going way beyond taste.* Wallace was certainly going to Longhorn with him if he decided to accept Kamarov's offer.

Here's the rub. For him the decision came down to duty and honor. He was a Landsman, a member of the family that ruled the Imperium for almost seven hundred years. He could no more say no to Kamarov's offer than surrender himself to the Goths. How to deal with Donna and Alex troubled him. He couldn't have any meaningful discussion with Donna before making this decision because of the distances involved, and, yet the outcome of his choice impacted them both in major ways. Not only did his decision put the three of them at risk as prime targets, but they would be separated from their family back on New Meyer. He was planning on taking them with him. The journey between New Meyer and Longhorn faced too many dangers to undertake without a significant military escort. On Longhorn they were all going to be isolated and cut off from friends and family. A visit home became highly unlikely because of the expense and risk involved.

Michael took a sip of the strong coffee, allowing the firm aroma and slightly nutty flavor to percolate through his senses. He permitted himself a smile. Earlier, when he had been alone for a moment, he had checked out Longhorn with a quick pulse of ShipNet. He hadn't investigated the planet's economy or naval contingent as one might have expected. Instead he checked out the coffee. Longhorn had a reputation for a good coffee product with many different flavors and blends. Another self-satisfied private grin. Coffee was one his guilty pleasures. At least his destination had decent coffee, even if the ShipNet reference was a few years old.

He shook himself and realized he was procrastinating. He turned his attention to his old friends and advisors. He studied their reactions. Shiro looked shocked yet thoughtful, his normally twinkling eyes shrouded in a mixture of emotions. Meanwhile, Emil looked amused, almost as if he had been half expecting something like this to happen.

No one said anything for a few seconds until Shiro pursed his lips in a soft whistle, followed by a slow exhalation. "Wow," he finally grumbled. After a moment he seemed to shake himself. "Your father and I talked with Emil of the possibility that during an Imperium collapse your father or you might end up as the highest ranking heir. We hoped the time would never come. The choices are just too difficult."

Emil still didn't say anything. He continued his silence, running his fingers through his graying mane. He sighed and said in an almost reluctant tone, "You must do this, Your Grace."

Michael grimaced. "I hoped you'd tell me something different even though I've come to the same conclusion."

"It's a death sentence you know," Shiro said. "A death sentence for you, the Duchess, and Alex."

"You don't trust Kamarov?" Michael asked.

"Kamarov I trust," Shiro replied. "I've known Niki for a long time. We go back to the Academy on Earth and we served as junior officers on ships together. He deeply believes, or at least he did believe, in honor and duty. He's had plenty of opportunities to become Emperor and hasn't taken them. The last exchange you had with him let us know that he understands that you won't be a puppet and you're still his choice. I just don't trust everyone else. Your Grace, you're going to have a bull's-eye painted on you by both the Goths and the Pretenders..."

"Shiro, Kamarov believes the Pretenders might lose if I, a Landsman, become Emperor. They have regular Imp units allied with them who might return to the fold once I'm declared."

"There's truth to that," Shiro agreed. "Some of the Pretenders are just ambitious men who want to be Emperor for the power and money and to fulfill their egos. They will resist and try to keep their power. A couple of the Pretenders want to fill the vacuum and try to bring some stability. Those will come into the fold quickly. Unfortunately, the Imperium will still be weaker. A couple of the Pretenders may seem to support you but they're really only biding their time. One misstep and they're back as saviors."

"So how do we work this?" Michael asked, realizing that he had already made the decision. He pulsed the AI, "Please have Master Guns report here."

"Who will you chose to replace you, Your Majesty?" Emil asked. "Your choice as both Duke and Emperor?"

Michael took a deep breath before answering. "Mitch. I don't know how my dear uncle will take the news."

Emil grinned. "I think if we get your sister more involved in politics we can force the Earl to reengage himself in the company."

A knock on the cabin door.

"Come," Michael said.

The door slid open and Master Gunnery Sergeant Ralph Goodson stepped through. He stopped in front of the table and bowed his head before stating in his firm New British accent, "Master Gunnery Sergeant Ralph Goodson reporting as ordered."

"Oh, knock it off, Guns. Grab a cup of coffee, and have a seat."

Goodson looked nervously at Murray who responded, "C'mon, Ralph, knock it off."

"Yes, sir."

If anyone saw Goodson for the first time out of uniform and were asked to guess his profession, a Marine would probably be their guess. To Michael, he looked as if he were born a Marine. Everything about him was square, his shoulders, his face, his jaw, and a flattened nose probably damaged in some brawl. His dark eyes held the intensity of a drill sergeant boring in on some hapless recruit. His black fatigues fit perfectly with all of the creases crisp and sharp. *He's more than just a spit and shine Marine. In his service prior to coming to New Meyer, he had accumulated more combat decorations than leaves on a tree.*

"AI, please request the Baron of Courtney's presence via avatar."

Michael needed to bring Mitch into the conversation. It would have to be done remotely because he didn't want *Courtney* to drop stealth to launch her captain's gig. *I should have brought him in earlier.*

A few moments later Mitch's avatar appeared, materializing near the hatch.

"Welcome aboard, Your Grace," Emil said with a smile.

Mitch started at the ducal address while Goodson looked purely nonplussed. "Emil, what gives with the Your Grace bit?" Mitch demanded.

"Isn't that the proper address for the new Duke of New Meyer?"

"What!!??" Mitch looked thoroughly confused. He looked at his cousin. "Ok, so what gives, Your Grace?"

"Actually the proper way to address me is Your Majesty," Michael replied with a smile.

"What the..?" Mitch asked.

"Okay, okay. This isn't fair. In a brief summary, the Imp Task Force is under the command of Admiral Nikolai Kamarov." Michael waited for the name to settle in. "He came here to bring me back as Emperor of the Imperium."

Mitch's mouth dropped open while Goodson immediately dropped to one knee and grumbled, "Forgive me, Your Majesty."

Michael motioned him to calm down. "Relax, Master Guns. I'm not Emperor yet. I apologize for the humor at your expense. On a serious note, Kamarov came looking for me. He believes the Imperium needs me as Emperor."

"Your Majesty, may I ask a question?" Goodson requested.

"I said knock off with the Your Majesty. Among us we'll keep the same informality we always have. Clear, Guns?"

"Yes, Your, I mean yes, sir."

"Better. Now what's your question?"

"Well, sir, how do we know that's truly the Admiral over there?"

Michael, Shiro, and Emil all stared at each other. "Wow, how could we be so stupid? Michael muttered. "AI, get me the Admiral on line immediately. Tell him I need him in a conference." He turned to Shiro while checking his implant. The two task forces were still two light-seconds apart. *Only four damnable seconds.* "You know him. Can you ask some private questions only the two of you would most likely know about?"

Shiro nodded, "No problem, Your Majesty."

"You, too?"

"Get used to it, Your Majesty." Emil advised.

Michael sighed.

Admiral Kamarov's avatar materialized near Mitch's. He looked around and his eyes lit up when he saw Murray. "Shiro! You old dog! So this is where you ended up! Excuse me, Your Majesty," he said to Michael, "if I say hello to a lifelong friend I haven't seen in ten years."

Shiro laughed, "Niki, you old codger. Do you remember that bar on Nigiri 3?"

"You mean the bar where you left with that red-haired barmaid and then I didn't see you for three days?"

"Yeah. I ended up marrying her," Shiro said with a grin, glancing over to Michael with a slight nod. "She's here with me on New Meyer."

"So how is Angie?" Kamarov asked.

"Still a fiery redhead."

"Good. Give her my love will ya?" He turned to Michael with a smile. "Well, did I pass?"

Michael burst out laughing. "I guess you did, Admiral."

"I tell you, Your Majesty, I'm going to like having you as Emperor. By your leave, Your Majesty?"

Michael nodded and the avatar winked out. He turned to Mitch. "Your thoughts, cousin?"

"I'm not ready. I mean, I just became Baron of Courtney."

"You'll do fine, Mitch. Shiro will help."

"Who are you taking with you?" Mitch asked.

"You mean besides my wife and son? Emil?"

Emil was a widower with no children, making things easy. He needed Emil.

The older man nodded. "Of course, I'll come, Your Majesty. My brother Edward will be a fine counselor for you, Mitch." He smiled. "I think he's a lot smarter than I am."

Michael turned to Murray. "Shiro, I think you need to stay. I'll have Niki Kamarov to run my military. Mitch will need you."

Murray nodded, looking a bit crestfallen, but he returned Michael's gaze steadily. "I understand, Your Majesty, and I agree, though I regret not going with you. I'd love to visit home again."

"Don't worry. I'm sure you'll have enough activity to keep you off the streets. Maybe we can arrange a visit home on Longhorn for you." Michael almost winced as he said that. Both men knew it was highly unlikely but served as a useful polite fiction.

Michael turned to Goodson next. "And, you, Ralph?"

"Your Majesty, are you planning to take the Duke's Battalion?"

"I don't think I can arrive with the whole battalion. Besides, what would that leave Mitch?"

"I agree, Your Majesty, but I think you can arrive with a reinforced squad, maybe even a platoon. They'll create a Guards Battalion for you where you set up your capital. So we can form the core, and I would suggest you ask Lieutenant Colonel Smythe to come along as your Guards Commander. He has the right kind of panache to pull it off. You'll need a personal bodyguard and I'd be honored to serve."

"Smythe?" Michael grumbled, picturing the flamboyant former New Britainer with the long flowing handlebar mustache and his flashy uniforms. Despite his obvious pomposity, he consistently showed brilliance in war games. *Smythe will be a good counter to Kamarov, our own flamboyant cavalry officer.* Michael grinned at the thought. "Good advice, Ralph. I'd be honored for you to lead my bodyguards, and I like the idea of Smythe as the head of my Guards. He's almost as flamboyant as Kamarov, a nice counterpoint. Shiro, start the process. Smythe is hereby promoted to Colonel."

Mitch spoke up, "Are you going to take *Cibola*?"

"Should I?"

"May I speak frankly, Your Majesty?" Mitch asked.

"Mitch, we've always been like brothers. Our relationship as Emperor to Duke will be no different." *We're not going to have much opportunity to converse once I leave. We both know that but I think we need the pretense of not losing contact.* He paused and looked at Emil and Goodson respectively. "If ever I don't ask for frank talk from my advisors and friends you have my permission to take me out and shoot me." He grinned. "No, this isn't a request, it's an order. So, Mitch, go ahead, shoot." He realized what he said and chuckled. "Er, I mean ask your question."

Mitch grimaced fighting not to smile at Michael's last comment. "I think you're handling this wrong. Every planetary leader we have met knew your father and where he came from. This may be his local area and things may be different out in the Imperium Heart, but somehow I doubt it. What I think you need to do, is to admit where you're from and arrive as your father's son, the son of the hero of Earth's defense, riding in on a white horse to save the Imperium." He paused for a moment.

Emil took the opportunity to speak up, "I agree with Mitch. This cover-up of Kamarov concerning where you're from will fail and do-nothing except undermine you."

"But New Meyer will be put at so much risk," Michael protested.

"So be it. As Emperor you can dispatch a task force to New Meyer and another one to New Brazil, and buy us some time." Emil gave a sly grin. "Those deployments have a way of becoming permanent with *Yakumo* modifying those battleships."

Michael sank back into his chair for a moment, thinking about the implications. "Ok, I think you're right."

Mitch continued, "Awhile back I was talking with Sanchez and his people as well as some of the folks from NMIT. They've come up with the concept for a new cruiser variant intended to support SOCOM. You know how we plan to modify all big gun cruisers by removing blast cannon turrets and replacing them with six Raptor hangers?" He waited for Michael's nod. "On this new version, two of those USVs will be attack shuttles. A *Raptor II* is roughly comparable in mass to one of our attack shuttles. With a modified hanger you could carry a platoon of Marines."

"I like the concept." Shiro said. "I'd feel a hell of a lot better about this if we had a ship with those capabilities. When we get the new capital ship dock built, the first ship will be a battleship modified in the same manner to serve as your Flag. It could probably carry your whole battalion and we can add a couple of TAVs."

TAVs or tactical aerospace vehicles were the equivalent of an in-atmosphere fighter aircraft that was also capable of planet-to-orbital travel. They provided ground support capability to escort shuttles down during a hostile landing. Their design limited their any use in deep space engagements because of a lack of armor, long-range attack capability, and acceleration.

"How do we protect all of our technology?" Michael asked. "Word of the USV, stealth, and missile technology will invariably slip out."

"If your immediate ships and escorts are from New Meyer as the Emperor's Squadron we can limit the rumors," Emil suggested. "The Emperor's Squadron will be an elite unit sworn to secrecy."

"In addition, I think we'll arm your ships with Stingers rather than Venoms," Shiro added. "Yes. They're a bit less efficient yet they'll still give you an advantage while keeping the Venom technology here. I think we can also downgrade the Manta on your ships. It will still be many times better than Imperium. The downgrades won't be obvious. This way, if the technology is captured or stolen, New Meyer will still have some sort of edge, as small as it might be."

"Won't those changes make the Raptors less effective?" Mitch asked.

Shiro nodded. "Slightly. I'm not too worried about the stealth. I still think they're hard enough to detect because of their small size. They should still be effective."

Michael nodded. "I like it, Mitch."

Emil said, "Best of a tough situation. If we can get Niki to buy in."

Michael grinned. "How can he not buy in? After all, I am the Emperor."

"Not yet you're not. Still takes ratification by the Senate," Mitch countered.

"Details, details. You remind me. Do I need to have a discussion with Niki about the Senate? How can it be reconstituted after Earth's destruction and considered legit? There is no way he's going to call a Council of Dukes with all of these Pretenders floating around. How am I to be ratified legitimately?"

He sipped from his mug, feeling the invigorating flavor of the coffee filling him with a sense of anticipation. *God, how I love challenges.*

Cruiser Cibola, Star System Leakpath One
3 April 685 IP

As the two fleets maneuvered to a rendezvous, Michael found himself engrossed in a myriad of details required for the transfer of power to Mitch. Even as Duke, he couldn't leave things to chance, reviewing plans after the first draft. At this level, he insisted he be treated as one of the team, not the leader.

His implant chronometer ticked 0200 ship time. He tried to stifle a yawn, but was unsuccessful. *I must keep going. I don't have time for sleep.* He yawned again. He sighed. *Maybe it's time.*

A discreet knock and Wallace stuck his head in. "A little warm milk, Your Grace, with a touch of medicinal brandy to help you sleep. It's 0200 hours and, if you'll beg my pardon, sir, but we need you coherent in the morning."

Landsman grinned. "Medicinal brandy, eh?" He then chuckled. *Medicinal brandy, my ass.* This was just Wallace's way to gently let him know that enough was enough. *He's probably right. I've hit the wall. Time to quit.* "Why thank you, Wallace. Your timing is perfect as usual."

A few minutes later he collapsed on his bunk and was instantly asleep, his last brief thought wondering whether Wallace had put something more than brandy in the milk.

When he awoke, the separation between the two task forces was a much more manageable light-second. Again a discreet knock and Wallace entered bearing a tray with a hearty breakfast of bacon and eggs with lots of coffee.

"Just fruit will do," Michael protested.

"You need your strength for today. I had to promise the Duchess that you'd eat right." He grinned, and whispered as if offering a conspiracy. "You don't want to mess with the Duchess, or is it Her Majesty now?"

"But I won't have time to work out today," he protested, patting his stomach.

Wallace gave him a paternal smile. "You'll be fine, sir. Trust me."

Michael sighed and gave in. Besides, the smell of the bacon and fresh coffee was making his mouth water. *No use fighting this. I'd never win. The things I do to keep the peace.*

After consuming the breakfast he had to admit to himself that he felt a bit more together this morning. He grinned. *Wallace knows best. I'm just the Emperor-to-be.* He squared his shoulders and contacted Kamarov implant to implant for a private conversation.

"Yes, Your Majesty?" Kamarov asked, sounding awfully chipper to Michael for this early in the morning.

"We have a few things to discuss before I embark on this little adventure of yours."

Kamarov laughed. "A little adventure? Interesting way of describing becoming Emperor."

Michael shrugged, his avatar duplicating the motion in the image projected in Kamarov's implant. "Let's be serious for a moment. How can I legitimately be declared Emperor? No Senate and no capital exist. I'm sure you don't want to open a quantum discontinuity like the Council of Dukes."

"Ahh, ye of little faith," Kamarov replied with his patented broad smile. "Our recently deceased Emperor may have been an idiot, but he wasn't a total one. At least, I could manipulate him enough to make him appear he had some semblance of intelligence. While he comprehended in a rough way the risks Earth faced, he never really believed what happened could ever really happen. Yet, with a push from me I guess he had enough inner sense to act. We created, in effect, a shadow government on Longhorn. We built an Emperor's palace there, ostensibly as a vacation retreat, but in reality a fallback should Earth fall. We added a duplicate Senate chamber, built for when the Emperor was residing in his vacation palace. No matter that you couldn't call it a vacation if you took the Senate with you. We had Senate Alternates selected in case the worst did happen. Fortunately the Heart Worlds are defended well enough. We didn't need to move any naval forces to defend Longhorn. That chute is now the most heavily defended chute in the Imperium. We enacted all this in a secret Senate session covered by an Emperor's Finding making it Top Secret. Any leakage of this to the media and the culprits would have been put in front of a firing squad. No trial required. Of course, the Pretenders who are Dukes know about it, but there is little they could do to stop it. That's one reason why these Pretenders as you called them hunted the Landsman heirs so diligently. They knew a legitimate alternate Senate existed to declare an Emperor."

Michael let out a small whistle. "Longhorn. Hmm. Why Longhorn?"

"It's in the Beta Canum Venaticorum chute that includes Shaiing. The chute's heavily defended and is one of the most industrialized chutes in the Imperium. The chute contains six Class One worlds besides Shai and Shinn, seven Class Twos, and six Class Threes. It produced eight per cent of the Imperium's industrial capacity prior to Earth's fall. In contrast, Earth's chute had only four. You can understand why the Goths haven't been able to raid the Longhorn chute."

Shaiing was the home of the Shai, the first race Humans had encountered in space, and one of the original members of the Coalition. They had been in space long before Humans. Their genetic make up made them non-aggressive, descended from herbivore primates never pushed to colonial expansion by population growth. They did not colonize despite having the whole chute at their disposal before Humans arrived. Their insular nature encouraged them to maintain the status quo. They did their best to avoid confrontation, making them superb diplomats and negotiators. Even after eight hundred years of contact with the more energetic Humans, the Shai had only a couple of colonies, mainly in uninhabited systems with large asteroid belts, to provide the home world with needed raw materials. They had one major colony world, Shinn, a Class-One world in the same chute but in a cul-de-sac system. They had turned the system into a virtual fortress, moving asteroids into position near the jump point exit and heavily arming them with robot-controlled weapons that would annihilate any hostile fleet emerging from the jump. This served as their hidey hole. If the Imperium collapsed they planned to pull back into Shinn and ride out any chaos. They maintained a large fleet of transports stored in space in their home system ready to begin evacuation to Shinn. The Imperium Navy maintained large fleets in the Shai system because of Shaiing's importance. Though a Class One world, Shaiing was not counted in the official tally of Imperium worlds. Technically, the Shai acknowledged the existence of the Imperium but they also existed as an independent Republic, with strong ties to the Landsman family going back to the earliest days of interstellar spaceflight.

"Longhorn itself is a Class One world. The system's second jump point leads to the Ohrian chute that is almost as industrialized. This is the true Heart Worlds area. There has not been a successful Goth incursion in over three hundred years, despite being one chute away from both the Earth and Meyer chutes."

"You don't think the Pretenders will challenge this Senate and demand a Council of Dukes?" Michael asked.

"They can do whatever they want," Kamarov growled. "The fact is we have the Emperor's genetic coding sealing the Finding as well as that of the President of the Senate. If they pushed the issue, the media would make them look like what they are, aspirants for personal power. As I said, a couple will come back to the fold immediately. They were in it to fill a void and had nothing to do with the heir hunt. Even that wasn't what people might think. We lost eight of the top ten heirs, and fifteen of the top twenty-two in the defense of Earth. Another stupidity of our past deceased Emperor. The rest, except for you, disappeared under suspicious circumstances."

"Makes you wonder if some of these Pretenders aren't in league with the Goth. You know the enemy of my enemy..." Michael said thoughtfully.

"Yes, Your Majesty, we talked about that too, There is no evidence," Kamarov replied. "I don't believe in coincidences," he snarled. "I expect you don't either. This just seems all too pat. Somebody is moving for a takeover, only we haven't figured out who it is."

"You mean where there's smoke there's fire?"

Kamarov shook his head. "No, I mean I don't believe in coincidence. Maybe one is just taking advantage of the situation created by the other. Light speed causes weeks or month lag times in info to communicate across the Imperium.. Too many things are occurring either simultaneously or so close together. Makes me doubt there wasn't at least foreknowledge." Then his face darkened as he continued, "Having knowledge and doing nothing to prevent a treasonable act is to me as treasonous as being a co-conspirator." His voice turned to a deep growl. "I am going to cut their balls off and feed them to them." Then a grin. "Then I'll really get mad."

Michael sighed. "Well, I guess our work is cut out for us."

Kamarov's grin turned feral, his teeth bared. "That we do, Your Majesty. That we do. By your leave, Your Majesty," With that he cut the transmission.

The future Emperor of the Imperium sat back in his chair and decided not to get on Kamarov about switching on and off so freely with his monarch. *It's a fine balance with him. Too little and he'll lack respect for me as being too soft, and too much and he'll consider me as a meddling micromanager seeking self-aggrandizement. I need to find that balance.*

Instead, he switched gears as he sent off the long delayed, dreaded message to Donna. *She'll kill me for making this decision myself and then she will be the dutiful wife and follow me to wherever this crazy show leads us.* He sighed and stretched, arching his back and using his right hand to massage his lower back as best he could. *I need to work out and get rid of some of this stress. A good gokaku-geiko with Goodson will go a long way work out all of the kinks and maybe reduce the stress a bit.* He used his implant to schedule a Kendo workout with Goodson in an hour. For his next task he needed to arrange a timetable for all the events leading up to their departure and for the departure itself. Kamarov had given him thirty-days. The Admiral threatened to leave with or without him. Michael didn't relish making the trip without Imperium protection. Even seven battleships didn't seem like enough although Niki had assured him it should be sufficient.

The ship's AI interrupted his thoughts. "Your Grace, Admiral Kamarov is back on the line."

"Patch him through."

Kamarov's avatar materialized a few feet away. "Your Majesty, I apologize for the abrupt way I left. I let my temper get the best of me."

Michael waved it away, and managed a wan smile. "I just finished a message to my wife."

"Oops, Your Majesty," Kamarov replied with a huge grin. "Infinitely more difficult than anything you'll do as Emperor."

Michael returned the grin. "There's a whole bunch of truth to that, Niki."

"Don't I know it?" Kamarov admitted.

"So, any comments on our change in plans?" Michael was referring to the plan he had worked out with his advisors. It was aggressive and bold, and, unfortunately risky. It would require Kamarov to leave two battleships at New Meyer and then reinforce them heavily with additional warships that would be turned over to Duke Mitchell.

Kamarov sighed. "It's bold. I'll grant you that." He sighed again. "Careful for what you wish for. You may get it."

"Does that refer to you or me?"

"Me," Kamarov replied with another grin, and then after a moment's contemplation, "and you."

Michael's grin grew bigger into a broad smile, "So, that means we have a deal?"

Kamarov sighed again, his eyes twinkling with what Michael read as a mixture of amusement and anticipation. "May God forgive me because I know not what I do." He paused. Michael wasn't sure whether the hesitation was real contemplation or just for show. Then, "Deal, Your Majesty."

"I guess I better get used to the sound of that."

CHAPTER 32

———◆———

J ESSICA LAY BACK IN THE cozy warmth of the covers and closed her eyes. *I must report this to the Goddess. She needs to know the Imperium has a new Emperor and a dangerous, competent one, at that.*

She used her training to calm her thoughts and concentrated on the image of the Goddess. She let herself float, picturing the Goddess's private domain. She felt herself drifting off, but gathered herself and re-focused.

After a few moments, she experienced a brief feathery touch, a trace of warmth and, an acknowledgement passing through her like a jolt of pure energy. She had no idea and couldn't care less about violating the physical laws of the universe as Humans perceived them. She had made contact. She couldn't call it a conversation but somehow she sensed the Goddess receiving the message. That realization led to arousal and a powerful orgasm coursing through her like a starship out of control. A few seconds later she slipped into sleep. She'd wake in the morning not really sure whether she had dreamt the whole thing. Jessica was content. She was doing her duty.

Argula City, New Barwick, Okra Star System
19 April 685 IP

The High Priestess sat up with a start. *A new Emperor! And a competent one. Don't these damn humans know when they're beat?* She sighed. *Of course not. This makes them such a good feedstock.*

She smiled again. *Rather be lucky than good.* Placing an Acolyte on a Class Three world such as New Meyer proved to be a real benefit. She could only subdivide and reproduce so many times. Using one of those offspring to spy on a Class Three world might seem like a waste to some, but her Sense of the Timeline had warned her about New Meyer. Her Sense once again had proven true. New Meyer was a Nexus that needed to be controlled. Jessica might only be an acolyte but she had already paid huge dividends. *This isn't good news.* She looked over at her sleeping husband. *Maybe he can take action and remedy the situation.* She nudged him awake.

"Waa?" the Granac asked sleepily.

"The Goddess just spoke to me," she said.

He shook his head and groaned. "Why does she always do it in the middle of the night?" he asked.

"The Goddess' methods and actions are not to be questioned," she replied sharply.

Her tone must have gotten his attention because he sat up straight and turned attentively towards her. "Yes, Mistress, of course," he replied. He bowed his head. "I meant nothing by it."

"The Imperium will have a new Emperor. A Landsman, no less."

His eyes widened. "A Landsman? But we got all of the heirs of any consequence! Anyone left is far down on the list. Our analysts believe the non-Landsman claimants can claim the throne without worrying about their lack of Landsman heritage."

"Well, apparently our information is wrong," she said, trying to keep her voice neutral. *This isn't his fault.*

"Who is he?"

"Duke Michael of New Meyer. Son of Alexander who died at Earth," she replied.

"Duke of New Meyer? A high enough Landsman heir? Nonsense. He's not even on the list," he replied, puzzled, checking his implant. ""The first Duke of New Meyer was from Argo, a world we control. I viewed the records myself when we first learned of Alexander running to the Emperor's aid."

"Well, those records must've been falsified," she replied. "It gets worse. Kamarov is still alive."

"What??!!"

She nodded. "He retrieved this Duke and is now taking him to the newly declared capital, Longhorn."

"Shit." He paused for a moment checking his implant. "I just checked the probable routes the Emperor must take to Longhorn. We can't get anything to intercept because it'll take too long to get communication to our forces."

"You doubt the Goddess?" she asked.

He looked shocked. "No, Mistress. Never."

"Are there Adepts or Acolytes with any of the forces in intercept range?" she asked, knowing the answer already.

"Yes."

"The Goddess will get word to them."

Yes, Mistress."

"Send me the expected routes and a list of all those forces with Adepts or Acolytes. The new Emperor will never reach Longhorn."

He smiled. "How can we lose, Mistress, with the Goddess on our side?"

She returned the smile. "Yes, how can we?" she replied. *If only I were truly a Goddess, then things would be so much simpler.*

CHAPTER 33

---◆---

Cruiser Cibola, Deep Space near Yakumo, New Meyer
19 April, 685 IP

MICHAEL STARTED AS DONNA PLAYFULLY poked him in the ribs. They lay in bed in the Admiral's cabin aboard *Cibola* after being reunited the night before upon his return to the New Meyer system. *Time to get up. I should have gotten up long ago, but hell, I'm the Emperor, right? Or at least the reigning Duke here. I can get up when I want.* He chuckled to himself. *Bullshit. I'm a prisoner to schedules like everyone else.*

Michael checked his implant to determine when *Cibola* was due to dock. *In about an hour.* The message from Takahashi indicated his new cruiser would be ready for inspection by the time he arrived. He thought of the conversation with Takahashi concerning his new ship.

"Your new cruiser is ready for your inspection. We suggest you allow her to spend a couple of more days in workup," Takahashi had informed him.

"No. Sir Badri," Michael replied. "We don't have the time. She made it through initial workup. You had to do-nothing to her engines or life support."

Takahashi appeared perturbed. "Your Grace, please. How can you call two days a workup? This is the first *Esteves*-class cruiser *Yakumo* modified. We didn't even modify her to the formally released plans. We used marked up conceptual plans."

"Sir Badri, sometimes you have to do things like that in war. I'm sure the Gods of Configuration Management won't strike you down. Besides, I have complete faith in your team. I just lack the time. I'm on a tight timetable."

Takahashi sighed. "Very well, Your Grace, as you wish. By your leave, sir?"

"See you in a few hours," Michael had responded and cut the connection.

Donna's voice returned him to the present. "So am I to forgive you or what?" she asked.

Oh, shit! I'm in trouble. Here it comes. "I thought you already did."

She smiled. "You'll be paying for this for a long time, you know."

Don't I know it? "Hey, you're now married to a future Emperor," he replied. *God, what a lame reply. That smile isn't one of sweetness. More like a cat playing with a mouse.*

"Is that supposed to be a good thing?" she asked.

"Well, it can be."

"Oh, really?" she countered. "I guess if you like being the target of assassins and the media, hundreds of light years from home."

"Sometimes I don't know when you're kidding or not."

She smiled again. "Good. But I know."

I wish I could interpret that smile. "We better start getting ready."

Cruiser Cibola, Deep Space near Yakumo, New Meyer
19 April, 685 IP

Cibola's shuttle glided from the *Yakumo* toward the nearby *Esteves*-class cruiser connected to the tender through a series of conduits, cables, and cherry picker type connections. Takahashi was still rushing to make a few last minute additions and fixes. The shuttle's small cabin was packed with Michael, Donna, Shiro, Mitch, and Emil. A nanny held their son, Alex, who was taking it all in with his wide gray eyes. Shiro and Mitch would be making the trip back to *Cibola* and New Meyer.

Shiro glanced at Michael, his eyes reflecting a bit of amusement mingled with seriousness. "OK, Your Majesty, what are you going to name her? We decided the reconfiguration to be significant enough to re-name her without angering the Gods of Ship Naming."

Michael couldn't hide his mischievous grin. "Any suggestions?"

"Your look seems to indicate, Your Gracious Majesty, you have something in mind. You might as well just tell us."

Michael's grin only grew broader as he chuckled at Shiro's combination of Your Grace and Your Majesty. "Well, you all appreciate that I'm a bit of a romantic."

"A bit of a romantic, Your Gracious Majesty? You?" Shiro retorted, returning the grin. "That's a bit of a gross understatement."

Michael's grin became the beaming smile of a proud father of a newborn as he revealed the name, *"Excalibur."*

Shiro grumbled, "King Arthur's sword."

Donna snorted. "Why don't you name her *Rocinante*?"

"Very funny," Michael replied.

"Rocinante?" Shiro asked.

"Don Quixote's horse," Michael snapped.

Shiro grinned. "So, Your Majesty," he said to her,

"Are you implying this whole journey is about tilting at windmills?"

"Let's not go there," Michael snapped again.

Donna leaned over and pecked her husband on the cheek. "I love pushing your buttons," she whispered in his ear.

Michael's response was muted as the shuttle floated upward relative to the tender, allowing a full view of the cruiser. She lay suspended in space, but somehow breathing power. He located the six hatches on her boxlike hull differentiating her from others of the *Esteves*-class. Four of the hatches had *Raptor II* USV's nestled in their berths. The other two, one on each side, housed the attack shuttles. There had been significant discussion about removing additional turrets and adding more USVs, but the interior layout of an *Esteves*-class cruiser wasn't conducive to so much internal change in such a short time.

The transport to carry dependents of the ships' crews and the Marines was moored next to the *Excalibur*. She also had the standard boxy structure of a large starship. Instead of Raptors, her eighteen hatches hid shuttles and automated container loaders. Hundreds of containers were stacked all around her exterior. *Spare missiles for the Raptors and our missile capable ships.*

The shuttle attached itself to the cruiser's airlock port. Michael waited for the shuttle's internal gravity field to align with the cruiser's. He stepped through the airlock to the sound of a Bosun's call. A recording of the Imperium anthem followed.

Newly appointed Captain Ronald Garrett greeted him, "Your Majesty, welcome aboard your flagship." He saluted. On board a warship Michael was treated as an Admiral, not the Emperor.

Michael counted the number of sideboys and realized it was the correct number for the Emperor, not a Duke. *I'll ignore the gaff though technically I'm not Emperor yet.*

"Ah, Captain, Your ship has a new name," Michael said, shaking Garrett's hand.

Garrett raised an eyebrow. "Yes, Your Majesty?"

"*Excalibur.*"

Garrett's dark brown eyes widened and then he erupted in a huge smile that seemed out of place on a face with otherwise stolid square features. "*Excalibur* makes us your sword." He bowed. "We are deeply honored."

"Oh, so now I'm King Arthur?" Michael mused.

Takahashi spoke up from behind him, his voice sounding like a refined New Britainer, "We'll arrange a quick christening ceremony. Have to do things right, you know."

"OK, make fun," Garrett groused. "These ceremonies go back fifteen hundred years."

Everyone else laughed and Michael clapped him on the back. "Ron, you're now Flag Captain to the Emperor. Don't worry. You'll have plenty of your precious ceremonies to participate in."

"Yes, Your Majesty," Garrett replied, still grousing slightly. "We'll take you to your staterooms."

Michael studied the Emperor's stateroom. Besides a master bedroom, Alex had a small room of his own, as did his nanny. The rooms, including a small kitchen, surrounded a large open area used for meals and entertaining. Wallace berthed with the crew but would still serve as Michael's orderly and cook. Michael smiled to himself. Wallace had been put out by being displaced by Alex's nanny.

"So what do you think?" Michael asked.

"Not bad. I suspect we'll be spending a lot of time here when you become Emperor?" Donna asked.

"I suppose so, at least until they build me a battleship where we can have a bit more room."

"I can't imagine how crowded it must be for your Marines and crew," Donna said.

Michael commanded the AI to bring up a crosssection

of the ship. It floated in the middle of the room. "Don't worry about the Marines, they're grunts and can well handle anything. We stripped out the magazines for the removed 'C,' 'D,' and 'E' turrets to use as shuttle hangers and a Marine area. The quarters are a bit cramped but usable. We also slightly reduced one of the propellant tanks to give them a workout/training room. They'll be fine. As for the crew, a couple of the junior officers will double up, but that's no big deal since I think they have it too easy anyway. The Imp Navy coddles its junior officers too much."

She rolled her eyes. "I hope you'll be a better Emperor than some I've studied. I've heard so much nonsense about what some of the past Emperors did."

He grinned lewdly at her. "I don't know. I like exercising Emperor's privilege. As I am about to do right now."

Her eyes widened as he stepped over to her. "Here, right now? Michael, they're waiting to begin the christening."

He laughed. "Let them wait. I'm Emperor and plan to test this new bed for suitability. Emperor's privilege."

He grabbed her and they both fell back on the bed, laughing uncontrollably. *It's sometimes good being Emperor.*

After a minute of kissing and passion she pushed him away, gasping for breath. "Your Majesty," she said, "You may be Emperor, but your duty to your subjects outweighs your whims." She stood and held out an arm to pull him up. "Wipe the lipstick off and then let's go." She added, "Your Majesty," with a sly smile.

He groaned and stood, adjusting his tunic and walking quickly into the bathroom to wipe off the lipstick imprints. He sighed. *I may be Emperor but that doesn't necessarily mean I'm in charge.*

CHAPTER 34

M ICHAEL SAT IN HIS COMMAND chair on the flag conn, musing about the past year. *A little more than a year ago I was looking forward to commanding a frigate. Then I became Duke for a year. And now Emperor. Talk about a whirlwind.*

The flag conn bustled with activity as the Emperor's Squadron aka Task Force One readied itself for departure. The Duke/Emperor had little to do, but his presence was still expected. Michael planned to follow his philosophy of leading from the front when practical. *At this point in the voyage I'm pretty much a bystander, a relatively useless appendage, but, so is the pilot on a shuttle during re-entry. The AI guides the shuttle down, but the presence of a live person reassures the passengers on board.* In case of an emergency, humans took comfort from the presence of a human pilot. Same for Michael in his current position. Garrett handled the details and would make the recommendation on when to depart. *I need to keep pace with the details so I can make an intelligent decision. I also need to be careful I don't get lost in the details.*

"Captain Garrett reports all ships ready for departure," *Excalibur's* com officer Lieutenant Judy Wong said through his implant. He pictured her in his mind, a short, stocky, dark-haired woman with an easy-going manner in private but all business when on the job. *Like most of my crew, she's the consummate professional.*

"Very well, thank you, Judy," he replied. *Here goes nothing.* He pulsed his acting squadron commander. "Captain Garrett," he said, "Initiate departure."

"Yes, Your Majesty," Garrett replied in a strong New Britain accent.

Rich Bassett had recommended Garrett to replace him when Rich had decided to stay at New Meyer because of his responsibilities as a leader of the New Britain community. Michael had agreed after reviewing Garrett's records. Ron Garrett had come to New Meyer as Bassett's exec on the *Sheffield*. Childless, he had lost his wife two-years ago to, of all things, an allergic reaction to a bee sting. She had been an avid mountain climber and had been suspended on the side of a cliff when a New Meyerian Tiger Bee had come out of nowhere and stung her. She had never shown any reaction to bee stings previously. By the time Garrett had made his way over to her she had died. *Getting away from New Meyer isn't a bad thing for him.*

Michael checked the display. Once he became Emperor the squadron would be designated Imperium Task Force One. Besides *Excalibur*, the squadron included frigates *Newberry* and *Rio Sinuoso*, corvettes *Vesta*, *Aguia,* and *Raven* and transports *Ward* and *Kinsey*. He had protested the presence of the two frigates. Mitch had been insistent. "They're a gift to the new Emperor from the people of New Meyer," he had argued. "We're getting two battleships, *Kremlin* and *Monticello*, from Niki. More than a wash,"

Shiro had declared. Michael decided not to argue. He wasn't going to win.

He sighed and sat back in his command chair. The ship stirred beneath him like a lithe cat awakening from an afternoon nap. He heard no real sounds, just imperceptible vibrations emanating through the deck and compartment. Soft murmurs filled the flag conn as reports coursed among the crew from the task force. Michael let the buzz fill him. He sensed no undue concern. He witnessed a crew doing its job competently and efficiently.

How am I going to handle Kamarov? He smiled to himself. *I'm sure he's thinking the same thing about me.* Over the years Michael had developed a strong working relationship with Shiro based on mutual respect. He had known Shiro for years. Besides being his tutor, he had been his father's fleet commander. *I've had years to work out a relationship with him. I don't have that kind of time with Kamarov, who is also a much stronger personality than Shiro.*

He had spoken at length about it with Shiro on the way back to New Meyer.

"Kamarov is going to be handful," he had said.

"No more than me," Shiro replied with a grin.

"Uh, uh, Shiro. He's used to manipulating Emperors to get his way."

"And I'm used to manipulating Dukes to get what I want," Shiro had said, his face completely blank before breaking into a wicked grin. "The difference between him and me is style. Me, I take on the persona of a kindly grandfather or professor. He's a lot more blunt. He's going to find it more difficult adjusting to you. He's used to working with sycophant Emperors, not one who understands what the hell he's doing and actually cares. He'll adjust and the two of you will achieve a balance. In the long run the Imperium will benefit from a strong relationship between you two."

"I think it's going to be a bit of a wrestling match," Michael had replied.

"Maybe so, but I believe you'll both be better off when you're done."

His implant quietly chirped a private notification. Mitch had also just departed the station heading back to New Meyer. He nodded his head and Mitch's image materialized. *I feel like I'm looking in a mirror.* The deep-set gray eyes regarded him frankly. He recognized the emotions in them as the same sentiments coursing through him. *It's more than looking in a mirror. I'm looking into my own soul.* Mitch had always been more than a cousin. *More like a brother and a best friend.* Someone he could always turn to for advice and support. The two of them worked out together regularly when they were on planet together and not away in space. They had sparred in a friendly competition in the New Meyerian version of Kendo and the New Israeli version of Krav Maga. They both bore their bruises well and the results had only brought them closer together. *Now this may well be our last real-time communication for years, if not forever.* The realization brought intense feelings of sadness and loss. *I'm losing something special I can't replace.* Part of him acknowledged the pending loneliness, a darkness touching his core being where there had been light and warmth. *Dammit. He's not dying, but it sure as hell feels an awful lot like it.*

"Cousin," he said, trying to control the emotions in his voice.

Mitch bowed his head. "Your Majesty." He seemed to be struggling for control also. He managed a weak grin.

"Goddammit, Mitch, knock off the Your Majesty bit," he grumbled, allowing a smile to release his feelings. Mitch's grin was infectious but Michael detected the pain behind the twinkle in his eyes. "Your Grace," he replied solemnly with a nod.

Mitch visibly winced. "Don't know if I'll get used to being called Your Grace," he admitted. "Too much, too fast. For both of us."

Michael nodded his agreement. "Yes, you're right," he

said, "and we're in for more of this, not less. Not going to get any better."

"At least I get to stay on my home world," Mitch said. "You're facing a complete upheaval with part of your life cut away."

"It's not like I'm dying," Michael said out loud.

"No it isn't, cousin," Mitch agreed. "This has happened throughout history when someone set out for a new world and left family behind. I hope we can keep the lines of communication open between Longhorn and New Meyer. At least we'll be able to exchange messages and stay in contact."

"I spoke to Niki about keeping the lines of communication open. He agreed to make it a priority." *For now. Who knows what the future will bring? The Imperium is stretched thin and can't afford the luxuries of catering to an Emperor's whim. We're probably never going to see each other again.* Mitch's eyes revealed he was thinking the same thing.

"Give my love to Claudia," Michael said simply. "You lucked out with her. She'll be a real asset."

Mitch nodded and sighed. "And give my love to Donna and Alex. Take care, cousin."

"You too, cousin," he said as the image faded away. "Take care of my world," he whispered out loud. "You, too, Carol." He and his sister had exchanged long-distance messages. She had stayed back on New Meyer to run the war effort and keep an eye on things. The com lag with New Meyer was just too long to hold any kind of conversation. *I'll miss you, too, Sis.*

He sighed and turned his attention to the flag conn.

Cruiser *Excalibur*, Star System New Meyer
23 April 685 IP

Michael stretched. They had departed *Yakumo* ten hours earlier to cross the five million kilometers to the jump point. Once they were well on the way he had begun exercises to meld the crew into a team. *They're young and not as experienced as I'd like. We don't have many experienced flag conn crew members in New Meyer naval units. We're all learning as we go along. Maybe we can get a couple of experienced personnel from Niki.* He listened to their conversations as they reacted to the current drill. *Not bad.* He grinned to himself. *As if I know. A year ago I was aspiring to command a frigate when my father returned.* The grin vanished as he thought of his father.

He sensed a stir through his implant as one of the Raptors roaming ahead detected an imminent breakout from the jump point. He watched the energy sensor readouts surge as the ship emerged from the jump point, followed by a second arrival.

"Two *Moscow-class* battleships," *Excalibur's* AI, nicknamed Harry, reported in his cultured New Britain voice.

Michael grinned. The ship's captain selected the personality for the ship's AI. Garrett had chosen the classic British "stiff upper lip" officer persona.

Michael checked the range. About a light-second or so. *Won't be too bad a delay.* "Patch me through to Captain Whitehall," Michael ordered. Whitehall commanded one of the battleships.

Whitehall's image appeared moments later. He was apparently anticipating the call. "Your Majesty," he said, head bowed.

Michael studied the image. *He's cut in the standard image of a typical New Britainer. Perhaps I'm stereotyping them. These New Britain officers seemed to be from the same template.* Squat build with a long face too big for its body. *Not quite the spitting image of Bassett but close enough. Sturdy and reliable. Almost a twin to Garrett.* Whitehall's personnel records backed up Michael's impression. His career, while not spectacular, had been solid. *I guess I can trust Mitch to his care.* He made his home on Longhorn having also escaped his homeworld's destruction. *Now he's migrating to New Meyer.*

"Captain Whitehall, welcome to New Meyer," Michael said formally.

"Thank you, Your Majesty."

"I think I'm still 'Your Grace', at least until the Senate says differently," Michael chided gently.

"Begging your pardon, Your Majesty," Whitehall replied without hesitation, "but with Admiral Kamarov's backing and you, the son of Duke Alexander, hero of the valiant defense of Earth and a Landsman to boot? I suspect your acclamation to Emperor will be one of the fastest in history. Besides, Your Majesty, the Admiral ordered us to address you this way."

"Of course," Michael muttered to himself, mentally shrugging. *Guess the old saying is true. You can't fight city hall. Anyway, it's not worth the effort.* "So I assume you received your orders? One of your battleships will proceed to *Yakumo* for modifications. Simple strap-ons of a new missile system. Are you aware of them?"

Michael opened a second window and an image of the two arriving battleships materialized. Both were massive boxy vehicles, each with thirty blast cannon mounted in triple 350 mm blast rifle turrets along the top and bottom of the hull (using the convention of up and down). The battleship's 19,000 tons dwarfed *Excalibur's* 9,000.

"Yes, Your Majesty. Admiral Kamarov showed us the records of *Harrier's* encounter with the Goths at New Brazil. Impressive. He also showed us records of Duke Mitchell's encounter with LeBlanc. Even more impressive."

Does Niki ever miss a trick? "Good. Your ship will receive a refit similar to what was done to *Excalibur*. We plan to keep some battleships intact because we need big guns in certain situations. Some of your big guns will be replaced by four Raptor hangers."

"Admiral Kamarov went over all of that with me,"

Whitehall replied, pausing for a moment. *"Excalibur, Your Majesty?"*

"This ship."

"You named her *Excalibur*, Your Majesty?" Whitehall was smiling broadly now.

Michael nodded. *Well, at least Niki didn't anticipate this one.*

"Smashing! Well done, I say," Whitehall said, slipping into his colloquial New Britain accent.

Michael had to struggle to keep from rolling his eyes. "I also assume the Admiral explained your two ships will become the core of the Duke's Battleship Squadron here at New Meyer? They'll be permanently assigned to New Meyer. Any officer or rating who doesn't want the assignment will be transferred back to the Capital prior to any refits. The two transports with me will return with your dependents."

"Your Majesty, I explained this to them already. They're a bit disappointed because they hoped to be part of His Majesty's Squadron. I'm proud that not one requested transfer. It's considered an honor, Your Majesty, to serve you by serving the Duke of New Meyer."

Michael didn't say anything, trying not to let his emotions show. He was suddenly acutely aware of the whirring of the air circulators and the other muted whisperings of the flag conn. "Oh, and, Captain, one more thing. I approved your promotion to Rear Admiral. You'll command the Duke's Battleship Squadron. Also, Niki and I agreed that additional capital ships will be joining you as soon as we can arrange it. You're aware that New Meyer will now have a bulls-eye painted on it. Admiral Murray will be counting on your support, Admiral."

His eyes lit up. "Thank you, Your Majesty. You can count on our support and best efforts."

"Just keep my cousin safe," Michael whispered as the image disappeared.

236

CHAPTER 35

Cruiser *Excalibur*, **Star System Back Door One**
28 April 685 IP

MICHAEL CONSIDERED THE CROWDED CONFERENCE room as the Imperium naval officers gathered around the conference table. An outer ring of chairs against the compartment's walls accommodated additional personnel. He could only make out scattered phrases from the buzz of conversations. He sensed most of the conversations were about him. *Not unexpected.* Part of him wished to be the proverbial fly on the wall to hear some of the exchanges. The other part acknowledged he was probably better off not hearing them. He had to work with these officers. They required time to adjust to a new Emperor and Commander in Chief.

Captain Garrett, who also acted as Michael's Chief of Staff, sat to his right. Kamarov and his Chief of Staff, Captain Adrian Hawthown, sat to his left. Garrett's position as Flag Captain was an honorary one while his designation as Chief of Staff was an actual staff position. Michael focused on Hawthown, pulling up his record through his implant. The Imperium Captain looked the part, distinguished, lean features with salt and pepper hair cut in the close-cropped style of the Navy. His brown eyes bore a spark of amusement as he caught Michael studying him. He just nodded and continued his conversation with the officer seated to his left, Captain Lucius Zhou of *New Shanghai,* a twenty-thousand ton all big-gun battleship. To his left sat Captain Aaron Chen of the battleship *New Canton,* sister ship to the *Shanghai.* Both captains regarded Michael with thoughtful expressions. *They're my most senior ship captains, and I must rely on them for support.* Their experience and seniority made them the natural informal leaders of the ship captains. He noticed the way the others deferred to them.

Michael continued his observations of those present, reciting their names to himself using his implant to register their faces so he would easily recognize them in the future. *One of the benefits of a neural implant, you never forget a face as long as you categorize it with a name.* Three other battleship captains, Abrahim Banks, Wilson Neumaier, and Karen Appia rounded out his senior commanders. After them came three cruiser captains James Longstreet, Arnold Esmaeel, and Lily van Dijk. The six destroyer captains Jerry Ming, Susan Jacobs, Caleb Bumgarner, Eric Hart, Jared Madera, and Jamie Hahn as well as the two Imp supply ship Captains, Dymytro Riabovil and Alyona Eremenko all sat in the outer ring. He had checked their personnel files supplied by Kamarov. All were extremely capable with a demonstrated high degree of loyalty to the Imperium. *I would expect nothing less from those handpicked by Niki.*

These, in addition to the New Meyerian captains, now formed the core of Task Force One, the Emperor's Task Force. He now placed his life and the life of his family in their hands. Niki acted as Task Force commander for the journey, but once they arrived at Longhorn a new permanent admiral would be assigned. Michael was considering suggesting Garrett but wondered whether he might need to get one from the Imperium navy ranks as a gesture of solidarity. He sighed. *God, I hate politics.*

"I'm glad to meet all of you in person. This'll be our last live get together until we arrive at the Capital. I'm designating this task force as Imperium Navy Task Force One, which, as you know, is the designation for the Emperor's Squadron. Some of you may think this is presumptuous of me because it's premature. I haven't been formally crowned by either the Senate or the Council of Dukes. Niki and I discussed this at length. I'm walking a fine line here of not wanting to appear as a Pretender but also needing to claim my right as a legitimate Landsman heir. We decided the latter trumps the former.

"I'm not going to the Capital to ask for the Crown. I'm going to Longhorn as the last known surviving heir to assume my rightful title as Emperor. I'm not giving anyone the opportunity to question this."

He paused and gazed around the table, meeting all of the seated officer's eyes. "Does anyone disagree? The Imperium can't afford a dispute right now. Admiral Kamarov expects the Senate to ratify me without much debate."

A chorus of "No, Your Majesty" filled the room. Michael wasn't the least surprised by their response. *Niki had briefed them.*

"By now you've met my Flag Captain, Captain Ronald Garrett. I know it's unusual for an Emperor's flagship to be a cruiser, but I'll explain my decision. *Excalibur* possesses some unique qualities and capabilities. Captain Banks, you thought this was going to be your position with my flag in the *South Dakota* since she is a survivor of Earth's Home Fleet. My decision is no reflection on you or your ship or your crew."

Banks didn't even blink his dark eyes though he did momentarily rub his long nose. Tall and relatively broad, he wore his dark hair in the standard military cut of the

Imperium Navy. "Your Majesty," Banks replied, "of course, we're disappointed. A ship named *South Dakota* has been the flag of Task Force One for three hundred years. We weren't at the Battle of Earth. We carried Admiral Kamarov's Flag in the relief. But you're the Emperor, and you will place your flag where you want. I also understand it's also a matter of trust. That's something, Your Majesty, we hope to earn. You have my full support. Welcome home, Your Majesty."

"Thank you, Captain. Your understanding is appreciated."

"Your Majesty, if I may?" Captain Zhou, an older man of Asian descent, asked. His hair had turned almost a white-gray tint lighter than his dark gray eyes. His face was slightly round but by no means fat.

He reminds me of a knife fighter. He's doesn't look like one you'd want to mess with. "Of course, Sir Luke," Michael replied. "Before you ask your question, I want to make one thing clear. In this forum you're free to ask just about any question you wish. Screw protocol and all that other crap." He glanced at Kamarov who sat quietly without comment. "I don't want you holding anything back for fear of offending me. We will face times when bluntness will be required to save our lives or the lives of those we're sworn to protect. In this conference room every plan is up for challenge. Every decision can initially be questioned here, but once I make a final decision then, of course, I expect it will be followed and obeyed. So what is your question, Sir Luke?"

Zhou glanced around and then shrugged. He was a small man and thin, yet his face radiated a force that had intimidated many an Imperium petty officer. "Your Majesty, every commander here reviewed the reports of Duke Mitchell's successes at New Brazil and at New Faroe. New Meyer has some technology we heard would be of use to us. Do you intend to share it?"

Michael took a deep breath. He had anticipated this question. As Emperor he was supposed to ensure the Imperium has the best technology to enable it to survive. As former Duke of New Meyer he believed the release of this technology could eventually spell doom for New Meyer. How could he tell them he expected to die as Emperor? How could he tell them he expected the final collapse of the Imperium to occur and his reason for accepting the Crown was to buy time for New Meyer? *I think Kamarov suspects this but has decided that I'm better than the alternatives even with my ulterior motives.*

He sighed as quietly as he could so as not to give a hint of his discomfort. "What I'm about to tell you is classified as an Imperial Finding. You're aware the penalty for divulging a Finding is death. Understood?"

Again a chorus of "Yes, Your Majesty."

"First of all, with one exception, the technology is not new." He paused, waiting for the surprise to settle down. "Of course, in a true sense, I'm spinning a phrase. We're dealing with old Imperium technologies long buried and forgotten, out of favor, or beyond current Imperium capabilities. We've revived and improved them."

Here comes the white lie. "My grandfather, the Duke of New Meyer, established New Meyer Institute of Technology to bring New Meyer's technology up to Imperium levels. He also intended New Meyer to act as a repository for technology. A couple of enterprising grad students started detailed searches of obscure New Meyer technology databases and uncovered the improved stealth and USV technology. We worked for twenty-five-years to recreate this technology. To accomplish this we had to raise our entire planetary tech base to almost Level One. New Meyer's tech base will now compare favorably with any of the Heart Worlds' in quality though obviously not in quantity."

He paused, making eye contact with most the men and women seated at the table. "Here are some details." The holo of a frigate came up. "This is our Type 1 Frigate, *Courtney*-class. *Newberry* is a Type 1 with four Raptor I's. Here is a Type II *River*-class frigate which is a bit longer and carries four Raptor IIs." He continued on, summarizing the two cruiser designs and giving a top-level description of stealth and the new towed arrays. He finished with a description of expected tactics. "Ok, so now be honest. How does all of this fit with current Imperium naval tactics and philosophy?"

They all glanced at one another. Finally Zhou spoke up, "It doesn't. Not even close." He sighed. "This will be difficult to sell."

"How difficult?" Michael asked.

Zhou appeared pained. "Very difficult. It goes too much against doctrine. They'll resist it to the core, even with Admiral Kamarov's endorsement. You're the Emperor and can order the doctrine changed. The bureaucracy and many of the Admirals will find excuses for not instituting it. We all know and understand the power of a bureaucracy to drag its feet." He grew animated. "Fighting with missiles? How ungentlemanly! No, Your Majesty, this will end up as a distraction. I'm reminded of the battleship versus aircraft carrier debate prior the Second World War back on Earth during the 20th century. I'm sure we all studied this in our respective academies. Even after Pearl Harbor many of the battleship Admirals and Captains simply refused to let go and acknowledge times had changed. People with a strong ideology or a deep investment in something are often more resistant to change even in the face of facts and data. I suspect this will be the case here."

Michael nodded his agreement. "Ok, so here's what we're going to do. We're going keep this classified under an Imperial Finding." He glanced at Kamarov and then back at the rest of them. "I'm a bit more pessimistic about how my ascension is going to play out than Admiral Kamarov. He believes when I'm crowned, many of the Pretenders'

Imperium forces will come over. I really hope he's right, but I'm not counting on this happening. I believe a couple of them will band together. Some may even team with some of the Goths. They're going to come after me and New Meyer in full force. If we survive this onslaught then the Imperium will stand a good chance of surviving. Because of this we must be cautious in using the new technologies. They will be introduced in stages to prevent their falling into our enemy hands. Therefore, the new technology upgrades will initially be limited to TSF One. Do any of you have a problem with this? I want straight answers here. In fact, I insist on it."

No one spoke up.

"We'll dispatch each of the non-modified TSF-1 ships individually back to New Meyer for upgrades. We'll use the cover of your being escorts. All of you won't go and all of you won't be converted because we need big gun ships, too. New Meyer can retrofit any of your ships in a matter of weeks. When TSF One is complete we'll determine what the next steps will be. By then we should have a better idea. Any comments, ladies and gentlemen?"

There weren't any. "Then you all agree and will abide by the Finding?"

A chorus of "Yes. Your Majesty," was his answer.

Hope I'm wrong and the Pretenders do come over, and the Imperium survives. He grinned to himself. *"Maybe I should enter the planetary lottery. The odds are about the same."*

PART II

EMPEROR

—◆—

"It becomes an Emperor to die standing."
Titus Flavius Vespasian – Roman Emperor, 69-79 AD

CHAPTER 36

T HE TASK FORCE EMERGED FROM the jump point into the New Portugal star system in good order. Michael listened to the flow of information from the flag conn through TacNet. *Where is the customs challenge? New Portugal is a Class Two world verging on Class One. There should be an active jump customs service.*

Kamarov ordered two frigates to scout ahead with their towed 22A arrays extended, not something normally done in friendly territory. The frigates each launched a Raptor to scout even further ahead. *Niki must be concerned too. Something is not right here.*

He opened a channel to the Admiral. "I hope you're seeing what I'm seeing, Niki. Or should I say what I'm not seeing."

The Admiral shrugged. He was ensconced in what had been meant to be Shiro's station. "No customs service. Earl of New Portugal is religious about collecting fees. They challenged us on our way here."

"This is reminiscent of Mitch's experience in New Brazil," Michael muttered.

Kamarov nodded and was about to say something when they were interrupted by *Excalibur*'s com officer. "In-coming com from New Portuguese corvette *Falcão Vermelho*."

"Put it on," Niki and Michael said simultaneously.

Niki's face was a combination of anger and shock. "I'm sorry, Your Majesty," he said in a tone indicating he obviously was more annoyed than sorry.

Michael decided not to take offense. "Get used to it, Niki," he said, referring to his being an active participant in command of the fleet.

"Careful what you wish for," Niki muttered.

Michael wasn't sure who Niki meant, so he decided not to comment.

The image of a naval officer materialized. "I'm Lieutenant Commander Jorge deGarcia of the New Portugal Customs Service. Who am I addressing?" he asked and then his eyes went wide. "Admiral Kamarov," he said, apparently recognizing the Star Admiral from his image. "I thought you were dead."

Michael grimaced. *Please don't. I'm sick of that comeback.*

"Well, you heard wrong. I'm Admiral Nikolai Kamarov and I'm escorting the new Emperor to the new capital of Longhorn."

Michael sighed in relief.

DeGarcia's eyes grew even wider. "Your Majesty."

Michael nodded in recognition. *Because of Kamarov's reputation, DeGarcia isn't questioning the existence of a new Emperor.* "What's the situation, Commander?"

DeGarcia's eyes narrowed. "An incursion of about one hundred and sixty-five Goth ships. Here's the strange thing. They split their force, with about sixty of them diverting to engage our system defenses. The rest are headed here on an obvious course to match orbits with the jump point. We believe they're coming out here to meet someone."

"Like us?" Niki asked. "Impossible. How could they have known about us and which path we'd follow? That requires FTL communication which is impossible."

Faster-than-light communications. For almost a thousand years people have tried to prove Einstein wrong about nothing travelling faster than the speed of light in our universe. As far as I know no one has. "We'll work on the how later," Michael replied. "Right now we need to know more about the situation here."

"There's a destroyer trailing the larger force heading here." DeGarcia reported. "The Goth force is about two million klicks away. Should be here in about three hours."

"How's the fight going in-system?" Michael asked.

"We're holding our own. Like I said they split their force. It's the Earl's belief the raid is secondary, maybe even a diversion. They're after something else. Your arrival here confirms that."

"How could they know?" Michael asked, repeating Kamarov's earlier question. "There is no way they could, not unless they had FTL communication, which is impossible." Then he sighed. "As I said, we can worry about the hows later. How many ships do you have here at the jump point?"

"Just our usual customs team. Battleships *New Lisbon* and *Garcia Menendez*, cruiser *New Braga* and eight corvettes. Because of the two jump points we keep our reaction force around New Portugal."

New Braga is similar to our Esteves class cruiser. Only marginal use in this upcoming fight. The two battleships could prove useful. "Can we avoid this battle?" Michael asked through his implant.

"No, Your Majesty. We came through the jump point on a high speed transit vector," came the quick reply from the fleet tactical officer. "We can't decelerate fast enough to jump back through the jump point. We can change course but they have the angle on us, even with our higher velocity."

Like a defensive back in football chasing down a runner. Michael pulsed his staff. "Do any of you disagree with this assessment?" A chorus of no's came in reply.

Kamarov's eyes widened. He spoke in a private channel, "I'm sorry, Your Majesty, they have us. We must fight, but our seven battleships against eighty cruisers is a mismatch we can't win, or even come close."

"Well, Niki, I guess you're going to get to see New Meyerian weaponry in action. Launch all Raptors," Michael ordered as calmly as he could.

Kamarov grinned wryly. "Not the way I would want it, but do you honestly think we have a chance?"

"Yes," Michael replied, with the germ of an idea forming. "I'm assuming they have no idea about our capabilities. I'm aware assumptions can get you in trouble, but I think this is a pretty solid one. Maybe not in the future, but now, yes. You're right. The odds are pretty steep, but not any worse than I would have faced as Duke of New Meyer resisting an incursion. Either the *Raptor* technology works or it doesn't. If it doesn't then we're screwed anyway."

"Why not use Manta and try to evade them?"

"Because I am Emperor and New Portugal is under attack. What do you think they're going to do if we evade them? How can I, as Emperor, leave an Imperium planet under siege like this?"

Kamarov stared at him. "You are your father's son."

Michael shrugged. "Is that an accusation or a compliment? As I said, you're going to see New Meyerian technology first-hand."

"I hope to hell you know what you're doing."

"Either it will work or it won't," Michael repeated. "AI, astrogation, plot a minimum time intercept course. Get us into missile range. Grav drive only. Max stealth," he said. A plan formed in his mind.

Kamarov's look was a combination of bemusement and concern. "Careful what you wish for," he muttered, shaking his head.

I'm starting to get tired of that phrase also. Michael grinned and pulled up the tactical plots, immersing himself in the Net. Within minutes more specific orders flew out to the Raptors. *Now how do I get us close enough to use our missiles?*

Then he saw it. He pulsed orders to the task force and settled back. *Nothing to do but wait.*

"Raptors in missile range," came the report over his implant, about an hour later. "Task force will be in missile range in fifteen minutes."

Michael acknowledged the report. *And in Goth kinetic round range ten minutes after that. Not much of a margin. By now they will have detected Kamarov's ships even with Imp stealth. However, if Manta is working they won't realize Excalibur and the frigates are here.* He listened on *Excalibur's* ShipNet to the sharp interchanges between the tactical controllers and the Raptors' AIs. The communication time delay had dropped to a fraction of a second.

He flinched as a series of loud pings came through his implant. *Settle down. You expected this.*

"They painted us with radar. ECW still holding," came another report. "They still think we're a larger force."

God bless NMIT's new electronic counterwarfare package. Michael grinned savagely. *They'd get suspicious of a Task Force with only five battleships moving to intercept a force their size.* "Weps, are the shipborne missiles ready?" he asked.

"Yes, sir. All of our Stingers are programmed with a seven-minute delay. Their Mantas all check ready. ECW is ready to cover the launch."

"Very well. Prepare to launch on my mark," he said. "Three, two, one, mark!"

Excalibur trembled as each of her sixteen rotary missile launchers spat six Stinger missiles in rapid succession. The missiles' gravitic drives oriented them toward their targets and then shut down. *Excalibur's* missiles were joined by forty eight missiles from the two frigates. The Raptors readied their missiles for launch. *Two hundred and twenty-four missiles. Pretty close to three missiles per Goth ship.*

"Manta holding," came the report over his implant. "No sign of their detecting the launch or the missiles."

"Missile range in two minutes."

Michael tensed slightly. Actually they were already in missile range. In space a missile didn't need to be powered to continue on a trajectory. Here the term missile range referred to full powered missile range. *I wish these were Venoms. Their shaped charge warheads are more effective. Unfortunately they're slow to make and too expensive to produce in the quantities we need because of the singularity generator required to form the Venom's shaped charge jet. EFP's are a poor man's shaped charge warhead. With Venoms I'd be sure of the kills. The EFPs have proven about seventy per cent as effective and we can make them almost three times as fast for half the cost. Still, I wish I had Venoms.* He sighed. *If pigs had wings...*

"Ignite fusion drive. Three gee deceleration."

He was safely cocooned in his command station, with the high-g protocol activated. His chair had reclined and morphed into a couch molding itself to his body. It reacted to pressure points to keep the high-g load evenly distributed and his body supported. His internal nanos had increased oxygen levels in his blood and speeded up his metabolism. His skeletal nanos stiffened his bone structure providing additional high-g support. Still, having the equivalent of three additional people sitting on your chest for fifteen minutes could be uncomfortable. He perceived the strain in the crew's voices, even though they were talking subvocally into their implants, which took little physical effort. The three-gravity deceleration was beginning to take its toll.

Ping! Ping! Ping! The pings were coming closer together. The Goths were getting ready to launch their kinetic weapons. *No echoes. Manta and ECW are working. They aren't getting real returns. They're seeing only what we want them to.* The Goth ships increased to four gravities in an attempt to overtake the Imperium task force. He wondered how long they could keep that up.

"ECW still holding. They don't have radar locks yet."

Suddenly the weight lifted from his chest. They had dropped acceleration to one gravity.

"Missiles are in range, Your Majesty."

Michael grimaced at the use of his honorific and then sighed. *Get used to it.* "Initiate missile drives on my mark." He took a breath. "Three, two, one, mark!"

Under the cloak of Manta the missiles activated their gravitic drives on overload and hurtled toward the Goth force at forty gravities, virtually invisible to all Gothic sensors. Slowly the missile image on the tactical tracker became fuzzy as they moved to a range where their Manta was also scrambling Imperium sensors. *Man, the Manta and ECW really work.*

"Missile launcher reload complete." *Excalibur* now had another ninety-six missiles ready for launch.

Michael nodded. He would hold them in abeyance until the results of the first salvo were determined. The Stingers were too valuable to waste on dead targets.

He held his breath as the missiles fusion drives flared like beacons on the tactical plot as they entered their final sprint. The ignition of their fusion drives, injected with anti-matter for additional power, produced visible signatures even Manta couldn't hide. Immediately the plot became muddled as the missiles' own ECW began to function. Hundreds of what appeared as drive flares appeared as the Stingers launched active decoys. *I wonder what it's like on board the Goth ships. Mitch told me he had these same thoughts at New Brazil.*

Then the universe seemed to explode as the missiles began to detonate. The tactical sensor image looked like something out of an old-fashioned fireworks display before it finally dissolved into total coruscating incoherence. *This isn't the fog of war. It's more like the flare of war.*

Slowly the sensors began to recover and the image solidified. Where there had been a hundred plus blips there were now many hundreds. *My God! Pieces of ships.* Most of the Goth ships that weren't broken into smaller pieces were tumbling out of control. Here and there a couple were still intact.

"Your Majesty, we have missile locks," Weps reported. He was obviously having difficulty maintaining his flat, professional reporting tone. Michael sensed the excitement underlying the statement.

"Take them out," Michael replied.

More missiles hurtled from *Excalibur* and in less than five minutes there were no more intact Goth ships.

"Poor bastards," Michael muttered. *I hate them for what they've been doing to the Imperium, and they killed my father. Still, they had no warning.*

Niki's comment summed it all up. "Holy shit!"

CHAPTER 37

THE HIGH PRIESTESS WATCHED HER husband and Chief Adept with a mixture of amusement and appreciation as he raged at his subordinates. The news of the Battle of New Portugal had arrived, setting off his tirade. She struggled to keep a calm expression and play the role of serene Goddess. However, she felt anything but placid now. She fully sympathized with her husband's rants. *This battle and its outcome should not have happened. I had no visions of it.*

She leaned back in her throne. *How could this have happened?* No sign of a decisive battle at this time had appeared in her visions of the timelines. *The battle itself is bad enough news but to learn Kamarov was still alive was even worse news.* She had sensed whisperings of a battle but not one so lopsided. *I never had a vision of killing the Emperor in this battle so why should I be so surprised? But I never sensed that Kamarov had survived the destruction of Earth.*

A new Emperor with Kamarov still alive is a major

setback. Over the past centuries, she had studied Human history to better understand her lifelong enemy. She grew to understand the role Kamarov was playing in the Imperium. Like many she had gravitated to the Roman Empire after seeing so many parallels. *Three strong men had kept the Western Roman Empire afloat in its last century of existence. Stilicho, Flavius Constantius, and Aetius. They did it as generals and strongmen behind the throne of weak Emperors. Kamarov is of the same ilk. He kept the Imperium together despite three incompetent Emperors. What little I've been able to glean about Duke Michael tells me he's not another of the incompetents.* The Granacian part of her shivered. *Kamarov with a competent Emperor could reverse years of progress in bringing down the Imperium.*

She shivered again. A mixture of dread and confusion coursed through her. *I never saw any of this in the timelines. Maybe a glimpse but of such low probability I discounted it.* Another thought brought fear. *Is someone else tampering with the timelines? Is that even possible? Or am I just getting old in this body and my visions are less clear?* She shook herself. *I need to address this all later. But now to the matter at hand. How did we lose that battle?*

She kept coming back to her original thoughts. *Were the reports wrong on the Imperium task force's size?* The Adept on New Cassus had been adamant. The report had come through without any doubt. He had personally interrogated the tramp captain who had brought him the news. The Granacian captain had watched the Human task force jump from the system, just as he had jumped in. He swore he wasn't lying. The Adept had used all of his Neary-enhanced abilities to discern the truth. The Granac was not lying or fabricating a story. He had observed exactly what he said.

Only five battleships. Another source confirmed the Imperium task force size. They had no reports of another force joining with the Humans. They would have needed a much large force to defeat eighty cruisers. *At least five or six times more than they had to have any chance. So what else could have happened?* She pulled up the personnel record of the Goth force commander. *Not necessarily brilliant but solid. Solid enough not to lose his task force to such an inferior force. Solid enough not to have his loyalty doubted.* He had beaten Imp forces a number of times before. Her husband was chasing the usual causes of the defeat, the obvious ones. *Larger task force. Completely incompetent command.* Neither incompetence nor treason sat well with the facts as she perceived them. One other possibility remained. One almost as unlikely as the other explanations they were pursuing. *New weapons technology? Such a technology would have to be truly revolutionary.* She was aware of no such advances in the many centuries she had fought the Imperium. She struggled with the concept. Imperium weapons technology was moribund. Even in the face of the Goth's string of victories over the last hundred years, the Imperium's solution had been to build more ships of the same type, not different. *The Imperium Navy prides itself on its traditions. I can't imagine the Imps ever accepting a new weapons technology without some sort of debate that would invariably end up public where I would eventually learn of it.*

Something new and revolutionary. She focused on that concept. *New weapons. Is this why such a small world as New Meyer had shown up so prominently in my visions of the timelines?* Too bad the Acolyte on New Meyer was on so low a level in thought capabilities. Her buddling would eventually grow enough to allow its host to become an Adept but not for another year or two. Jessica, wasn't that her name? Jessica couldn't get complex ideas across interstellar distance. Getting word of the new Emperor had been difficult enough to glean from the contact.

I must get a true Adept to New Meyer. Meantime, she had to deal with the new Emperor. *A high level Adept to*

Longhorn is now a priority. She had to avoid getting caught up like her husband in the frustration of the defeat. She had to keep the long view. *I've worked eighty years to get to this point. This is just another bump in the road.* She just hoped that was true and not a rationalization. *New weapons technology.*

CHAPTER 38

MICHAEL LOOKED DOWN AT HIS new home planet on a holo display in his cabin. Donna stood next to him with a squirming Alex in her arms. "Alex! Settle down or no treats," he snapped. *After four months aboard this ship I'm looking forward to a new home.*

The two Marines who had entered the new Emperor's compartment to escort them to the shuttle looked at each other and grinned. Master Gunnery Sergeant Goodson whispered to Donna, "I'll take him, Your Majesty. He likes my uniform."

Donna relented gratefully and handed the fidgeting child to the burly sergeant. The youngster settled quietly in the Marine's arms, fascinated by the brass buttons on Goodson's dress uniform.

Michael hid a smile. Seeing Alex as a favorite of these hardened warriors seemed incongruous. He shook his head in wonder remembering Goodson on his hands and knees playing with the youngster yesterday when an hour before he had been practicing ways to kill a man silently. *We just pigeonhole people too easily.*

Longhorn was located in the Beta Canum Venaticorum system, 27 light years from Earth. Also the third planet in its system, Longhorn was slightly further from its sun than Earth and massed about 89% of Earth with a corresponding lighter gravity. Chara, the star's official name, was more massive and about 15% brighter than Earth's Sol. Longhorn exhibited a generally warmer climate than Earth but still comfortable because of a less eccentric orbit. Though the planet and its asteroid belt were less metal rich than Earth, Longhorn still comfortably supported a population of ten billion in a Class One civilization

Task Force One, or TF-1 as it was now called, hung in geosynchronous orbit over Longhorn's main continent. While Longhorn couldn't be classed as a garden planet like New Meyer, it was only slightly less inhabitable than Earth. Early colonists had suffered grievously from allergens present in the planet's ecosphere. This inhibited early development, requiring all colonists and visitors to undergo anti-allergy treatments. The settlers spent almost fifty years in a mini-terraforming effort. Much of the planet's flora and fauna were now Earth-derived, addressing the allergy problem. A visitor from Earth would recognize many of the species and not suffer a serious allergic reaction.

A Marine non-com's image appeared in his implant. "Your Majesty, *Hengroen* is ready."

Michael had named the Emperor's gig *Hengroen* after King Arthur's horse to make it consistent with the cruiser's new name. *Are we taking this whole King Arthur thing too far?* "Thank you, Sergeant." he replied. He turned to Donna and asked, "Well, are you ready? Here goes nothing."

She tried to smile reassuringly. "I'm sure it'll all work out. So far, the response has been positive."

"I think they're in a state of shock. Niki has done a good

job of feeding the media. I'm being shown riding in on a white spaceship to rescue the Imperium. Once they've had time to think and digest then I'm not sure what's going to happen."

She giggled. "Isn't what they're saying the truth? They not only have an Emperor now of true Landsman blood, but one who is a fighter and a leader, one who led small helpless New Meyer against the onslaught and chaos." Her voice changed as she imitated a Media personality back on New Meyer. "And, no less, he's arriving on a ship named for King Arthur's sword. Who better than King Arthur to provide hope in this time of chaos?"

"Knock it off, hon. I don't need this from you, too." He wheeled and exited the cabin.

She rolled her eyes and followed him out, still giggling to herself. A mixture of emotions swept through her. She put on a brave face to support her husband and to play the role of the stoic wife of the future Emperor, but deep down she was terrified. She couldn't look at Alex without feeling guilty for putting their child at risk. Part of her realized if Kamarov hadn't found Michael and offered him the throne, they would have been at serious risk for a long time at New Meyer. The danger seemed so much more flagrant and more imminent now. *I'm so proud of Michael and love him even more for his sacrifice and his internal strength. Yet, I'm furious with him for making this critical decision without me. Yes, Michael had been working with a time limit while located in a different star system. None of this altered the fact that he made the decision without me. Now I have to live with the consequences.*

So now here she was, about to arrive at her new home as Empress-to-be of a dying empire. Her husband was going to swear to serve and protect this empire. Yet deep down he believed the Imperium hadn't a chance in hell of surviving. Like his father, he didn't shirk his perceived duty. *He's trying to stem the raging hordes with a fly swatter. Is that why I love him so much? The chivalrous knight on his charger? Or was he really like one of those Kamikazes she had just finished reading about in her military studies? No matter. I tied my fate to him and am destined to follow him where he chooses to go.*

They settled into the heavily padded couches on the shuttle and waited for the ride down to the planet's surface. The gig smelled of purified, recycled air, and was slightly on the chilly side. Alex was strapped into a child's seat next to his mother while Emil sat next to Michael. Kamarov, who had joined them in the shuttle, sat in the row behind the Emperor. Despite the remodeling, it still seemed small and cramped, with six rows of two by two acceleration couches.

"You ready for this?" Emil asked, referring to the oncoming media circus, not the reentry.

"As ready as I can be," Michael replied and then grinned. "But are they ready for me?"

"God help them all." Emil muttered. "They don't know what they're in for. I suspect Niki is regretting his selection already."

Michael laughed. "He got what he wished for. Now he's going to have to deal with me."

"Personally, I think, Your Majesty, I'm lucky," Kamarov yelled over from his seat.

"Geesh," Michael whispered, "Either he's got this shuttle bugged, or he has one great set of ears."

Kamarov merely grinned.

A slight lurch and the gig fell away from *Excalibur* in a long, lazy arc into the atmosphere. Retrorockets fired briefly and the shuttle plunged deeper into the atmosphere, its nose at a high angle of attack to present the protected underside to the increasing drag from the atmosphere. A two gravities deceleration pushed everyone else back in their seats with enough force to start Alex bawling.

"At least he'll pop his ears," Michael remarked to Emil.

Emil didn't answer but concentrated on breathing under the seemingly increased weight on his chest. He did manage a weak grin and a slight nod. Michael relaxed, using his Navy training to handle the increasing gees. He wondered if they should have tranqued Alex as the cruiser's flight surgeon had suggested. The gig's AI had been instructed to take the most gentle reentry path available, using the gravitic drive to follow the right glide path. *Reentry is never gentle.*

The media worried him. Word of their victory at New Portugal filled Longhorn's P-Net with all kinds of chatter. Kamarov, in an effort to keep the New Meyerian technology under a tight wrap of secrecy, had alluded to a load of standard anti-ship mines the task force had deployed. He also referred to Michael's tactical brilliance in luring the Goth ships into the field. *No talk of secret weapons for the moment. Wait until they see Excalibur and the frigates. We have another cover story that Excalibur carries eight Marine attack shuttles in support of the Emperor. How long the cover will last is anyone's guess.*

The gig shook and bucked slightly as its wings bit into the atmosphere. Alex immediately stopped crying and began giggling. Michael shook his head in wonder. *Alex must think it's some kind of game. Now, if I could only do something similar with the butterflies in my stomach.* The P-Net had already declared him Emperor even if the Senate hadn't gotten around to it. Their landing at a public field instead of the Navy base allowed better access to the arrival ceremonies. He expected a circus when they landed. *Well, Kamarov seems to be orchestrating this pretty well. He limited contact with me during the flight in, thereby building anticipation for this moment.*

As Duke of New Meyer, he had to deal with the media on a regular basis. Being a Duke was not the same thing as being an Emperor. On New Meyer he had a relatively friendly P-Net. They respected the office of Duke and offered some leeway due to the dangers New Meyer faced. His father had worked hard to cultivate P-Net contacts and play down the popular cult following.

On Longhorn, he was likely facing potentially hostile P-Net bloggers who would love to do-nothing more than disprove the Emperor's credentials, or to find something unsavory about him. He and Donna were now the Royal Couple, destined to be followed everywhere. *Poor Alex. They'll eat him up.*

He faced a more important question. *How will the bureaucracy react to an Emperor who is used to getting things done? To complicate the situation, the current government has been acting without an Emperor. How will they respond? And how will the military?* He closed his eyes for a moment and tried to think of the Manor back on New Meyer as a way to disrupt this train of thought. He had gone over these questions a hundred times with Emil and by himself. He found no simple or optimum answers. Life was sure to be interesting in the near future, more likely for the rest of his life, as short as it might be.

He had tried to pick Kamarov's brain but the Admiral had remained strangely evasive. *Kamarov doesn't know either.* The last two Emperors Kamarov had served had been basically do-nothing sycophants who allowed both Kamarov and the bureaucracy pretty much full rein. Kamarov probably recognized Michael as being different. *Does Kamarov think of this as good or bad, or just a problem to be solved?*

The shuttle emerged from its reentry-induced plasma cocoon into a bright blue sky dotted with the spidery white filaments of cirrus clouds. Michael heard Alex cooing as Donna pointed out the clouds. He smiled and relaxed, enjoying the few moments of solace and quiet before the storm of media. He glanced out of the corner of his eye at Emil. The older man appeared relaxed and lost in his own thoughts. *We're not looking forward to the next few hours, are we, old friend?*

The gig settled down onto the concrete pad, its underjets supplementing the gravitic drive. Throngs of onlookers ringed the field. Michael looked out from his window and steeled himself for the onslaught. Civilian police, reinforced by a company of Marines in dress blacks, held the crowd back.

The door to the shuttle swung open and Goodson's Marine detail stepped out first. Goodson paused for a moment, taking in the crowd and then started down the steps. Once the eight Marines, the number required for a head of state, formed a sideboy-type honor guard at the foot of the stairs, Kamarov exited and began the climb down to the sounds of a band playing the Imperium Navy's anthem, *Jetting to the Dark Skies*. The Marines snapped to attention and presented arms, while a roar arose from the crowd. Kamarov paused midway on the stairs and raised an arm to wave. The crowd's roar grew louder. As quickly as the noise had risen, it fell to nearly complete silence as Michael stepped out with Donna and Alex. Almost as one, the entire crowd dropped to one knee. The band played the Imperium Anthem. Michael nodded and they all rose. Shouts of "Long live the Emperor!" started and expanded outward through the gathering until carried by thousands of voices.

Michael leaned back and whispered to Emil who followed them down, "Can it be this easy?" The crowd's din almost drowned out the whisper.

"They're looking for deliverance," Emil whispered back. "They know you won a decisive victory at New Portugal. You're a glimmer of hope."

"Glimmer is the right word," Michael muttered as he continued down the stairs.

A tall, older, distinguished-looking man with white hair stepped forward and bowed as Michael stepped off the stairs. The music stopped and so did the shouts. A silence settled over the field.

"Your Majesty, I'm the Duke of Longhorn, Richard Jimenez y Lewis. I welcome you to our world." He spoke softly since his words were being carried to the implants of everyone else present and most of the planetary population.

Now what does an Emperor say to that? The stock reply would be to say one is honored to be here. However, some might think that statement demeans the position of Emperor. Emperors aren't honored to be on a world, the world is honored to have the Emperor. Most of the other responses he considered sounded arrogant to him. He chose a neutral course. *Dammit, I should have listened to Niki and choreographed this more.*

"This is a beautiful world you have here, Your Grace," Michael improvised. "I can see why it's the next Imperium capital. Thank you for acting as custodian of the Empire during the recent troubles." *I think I got that right. I simply refuse to use the Imperial We.*

Lewis bowed his head in acknowledgement as a roar of approval arose again from the crowd. Lewis raised his hand to silence the crowd. "Your Majesty, I also have some information for you. I am pleased to officially inform you the Senate in secret session has already approved your ascension to the throne."

Can it be this simple? Or are they so desperate?

Michael looked out at the crowd, realizing he had to say something. He decided to use basically the same speech he had used when becoming Duke. That was one advantage of the relative isolation of New Meyer. *No one here has heard it.* He began, "There is no need to tell you all I'm grateful for your support. We face many grave challenges..."

The response was the same as on New Meyer. The crowd cheered, and the shouts of "Long Live the Emperor!" rose to a crescendo. *Maybe not as memorable as "I shall return" or "a day that will live in infamy" but it served its purpose.*

He waved away the press and promised a news conference after he was settled.

Michael hid his distaste as he climbed into the gravitic sled to take him to the palace. The profligate use of such sleds for transportation confirmed his impression of Longhorn as a Heart World that was impossibly wealthy when compared to New Meyer. Despite the planet's vast wealth, he had the sense that they lacked a sense of urgency and weren't devoting enough to the war effort. *My God! Don't they realize Earth was just destroyed and the Imperium is in danger of collapsing? The drives for those gravitic sleds could be used on Raptors. He sighed to himself. Maybe I'm being judgmental. After all, at this point they don't have Raptors.*

He looked around at the plush interior with its padded reclining individual leather seats and couches and the mahogany-like tables. *This is really comparable to a standard corporate executive craft though larger.* It was more elaborate than the Duke of New Meyer's jumpjet or copter but then this was the official sled for an Emperor. He sighed. *Get used to it.*

A short stocky man with jet-black hair and the standard Imperium bronze skin with bright blue eyes, greeted him as he stepped through the open door, "Your Majesty, I am the Palace Chamberlin, Jeremiah Crowe. I welcome you to our world."

Michael glanced back at Wallace. Crowe caught the look and understood. "I'm looking forward to working with Mr. Wallace, Your Majesty. I'll stay on to help if you'd like."

He and Wallace had talked about it and Wallace fully understood his role. Michael needed to evaluate Crowe before deciding whether to keep him or not. Wallace had told him the two men had been chatting for the two days TF-1 had been in orbit. *A good sign.*

"He seems like a good man, Your Majesty," Wallace had

told him. "He knows the territory and what it is to serve an Emperor. I'll have no problem working with him."

Michael saw it as a temporary fix but Crowe knew his way around the Imperial world. By making Wallace his personal chamberlain he kept Wallace close to him and more responsible for his family's personal comfort and safety. "Jeremiah, you'll stay on and help run the household as Majordomo. Wallace will be my personal chamberlain."

"As you wish, Your Majesty."

Michael nodded. "We'll get together and chat a bit once I'm settled in."

"Very good, Your Majesty. This way if you please," Crowe said, guiding the new Emperor to a larger overstuffed chair with nanos to contour the seat to him.

The sled lifted off and began its flight to the palace. Gleaming towers two or three hundred stories tall glistened in the bright sunlight like thousands of polished mirrors as the sled skirted the city. Capital City was a decent sized metropolis of about twenty million. *What a boring name!* He made out high-speed maglevs weaving their way through the heart of the city. New Meyer had similar trains but they were limited to cross country, inter-city runs, not as a primary people mover inside a city. He observed only a few highways, unlike New Meyer. The sky, on the other hand, was filled with hundreds of gravitic powered craft. *With civilian gravitics who needs highways?*

Michael spotted a couple of the buildings mounted on gravitics, hovering above the city like some overbearing pagan gods. He shook his head at the waste of energy, wondering if maybe the problem was with him. New Meyer didn't allow gravitics for civilian uses, citing the need to build the fleet. They were too expensive and too complicated to build for just a rich man's whim. But here on a Heart World, maybe because the industry was so advanced and efficient it wasn't an issue. Yet the Imperium was being squeezed by so many forces He just couldn't justify the laxity and lack of purpose he sensed.

Don't they understand the precariousness of their situation? Heart World or not, the Goths had shown resourcefulness and ruthlessness in penetrating the heart of the Imperium and sacking planet after planet. The Imperium is in shambles and slowly splitting apart and people here were carrying on as if nothing were amiss. When he had scanned P-Net while in orbit he had found the blogs spent more news time on the sexual activities and exploits of some of the planet's wealthier people than on the war news. He had asked Emil about that two days before and received a shrug.

"Maybe things are so dire they need the escape," Emil had mused.

"More like sticking their heads in the sand," Michael had muttered, resisting the impulse to say up their asses instead.

"Lighten up, Michael," Emil had whispered. "These are people who are trying to live out their lives with some sense of normality. If they need a bit of escapist fare to help them get through the day, then why not?"

"Because it takes away from the war effort," Michael had said through gritted teeth. "We're fighting for our survival here and we don't have time for this foolishness. Any day now a force of..."

"Goths will come roaring through the jump point," Emil had interrupted. "Do you honestly believe, Your Majesty," Emil had continued, "that if the people who you're bitching about paid full attention to the war and nothing else, it would make that much of a difference? Their factories and spacedocks are running full tilt as it is."

"Efficiency," Michael had replied. "I bet we could increase their ship production by twenty percent."

"Yes, we probably could," Emil had replied. "However, the survival we're fighting for isn't just being alive. The war is for our way of life. This is a long term war, not one over in a year or two. If we survive by giving up all we have, then have we really won anything?"

Michael sank back into the soft padding of the chair. *Emil didn't get it. The people of the Heart Worlds are soft. They aren't willing to make the same sacrifices as the hardier people of New Meyer were already doing. That's why the Imperium was not going to survive. They had lost their sense of sacrifice for the greater good.*

The prime example of this was coming up ahead. *The Emperor's Palace:* A fairy tale of tall silvery spires, lush green landscaped grounds of colorful flower gardens interlaced with small ponds and waterways. *The gardens are truly magnificent.* He grimaced. *Another extravagance.* The whole palace complex contained twenty buildings all covering more than four square kilometers, suspended by gravitics a thousand meters over the countryside. He wondered how many battleships could be powered by the gravitics used for the palace. *Well, I might soon find out if I have my way.* Seeing the palace was no surprise to him. It had been included in the briefing packet Kamarov had downloaded while they were still in Back Door One.

Kamarov had also downloaded a good portion of the Longhorn Net to *Excalibur's* AI. Michael had scanned the P-Net looking for a likely place for a new palace, one modeled more on New Meyer's much less extravagant Manor House. He had picked out a two thousand acre site in one of the national parks for the Emperor's new manor. This floating palace was going to be scrapped, if for no other reason than to make a point and set the tone. It was a hangover from the previous Emperor's extravagance, who had ordered it built-in case he had to flee Earth.

Things are going to change.

CHAPTER 39

Emperor's Palace, Longhorn System
30 August 685 IP

"**G**ODDAMMIT! AM OR AM I not Emperor?" Michael growled, trying desperately to keep his temper under control.

"Yes, of course, Your Majesty," soothed Chandraja Al-Haidar, current First Minister of the Imperium Senate. "Please, you must understand, the Palace is a symbol of the Emperor and the Imperium. Tearing it down will just remind people how bad things are."

"That's the whole goddamn point! Things are bad! The Imperium is in danger of collapse. Worlds are being lost. The Imperium is fracturing." Michael paused and took a deep breath to gain control of his anger. He clenched his fists for a moment. *They don't seem to appreciate how deep in shit they are. Their attitude is so frustrating.* He glanced over at Emil who shook his head slightly to tell him to back off a bit. Michael sighed and plunged on, determined to get through to this woman and through her to the rest of the Heart Worlds. *Al-Haidar means the lion in Arabic. She certainly isn't one.*

"Madame Minister," he retorted, letting a trace of anger show. "I'm going to be firm on this. I know many of you consider me a provincial from one of the Border Worlds. Therefore, I supposedly don't understand the more sophisticated ways of the Heart Worlds. I can't do anything about where I'm from or what you think of me. I'm Emperor. The decision is mine."

"Your Majesty, please. You've only been here a couple of months and you need to become acclimated. We have our ways of doing things."

Michael shook his head, before finally speaking through clenched teeth, "No. You must become acclimated to me. I'm the Emperor."

She started at his response. "Get acclimated to you, but..."

He interrupted. "What must I say to light your jets and for you and your supporters to understand what dire straits you're facing?"

"Your Majesty," she protested, "we do understand the mess we're in. Why do you think we voted you in so quickly? We'd be pretty dumb and blind not to see what's happening to the Imperium. We need symbols. The Imperium is favored with an Emperor again. One who won a great victory over our enemies. Your palace is a symbol of your office and a symbol of the Imperium's greatness, giving our people the hope we can carry on and win. If you come in and dismantle it, saying things are so bad that we need to retrench, they're going to say what's the use? If the Emperor can't have his official palace because things are so bad, then we've already lost. The people will only think it's a matter of time before the Imperium collapses."

Michael leaned back for a moment. "Madame Minister, I get everything you said and admit your point of view bears some merit, but I believe a leader must lead from the front. He must at least be willing to make the same sacrifices he is asking of his people. I am addressing the

Imperium in a couple of days. Sacrifice will be the theme of my speech. You can't fight a war without sacrifice. You can't fight half-heartedly and expect to win. So, I am signing the document. Tomorrow we'll begin taking bids on building the new manor. It will be complete in three months. When the manor is finished the palace will be dismantled and sold for use in the war effort. I've made my decision."

Al-Haidar sat back for a moment and studied her Emperor. She was a striking woman with jet-black hair and large dark eyes that could go from a twinkle to laser beam seriousness in a mere flicker. Her skin, darker than the Imperium norm, was smooth and silky, unblemished by her age. Her reputation indicated she had never used her beauty for gain.

She bowed her head. "Very well, Your Majesty. Maybe you understand something we don't. I hope to Allah you're correct. I will, of course, support your efforts."

"Thank you, Madame Minister. Can I offer you some more tea? I want to discuss some other items with you."

She nodded with a faraway expression in her eyes. He poured her tea from a simple china teapot, a New Meyerian family heirloom that dated back to when Meyer, New Meyer's parent world, was the Imperium capital. Michael refilled his own mug with coffee and continued to study his First Minister. She was native to Longhorn but not from one of the noble families. She had worked her way from a mere corporate auditor to First Minister of the Imperium Senate in thirty years, having served as an at-large member some six years earlier. Michael wondered how much her auditing background helped her get ahead by uncovering dirt on her superiors. She had cultivated an image of integrity and as a representative of the common person. She was the first commoner First Minister. The honor often went to some Earl or Duke, which spoke to her capabilities and reputation. Even the peerage respected her. He made a note with his implant to investigate at least knighting her.

"Madame Minister," he said gently.

She looked at him, startled, "Your Majesty, I apologize. I..."

He waved her apology off. "No need, Madame Minister. First of all may I call you Chandraja? You and I are going to be working together a lot and I think we need to drop the titles. You may call me Michael in private."

"I couldn't, Your Majesty. Such informality is," she fumbled for the word, "is inappropriate."

"I prefer informality with close and trusted advisors. I find titles get in the way. As I said, we're going to work together long hours to reach agreement on many issues. Some we'll agree on and on some we'll disagree. I find titles put a barrier between people and get in the way. Yes, I am Emperor and you're technically my subject. I hope you'll become a trusted advisor and I want your honest opinions. I don't want to be surrounded by cup holders who tell me what I want to hear or what they think I want."

"I'm honored, Your Majesty, but I'd still like to keep the protocols."

"I understand. okay, Madame Minister. Now let's get down..." He straightened up as a message from a drone came across his implant. A breakout of an unknown fleet in the Severus system. He saw her stiffen, too. She must have received the same message.

Their eyes met and she nodded and stood, "Your Majesty," she said, "I will leave you to let you deal with this emergency."

He shook his head. "Stay, you are now part of my Emergency Security Council."

"Emergency Security Council?" she asked, apparently puzzled.

"Yes. A new organization I was going to put in place for just this sort of thing."

The door opened and Colonel Sir Bernard Smythe strode in along with Emil. Michael waved them to the conference table. They seemed surprised at Al-Haidar but said nothing. Kamarov strode in next, noticed the First Minister, raised an eyebrow, gave a slight nod of approval, and sat.

Michael bristled slightly at Niki's approval. *I don't need his consent or endorsement. I'm the Emperor. He needs my approval.* He calmed himself, and spoke, "This is the beginning of an Emergency Security Council I will call in times of crisis. I'll let you know who else I want on the committee. With the First Minister present, I can get some legislative support up front. I'll probably add the Ministers of Defense and State. " *Though with Niki and Emil why do I need them? Because of protocols.*

"I like it," Emil said. "Certainly improves lines of communication."

Michael gave his old advisor a hard look. "Thanks for your approval, Emil," he said with a trace of sarcasm. "However, I can't claim it as a new idea, just one my predecessor never used."

Emil's eyes widened, "Your Majesty, I didn't mean to be presumptuous."

Michael took a deep breath and exhaled. "I'm sorry, old friend, and I didn't mean to be so sharp." He paused before continuing. "Anyone not view the message? Anything you can add, Niki?"

"The task force was squawking Imperium codes," Kamarov said. "Follow up message indicated a Task Force commanded by Duke Wolvein."

Thanks for repeating what we all knew. I asked for new info. Like how in the hell did Wolvein get within two jumps of Longhorn without us hearing about it? "Do you think he comes here to challenge?"

Kamarov shook his head. "Not militarily with only

seven battleships. I can't imagine him challenging you politically. You're a Landsman and he's not."

"So what the devil does he want?"

Kamarov shrugged. "Another message coming in for you now."

"Let's all look at it." Michael ordered the palace AI to distribute the message.

Wolvein's image appeared. His avatar sat behind a desk in his cabin aboard his flagship, so only the upper half of his body was visible. Small in stature, his squarish face exhibited the beginning of the wrinkles and smudges of aging. Nanojuvenation provided life extension but not immortality. Nature had never intended humans to live forever. While nanojuvenation extended and smoothed out the aging process, the human genome still limited lifespans to 120 years, even with biomechanical assistance. The brain offered the biggest obstacle and Imperium technology still had not completely broken down the function and rejuvenation of brain cells and neurons. If there were a God he or she had done a good job in building limitations into the human body that even nanotechnology and biogenetics could not overcome.

The message had been recorded six hours earlier for its long journey across three star systems. Wolvein bowed. "Your Majesty, I have just come from New Meyer." Michael tensed waiting for some kind of awful news, but Wolvein continued on, "I had a nice little chat with your cousin, the Duke. He sends his best wishes and wants you to know that all is well there. He informed me of your ascension to the throne. I've been out of touch for a couple of months and had not heard. I decided that my next step before returning home was to offer my allegiance to you and reaffirm my dedication to the Imperium. With your leave, Your Majesty, I request an audience with you to offer my fealty and strengthen the bonds with the Imperium. Duke Wolvein out."

"Can it really be this simple?" Michael asked out loud, not realizing he was vocalizing his thoughts.

Emil was the first to respond, "I'm not surprised, at least not completely." He stopped, not wanting to reveal what he knew in front of Kamarov.

Kamarov looked a bit surprised. "I'm not sure what to make of it. Overall, I think we must take it at face value. Still, we must keep our guard up."

Michael nodded, "I agree. Niki, who is the new head of Imperium Intelligence now? Her name escapes me."

"Countess Huffman, Your Majesty," Kamarov replied.

"I want her at these meetings."

Kamarov stiffened slightly but nodded his assent. Michael caught the slight reaction. *So you want to screen intelligence to me? Well, it ain't gonna happen.*

"Admiral, make arrangements to escort his flagship here when he arrives in the Longhorn System. The rest of his task force stays at the Chara system jump point. They're still at least two months away."

Kamarov nodded. "Yes, Your Majesty."

"Emil, please work to make arrangements to greet the Duke as an ally. Stay alert until I meet with him. I want us to err a bit on the cautious side. As I said, this seems too simple."

Emperor's Palace, Longhorn
30 August 685 IP

"Countess Huffman has arrived, Your Majesty."

"Show her in, and show in Admiral Kamarov, Ministers Aurelis and Al-Haidar, and Colonel Smythe when they get here."

"They're here, Your Majesty, but Minister Aurelis thought you might like a few moments alone with the Countess first," Wallace replied.

Michael sighed. "Ok, send her in and I'll let you know when to send in the others."

The door opened and the Countess Xandra Huffman entered. She was a tall, lithe woman. Her hair showed early signs of graying. She wore it cut short but still fashionable.. She appeared to be a mixture of contradictions. On one hand she seemed secure enough not to dye or nanoreconstruct her hair. But at the same time, her skin, however, was smooth with little sign of aging, the obvious result of nanocosmetics and anti-aging drugs. *She's packaged herself to play a role.* Her gray hair gave her a slightly matronly look to disarm and gain people's trust, yet she had reconstructed her face to make her a bit more alluring to men. *Attractive but not enough to be a threat. The image suits her in the role she plays and in her position as intelligence chief.*

Her dark eyes sparkled with a deep ingrained intelligence and awareness as she coolly studied Michael. Then she bowed and spoke in a strong, yet melodious voice, "Your Majesty."

"Take a seat, Countess. I don't stand on ceremony."

"So I was told," she grumbled.

"What else were you told?" Michael asked.

She smiled demurely. "You can't expect a woman to reveal all her secrets on the first date, can you, Your Majesty?"

"No, unless one is the Emperor," Michael replied.

She bowed her head. "So far my info on you has been correct. Straightforward. Unpretentious."

"Is that all?"

As she hesitated, Michael held up his hand. "This is totally unfair of me. If you're going to be the head of my Intelligence Service, then I need to trust you."

She pursed her lips. "So this was a test, Your Majesty?"

Michael laughed. "You've been talking to Niki, I see."

She returned his laugh with a tight smile. "Your Majesty, if that's what you think, then I agree."

"Ah, protecting your sources." He grew serious for a moment. "I'd better not find any of my offices or living quarters bugged. That's something I won't tolerate."

She studied him for a moment, her eyes shining. "Your Majesty, I guarantee if I wanted you bugged you'd never find it." Then a bit of a mocking look. "Bugging you would be illegal, wouldn't it?"

No wonder they call you the Countess She-Wolf. Michael leaned back in his chair and studied her. She did not wither under his gaze, but just looked at him calmly. "Countess, you obviously have an edge on me. You've been here a long time and I've just arrived. You've had years to build contacts and agents. I've had a couple of weeks." He paused and stared at her coldly. "But I have a different edge. I'm Emperor. So, once again, do you have my quarters and offices bugged? This is not one of those little tests Niki told you about. This is serious. You answer me truthfully and you'll become a trusted advisor. You lie to me and I promise you won't do it again. Dead Intelligence Chiefs don't lie."

Her gaze was unperturbed. "Your Majesty, on my honor, I have not bugged your quarters or offices. In fact, I can guarantee you that no one else has. That's part of my job and I take it seriously. I know some call me the Countess She-Wolf. Well, good. Better they fear me than ignore or defy me." She paused and bowed her head slightly. "Your Majesty, I'm on your side. Believe me when I say in all honesty if the Imperium is to survive we need you as Emperor. Of that I am sure, and this meeting just removed any doubts."

Michael nodded and then spoke into his implant, "Send the others in."

The four visitors entered, followed by Wallace with a steaming pot of coffee, a pot of tea, and a plate of small finger rolls. The aroma of the coffee filled the room like a welcoming friend. Michael motioned them to sit on the two couches facing each other perpendicular to his desk. Wallace laid the tray on the table between them and offered them all coffee or tea

Once they were all settled in, Michael began. "As I've explained, I've selected all of you along with the Empress to be my Emergency Security Council." He paused to let them absorb this statement. "I know that some of you have known me and of me for only a short time. We're in a tough situation here and some quick decisions on who will be my close advisors need to be made. I don't have the luxury to make these decisions over time. I suspect I'll add one or two others." He smiled grimly. "But for the moment you will do."

He waited for comments. There were none. He looked at his Intelligence Chief. "Countess, why don't you fill us in on what you've learned about the alliance between Dukes Javez and Ingrahan and the so-called King T'Kiel."

"Your Majesty, it's not an alliance yet. It's more of a trade agreement and mutual nonaggression pact." She paused, "The troubling thing is that Duke Javez's and Duke Ingrahan's actions give tacit recognition to T'Kiel. They recognize him as a legitimate ruler of what used to be Imperium territory. And yet, they claim it's not an alliance. In fact, I've got credible reports that the two Dukes and T'Kiel plan to visit here in the near future and pay their respects to Your Majesty."

"So what do I do about T'Kiel?" Michael growled. "If I receive him I've just legitimized his rule. If I don't, I'm obligated to take those worlds back with a commitment we can't afford at this time."

"I'm not sure you have a choice, Your Majesty," Kamarov declared. "As you so aptly pointed out we can't afford the commitment to take these worlds back. We just don't have the resources."

Emil was shaking his head, "You're in the same position that the Western Roman Empire Emperors back on Earth were in after the Germanic influx beginning in 379 AD. Their forces were stretched too thin to resist the Goths. Rome was sacked in 410 and the Western Empire never regained its impetus to take back the lands lost. A series of Germanic kingdoms rose inside the Empire that stabilized things for a couple of decades. While the Western Roman Empire eventually dissolved, the recognition of those Germanic kingdoms bought them some time. In fact, these Germanic tribes adopted Roman ways and became part of the Empire. They helped defeat the Hun Invader, Attila, in 450 AD. However, in the end, the Western Empire dissolved."

Michael grinned at him. "You're a big help, Emil. Have any really gloomy analysis?"

They all chuckled at that.

"Seriously, Michael. Let's look at what you directly control. Certainly the Heart World chutes and probably seven or eight other chutes, including the New Brazil- New Meyer Chute. That's about fifteen hundred worlds. On the positive side, you control the Heart Worlds which gives you immense manufacturing and technical resources. I suspect there are more chutes that would swear allegiance if we can regain contact with them. I'd guesstimate you can claim three thousand worlds, of which two hundred are Class One or Two. That is by far the largest percentage of the advanced industrial worlds. Three thousand worlds are still well short of the ten thousand that made up the Imperium at its peak, but it would be a large portion of Imperium wealth and resources."

"I can add to your woes, Your Majesty, if you'd like," the Countess said with a wry smile.

"Hey, I'm not a masochist," Michael protested. "What else do you have?"

"We're facing an issue of Goth kings wanting to join the Imperium."

"Why? I thought they hated us," Michael asked.

"Because we still represent legitimacy," Emil interjected. "Many Goths may hate the Imperium, but they're also jealous of us and our society's wealth and affluence. Same way as the barbarians hated Rome and yet still adopted Roman ways."

The Countess did not look pleased at Emil's interjection, but continued on as if nothing had happened. "Your Majesty, we have information that another Goth king is interested in joining the Imperium. His name is T'Zar. From what we can tell he controls about two hundred Imperium worlds, with six of them pretty heavily industrialized. But more importantly, he controls twelve major food production worlds that provide beef and grain and agricultural products to the Imperium."

One of the surprises of the interstellar economy as it grew and matured under the Coalition and later the Imperium was the importance of food and agricultural trade. Pre-spaceflight and early Coalition economists always assumed interstellar travel would be too expensive for trade involving agricultural exports. Then it was discovered that gravitic drive reduced travel costs enough to make the exports commercially viable. Not all worlds were anywhere as fertile as Earth. Even with terraforming and genetic engineering there always seemed to be a shortage of food, particularly meat. Millions of years of evolution had conditioned humans to be meat eaters and the need to raise cattle had never gone away. Livestock requires vast amounts of land and as worlds industrialized it always became a battle between agricultural resource requirements and living space.

"What do we know about T'Zar?"

"A Granac. A minor king in the Goth hierarchy. From what we can tell his rule has not been all that bad. He did confiscate some lands and corporations for his nobles, but overall he has done a reasonable job of emulating Imperium rule."

"So it begins," Emil muttered.

Michael looked at his old friend and advisor. "You really believe this Rome analogy thing? That we're trotting down the same path?"

"History repeats," Emil said, "and you are faced with the same lack of choices they were with the same inevitability. You don't really have a choice. Because of trade disruptions due to Goth conquests, the price of food on the Heart Worlds has skyrocketed, leading to other inflationary pressures."

"I can't agree more," Al-Haidar interjected. "It's the number one complaint that planetary legislatures are receiving. It's made its way up to the Imperium Senate. No one's starving yet but the Heart Worlds' economy is stalling a bit because of inflation."

Michael looked thoughtful. "So what you're saying is that we're caught in the same historical squeeze as the Western Roman Emperors." He paused and looked at the Countess. "And what does T'Zar want? What are his demands?"

She smiled grimly. "Recognition. He wants to keep his title as King. He also seeks recognition as an Imperium Duke."

Michael grimaced. "And what do we get out of it?"

The Countess shrugged. "He says complete fealty. He claims he has a large number of ships loaded with meat and agricultural products in orbit, ready to come to the Heart Worlds."

Michael grunted. "And we end up with an Imperium made up of petty kingdoms."

"That's about the short of it," Emil said.

"I'm sure there are more T'Zars out there," Michael mused. He looked over to Kamarov who had been listening to the conversation but had not contributed. "Niki, what are your thoughts from a military perspective?"

"Right now there are probably two thousand worlds

under Goth control, possibly as many as six thousand, though I doubt the number is so high. We've lost contact with that many worlds. Our best estimation is that a good number of those are smaller worlds who have lost their jump capabilities or at least are not regularly visited. Still, it's a frightening prospect that we have lost contact with that many."

Michael leaned back, looking at Emil. "It starts. My father estimated that more than half of the worlds if not three-quarters will lose spaceflight if they lose contact with the Imperium. There are not many New Meyers out there, Tier Three worlds with the industrial capability to build gravitic and jump drives. This is why he called it a dark age. And many of those that lose spaceflight will be hard pressed to keep even a modicum of technology."

He let out a sigh. "So what do we do? We can allow T'Zar in and try to hold on longer. Is the Imperium really salvageable? Or should we be looking to retreat and consolidate around the Heart Worlds and the territory we can defend?" He looked at each of his advisors, wishing Donna were here, but she was off on a publicity tour to the other Heart Worlds and currently too far away to participate. "So which is it?"

Al-Haidar was the first to respond. "Your Majesty, we certainly must try to recover some of the worlds. We owe it to them." All of the others nodded in agreement,

Michael reached a decision. "All right, bring in T'Zar and let's meet this fellow. Also, let's bring in our two errant Dukes and T'Kiel. The one thing I won't condone is some of our Dukes moving off and instituting agreements with other entities without Imperium approval."

Emil nodded. "As you wish, Your Majesty."

CHAPTER 40

BARON GREGORY LAZOUR OF ESPOIR Nouvel watched the approaching female customs agent with only mild interest. Her customs uniform did little to emphasize her body. *A bit on the pudgy side.* As she drew closer her bright blue eyes attracted him. He reached out and tasted her emotions, his Neary smoothly integrated with his own thoughts. *Not good.* Espoir had been out of contact with the Imperium capital for a couple of decades, and, therefore, represented a potential threat. Her emotions tasted of concern and a desire to be thorough with him. *I can't afford a real detailed investigation. I need to get by her examination without any fuss.*

"Your purpose visiting Longhorn?" she asked.

He smiled his most radiant smile while gently pushing on her emotions. Her eyes widened slightly as her attraction for him increased. He shouldn't take her here, even in the privacy of his cabin. *Requires too many explanations.* So he limited his influence on her, though he perceived her nipples already hardening. He continued tracing her pathways and found one glowing red in his mind. *She has a submissive streak and hides behind her uniform.*

"To reestablish contact with the Imperium," he replied, bowing. "Baron Lazour of Espoir Nouvel, or New Hope in English, at your service." He pushed on the red.

She blushed. "Reestablish contact with the Imperium," she repeated.

To take control of your Empress, but I can't tell you that. "My brother is Count Lazour, ruler of New Hope. He sent me to swear our world in fealty to the new Emperor." He smiled. "I'm amazed how fast the word of the new Emperor has spread. We're returning to the fold." He now slid down deeper into her mind and pushed again, this time to make her more trusting. *I'm not a threat. You know that to be true.*

"Well, your Espoir Nouvel is not on the proscribed list, so I welcome you to Longhorn. Is there anything I can do to make your stay here more pleasurable?" She licked her lips, her posture changing to a more provocative stance with one hand on her left hip.

Gregory smiled, trying to make it warm and not feral. *This is almost too easy. How can I resist such a tasty morsel? Maybe I'll take her. I don't think the High Priestess will mind this little diversion and I should be able to control her ship's response. Besides, I need a feeding, even a partial one. It's been too long.* As an Adept in the Neary religion with a fully Merged Neary, the Goddess gave him freedom to enjoy himself. Anyway, having a customs agent under his thumb could prove useful.

He tasted her mind again and pushed much harder. *Almost no resistance. A natural submissive.*

"I see you're nearing the end of your shift. Why not stay a while?" he whispered in his best Influence Voice. "You can send word I have some property you need to examine." He suppressed a grin at the double entendre.

She nodded, dropping to her knees and working the zipper on his trousers while activating her implant to inform her ship of her plans to stay. Her heightening emotions changed her taste to hot and spicy. *What have I liberated here?* This time his smile was feral. He pressed a bit harder on her mind and began to convert her to his devoted servant while feeding back her own excitement. *Yes, she'll supply a good feed.* He grinned. *A snack. I can't afford a dead body on the ship nor can I weaken her enough so she can't leave the cabin. She'll probably call in sick tomorrow, but she'll be able to make it back to her own ship.* He grinned. He passed all her defenses and searched her memories by tracing more of her emotional trails. *Ah! Very good.* He planted a desire for her to spend her two week leave next month with him on Longhorn. *Gives me an opportunity to work on strengthening her programming while feeding a little more.* His own arousal began to feed back to her. *She's not bad with her mouth. Uh, mmm, in fact pretty damn good.*

She disengaged her mouth and stood, slowly undressing. *She's not as pudgy as I first thought. In truth, she's cute, just big-boned.* She stood naked, allowing his inspection. He fed his approval back to her. *I must've picked up her self image earlier. I'll change that. If I do it right she'll become really useful.* His own arousal grew. *Yes, valuable in many ways.*

He led her into the cabin's small bedroom and pulled her down on the bed while quickly shedding his clothes. Her mouth found his and she groaned as his probed. He slid into her. She orgasmed. He ingested a little of her life force as the orgasm amplified her essence. He embedded the need to be devoted to him and then embedded the image of the Goddess as her Goddess. He'd work on the latter connection when she visited him next month. Now it was enough just to plant the idea. *My first Imperium Service convert in the Longhorn system. I hope to add many more, ending with the Empress herself.*

Enough of this. Now I can enjoy her. He sipped as she came again.

CHAPTER 41

THE DEEP RUMBLING OF THUNDER portended the arrival of a late summer storm on a slow, gray Saturday. The new Emperor had decreed this to be a quiet weekend, with no formal activities planned and many of the staff given the two days off. A few isolated rectangles of light where a few essential personnel toiled lit the otherwise darkened corridors.

Even the section of the palace housing the private quarters of the Emperor remained slow and hushed despite his presence. Emperor Michael VI sat in his private kitchen on a stool at one of the islands used for food prep. He sliced off chunks of a freshly picked, green skinned apple and absently popped them into his mouth. A glass of white wine sat on the counter next to him, along with a small block of cheese. Every couple of minutes he reached over and sliced some cheese, and finished with a sip of wine. A bowl of apples sat on his left. A pie baked in a timed oven, filling the kitchen with the smells most associated with a cold winter day at grandmother's house, not a balmy, wet,

August Saturday. He ignored the kitchen staff huddled over in one corner, apparently unsure of what to make of an Emperor who sat on a stool in the kitchen and carved chunks of an apple himself.

He enjoyed the quiet moment and tried to let his mind wander to things other than the affairs of state. The uniformed man pacing back and forth in front of the island interrupted his attempt at tranquility.

"Dammit, Niki, sit down and enjoy some of this cheese and wine. You're making me dizzy with your pacing," he grumbled with a smile belying the tone of his voice as he popped another piece of apple into his mouth.

Kamarov stopped and turned. "How can you be so calm?" he asked with exasperation in his voice. "You're the one preaching urgency and now you're sitting here calmly munching on some food."

Michael's smiled. *I enjoy pulling Niki's chain.* "Niki, the alliance is a rumor. Consider how wrong we were about Duke Wolvein."

"Were we? On the day Duke Wolvein arrived in this system to supposedly swear fealty to you, we learned two of the other Pretenders signed a mutual defense pact and allied themselves with a Goth King! I don't believe in coincidences and I don't believe they're only rumors."

"Come on, Niki! Wolvein was in space for months and went to New Meyer first. Even the rumors don't have the alliance forming so soon. Besides, the alliance is only a rumor."

"As I said, I don't believe in coincidences." Kamarov stopped in front of Michael. "You're the one who is telling everyone else to be on guard and to be more prepared. Yet here you serenely sit, eating cheese and wine and a damned apple, acting as if nothing were happening. I tell you I don't trust Wolvein, particularly in light of Javez' and Ingrahan's agreement with T'Kiel. Why can't you make the connection?"

Michael sighed. "Niki, now tell me what is really bothering you? It certainly isn't Wolvein. Does the rumor of an alliance between two second-rate Dukes and a second string Goth king bother you so much?"

Kamarov took a deep breath. He glanced over at the kitchen help. Michael turned and nodded to them, "Take a break."

"Yes, Your Majesty," the Chef mumbled and hurriedly led his embattled troupe as if retreating from an onrushing alien horde.

Michael stood and walked over to one of the cabinets where he pulled out an identical goblet to the one on the counter. He handed it to Niki and ordered, "Sit, and join me with a glass of wine."

"Yes, Your Majesty," Kamarov replied.

"Now what the hell is burning you?" Michael asked.

Kamarov sighed. Michael interjected, "Out with it."

"Your Majesty, this is delicate."

"So much for the forthrightness we talked about at Back Door One."

"The arrival of Duke Wolvein scared the hell out of me."

Michael raised his eyebrows. Kamarov continued on, "His task force was not a threat at all. He had seven battleships. Our jump point forces contain one hundred and fifty-four at each jump point and one hundred and fifty more as a quick reaction force. So he wasn't a threat. What if it hadn't been him? What if it were a true Goth incursion? We're still undermanned, you know. Even with your New Meyerian ships we'd have a tough time repulsing an incursion the size of the one that took Earth."

"Yeah, so what's new about that?"

"You, Your Majesty. You're here now as Emperor and that makes us a big target."

"Welcome to my world, Admiral," Michael replied with a grim look.

"My concerns go beyond that. Your New Meyer has

technology that may well allow the Imperium to survive and you're not willing to give it to us." He paused before asking, "Michael, yes or no, are you Emperor of the Imperium?"

"Yes, I am," Michael replied.

"Are you dedicated to the Imperium's survival?"

"I wouldn't be here if I weren't," Michael replied again.

"As dedicated as you are to New Meyer's survival?"

Michael took a sip of wine before answering, "Are you asking if I'm willing to risk the Imperium's survival by holding back on New Meyerian technology?"

Kamarov didn't answer. He too took another sip of wine while reaching over and slicing a piece of cheese.

Michael continued, "I'm going to answer you as I did before. I don't think the Imperium is ready for the technology. NMIT took us twenty-five-years to come up to speed on technology, and I guarantee you, New Meyer does not lag Longhorn at all in technology. We may be a Tier Three world in population and size of the economy but we're not in technology."

"Your Majesty, with all due respect, that's BS and you know it. If you believed what you just said about it taking twenty-five-years, then what are you afraid of? The Goths won't be able to duplicate Manta. You'll have a twenty-five-year head start on the rest of the Imperium. The real answer is you're here to buy New Meyer time, aren't you?"

"No, not in the sense I think you mean," Michael replied.

"Then in what sense?" Kamarov demanded.

Michael's gaze never wavered as he replied, "I don't disagree with my father and grandfather on all their plans. I believe the Imperium is doomed as an entity. When? That's what I don't know. I also believe you and I have a decent chance of changing the result, or at least delaying the Imperium's demise for a long time. I'm here to give the Imperium the shot it deserves." He paused, looking even harder at Kamarov before continuing. "The longer the Imperium survives the better chance New Meyer has of surviving. I see a corollary of sorts. The longer the Imperium survives the better the chance that whatever comes after the fall won't be some giant galactic medieval time where chaos reigns. The survival of New Meyer relates to that particular goal. They're not mutually exclusive."

"Then why won't you share these technologies with us?" Kamarov asked. "You're sharing them with New Brazil aren't you?"

"Not in the way you think. We haven't given them the technology, just the hardware." Michael went on to explain the deal he cut with Sakomoto.

"Why not make the same deal with us? You're worried about it getting out of your control?"

Michael nodded. "Truthfully, I'm torn. If we introduce the technology here we can lose control of it. Maybe the Goths won't be able to take advantage, but I worry about other Imperium entities like this alliance you're so hot about."

"The technology will give us an edge," Kamarov asserted. "Our enemies won't stand a chance."

Michael shrugged. "Niki, you agree we can't introduce the technology instantaneously. The Navy bureaucracy and the battleship captains won't support that kind of change so quickly. You agree no security is infallible."

"I'm not so sure. Look at the Manhattan Project during World War II on Earth."

"Yes, the Manhattan Project. The moment the nuclear bombs left their isolated laboratories for deployment, America's enemies, the Soviets I believe they were called, stole the technology. A couple of spies handed the Soviets the American's A-bomb plans. We can't risk our weapons know-how falling into our opponent's hands." He stared at Niki. "I admit this technology is the only thing New Meyer has going for it to survive. I can't risk any of the technologies falling into other hands."

"So you admit New Meyer's survival rates ahead of the

Imperium's survival in your priorities." Kamarov appeared disturbed and disappointed to Michael.

"I told you they're not mutually exclusive," Michael replied. "I'll admit I'm torn about what to do. I want to share something with you." He paused for a moment. "AI!" he verbalized so Kamarov heard the command.

"Yes, Your Majesty?" the disembodied voice replied.

"Play file EM-1 and channel to Admiral Kamarov also."

A few second later Mitch's image appeared and the kitchen faded into the background. The image was visible only to the two men through their implants' connection to their optic nerves and they listened through the audio nerve connections. "Greetings, cousin. All is well here at New Meyer. We had a bit of a scare when Duke Wolvein appeared in force at our jump point demanding the identity of the destroyer of LeBlanc's task force. He called himself Emperor." Mitch grinned. "I disabused him of his pretentions. When I told him of your ascension, he actually seemed thrilled a Landsman was back on the throne. He agreed to transport this message for me. Oh, by the way, Edward warned me Niki has a blind spot concerning Wolvein due to his losing the competition for the Duke's wife."

Michael glanced over at Kamarov. The Admiral's face darkened but he waved to keep the message playing.

"Oh, and Claudia is pregnant. We decided to set up an heir now just in case. She's early on but the P-Net is in heaven with the news. She reminds me so much of Donna. I guess we're both lucky men."

Mitch paused before continuing, "The new spacedock work has been accelerated. I think recent events had an effect on Congress. Also, New Brazil played a big role, as well as your sister. We plan to complete the spacedock in four months now.

"I rethought our last discussion about the disposition of New Meyer technology. In my humble opinion, we should go ahead and share some of the technology with the Imperium. We should cut a New Brazil-type deal with them. Carol agrees and so does Shiro. I'm dispatching two converted New Brazil cruisers and four frigates to reinforce your squadron." He held up his hand as if to forestall Michael's protests. "You're our best chance of survival, Michael. Those ships will help. As I said we got the spacedock working and *Yakumo* is doing a brilliant job of cruiser conversions. I feel comfortable in making this tribute to my Emperor. Besides I expect a couple of battleships in return.

"So how is it to be Emperor? What is Longhorn like?" He grinned, "Are we really backworlders? Take care, cousin. Be safe and give my love to Donna and Alex. Mitch out."

As the image faded away Michael turned his gaze back to Kamarov. "So you see things aren't as cut and dried in one direction or the other. Mitch believes as I do. The longer the Imperium survives the more chance New Meyer has. Of course, if we can restore Imperium power fully then New Meyer's survival is far less problematic. Do you believe we can restore all the Imperium worlds?"

Kamarov shook his head, "No, Your Majesty, I don't, at least not in our lifetimes."

"Will you guarantee the Imperium will protect New Meyer from outside incursions?"

"You damn well know we can't guarantee anything of the sort, Your Majesty."

"So now you understand my dilemma. I'm not saying New Meyer is the phoenix if the Imperium falls though that was the goal of the original plan. Tell me, Niki, do you believe the Imperium can even survive with enough influence to bring stability back to this sector of the galaxy?"

Niki sighed. "Not until after many years of war."

"How long do you think the ISDF can hold the Shaallit at bay if the Imperium falters?"

Niki looked thoughtful. "They've been pretty self-sufficient for the last few centuries, so I think they can keep things in control for a while."

"How long do you think before the ISDF leadership start exerting themselves to fill the power vacuum? Somewhere along the line they may decide to become a player. Right now they may be the single most powerful entity left."

"True, Your Majesty, but their mission limits their flexibility. With all those systems to protect to keep the Shaallit at bay they may have a large fleet but they also face large commitments."

Michael nodded in agreement. "I can't argue with your point except we really don't know what ISDF's ship production capabilities are. Quite possibly they may be able to produce enough to hold the frontier and still make some moves. We've let them become too independent. I'm not sure what control we have over them now."

It was Kamarov's turn to nod. "Yes. Our contact with them became much more sporadic in the last decade." He sighed and looked straight at Michael. "So, Your Majesty, what are you going to do?"

Michael shrugged again. "I told you when we began this thing I will be my own man. That doesn't mean I can't listen and take advice. The so-called Plan my grandfather and father instituted went awry long ago. Clausewitz was right about no battle plan survives first contact."

"And?"

Michael sighed. "Let me think on it."

Kamarov nodded. "Your Majesty, in the meantime, I'll make arrangements to send help to New Meyer in building their spacedock when we send those ten battleships to them. We'll benefit if we strengthen New Meyer's position, not only because of your mental health, but because they can help bring stability to their surrounding chutes. I'll also send word to welcome those New Meyerian ships that are on their way. Based on what we did at New Portugal those ships will be welcome."

"Thank you, Niki," Michael replied.

Niki grinned. "Just don't take too long to make up your mind. We don't have a lot of time."

Michael merely nodded.

CHAPTER 42

MICHAEL SAT AT HIS DESK awaiting T'Zar's arrival. *T'Zar might misconstrue my not meeting him at the spaceport as an insult and decide to leave. A risk, but one I needed to take.* T'Zar's visit was being kept secret until he determined whether to bring T'Zar into the fold. If he decided against bringing T'Zar into the Imperium the meeting would stay secret. He shrugged. *I'll take my chances.*

"T'Zar arriving," said the office's AI in a clipped precise New Britain accent. Michael hadn't bothered to change the AI's personality. He sort of liked the butler persona.

T'Zar entered and bowed his head in respect. "Your Majesty."

Michael studied the alien, the first time he had ever met a Granac in the flesh. *He's not quite what I expected. I understood they were stockier and their skin yellower. His nose is too sharp, almost Human. Not nearly as flat as I understood them to be.* A thought occurred to him. He pulled up the intelligence report and sure enough he found the data he wanted. *He's part Human!* Successful breeding between Granacs and Humans had long been recognized as possible. Here stood a walking example.

Michael collected himself and nodded. "Welcome, T'Zar." He motioned the Granac to sit in a chair in front of his desk. Another part of his power play. "What can I do for you?" he asked without any preamble or pleasantries.

"Your Majesty, thank you for seeing me." T'Zar's English was not perfect, but not deeply accented either. His low pitch caused him to swallow some of the vowels. "I appreciate your getting to the point rather quickly. Good. I'm here to petition the admittance of my kingdom into the Imperium."

Michael studied him for a moment before answering. "Your kingdom? You're offering me the two hundred worlds you took from me? Worlds you took illegally and through the use of force?"

The Granac shrugged in an almost Human gesture. "I believe, Your Majesty, using an old phrase from your own people, possession is nine-tenths of the law. You could, of course, come and take them back from me. I suspect the Imperium has enough ships to do so but not without weakening your ability to address more pressing needs. Furthermore, a battle for my kingdom will put the worlds you need at risk. My ships in orbit around Cassia are loaded with eight hundred thousand tons of beef and other staples ready for shipment. I can provide you two hundred thousand tons on a monthly basis as tribute, plus four to five times that amount in trade. In return, I want recognition as a Duke of the Imperium. I promise to swear fealty to you."

"And if I don't grant this?" Michael asked

"I'll sign up as a member of the Outer Worlds Alliance. Most of the foodstuffs will go to them."

Outer Worlds Alliance? So, Javez and company are in league already. I understand now why they've been so slow in acknowledging my summons. This validates the Countess's' information. Michael exhaled softly to himself to ease the tension rising in his stomach. "What do you get out of this if I accede to what you ask?"

"An enlightened ruler. Imperium protection, Your Majesty. Access to Imperium markets," the Granac replied. After a pause, he spoke, "Recognition and some legitimacy. As a crossbreed," he frowned at his own term, "I'm limited in what I can hang on to inside either the OWA or within what you call the Goth Alliance."

"Download a map of the worlds under your control," Michael ordered.

The map materialized and the room faded from view as Michael's implant transmitted the image directly to his optic nerves. *The worlds shown in the map constitute three chutes. They also provide a bridge to two hundred more worlds cut off from the Imperium for decades.* Michael realized his options were narrowing. He studied the map. *One Tier One world along with three Tier Twos. Remainder are Tier Threes and Fours. These chutes were colonized from Earth. These chutes are similar to NBNM in makeup but with more habitable worlds.* He suppressed a twinge of homesickness at the thought of his home chute.

"You're willing to swear publicly before your deity your fealty to me and the Imperium?"

"Yes, Your Majesty. I converted to Christianity and I will swear before God my fealty to you and the Imperium."

Michael hesitated. *Can it be this easy?* He grinned to himself. *I've been asking that question a lot lately.*

"I want to join the Imperium for another reason," T'Zar added.

Michael raised an eyebrow. T'Zar appeared uncomfortable but continued. "I converted to a form of your Human's Church of the Universal Creator. You must be aware this church believes in multiple visits by the Son of God to different races to bring Enlightenment, under many guises. For you Humans his name was Christ."

Michael nodded, not sure where the Granac was going. T'Zar took a deep breath and then continued. "I believe that the leadership of the Goth Alliance has fallen under the sway of a cult religion of the Goddess Nearyahn. Al'Rik O'Rathll, our Grand Leader, is married to the High Priestess of this religion as was his father. He is working to make this the official Goth religion. Your Majesty, I fear there is something evil about this priestess. She claims to be the embodiment of the Goddess, similar to those who believe Christ was of God. There are stories of, um, I guess you might call demonic possession. I realize you Imperials think of us, Goths as you call us, as barbarian rubes. You're wrong. We've adapted many of your ways as a result of our conquests. We've educated our youth using your schools and teachers. This religion is a cult. Nearyahn is winning converts throughout Goth-dominated worlds. The stories about Nearyahn also tell of priests of various Christian faiths being brought forth to meet this High Priestess in private and coming out of the meeting converted and devoted to the Goddess. Pious and holy men swearing instant allegiance to a Goddess spouting opposing beliefs to their faith in Christ.

"I understand the Imperium requires freedom of religion, but I beg of you to please investigate this religion and consider banning it." He paused and gazed straight into Michael's eyes, his own indigo eyes deep and troubled. "Your Majesty, I must propose one condition to my swearing fealty to you. You must allow me to outlaw the Nearyahn religion in my kingdom. Please, Your Majesty, I beg of you. Any other religion is welcome in our worlds." He gave the equivalent of a wan smile. "Even those of yours preaching Goths as agents of the devil."

Michael nodded, fighting not to show puzzlement and disbelief. He summoned the new robotic butler, Sawyer.

"T'Zar, I will think about this and meet with my advisors. Sawyer, take T'Zar to his quarters. I'll summon him when make a decision."

As soon as the door slid shut behind them another one opened and in walked his Privy Council. He waited for them to be seated. "You catch all of that?"

They all nodded. "Do you think his crossbreeding is the source of his desire to join the Imperium?" Michael asked. "I'm no psychologist but it seems pretty obvious to me."

Emil responded first, "A strong possibility. I gather he hasn't received much acceptance among his Goth contemporaries, which surprises me. The Goths are a mixture of at least three different races."

The Countess spoke up, "They're organized in tribes running pretty much along racial lines."

"Tribes?" Michael asked. "We keep treating them as if they truly are barbarians. We're all aware that's not true. Barbarians don't man spaceships and don't run technology. I find the tribe designation to be out of place."

"You must remember their background," the Countess replied. "Some of the original Human worlds were settled as prison worlds early in the Imperium. At some point they were cut off from the Imperium during the Shaallit Wars of the 3rd Century. They slid back a bit before climbing out. The Granacs are a clan-oriented society, while the Braum are pack-dominated. So the idea of tribes may not be so farfetched. 'Tribes' is an Imperium term, a rough translation of a word they use. Kingdoms might work just as well."

"What about this religious thing?" Michael brought up. "It's against the constitution to ban a religion. Yet, he seemed really scared. Any of you familiar with this Goddess of Nearyahn?"

The Countess nodded. "Our Intelligence Service tracks Nearyahn. Strange stories circulate about the religion. We dismissed most of those as the usual P-Net conspiracy theories. However, I can't explain why two of our agents were captured, brought in front of the Priestess in a private meeting, and then turned. We lost two of our intelligence networks as a result. We didn't know what to make of it. Combined with T'Zar's stories of those converted Priests, I think we must investigate."

"Then I suggest finding out about this religion becomes a priority, My Lady." Michael ordered. "Meantime, do we accept him?"

"Recognizing him opens up two hundred worlds beyond his," Smythe said, speaking up for the first time.

"Niki?"

The Admiral shrugged. "Not much choice, Your Majesty. As Colonel Smythe pointed out he opens worlds to us, two hundred we won't have to protect. We'll leave that to our new Duke T'Zar."

"Emil?"

The older man rubbed his newly grown beard. "I'm not sure if history is going to repeat itself but I agree about the lack of choices."

The beard makes him appear old. He believes it makes him look distinguished. "Countess?"

She shrugged. "As everyone else said, not many other choices."

"Madame Minister?"

Al-Haidar took a moment before answering. Then she sighed and said, "I agree."

"Empress?"

The Empress Donna Landsman gazed at her husband thoughtfully. She shrugged and smiled, "Are we, as Humans, doomed to repeat history?" She sighed. "Be that as it may, with the limited options facing us at this time, I agree."

"What do we do about this religious issue?" Michael asked.

"Turn a blind eye. Accept his fealty and let him do as

he suggested," Emil replied. "Meantime, we investigate the Goddess of Nearyahn. If we receive a complaint about religious intolerance we'll be forced to investigate. We may be following a dangerous slippery slope but something about him convinced me he's truly afraid of Nearyahn. With the Countess' tidbits I believe there may be something to this."

Michael sighed. "I don't feel comfortable allowing him to ban a religion. Freedom of religion is an underpinning of Imperium law." He shrugged. "I keep talking about dangers and threats. Well, this may be one we need to understand better. I think we'll follow Emil's suggestion for now. This Nearyahn religion is now the subject of an Emperor's Finding classified top secret. Countess, please make this a priority."

We're following a treacherous path here. Allowing some of the Goth to join the Imperium eliminates or reduces warfare. In doing so do we weaken the Imperium's basic fabric? He now understood Emil's description of the dilemma faced by the Western Roman Emperors in the Fifth Century. Something his father had once told him popped into his mind. Converts to a religion often became the most religious and immigrants to a new country the most patriotic. So maybe T'Zar and his ilk will turn out that way. *Maybe. Or maybe the whole thing is a ploy by others to weaken the Imperium.* He mentally shrugged. *Only time will tell.* "So we're all agreed?"

A chorus of "Yes, Your Majesty" was the response.

"Emil, take care of getting the directive released to the public. Work the spin carefully. Madame Minister, you'll work Congress?" Both nodded in the affirmative. "Anything else?" he asked.

The Countess stirred, glancing at Kamarov. "Admiral, do you remember Admiral Denham Swann?"

"Swanee? Of course, I do." Kamarov seemed a little

surprised. "MIA for six or seven years now. Hero of the battle of Calderus Five. Why?"

The Intelligence Chief seemed a little uncomfortable. She turned from the Admiral to her sovereign. "Rumors are circulating concerning him." She hesitated before continuing. "Admiral Swann is not dead. In fact, far from it."

"Great news!" Kamarov exulted. Then he saw the look on the Countess' face. "So what's the bad news?"

"Reports show Swann behind the OWA. Intelligence reports indicate he fought a couple of battles and has a large number of Goth kings swearing fealty to him."

Kamarov sank back in the chair. "Why, that SOB has actually done it. Do you realize he's one thirty-second Landsman? His grandmother was the fifth daughter of some minor noble. Back at the Academy he used to say wistfully how if he were Emperor he'd fix things. We all treated it as the meanderings of a young officer being beaten to a pulp during the first year. But I remember now he brought this whole thing up again when we were serving together on the old *Agincourt*. He had remarked how unfair he found the law requiring heirs to the throne to have a direct line to Emperor Michael I."

The Countess appeared sympathetic, an unusual gesture for her. "I know he was your friend, Admiral, but I have worse news. Same reports implicate him in the Landsman assassinations in the past two-years. The report also hinted he planned the attack on Earth. I think the last is probably stretching things."

Niki sighed, his normally hard features softening. "Would ol' Swanee do something like this?" he asked, almost as if he were trying to reassure himself. He turned to Michael. "Your Majesty, this changes things. We're going to have to do something about this OWA."

Michael nodded. "Yes. Do you think T'Zar is part of the plot?"

"No, in fact, he may be here as a result of the pressure to join and he doesn't like what he sees," the Countess answered. "Of course, I can imagine a scenario where his joining the Imperium is a ruse. Oh, I forgot another interesting tidbit. Rumors have Swann married to a priestess of a new religion."

"Nearyahn?" Michael asked.

"I don't know."

"This should move the investigation of Nearyahn to the top of your list," Michael ordered.

The Countess nodded. "I agree, Your Majesty."

Michael shrugged. "Sometimes you just have to do things on faith that someone is worthy of your trust. Anyone want to change your previous vote about T'Zar?"

A chorus of "No, Your Majesty."

"Very well. Emil, start the arrangements. Let's do this quickly." He glanced at his wife. "You'll work with Emil and the PR ministry to handle P-Net?"

"Of course, Your Majesty," Donna replied.

"Thank you, all."

Donna stayed behind as the others filed out. She walked over to him, perched herself on the arm of his chair and asked, "How are you doing, honey?" She began rubbing the back of his neck with her right hand.

"Mmm, much better now," he grumbled.

She leaned over and nuzzled his neck a bit. He inhaled the sweet fragrance of her hair. *Vanilla.*

He pushed her away and gazed deep into her eyes. "Ok, my love, what do you want?"

She smiled demurely. "Moi? What makes you think I want anything?"

He grinned at her. "We've been married long enough. I know when you want something."

She laughed. "You only know because I let you know."

Michael rolled his eyes. "Yeah, sure. I know you want something now. Makes no difference whether you're letting me gain an inkling through your feminine wiles or whether I figured this out all by myself. So do you want something enough to make googly eyes at me in the middle of the day?"

This time she rolled her eyes. "Whatever. Here's what I want. I want you to take a break. This weekend. Let's get away from here and be alone."

He shook his head. "We can't be alone. Security."

"At least we can be away from here. Yes, things are tough, and I suspect they're going to get tougher. So let's break away while we still can."

"Where do you want to go?"

"The Ranch."

"The Ranch? What's that? They haven't even started on the Manor yet."

"I discovered that a former planetary Duke built a small retreat out near Lake Sipparo for VIPs. It's actually a working horse ranch. The bureaucracy, in all its wisdom, has maintained it in working order. I'm sure Alex will love a visit there."

Michael exhaled. "Sounds wonderful. okay, you twisted my arm. Go have Crowe make the arrangements."

"No need, I already spoke to Crowe and Wallace. Arrangements are being made as we speak."

Yeah, who's really Emperor here?

CHAPTER 43

Emperor's Palace, Longhorn
16 November 685 IP

DONNA ROLLED HER NECK AS she stretched. Even the chair's nanos didn't keep her from stiffening after hours of digitalwork and meetings. She sighed. *Last meeting for the day.* Some Baron from a small world wanting to reinitiate contact with Imperium.

The door opened. In walked a tall, broad-shouldered man with shoulder-length dark hair and eyes alive with a power that attracted her gaze. She thought he was the most handsome man she had ever seen. She shook herself and took a silent breath. *Careful girl, you're not a schoolgirl any longer.* She forced a picture of Michael into her mind.

Gregory released some pheromones from his modified glands and observed her reaction while tasting her emotions. Her eyes widened slightly and he tasted her heightened sexual response. At the same time he tasted her resolve as she focused on her husband. He thought about another dose of pheromones and maybe pushing a bit harder but changed his mind. *She's a strong one and won't be easy. I need to do this without damaging her. With her resistance the risk is too high. Let's just start with some simple acceptance and even a little sympathy leading to friendship. I really don't need her full conversion until the Emperor is dead.* He bowed. "Your Majesty, I am honored that you have taken time to see me. I know you and His Majesty are busy. I appreciate your finding a few moments to spare with an envoy from such an inconsequential planet as Espoir Nouvel."

"No planet is inconsequential," she replied, adding warmth to her voice. "Tell me a bit about your world." She motioned for him to sit in one of the overstuffed chairs in front of her.

A natural response without any push from him. He sensed her frustration with the tedium of digitalwork. He smiled warmly. "Your Majesty, you certainly have more important things to do."

She shook her head, interrupting him. "No, please go ahead. I can use the distraction."

This time he pushed, feeding a little of his handsomeness again. "Very well, Your Majesty. A group looking for a less harried, urban existence from New Paris settled Espoir a hundred and fifty years ago."

She grinned. "Sometimes I can sympathize with that impulse."

He sensed her warming to him, if only in a casual manner. *It's a beginning. No need to push too hard. I just want to make sure she wants me to come back for more discussions. One step at a time.*

Garcia-Mankin Office Building, Capital City, Longhorn
18 November 685 IP

Gregory was ushered into her office with little fanfare. After all, he came from a minor world no one had heard from in years and felt fortunate to be granted the meeting. *Her insistence on using a live assistant made making the*

appointment easier. Samantha became my second convert.
He grinned to himself. *I'm still recovering from my night with Sam.*

The woman seated behind the desk looked up as he walked in. He entered the outskirts of her mind. *All business.* He explored a bit more, probing. *Promising. Highly repressed. I can use that.* He pushed, tasting the changing emotions as he went. *This will be much easier than the Empress. Much, much easier.*

The stately woman rose from her high-backed chair and extended her hand. He took it and bowed his head. "Welcome, Baron," she said, her eyes regarding him with frank curiosity and possibly something else.

"My Lady," he said, bowing again.

He pushed again, finding her weak spot. A risk but he sensed an opportunity. He tasted the repressed sexuality and desire. He found her brittle and ripe for the taking. No depth to her resistance. *Not like the Empress.* He released more pheromones.

She motioned him to sit, her eyes widening in response to the pheromones as she sat back down. She just sat there returning his stare, her eyes unfocused. He decided to go for broke and pushed hard. Her emotional barrier crashed inward, leaving her wide open and defenseless. He pounced mentally and met no opposition. He drove her desire and lust and added another shot of pheromones.

"We must be alone and this meeting kept secret," he ordered.

She stood. "AI," she said in a voice that almost squeaked. "Cancel all my meetings and allow no one in. I have a high priority from the Emperor and do not want to be disturbed. Password Code Zero Alpha Omega Eight, Priority Alpha Four. Shut down all recording devices including yourself."

"Yes, My Lady."

He watched as she slowly began to peel off her jacket. A well-preserved, decent body with very feminine attributes revealed itself to him. Her trim figure indicated she worked out regularly and kept herself in good shape. She stripped off her underwear without any hesitation or embarrassment and walked over to him. Her breasts were firm and her nipples hard. She straddled him as he sat in the chair. Her mouth was warm and wet. "How may I serve you, Master?" she whispered in his ear.

Gregory couldn't believe how little time and effort her domination required. *So quick. So easy.* The so-called Countess She-Wolf had folded in no time at all. *The Head of Imperium Intelligence belongs to me.* He checked his resident Neary. The complete Merging between a Human and a Neary often took up to a year. He was far enough along so the Merging seemed natural to him.

Yes, I have enough available for a splinter. She's ready and it guarantees me control. The Countess undid his trousers. He pushed mentally against her open mind and felt it yield again. He fed back to her all the sensations he experienced and her own emotions. She began grinding against him, moaning. She came immediately and violently as if she were letting out years of repressed desires. She continued thrusting her hips, her breathing coming in rapid gasps of exhilaration and pleasure as she built to another climax under the torrent of the feedback of her own excitement. *She's ready.* He waited till she shuddered in release again. At the height of her spasms he inserted the splinter and felt it enter her brain. She climaxed again, the passion exploding in her mind like a torrent of brilliant light.

He didn't let her stop but forced her to continue riding him. His left hand came up and cupped her cheeks forcing her to look up directly into his eyes.

"You belong to me," he said and pushed mentally.

"I belong to you," she repeated her eyes wide and glassy.

"You belong to me."

"I belong to you."

"You find it natural to belong to me. You believe in the Goddess of Nearyahn. She is your mistress as she is mine. These are natural and undeniable truths."

"I find it natural to belong to you. I believe in the Goddess of Nearyahn. She is my mistress," she repeated, her hips still in motion. Her voice strained with the desire to let go again but he suppressed it.

"You are loyal to the Goddess of Nearyahn not to the Emperor of the Imperium." He let her release again as she responded.

"I am loyal to the Goddess of Nearyahn not the Emperor of the Imperium," she screamed as she rode the waves of pleasure, her mind wide open to him.

"You love me," he said, not letting her stop and now preventing her from another release.

"I love you," she said, mewling as lust overcame her.

"You love me no matter whom I'm with or if I marry someone else."

"I love you no matter whom you're with or if you marry someone else." She groaned in desire, her hips moving almost of their own volition now.

"You'll help me kill the Emperor so I can marry the Empress and convert her to the Way of the Goddess."

"I'll help you kill the Emperor so you can marry the Empress and convert her to the Way of the Goddess."

He prevented her from the release she so wanted. "You're dedicated to this and find it right."

"I'm dedicated to this and find it right." Her voice broke and her eyes, now tinged with violet, pleaded for relief.

"When you cum you're mine and this is all truth to you not to be doubted. This is your new reality. You will still work to make the Imperium safe as you do now to keep prying eyes away from you. Only now you will strive for the goals I set for you. You will help me kill the Emperor and marry the Empress. You will tell no one of it. Now cum!"

She cried out in pleasure, bucking violently and

screaming before passing out as her whole body spasmed. Her final throes pushed him over the edge. He let out a loud groan of his own, sinking against the back of the chair. *Thank the Goddess she has a soundproof room.*

He slid her gently to the floor, taking care not to let her fall. After re-buttoning his trousers, he lifted her up and put her on the office couch. He slowly dressed her and then left. She would wake a few hours later completely devoted to him. She would work as she always did for the good of the Imperium. He would need to reinforce these commands almost every day until the splinter consolidated enough, maybe in two months. He grinned again. *The things I do for the Goddess.*

The splinter he had inserted was not a buddling, just a tiny non-fertile piece of his Neary. It would gain and hold control but never grow enough to reproduce or become a full resident Neary. She would never experience the full benefits of a Merging like he had. She would always be linked to him and subservient to his wishes. *She must have enough freedom to be herself in terms of maintaining the trust of her colleagues and the Emperor, but not enough license to even contemplate resistance. A fine balance.*

Unlike the High Priestess he couldn't afford much in the way of splinters. He was still only an Adept. The Head of Imperium Intelligence was a high enough target to make it worthwhile to use one of his precious splinters. *The Goth Alliance controls the Head of Imperium Intelligence.* He had to smile at his conquest.

The next splinter will be for the Empress. *Mistress will be ecstatic. First the Countess, then the Empress.*

CHAPTER 44

"H E WHAT?" BOTH MICHAEL AND Kamarov exclaimed simultaneously.

Michael had watched the storm move in since early morning. The morning began with the promise of a delightful spring day with clear blue skies blossoming from the dawn's reds and pinks of sunrise, like a flower opening its petals to the sun in all its golden glory. Cool breezes wafted the fragrant scents of springtime across the palace's lush gardens. Then, as so often at this time of year in Capital City, the skies darkened. Tall, black thunderheads with peals of rolling thunder and eye-hurting, dazzling flashes of lightning rolled in from the west. A howling wind slammed the rain sideways. The palace, suspended on gravitics above the city, trembled slightly.

"He did what?" Michael repeated, this time framing his response with cold, icy hardness. He stared at his coffee cup for signs of the palace's movement in the wind. *Rock steady. City engineers claim the quivers are imaginary. I wish Swann was, too.*

The Countess Huffman eyed them both coolly, before continuing, "Swann declared himself Emperor of a New Imperium. The OWA is now the New Imperium. Swann says he's tired of dealing with Pretenders. According to him, genetic tests can be faked. He claims Your Majesty is not truly a Landsman. He points to the Imperium's own databases showing Duke Alexander as the Duke of a world overrun by Goths, and later given New Meyer as consolation."

"Victim of our own machinations," Michael grumbled. "Oh, what a tangled web we weave." *That was a cover story of New Meyer's founding to hide the Plan that my grandfather created. The one I wanted to change because isolation doesn't work. Well, that's Mitch's problem now.*

He paused to study the Countess. She seemed different. Her eyes seemed to be warmer. He smiled to himself. *Maybe she found herself a man.* "I can't imagine Swann gaining control of P-Net Media to do this. P-Nets are way too diversified. He hasn't been in power long enough. There are just too many independent blogs on planetary Nets these days. How is he pulling this off?"

"By a campaign of half-truths and innuendos," she replied. He's brought some stability to New Imperium space. As a result, his popularity right now is the same as yours here. One more thing. He's married to a Nearyahn Priestess."

Did I sense a quaver in her voice when she said Nearyahn? Is she all tangled up in a wave of rumors like all of us? "Shit." Michael said and sat back in his chair.

The Countess gave one of her rare smiles. "Some things are going well, Your Majesty. Heart World warship production increased to a new peak in the past two months. We've reinforced many Imperium worlds. The two hundred *Whitman*-class transports you ordered pulled out of space storage are opening trade routes with chutes previously out of contact with us. Over eighty star systems previously unprotected by regular navy ships now have Imperium warships as well as regular runs with the Heart Worlds."

"I guess that's good news," Michael admitted, "but it pales in comparison. Swann has declared himself Emperor of the New Imperium, an organization of his own making. Almost two thousand worlds now swear fealty to him. This is something I can't allow."

"History repeating itself," Emil grumbled.

"We're not the Roman Empire," Michael retorted. "I'm not going to allow the Imperium to be split in two, with two Emperors."

Emil responded with a smile, before growing serious. "What do we do about it?" he asked.

After a pause of several seconds while everyone else looked at each other, Emil finally answered his own question. "I guess we need to take some action. I think the only effective action will be military."

Michael sighed. *There it is, out on the table.* Actively attacking former Imperium worlds. *Civil war is something I wanted to avoid. They never solve root cause, just bury them for future generations to deal with.* He turned back to the Countess. "Tell me more about Swann's popular support."

"We're tied pretty well into their media though we lag by a few months because of the distances involved. The blogs are running in favor of the New Imperium more than ten to one. Conversions to Nearyahn are also on the rise. These aren't the Heart Worlds, Your Majesty. Support for the Imperium in the OWA eroded over generations of neglect and Goth raids. I can guess what your next question is going to be. They don't have many regular naval units. However, they do have quite a few Goth units and many Planetary Reserve units. I'd say a New Imperium fleet will be more than sixty percent Goth."

Michael's eyes furrowed. *Her voice quavered again at the word Nearyahn. Wonder what that means?* "What happened to all of their Imperium Navy units?" Michael asked.

"They fought a long extended battle against the Goths over the centuries with limited reinforcements. Past Emperors never replaced the losses. They do have Planetary Guard units, but we don't know much about their quality."

Michael turned to Kamarov. "And the Imperium Navy? Do you have a contingency plan for something like this? A large breakaway declaring independence."

"Your Majesty," Kamarov replied. "We go in and kick their asses and take back our territory!"

Michael chuckled. "I wish things were so simple, Niki."

"Ah! But they are," Kamarov retorted.

"The devil is in the details, Admiral," Michael responded with a smile.

"True, Your Majesty. We've been working on a plan. I can share the highlights with you tomorrow. The plan will be ready for release in a couple of weeks."

"Make it sooner. A week. I don't look forward to civil war but I'm not one to procrastinate. I can't allow anyone to secede from the Imperium. No one. Understood?"

A chorus of "Yes, Your Majesty" was the response.

"Niki, I want a plan by the end of the week." Kamarov nodded. "Emil, I need a good speech. Something with meat on it to inspire the P-Net. I'm going to war over the principle that no one is allowed to secede. This has to be made clear to the Imperium as a whole." Emil nodded. "Countess, prepare an update on their ship estimates and any reports on deployment even if the reports are weeks or a month old. We'll make do with what we can get." He turned to Al-Haidar, "Madame Minister, I want to address the Senate next Monday."

"Yes, Your Majesty, I'll arrange it."

"And what do you think the response of your colleagues will be?" Michael asked.

Al-Haidar looked thoughtful. "I think most will give you

support. Some will think we should concentrate on the Goth menace."

"As I thought. Emil, we must make the case that we can't let this secession happen and it must take precedence over the Goths for the moment. In fact, the two are now entwined. The New Imperium is really a Goth government in disguise. Don't bring up the Nearyahn sect. A crusade against a religion would be a hard sell."

"Understood, Your Majesty," Emil replied.

"Lots of work ahead of us. Let's get to it."

Hotel Alamo Fairmont, Capital City, Longhorn
22 Nov 685 IP

Gregory closed his eyes and let the images of the meeting fade away. The Countess' splinter had settled in well and formed solid connections with her brain. The splinter had accomplished its task without causing her any visible discomfort. No headaches or anything forcing her to seek medical care. *I have enough control now for my needs.* He allowed himself a smile of satisfaction. *I've unleashed a lioness in bed after many years of repression. Her passion and ardor make up for her age.*

Now to report. He focused his mind on an image of the High Priestess and closed his eyes. A moment later he sensed her presence. Sinewy tentacles of her caress sent shivers down his spine. *To be able to do this over four hundred light years still blows me away. I'm sure there's no physical explanation of how this works*

"Ahh, Gregory," she said with a trace of a smile causing more shudders of pleasure through him. "How are things in Capital City?"

"Delightfully decadent," he replied with another smile.

"Don't enjoy yourself too much," she cautioned, her voice hardening, "I didn't send you to Longhorn for a vacation."

This time the quivers were not those of pleasure.

"Of course, Mistress. I'm calling with some news. I just watched a Privy Council meeting through the Countess's eyes. The link with her splinter is working perfectly and she had no idea I was present. They're going to attack, Mistress, to take back Imperium worlds. They're aware of the existence of Nearyahn but are only vaguely aware of the threat. I'll influence the Countess to allay their fears on that account. I must be cautious, as you're aware, or she'll lose credibility. My intention is to slow down their awareness of Nearyahn. I'm working to increase P-Net support for the freedom of religion clause in the Imperium Charter to make outlawing Nearyahn more difficult."

"Very good," the High Priestess said.

Ripples of pleasure coursed through him.

"Which worlds do they intend to take back?" she asked.

"The New Imperium."

"Oh, they do, do they?" she snarled. "Do you know when?"

He shuddered at her ferocity. "They don't know yet themselves. Kamarov is supposed to provide a plan next week."

"Understood. Keep me informed. I need details so we can arrange a few surprises for our young Emperor."

She smiled again and a brief paroxysm of sheer joy verging on sexual release surged through him. "Well done," she said and cut the connection.

He exploded in orgasm.

Argula City, New Barwick, Okra Star System
22 Nov 685 IP

The High Priestess sank back in her high-backed throne and summoned her husband. Things were coming to a head much sooner than her visions had indicated. Attacking the New Imperium? *Damn these Humans. Why does dealing with them always mean you move along the less probable timelines into the future?* She sighed. Plans must change.

She brought up an image of known space through her neural implant and studied the three dimensional representation. *I was right. This new Emperor is going to be a problem. Yes, he's his father's son.* This forced her to pull forces from the New Meyer attack to counter the Imperium invasion. *Fortunately, from what I'm getting from Jessica I don't think New Meyer has as much of a navy as I thought. The attack on New Meyer can do with less. Now we'll attack first and see how this Emperor reacts.*

CHAPTER 45

"WE'RE READY WHEN YOU ARE, Your Majesty," Kamarov's voice, as steady as ever, said through his direct link to the Emperor. "We can proceed to jump anytime."

Michael viewed the virtual image of the massed fleet produced by a scouting Raptor's Twenty-Two. He studied the vast armada of ships spread out across thousands of kilometers of space floating peacefully in the dark coldness of the outer reaches of this star system. *Nothing peaceable at all about these ships.* The task force was comprised of powerful warships, a vast fleet designed to engage and destroy the enemy. One hundred and thirty standard Imperium battleships, eight of which had been modified with strap-on missile launchers. *Ninety-six Stingers.*

Excalibur seemed dwarfed by these monsters, and yet the cruiser's own mass and steadiness proved comforting in her own right. He wouldn't trade her for any of the battleships. Three other USV-modified cruisers had arrived from New Meyer and were now part of Task Force

One. The fleet's cruiser force, outside of TF-1, included eighty of the all gun older style cruisers. A quarter of these had hastily improvised strap-on missile launchers. *Another 120 Stingers.* TF-1 now included eight frigates, adding their Raptors to the mix. Sixty fleet destroyers provided escort and scouting. In addition he had thirty ships provided by T'Zar, thirty Goth-barbarian cruisers with their nasty kinetic projectiles. Michael grinned at the irony. *If my father had this force at his disposal Earth would never have fallen.*

He gave the mental equivalent of a sigh. *I'm not using these ships to attack the Goths. I'm actually starting a civil war. Am I hastening the collapse of the Imperium or am I strengthening it in the long run?* The Privy Council had argued this incessantly for the past six months and had not come to a unified conclusion. *Ultimately, the decision was mine. I can't tolerate an organization calling itself the New Imperium led by a man who declares himself Emperor. Especially one who might be under the influence of the Neary.* A new ambassador from New Meyer, the Ambassador Baron Rio Grande Cristina Cardoso, had arrived with dire warnings about the Nearyahn Religion.

Kamarov repeated his message.

"Understood, Niki. Just give me a minute," he replied, trying to keep the mixture of excitement, fear, and anticipation out of his voice. *Are we ready to do this? Civil war?* This whole mission was a gamble, dependent upon surprise, something difficult to achieve when gathering so many ships *A balance between adequate force and secrecy. If I took additional ships their absence would be even more obvious to anyone watching.*

His com officer pulsed him. He turned his attention to her. "Your Majesty," she said with a professional coolness to her voice, "I'm sorry to intrude. We received a lascom from *Fenris* at Jump Point Two. Marked urgent for you and Admiral Kamarov."

"Ok, pass it on."

An image of a frightened looking Asian woman appeared. "We're facing a massive incursion in the Ocarius System. Hundreds of Shaallit ships. I don't think we can hold."

"Your Majesty," the com officer added, "*Fenris* reports the message was delivered by a long-range com drone and repeats over and over again."

Shit. Why did the Shaallit pick now to attack? Of all the worse luck. Well, I have to deal with it. Michael checked the stellar map, puzzled. Why Ocarius? The path made no sense if they were attacking Longhorn. The path was too winding, adding months of travel, giving me time to respond. Too many intervening jumps to make this an attack on the Imperium capital. Almost tangential to the Heart Worlds as if they're trying to cut them off from a portion of the remaining Imperium worlds.

That last thought brought it into focus. The incursion aimed to cut New Meyer off from the Imperium. New Meyer might even be the target. Why New Meyer? *If they learned about the new technologies, they may be attacking before we became too strong.*

"Not we, but they," he muttered under his breath. *I must remember I'm Emperor now not Duke of New Meyer.*

He sat up straighter. The implications, or at least the inferences, were not good. *How could they know about New Meyer? Coincidence? Or is this all coordinated with the New Imperium?* Swann had allied himself with some Goth kings but would he stoop to ally with the Shaallit? *I'm treating with the Goth kings, too. Doesn't make me more likely to make deals with the Shaallit.* How much influence does his Neary wife have on him? Michael took a deep breath. *No matter. I must respond.* He studied the star map. By some coincidence, Shepherd II sat only two jumps away from Ocarius. A little under a four-week journey. *By then the issue would have been decided. Either the ISDF holds or the Shaallit move on.* In reality, his ships were likely to meet the Shaallit in the next system, if the Shaallit were coming this way. *They would be if they were looking to cut off New Meyer from the rest of the Imperium. Only three jumps to New Meyer from here.*

He spoke into his implant, "Niki, you got this?"

"Yes, Your Majesty," came Kamarov's reply. "I believe they're targeting New Meyer."

"Maybe," Michael admitted. "I thought that at first. Now I'm not so sure. I'm thinking more of Horns of a Dilemma approach. If they come through here, the Shaallit can turn either toward the Heart Worlds or toward New Meyer. The dilemma requires us to choose one or the other."

Kamarov grinned at him. "Shiro would be proud that you listened in Tactics 101." Kamarov's face furrowed for a second. "You understand we can't split our forces and intercept them and still attack the New Imperium."

Michael nodded. "Isn't that the meaning of Horns of a Dilemma?"

"Correct, Your Majesty. If we split our forces they can defeat us in detail. We must respond to the greatest threat first which in my opinion is the Shaallit incursion. I think Swann will follow suit and try to take advantage. We certainly can't let a Shaallit task force run freely inside the Imperium. I don't believe the planetary or even chute defenses can handle this incursion unless the ISDF does a good job of heavily damaging their forces. Too many undefended star systems around to provide a breather for any Shaallit force breaking through. So it's up to the ships here to stop them."

He bowed his head. "Your Majesty, with your permission I'll get the orders in play. We'll depart in an hour. You should head back to Longhorn with TF-1."

"No way," Michael retorted. "You need TF-1 ships, particularly the *Raptor*-capable ones. Like you said we can't afford to divide our forces."

"I'm not risking the Emperor and I'm not sending you

back unprotected. TF-1 represents a small fraction of our forces. I'm not going to lose another Emperor, Your Majesty. Not on my watch." Kamarov said. "Don't let it go to your head, but the Imperium needs you."

"Sending me back?" Michael snapped angrily. "Niki, I remind you I'm Emperor. Understood?"

"Yes, Your Majesty, I understand. With all due respect I don't think it's wise to put you at risk."

"Let me remind you that one of the primary purposes of the Emperor is to act as a war leader."

"Yes, Your Majesty, but Emperors don't always lead from the front. Do you believe I am capable of leading the fleet into this battle?"

"Of course, I do, Niki, or I would have fired you a long time ago."

"Then let me do my job. Your Majesty, your job is organizing the defense in case the New Imperium or Goths decide to take advantage and launch their own strike at us." He hesitated, "Or if I fail to stop them. Plenty of resources remain in the Heart Worlds. They must be organized and they need leadership."

"But..." Michael started to say.

"Your Majesty, there are no buts. I know this poses a threat to your home world. You must decide now whether you are Emperor of the Imperium or still Duke of New Meyer."

"Not fair."

"Fairness has nothing to do with it," Kamarov replied. "We've had this discussion before. Are you Emperor, Michael? Are you dedicated to saving the Imperium or is this an excuse for you to buy time for New Meyer?"

Michael sighed as he realized Niki was right. *I am Emperor and I swore an oath.* "Very well. I guess you'll have all the fun."

Niki nodded. "If you want to call this clusterfuck fun. You know I'm right. I don't need to go into battle worrying about you. We may have to take a stand and I can't do that with you present. You need to head back to Longhorn to rally support. I repeat. Our other enemies are going to take advantage of this opportunity. If Swann doesn't then he's a fool and we needn't worry about him. The Swann I knew will be all over this. You should also take T'Zar's ships back with you."

"So you think this could be a coordinated offensive?"

Niki shrugged. "Maybe, although I doubt it matters. Even if this whole thing isn't coordinated, Swann will be supplied with a golden opportunity. Like I said, Swann is too sharp to pass this up. Same goes for the Goths."

Michael nodded. "You sure you want me to take T'Zar's ships with me?"

"You can use him as a quick reaction force. Besides T'Zar may need them. I wouldn't be surprised if he's targeted."

"OK. We'll depart after you," Michael answered. "However, I'm giving you *New Landsman City, Tyler River, and Caton River*," he said, holding up a hand to forestall Kamarov's protest. "A cruiser and two frigates. Replacements from New Meyer are probably waiting for me back at Longhorn. You need those Raptor-capable ships more than I do right now. We both know you're going to be outnumbered."

Kamarov sighed audibly in obvious resignation. "Very well. Good luck, Your Majesty."

"You too, Niki. Godspeed."

Michael looked down at the coffee cup he was unconsciously holding. He took a sip and almost spit it out. Not up to Wallace's usual standards. It had an unusually bitter taste.

CHAPTER 46

THE IMPERIUM TASK FORCE EMERGED from the jump in relatively good formation. Star Admiral Nikolai Kamarov immersed himself in *Dreadnaught's* TacNet, downloading the incoming reports as the task force's AIs recovered from the jump. The first good news arrived. No enemy ships waiting for them at emergence. They hadn't jumped into the teeth of a Shaallit task force. He had jumped without waiting for reports from scouts sent ahead. Time had not been on his side.

As he studied the tactical displays his mood changed. He found no sign of the Shaallit ships. *Are we too late? Did they jump out of here already? If so, where are they headed?* He thought of another potential scenario, one he didn't like at all. *They're still here but waiting in stealth for the right moment to pounce.* He had little data on the Shaallit's current stealth capabilities. *What if they discovered the same technology as the New Meyerians? Do I release the crews from GQ or leave them bundled up?*

Only a couple of his ships had the New Meyerian

stealth system installed. Still, even standard Imperium stealth was better than nothing. His battle sense tickled. *I still don't know what I'm facing.* He pulsed "Burly" Jake Johnson, his chief of staff. "Jake, order all ships to stealth and to remain at GQ. Launch all Raptors. Full scouting mode. We're looking for a stealthed fleet. Signal all ships, gravitics only, no fusion drive. Let's hold position. I don't want to venture too far until we learn whether we missed them or they're hiding. Maybe we got lucky and beat them here. Review the breakout. The Shaallit probably engaged stealth immediately on detection of our breakout."

Depending on the timing, we're either a cork in the bottle or an afterthought. No way of knowing until he detected the Shaallit ships or received word he was too late. *I still don't know what I'm facing.* He submerged himself deeper into the task force TacNet, doing his own mining for data. *The tickle won't go away.* The ships were dispersed closely enough to allow a completely integrated network, permitting him to enter the nets of other ships. He looked over the shoulder of one of the Raptor directors aboard *Tyler River. About a quarter light-second delay.* He listened to the clipped tones of the AIs responding to the director's commands and queries. *I was born fifty years too early. Oh, to enjoy the freedom of the Raptors roaming across an entire star system. Or almost as good, to be captain of one of those new frigates.* He became a naval officer to command warships in battle. Instead, here he sat, an almost useless bystander, kibitzing when he gets the opportunity. *To be back in the captain's chair...*

Johnson interrupted his thoughts. "Admiral, we've received a general broadcast from the ISDC corvette *Takanami.* Her IFF code is old but definitely Imperium, Sentai Haramaki. The outlier connectors still work. She claims she's trailing a Shaallit fleet of three hundred ships about ten light-seconds out. Message includes their last course. The Shaallit went stealth when we jumped in and she lost them."

Ten light-seconds, about three million miles. We made it by an electron's hair. "Jake, what are the chances this is legitimate and not a Shaallit ruse?" he asked.

Johnson didn't answer for a moment. "Admiral, as I said, the code outliers work, though the code is old. The way contact's been between the Imperium and the ISDF, I wouldn't expect the Sentai to have the latest codes. Maybe the Shaallit got their hands on the code and are using it as a ruse, but I don't think so. *Takanami* probably had to do a wide broadcast rather than tight beam because she can't detect us either at that distance with us in stealth."

Niki nodded. "I think you're right. Let's go on the assumption right now it's legitimate and not let this opportunity go to waste. Have a couple of Raptors check that area out. Maybe we caught a break and maybe the new TA-22As will be good enough to pick up our Shaallit friends now that we know approximately where they are. If not we may have to risk a couple of radar pings. Let's keep the task force at GQ. I realize it's uncomfortable. I just don't know who's hiding out there. However, let's get the crew fed. Rotate the crew, leaving most of the crew in their cocoons and giving a twenty-minute break to a fifth of the crew."

Johnson's avatar nodded, "I'll pass the word."

Johnson's avatar blinked out, leaving Niki alone in his cocoon with the quiet whisperings of the air circulator. *Am I crazy? Three hundred ships. And I have a hundred and ten battleships. Have I lost my fuckin' mind? These aren't Goths with their toy cruisers. These are Shaallit with technology comparable or superior to the Imperium's. Will the New Meyerian technology make up the difference? Do we have enough of it to make an impact?* The tech had been extremely successful in the three instances it had been used, but that was against rogue Imperium ships and Goths. *What is the capability of these Shaallit ships?* The fact that they got past the Sentai didn't bode well, unless by sheer numbers. *God, if so, how many ships did they start with?*

He closed his eyes. *It's a good day to die.* The phrase popped into his thoughts. He didn't identify the phrase immediately. Then he grew angry with himself. *I prefer the quote attributed to ancient General Patton. "No bastard ever won a war by dying for his country. He won it by making the other poor dumb bastard die for his country." More to my taste. Or just more of my public persona? The tough old bastard I love to play. Am I not allowed to feel fear? About an hour or so to go before we engage. If we wait for them, then about three hours.*

"Admiral, another message from *Takanami*. Message is real short. My guess is she's worried about being detected. She says there's an ISDF Task Force about three days behind in pursuit. No details on its size or make up. So far nothing showing up on our arrays which means they're running in stealth, too."

Too far away to do any good. "Very well," Niki replied.

"Admiral! Breakout behind us! Task force squawking New Imperium!"

Fuck! What now? Did Swann sell out to the Shaallit?

The GQ alarm reverberated through the ship. *Not much of a break for the crew,* He opened a window to the *Dreadnaught's* detection station and looked over the tech's shoulder. The displays just cleared from the jump radiation. *Fifty-seven ships with twenty-five battleships.* He looked at his own ships' disposition, searching for the right vessel to challenge the incoming fleet.

"Have *Fennel* challenge them," Niki ordered.

Fennel was an old *Flower*-class corvette, a class of small escorts. Even smaller than the *Hawk*-class, their namesakes served as a mainstay of the Battle of the Atlantic back in twentieth-century Earth. *Another nostalgic Emperor.* Six of them monitored the jump point. He viewed them as expendable and detached far enough away to minimize the risk of revealing the task force's location. Their crews knew they were expendable and yet they still volunteered.

He fretted as he waited to hear whether he had another hostile force to deal with. *Fennel* was too far away and too technologically obsolete to be included in the task force's Net. He fidgeted, hiding behind his mask of being the unflappable Admiral. *I've learned to hide my impatience from the outside world.*

Two minutes later an image of a youngish, dark-haired man materialized. "I'm Rear Admiral Avram Chen of what you call the OWA and what we call the New Imperium." Then his eyes widened with recognition. "Admiral Kamarov! We heard you're alive."

A quick perusal of data files through his implant brought up images of a young, dashing commander at some obscure function on an outer world about fifteen years ago. He had pegged him to be a future Flag officer at the time. *I guess I haven't lost my touch in judging talent.*

He resisted the cliché concerning rumors of his death. He decided to be blunt. "So, Admiral Chen, what are you doing here?"

"Defending the Imperium, by whatever name the politicians call it. We can't allow the Shaallit to run free in Imperium space."

I wish I believed that. "You have orders to support me?"

"No, Admiral, no orders. I'm an Imperium officer and no one needs to tell me what my duty is. New Imperium, Imperium, whatever name, Shaallit are an enemy of our race."

Niki sat back in his padded seat, allowing the nanos to massage his aching muscles. *If Chen had indicated Swann had ordered him then I'd be suspicious. This is Chen acting on his own, responding to his oath as an Imperium officer.*

Chen's tone convinced him. He viewed himself an Imperium officer and recognized his duty. *There are still officers left of this caliber in the Imperium Navy. Maybe the Imperium by whatever name we end up calling it has a chance with men such as this.* "Very well, Admiral Chen, welcome to the party. Jake, find a place in the formation for Admiral Chen's task force."

"Contact! Abby Raptor from *Northfork River*. Large fleet exactly where *Takanami* said they'd be."

"OK, now we know. Jake! Let's go kick some Shaallit butt!"

Battleship Dreadnaught, Star System Tsang's Delight
15 March 686 IP

Niki viewed the closing fleet with an almost detached sense of unfurling events. Shaallit stealth appeared roughly equivalent to Imperium levels, not anywhere as good as New Meyer's Manta. He scrutinized the numbers as the Raptors and the task force's Twenty-Twos formed a detailed picture of the on-rushing Shaallit fleet. *Takanami's data is wrong.* The Shaallit fleet numbered closer to four hundred and fifty ships, with more than two hundred fifty battleships, each easily matching their Imperium equivalent in firepower and armor.

As the picture formed from the incoming data a more ominous scenario emerged. The Shaallit battleships at the core were something he'd never seen before. They massed fifty percent more than the *Moscow-class* making up the majority of his heavy warships and about forty-per cent more than his five *Dreadnaught*-class ships. Much of their mass seemed to be in armor. *I wonder how effective the New Meyerian Stingers will be.*

Thirty Raptors launched their Stingers against the outer ring of smaller battleships. Even at this distance he observed the Shaallit area and point defense weapons respond as bright pinpoints of ruby light detected by the Task Force's arrays. About a third of the Stingers made it through. Now familiar blossoms of nuclear fire indicated the Stinger warheads detonating. EFP projectiles were invisible at this range. However, their impact with Shaallit armor appeared as smaller gas plumes, glowing like a dying red dwarf star. Forty battleships died as another twenty spun away out of control or unable to keep up.

That opened a gap into which his thirty remaining Raptors plunged, their Manta and ECW systems working hard to scramble Shaallit radar. Niki viewed Manta's effectiveness via updates received from the Raptors through their controllers on the frigates and cruisers controlling them. Three Raptors died before launching. Small pinpoints of light indicated Stingers dying as the Shaallit defenses worked. Seventy-five Imperium missiles struck forty-eight of the Behemoths, the new nickname for the giant Shaallit battleships flowing across the TacNet. *Not nearly enough Stingers.* As the tactical screen cleared from the aftermath of the attack he counted ten of the Shaallit Behemoths destroyed and twenty more veering off. *Shit! Not enough.* The New Meyerian technology had proved less effective against the Shaallit than against Imperium and Goth ships. *If I had more Raptors I could have evened the odds. Maybe their Venoms might be more effective. Damn you, Michael, and your stubbornness. We needed all that technology.*

The Shaallit task force rolled on and struck the Imperium formation.

Battleship Dreadnaught, Star System Tsang's Delight
16 March 686 IP

The fog from the fire suppressant sprays dissipated slowly, allowing Niki a clearer view of *Dreadnaught's* flag conn. Medical teams toiled to remove the few living casualties and numerous remaining bodies. Damage control personnel in their bulky armored spacesuits struggled to restore control over many of the ship's systems. Surviving flag conn crew remained in their cocoons, also working to restore tactical operations. Sporadic data from TacNet made control difficult. Niki checked *Dreadnaught's* condition. A direct hit on ship conn by a Shaallit kinetic weapon also caused the havoc on the flag conn. *Dreadnaught* was being conned from the backup, some thirty meters away aft.

Niki shook his head to clear the fuzziness, ridding himself of the aftereffects of the shocks to his body in the past half hour. The great battleship had been pummeled by overwhelming numbers of Shaallit battleships flowing past toward the jump point. He had discovered three of his battleships were required to kill one of those Behemoths. *Numbers I can't afford being so outnumbered.* The Imperium task force strap-on missiles had come as a surprise to the Shaallit and accounted for another twenty-five of the Behemoths. *Still, it's like trying to stop the tide at a beach using wire mesh.*

He sighed and re-opened his TacNet window that had faded to black a moment before. The delay in opening reflected the overall damage to *Dreadnaught's* systems. The ship's AI struggled to provide him concise data with many of its sources damaged or destroyed. *Not pretty.* However, *Dreadnaught* was still capable of fighting. Her strap-on missile tubes were expended but two of her 300mm blast rifle turrets were still operational. She now stood toe-to toe pounding it out with two of the smaller Shaallit battleships in far worse condition than she was.

Most of his battleships appeared on TacNet as shattered hulks tumbling through space for eternity. A much larger number of smashed Shaallit hulls were also visible. He had placed his ships in their path and the Shaallit ships had simply rolled over his by their sheer numbers.

Even the vaunted New Meyerian technology couldn't stop the onrushing Shaallit force. *I didn't have enough. Another twenty frigates and we could have stopped them.* Shaallit technology and ship design seemed superior to Imperium technology in detecting stealthed New Meyerian ships and their deadly missiles. Still, the New Meyerian ships gave a good account of themselves and their marvelous AIs had adapted to the Shaallit capabilities. The Raptors learned to devote more missiles to each Shaallit warship and to use their stealth and decoys more effectively. They had made the Shaallit pay dearly.

I need a cup of tea. An image of the electric samovar always percolating while he was on the bridge competed with the open e-windows for his attention. He sighed. *I can't get tea while I'm in the GQ cocoon. Besides the samovar's no longer there.* The image morphed into a shattered urn spattered across the deck by the kinetic weapon that had taken out the conn. *I had that samovar for almost thirty years.* He sighed again and pushed all those images away.

He turned his attention to the screen showing Chen moving the remainder of his battleship force to intercept a Shaallit force of over sixty ships making a break for the jump point. Niki had no idea how many Shaallit ships had already jumped. He winced at the count. Chen only had twelve undamaged battleships left and four others in some semblance of fighting condition. Three Raptors, the last still with missiles, and acting on their own, moved in to aid the New Imperium admiral. *Too little too late. Well, those green-skinned bastards are not going to get through untouched.*

He reviewed his message to the Duke of New Meyer he had sent earlier. Those Shaallit were not headed for Longhorn. Their exit vectors in their jumps out of system pointed at the next star system on the way to New Meyer. The message using lascoms to cross star systems and pre-placed message torps for the jumps would beat the Shaallit force by two or three weeks. "Your Grace," Kamarov's message said, "the Shaallit have excellent point and area defensive weapons on their large warships that can be effective against the Stingers. They also have a new class of battleship out-massing even *Dreadnaught* by thirty percent or more. They have escorts dedicated to missile defense. They also use large multi-frequency phase radars in a network that, while it can't completely break down your newest stealth, it does a damn good job on standard Imperium stealth. Our Raptors and Stingers are just not as effective against the Shaallit as they were against Goth or other Imp forces. Our one big advantage is your new stealth. The Raptors are not as effective as we needed. We ended up expending most of our Stingers, taking out over one hundred battleships but not enough of the Behemoths. It then came down to an old-fashioned knock-down battle between big guns. They had more guns than we did. Again, your new stealth came in handy and helped even the odds.

"There were more than four hundred ships in the Shaallit force. We just couldn't stop them all. I'm afraid you're going to have to deal with what gets past us. Right now we're in survival mode to see what ships we can resurrect to hold off the remaining Shaallit ships, some of which are in as bad shape as we are." He knew the last was a white lie as his implant highlighted a brand spanking new, untouched Shaallit Behemoth engaging *Dreadnaught. I guess it is as good a day as any to die. Still, I made a lot of those Shaallit bastards pay with their lives for their Emperor-Protector.* "May God Speed, Your Grace. Long live the Imperium." Then his world exploded.

CHAPTER 47

Longhorn System, Emperor's Palace
26 April 686 IP

THE EMPRESS DONNA ARIEL LANDSMAN considered the gathered members of her husband's Privy Council. *Excalibur* with Michael aboard was in system but still two weeks away. She had exchanged messages with Michael about the incursion. Lightspeed time lag made it impossible for him to participate in the meeting. Still no conclusive word on the Battle of Tsang's Delight. *Notification taking so long means bad news.*

She had become more comfortable sitting at the head of the Privy Council these past weeks with Michael out-system. She found the military less alien due to recent training in military matters by Shiro back on New Meyer. Since arriving on Longhorn, Kamarov and his deputy, Kevin Cervantes, had provided instruction. The military download to her implant when she became Duchess had been a shock at first because she had no prior military training. The conflict between the military and her medical training required assimilation over time. She grew to both hate and love the tactical simulators as part of her training.

They forced her to reconcile her new military knowledge with her older medical and physician temperament. She found it painful at first. *I'm a healer not a warrior. I had to get past that. I came to understand the methods I use to cure a disease are not so different from leading ships into battle.* Both required life and death decisions. The preparation enabled her to assume her role of Empress as a ruler and not just a First Lady in the old Earth USA sense. *I wonder if Claudia is doing as well with this stuff as I am.*

She turned to Kevin Cervantes, Vice Star Admiral, who was sitting in for Niki. "So no word yet from Admiral Kamarov?" she asked. *Stupid question. They will tell me as soon as word arrives.*

"Only tidbits, Your Majesty. Nothing firm other than we know Star Admiral Kamarov fought a major engagement."

She turned to the Countess with a raised eyebrow. The Intelligence Chief replied with a shake of her head, "Nothing to add, Your Majesty. Sir Cervantes would have better info on this than I would."

Something in the Countess' tone caught her attention, "Ok, Countess, I can see you want to add something."

The Countess gave a slight shrug. "We've been getting reports about some stirrings in the New Imperium and in other areas of Goth controlled territories. Nothing firm, just whisperings of fleet gatherings and pending actions." She paused, her eyes narrowing as if she were in thought. "I wouldn't worry about it. We get these all the time." Her voice sounded strangely thoughtful.

Donna caught a momentary look of puzzlement on Cervantes' face. *He's surprised the Countess blew off the warnings. I must admit this is not like her.* She smiled to herself. *Perhaps the rumors of her having an affair are true. She seems less high-strung and more relaxed. I wish I knew the identity of her lover.* She had to suppress a giggle. *I certainly can't ask Imperium Intelligence to find out who it is, can I?* She considered for a moment. *I'll ask Gregory if he's heard something. He's wormed his way into the upper levels of government here. Not bad for an outworlder.*

"We've put all forces in the Imperium on alert," she said. "Any other recommendations?"

"None, Your Majesty," the Countess replied. "As I said, probably nothing to worry about."

She glanced at Emil. "Your thoughts?"

Emil replied in a quiet voice, "I think you're doing everything you can. All Planetary Guard forces are on alert. Reserve units are being activated. I don't think you can do much else, Your Majesty, without panicking the population and running the risk of crying wolf."

She received similar affirmative responses from Al-Haidar and the newly appointed Minister of Defense, Phillip Stirling.

She sat back and took a deep breath before continuing. "I'd like to think we can do more, but we're doing what we can. The Emperor and I agree with your assessments. I ask you to remain alert and keep pushing your people. I believe the shit is going to hit the proverbial fan and the future of the Imperium may be decided soon. Just the gut instinct of someone new to Imperium affairs."

"Sometimes gut feelings are all we have to go with, Your Majesty," Cervantes said. "That's why we have people and not AIs running the government."

Donna smiled, "Thanks, Kevin, I really hope I'm wrong."

"So do we all," Emil grumbled.

CHAPTER 48

———◆———

"Your Majesty, if you please."

Michael opened his eyes and glanced at his implant chronometer. *Well, at least I got two hours sleep.* They had arrived back in Longhorn system six hours ago. He had given the crew a few hours stand down before resuming the journey to Longhorn.

Garrett's image floated in front of his eyes. "Another incursion, Your Majesty. LC-82. Approximately two hundred Goths."

Michael pulled up the system from the ShipNet database. *Longhorn Chute System 82, a small uninhabited star system. They couldn't have picked a worse place for us. A small red dwarf with no planets and jump points thirty million kilometers apart. Only forty-four or so hours to cross that system.* The external jump point led to a chute that connected to a chute with no major populated star systems and not in any direct trade route path. *Just used by tramp freighters to a few mining worlds further on.*

"It gets worse, Your Majesty. The Goths jumped into LC-82 more than thirty-eight hours ago."

"What? And we're getting the word now?"

"It's sketchy. Our best guess is the Goths jumped a Q-ship into the system first, disguised as a tramp freighter. She took out the corvette *Green Pieohawk*, the only warship we have on station there. We received this warning because one of our new *Whitman* freighters happened to jump into LC-82. She survived long enough to get the message out."

"Shit. We only have a few hours before they've crossed the system." *Damn. LC-82 was slated to get a covering force in a couple of months. I warned the Senate.* From LC-82, the Goths could jump into any system in the chute including Longhorn itself. *Can I allow local star system forces to deal with the incursion? I stripped the regular Navy units to support our attack on the new Imperium. Except for TF-1 I only have Planetary Guard units remaining.*

He messaged Vice Admiral Miguel Zavala, commander of the Planetary Guard at Jump Point One. Zavala was aboard the battleship *Sam Houston*, the traditional flagship of the Longhorn planetary guard. She was an older well-kept, all-big-gun ship that had been upgraded with New Meyerian stealth. The Longhorn Planetary Guard consisted of one hundred and fifty battleships. Unfortunately fifty were on-guard at the other jump point, and were, therefore, a month away. *Fifty at this jump point. Fifty around Longhorn as a reaction force two weeks away.* Only six of the fifty here had temporary Stinger strap-ons while the rest were typical all-big-gun battleships. *Fifty battleships plus TF-1 against two hundred Goths. Not bad odds. It's the smaller worlds I'm worried about.*

"Miguel, I'm going to jump into Eighty-Two with TF-1."

Zavala's face darkened. "Your Majesty, if I may?" Michael nodded. "I believe that's inadvisable. The risk to you is too high. All the inhabited systems in the LC chute have significant forces. We can send a reaction force to whatever system the Goths jump into. That way we can combine forces to counter the incursion."

"That's not entirely true. You're only talking about the Tier One and Two worlds. There are twenty-five Threes and Fours not nearly as fortified." *And your attitude is typical of many of the Heart Worlders – only the Ones and Twos are of any concern.* "Miguel, this is not open for discussion. You will provide me with ten big gunners as support. We'll depart in two hours."

Zavala's squarish face was impassive though Michael sensed the disapproval in his brown eyes. "Yes, Your Majesty," Zavala replied. "By your leave."

He pulsed Garrett through his implant. The Flag Captain had opened his mouth to say something. Michael held up his hand. "Don't you start with me. I gave you your orders. We depart in two hours."

Four hours later and they still weren't ready. "This is unacceptable, Admiral," Michael said, using Zavala's rank to express his disapproval. "What is taking so long?"

Zavala looked pained. "Some of their officers were on other ships visiting or conducting business. We also topped off hydrogen."

"Topped off hydrogen?" Michael exploded. "We're jumping and I don't expect much maneuvering. We need to get through that jump point before the Goths get there."

Zavala recoiled. "Many of the ships are below seventy percent. Some below fifty."

Unbelievable. "Your ships here on alert allowed themselves to drop below fifty percent, or even seventy percent? That violates regs older than both of us combined."

"You must understand, Your Majesty, until recently, we were only a reserve force. They only became the primary defense force when you pulled the forces to join Admiral Kamarov. They're not fully adjusted to their new role."

They became the primary force months ago. Not enough time to adjust? Michael calmed himself, suppressing the impulse to fire him on the spot. "We'll discuss this later. I want you to light a fire under those ten Captains. I want those ships in line in fifteen minutes. I don't care how much hydrogen is in their tanks. And I don't care if they're crewed by midshipmen. We leave in fifteen minutes. Understood?"

"Yes, Your Majesty," Zavala replied stonily.

Did he drag his feet on purpose? Task Force One was ready in less than an hour, but I need the big gun support. I held our departure until the Planetary Guard ships were ready. I'm going to fire Zavala's ass when I get back and find someone who can turn these Planetary Guard buffoons into real Navy. He frowned. *If I get back.*

Fifteen minutes later on *Excalibur's* flag conn, he watched the last of the ten arriving battleships maneuver into formation. *What are we jumping into? I should have sent another scout ahead. There's none for it.* "All right, let's jump," he ordered.

The GQ klaxon blared as they readied for the jump. *No use taking chances.*

Cruiser *Excalibur*, LC-82 System
26 April 686 IP

They materialized into a fleet commander's worst nightmare.

Kinetic projectiles and blast cannon beams slammed into the lead ships within one minute of emergence. All of the task force's battleships and cruisers took fire. Even *Excalibur*, screened by four battleships, was under attack. Alarms screamed their warning through Michael's implant, momentarily deafening him. AI's desperately responded with point defense fire. Michael found himself powerless to do anything. The attack happened so quickly only the AIs reacted fast enough, determining it was too late to use decoys and jammers. Radar guided tri-barrel point defense lasers firing eight hundred pulses per second opened up on the incoming projectiles. Despite the short response time, they performed creditably intercepting the incoming projectiles.

Excalibur shuddered and bucked like a dying horse as she took four hits immediately, her thin cruiser armor offering only marginal resistance to the nanohardened submunitions. Four more hits followed. The submunitions sensed the soft target and went into alternate mode. Once inside a ship's compartment a fuze triggered the explosive charge, sending razor sharp shards in all directions. Some of them reacted with the compartment's atmosphere to flare into super-hot flame. No one inside a penetrated compartment could survive, not even inside their cocoons.

The Goths made only one mistake by following their doctrine of attacking the task force's larger ships and virtually ignoring the escorts, in this case the New Meyerian frigates. Thus, the ten Planetary Guard battleships served a purpose. They became cannon fodder, drawing fire away from the smaller Raptor-capable ships. All six frigates at the first alarm launched their Raptors. Standard policy required them to be ready for launch after a jump, just for reasons like this. Once their Raptors were released, all the EM rotary launchers began flinging Stingers at the Goth ships. By the time the frigates began to receive some attention from the Goth cruisers all of their missiles were en route. The Raptors had also launched, acting on their own as the frigates began dying.

The Goths simply had no adequate defenses against the stealthed missile onslaught and they died.

Michael sensed the Raptors launching their missiles through the still operating TacNet. *Good...* He never finished the thought as a kinetic projectile penetrated the flag conn and exploded two meters from his cocoon.

CHAPTER 49

———◆———

Dreadnaught Chisholm's Trail, Deep Space, Longhorn System
24 May 686 IP

THE SHIP BEARING THE SHATTERED body of Emperor
Michael VI emerged from the jump point precisely
on time. The response across the Longhorn System
required preciseness because all the planned events were
tied to *Excalibur's* expected arrival. Einstein's light speed
limitations made a simultaneous reaction impossible. On
board the ships of the Planetary Guard, bosun's whistles
rang out with "Head of State Arriving." On Longhorn itself,
alert sirens wailed and the P-Net displayed the Emperor's
image for two minutes of silence.

The new Empress Regent Donna Ariel Ben-Levi
Landsman stood at attention along with the crew of
her newly designated flagship until the completion of a
muted rendition of "Hail to the Emperor." She struggled
to maintain a stoic visage for the outside world despite
the tears welling up in her eyes. *I'm not going to yield to
the grief.* With sheer force of will she squashed any visible
tremor. *I'm Empress now by Michael's will and I'm not going
to give any of the Senate and P-Net naysayers the slightest*

opening. The reactions of some Senators and P-Net bloggers pissed her off. After a thousand years of Humans in space a sizable conservative minority on Longhorn still believed women should not be permitted to serve as Emperor. They actually claimed a woman's emotions and hormones rendered them incapable. *I thought the Neanderthals had died out fifty thousand years ago.*

One group of bloggers, including eight senators, called for Mitch to become Emperor as the next Landsman in line. Michael's will expressly forbade Mitch becoming Emperor. According to the will, stated in no uncertain terms, she was to serve as Empress Regent until her son reached the traditional age of thirty. *Some idiot Senators even wanted to make the Earl of Newberry, Michael's uncle, Regent.* She snorted to herself. *They seemed to think any man was better than a woman. Fools. They'd deserve what they'd get.*

The smashed hulk of the *Excalibur* began its slow passage down the system's gravity well, lumbering at a half gee towed by two tethered tugs. *Chisholm's Trail,* now the Empress' flagship, trailed behind, followed by the other survivors of the battle. She settled herself in her flag chair for the long journey, sipping a cup of hot cocoa provided by the ship's Chief Steward, Gerald Newcombe. The cocoa's sweet fragrance wafting from her favorite mug seemed a bit dull today. She drank mechanically, something to do, something to fill the time. The Imperium had lost its Emperor but she lost her husband, her lover, her soulmate, and the father of her child. She found little opportunity to mourn. The affairs of state didn't permit it.

I can't spend the whole three-week trip to Longhorn in this chair. At some time I'll have to go to my cabin. When I do, I'll lose it and have a breakdown. That's okay. I must let the emotions out sometime. I need to finish mourning. But can I regain control? If she didn't then she'd be the weak-willed woman portrayed by her political opponents.

To make matters more difficult, she lacked a real support structure for the journey to Longhorn. *My real support is back on New Meyer.*

"Your Majesty," Cervantes whispered through his implant, his voice soft and sympathetic in tone, "you really should go to your cabin. If I may be so blunt, no one will think less of you for it." She had designated him the new Star Admiral.

Tears welled up as she struggled for control. She forced them back by sheer will. "Thank you, Kevin, I will. Just not right now. I still have work to do."

Her implant beeped and the image of Flag Communications Officer Lieutenant Sofia Morales-Jones materialized.

"Yes, Sofia?" she asked, leaving the link to Cervantes open.

"In-coming message, Your Majesty."

"Lieutenant, I thought I left orders not to disturb Her Majesty," Cervantes snapped.

"Yes, Admiral, you did. In my judgment she needs to take this one. It's from Admiral Swann."

"Okay, Kevin, I'll take it," she replied, the firmness of her voice masking her pain and despair.

Swann's image materialized. Donna left the link open to allow Cervantes to view the message. The background data to the left of the open window indicated the message had arrived through LC-82, relayed by one of the Imperium's pickets in the system.

Donna studied Swann's image, a stocky man with a swarthy complexion darker than the Imperium bronze norm. His brown eyes glowed with an intensity reminding her of Michael. The rest of his features were nondescript as if they had been sculpted from the statistics describing the Imperium norm.

He spoke in a deep bass voice, "Your Grace, my apologies for interrupting your grief with the affairs of state. First, let me offer my condolences on the loss of your husband. We may have had our differences about who is truly Emperor. However I respected him and the work he accomplished in strengthening your part of the Imperium. Second, I assure you I had nothing to do with the Goth and Shaallit incursions. You must be aware that my force was headed your way. Please be assured we tried to intercept the Goth force before it penetrated your so-called Heart Worlds. As your scouts will have certainly informed you, my force is heading back to our New Imperium capital. I believe my intentions to defend the Imperium were made clear by Admiral Chen's actions at Tsang's Delight. I will allow you time to mourn and then we need to meet. With your husband dead, I think you understand the benefits of reuniting the Imperium. Again, my condolences, Your Grace."

Donna had turned a bright red and issued a series of expletives that even the saltiest of *Chisholm's* marines would have had difficulty duplicating. Cervantes let her rant, sitting impassively, only a slight blush indicating his reaction to her vehement explosion. Finally she calmed herself. "That sanctimonious son of a bitch," she spat. She focused on Cervantes. "How can we know whether what he said about trying to head off the incursion is true, or whether his force was a follow-up to take advantage?" She stopped and her eyes narrowed. "Maybe what our frigates did to the Goths gave him second thoughts."

Cervantes still didn't say anything, apparently intent on letting her anger run its course. She continued, "The reference to Chen. Niki's last message made it clear that Chen was acting on his own. Suddenly, Admiral Swann is the great protector of the Imperium.

"And to address me as Your Grace and imply that with Michael dead I would be more willing to acknowledge him as Emperor." She stared at Cervantes. "Now you appreciate why I can't let go right now. I'm going to take that bastard down, cut off his balls, and feed them to him." Her demeanor changed as she took a deep breath. She continued with deadly calm, "Admiral, we have work to do. We can use this trip back to Longhorn to plan our response." She paused again and sighed. "However, you're right, too. I need to get some sleep." She glanced at the time at the bottom of the open window. "Staff meeting at 1000 hours tomorrow. I want a status summary and recommendations. Good night, Kevin." she said, switching her implant off.

She stood up and exited the bridge. *I can't even talk to Greg with this damn com lag. I can use a friend and some light conversation. He's been such a help. I'll look him up when we get back.*

Deputy Star Admiral Sir Kevin Cervantes exhaled visibly as the e-window closed. He sat back and glanced around at the *Chisolm's* spacious flag conn. Her tirade had been implant to implant and had not been witnessed by anyone else on the bridge. What did her eruption tell him about her? *The venting concerned more than just the Swann message.* He couldn't imagine what she had been through. Uprooted from her home on New Meyer, dragged here to Longhorn, and immediately immersed into the frustration of court politics as her husband became Emperor. Then she loses her husband and suddenly finds herself Empress of an empire in mortal danger of collapsing. Many at the court considered her a frontier rube who had no business being in charge.

He gave a mental shake. *No, she's no more a frontier rube than her husband had been. T*he two of them had revitalized Longhorn, kicked it off its lethargic ass, and generated some sense of urgency, and, more importantly, hope. *So the question is, could she carry on in her husband's place?*

He forgave the outburst. *Her way of regaining control as witnessed by the way she shut it off at the end.* The more he reviewed her actions since her arrival on Longhorn, the more he regarded her as a strong leader, well suited for the job. *Yes, she will do fine,*

No one on the busy bridge heard Cervantes mutter, "The Imperium is in good hands. We may survive this yet."

CHAPTER 50

THE HIGH PRIESTESS OF NEARYAHN stared at her Adept husband with rising anger. "I gave you simple orders. You had more than adequate forces and yet you failed. Longhorn still stands and I'm not hopeful we'll be successful in taking down New Meyer."

This time he didn't cringe. She hadn't filled the room with her pheromones to muddle his thinking. She wanted him in condition to talk and reason. He returned her gaze with a bit of defiance. "We followed the plan, Goddess. We still don't know what happened. Somehow, some of the ships in the Emperor's squadron survived the ambush and none of our ships did. Makes no sense. The cruiser left at the jump point to monitor the battle and report back in case of a defeat provided little insight. She detected vast amounts of radiation at the site of the battle, more than could be accounted for by normal spaceship-to-spaceship engagements, but offered no explanation. Our techs are still studying the data but hold little chance of discovering what actually happened." He brightened. "On the other hand, we did kill the Emperor and Kamarov. This could turn out to be a mortal blow to the Imperium."

She sighed. *He's right. Something is going on that we don't understand. New weapons? A secret source of ships?* "You're right, husband," she replied more amicably. "I'm being unfair. Maybe we didn't gain all of our objectives but we did kill the two leaders who revitalized the Imperium. Without Emperor Michael, the Imperium will lack direction. The loss of Kamarov for real this time beheads their Navy. They lost their best military mind and a symbol.

"As for New Meyer, maybe the pending attack will be successful. Our sources tell us their navy is still quite small. We'll see how that goes. Meantime, Husband, you must rebuild your forces. We lost too many ships and are at risk from our own internal issues, no less the Imperium. In case we don't succeed, I set other plans in motion. This time, they're more sneaky and subtle." She paused and grinned at the thought. *I've heard Humans say the direct approach is not always the best.* "Other paths can lead to victory. The Empress will be more vulnerable to Gregory now. He will soon be in a position to insert a splinter and then she will be ours. Having both the Empress Regent of the Imperium and the Protector of the New Imperium under our control will certainly put us in a position to reach our goals." *I will at some point enjoy the Empress as a tasty morsel and Gregory will become Emperor of what's left of the Imperium. Then I'll find a Human female to inhabit and become Empress. Sorry, Husband. Business is business. I'll find you some cute female priestess to replace me.* She sighed. *Even then these Humans won't succumb easily. But in the end they will be our feed cattle.*

COMING SOON

LIBERTY'S CHOICES

New Landsman City, New Meyer
12 June 685 IP

A SMALL PART OF THE BILLION-YEAR-OLD being, referred to as One by his fellow Passimians, materialized in the empty, dimly lit alley between two buildings in New Landsman City. Reality washed over him, a torrent of contradictions of vibrations, ambiances, and perceptions. An icy cold wind sliced through his light outer garment and a mixture of snow and ice assaulted his face. For a moment, he stood rooted, resisting the assault from the material nature of becoming a corporeal being. He found the feelings both exhilarating and overwhelming at the same time. He wondered if the Passimians had given up too much with the Discorporation.

He closed the brown eyes of his human form, shutting out much of the extraneous input. His outer garment changed to a long, heavy parka. A knit ski cap materialized on his head. The cold receded. He squashed many of the sensations and impulse by sheer will and regained his composure. He glanced down at the broken pavement. A thin layer of snow covered the ground. He elected not to worry about boots.

He studied his location on the timeline and grinned. *I guess we Passimians aren't as omnipotent as we'd like to think. In Human terms I missed my target by three hundred meters and four hours.* His Human persona of Dr. Jamian Loregos, supposedly a former Professor of Bioelectronic Integration at the University of New Largos hefted his backpack, picked up his battered brown suitcase, and walked out into the bustle of New Landsman City. He used the new Portal attached to his implant to block out the assault of advertising from the various establishments he passed. The entrance to his destination, a medium-rate hotel in the city's immigrant district, glowed in a garish orange of LED and holographic images at the end of the block.

To anyone checking, the spaceport and customs computers recorded Dr. Loregos arriving on a refugee ship some six hours earlier. All of his required data was in order. Imperium records showed he had been recruited by the New Meyerian Intelligence Service to migrate to New Meyer. TSP work schedules showed him starting a new job tomorrow in the Implant Research Section at the TSP Plant #1.

He sighed. If things went according to plan, he would have access to the people he needed without manipulating too many minds. He hated taking advantage of these Lesser Races, but sometimes he faced little choice. Tomorrow afternoon he had simultaneous meetings with his three targets, requiring him to assume three Human personae at the same time. A challenge for even a Passimian but one he could meet with only modest effort on his part. His Dr. Loregos persona was scheduled to meet with Carol Landsman, target number one. *I'll ensure Dr. Loregos is given some distant, remote assignment so if I need to return my presence will not have been missed here when I return to my own existence. I will have done what I could for the Humans. What they make of it is up to them.*

After the brief formality of using his Human implant to register and pay, he dropped his bags in his room and relaxed on the bed, his eyes closed. He reached out with his mind and found the first implant of interest. He followed the bioelectronic pathways to the core programming. He expended only a little effort to change reality. This allowed the extra programming to appear in the subject implant. The software updates proved easier than the additional neural connections to the brain. *Humans are more complex than we Passimians arrogantly believe.* He moved to the next implant of interest. The targeted three implant modifications in place, he moved on to the first selected AI. He found this a much easier task as he only inserted some false data into its memory. When he finished with the AIs, he found the other Humans whose perception of reality he needed to alter to allow his plan to move forward without interference from other Humans. He was ready.

He rose from his bed and left the room. Outside in the corridor, he turned the corner and transported across eleven hours and eight miles. He materialized in an elevator at TSP headquarters arriving on the floor containing Carol Landsman's office. The guards downstairs remembered reviewing his identity, as did the plant's AI. The elevator's mini-video also had records of him entering on the main floor. *If Humans guessed at my true capabilities they would consider me a God. I can't allow that.*

Carol's live administrative assistant, Julia Puentes, smiled at him as he exited the elevator. "Go right in, Dr. Loregos, Ms. Landsman is expecting you." Carol had insisted that peerage ranks not be used while at work.

Julia never considered how this man had arrived without a coat or hat in this weather. She ignored that he showed no sign of the heavy snow falling outside. To her, all appeared fine as she pulsed the Office-Net to open the door to her boss's office.

Carol stood and greeted him. "Please take a seat, Doctor." She studied him with frank curiousity.

Loregos smiled at her and sat. "Ms. Landsman, do you greet all new TSP employees?"

"No. Only those at a senior level or with a special talent."

"Of which neither apply to me. Then why are you seeing me?"

Her eyes furrowed at the thought. "My implant's AI informed me of the meeting," she replied, appearing puzzled.

"Was it on your calendar when you checked three minutes ago?" He contacted the O-Net AI and blocked all monitoring equipment in the office. He wanted no record of this.

Carol's eyes narrowed before widening in surprise. She jumped up. "Who are you? How in the hell did you get in here?" She tried to call security but found she couldn't trigger her implant or even move. Against her will she sat back down.

"Carol, I'm going to call you by your given name to keep things more personal. I arrived on your world a few hours ago. I'm not human nor even a corporeal being. I took this form to make it easier on you. My true appearance is something you don't need to worry about, and is not your concern. What is your concern is why I'm here. You also sense everything I'm telling you is true. I'm not using some sort of mind control to force you. Instead, you sense the truth of what I'm saying. In fact, didn't you sense the falsity of your employee, Ratzger I think his name was, even though you had no reason to do so? You just knew his intentions were dishonest, didn't you?"

Carol nodded, her eyes wide. He continued, "You sensed his emotions directly, not realizing at that moment what you were doing. I modified your implant while you were sleeping last night to enable this new capability." He held up his hands as she tried to rise again. "Use this new sense of yours. You know I'm telling the truth, don't you?"

She nodded, sitting back down. She took a deep breath. "Ok, who are you and what do you want?"

"I represent a race a billion years older than yours and far ahead of you Humans. We typically don't pay much attention to the affairs of what we call the Lesser Races, preferring to let nature take its course. However, we've identified a number of races, among them Humans, with potential to grow beyond their current capabilities and physical existence. As the youngest of my race I'm assigned to keep an eye on them. During my studies I uncovered a threat to the existence of your race requiring our intervention. I'm here to give you tools to protect yourself from this danger."

Carol sat back on the couch. "I somehow perceive you're telling me the truth. You've shown amazing abilities to warp reality to your needs. How do I know this new so-called capability you've given me works in relation to you, and that you're not just manipulating me?"

One/Loregos shrugged and smiled. "Some things have to be accepted on faith, like the burning bush. Besides, if I had sinister ends in mind why go to all the trouble of convincing you of my good intentions when I could simply will anything bad I wanted? Carol, your new implant gives you the power to resist my control of you."

Carol found herself powerless to move again, though this time she could still speak. He continued, holding up his hand in a human-like gesture, "Carol, I need you to relax and focus. You'll find a new Portal in your implant. Open it."

She took a moment to locate the electronic gateway. Her implant's AI didn't even admit to its existence. She thought of the Portal opening and somehow magically it did. The torrent of emotions flowing from the portal almost overwhelmed her.

"Focus, Carol, and separate them. You'll find you can block all or some of them."

She concentrated and identified Julia's and his emotions amidst a tide of others. Somehow, by sheer willpower, she pushed all of the others out of the way and focused on his.

One/Loregos smiled, though the smile appeared

mechanical, with no emotion behind it. "Very good, Carol. Now I want you to continuing focusing on the energy emanating from the Portal. Not the emotions themselves, but the Portal's underlying strength and power allowing you to sense them. Yes, very good. Now harness those qualities to will yourself to move."

Carol lifted her hand to brush a strand of dark hair from her eyes. She still sensed the impulse emanating from the being sitting across from her encouraging her not to move. He nodded at her and something changed. The universe seemed to twist. Dr. Loregos became the most handsome, sexually appealing man she had ever met. She fought her sexual attraction to him, unable to resist this godlike being in front of her. The world twisted again. Her breathing quickened as her body responded with uncontrollable arousal. The impulse to undress and go to him seemed so natural. She removed her jacket and began undoing the top button of her blouse. A small part of her mind protested and instinctively reached into the Portal. The sexual arousal disappeared and he turned once again into a plain, non-descript Human.

Again that blank smile. "Very good," he said. "Your new enemies use those urges in that manner to control humans. I apologize but you needed to learn how to respond."

Carol struggled to calm herself by slowing her breathing. She still sensed the heat emerging from the alien but now ignored it. At some level she fathomed this was not an attempt to take advantage of her but a lesson of some sort. Her connection to the Portal seemed more natural now. "Who are these enemies of ours?" she demanded. "Not the Goths or rogue Imps? Or even the Shaallit?"

"No, you're correct. Your biggest enemy is one you may not even be aware of, a religion worshiping the Goddess of Nearyahn. I know religious freedom is one of your Imperium's core tenets. That's one of the first steps toward reaching the freedom of my race. Despite the basic goodness of that tenet, you must ban this religion in your chute and on any world you control. Otherwise, the Neary will destroy you."

She frowned. "Banning a religion will be a difficult sell to Congress."

"Nonetheless, you must find a way without revealing my race's existence or the power of your new implant. I took steps to ensure no physical recording of this meeting exists. You'll remember this meeting and what occurred here. I need your conscious support and your free will. Some of my race are less discriminate about influencing members of the Lesser Races. Of course, that's when they even deign to pay attention to you at all. I believe differently and try to respect you by minimizing my influence." *Until now.*

He held up a package about thirty centimeters on a side. "This is my gift to you. I can't explain exactly what it is or what it is does. In terms you can understand, consider the Cube a piece of me dedicated to one thing, modifying additional implants as I did yours. The Cube draws limited amounts of energy from the surrounding environment and is therefore limited as to how many implants it can modify. Five per month is the limit. Contrary to what you think I'm not omnipotent and I'm not God. So five conversions a month is all I can offer you. I downloaded a suggested screening process into your implant. As you learn more about the Portal's new capabilities, you'll realize why you must be selective in determining who gets access. I also modified the Duke's and Duchess's along with yours. You need to decide who else you want. I suggest you put the Duchess in charge of the responsibility for selecting the Portal recipients.

"The Cube is not exactly alive in your terms but that's the best way to describe it. Your implant, if removed, will appear to your people like any other implant. You don't have the technology to detect the modifications I made. Your implant's AI is not aware of the Portal. No bioelectronic interrogation will uncover anything different from the norm. The modifications were absorbed by your brain as it tied into the modified implant. Once this happens, you can replace the implant if required and reconnect with the Portal. Any attempt to slice that part of the brain away connecting with the implant will destroy the Portal's capability and any trace of its existence. You'll detect no changes in the brain. I set it up this way for your protection, to keep the technology from falling into your enemies' hands, and to keep the technology away from your race. You're simply not ready for it. I stretched the rules by giving you this power to assure your race's survival. Now the rest is up to you." He smiled and was gone.

Carol sat for a moment before using her implant to pulse Mitch. She was surprised by his immediate response even though he was twelve million klicks from New Meyer. Her connection was different. *I'm mind to mind with him.*

"Mitch, what just happened?"

She sensed the quizzical nature of his response. "You tell me. You went through it, too."

Claudia tied in also. She seemed puzzled and a bit frightened. "He appeared in my cabin wearing the uniform of a steward," she said.

"She appeared to me as a female steward," Mitch said. "At one point she was the sexiest women I had ever met." He grinned wanly at his wife. "You don't want to look and sound the way she did. She oozed sex."

"He did the same with me," Claudia said, blushing. "At that moment he was the sexiest man alive and completely irresistible." She glanced at Mitch and grimaced. "You weren't important. Only being with him was important."

Carol sensed their discomfort as they grappled with their emotions. She sighed and grinned wanly. "He said that the Neary used the sex thing to control Humans. I suspect they can probably do the same with the Granacs and Shaallit since they're so similar to us. I wonder how deeply into the Goth leadership this Neary influence has reached." She paused and exhaled. "I think something changed dramatically. I'm just not sure exactly what."

Mitch grinned back at her. "A bit of an understatement."

Claudia looked at them both, "My God! What else can these things do?"

"I guess we'll learn as time goes on. That should be fun," Carol added sarcastically.

"Fun is not the right word, cousin," Mitch replied grimly.

www.ingramcontent.com/pod-product-compliance
Lightning Source LLC
Chambersburg PA
CBHW051528250626
47156CB00001B/278